RED SKY LAMENT

Also by Edward Wright

Clea's Moon
The Silver Face

RED SKY LAMENT

Edward Wright

ORION

First published in Great Britain in 2006 by Orion,
an imprint of the Orion Publishing Group Ltd.

Copyright © Edward Wright 2006

1 3 5 7 9 10 8 6 4 2

A CIP catalogue record for this book is
available from the British Library.

ISBNs 0 75286 929 9 (hardback)
0 75286 930 2 (trade paperback)

Typeset at The Spartan Press Ltd,
Lymington, Hants

Set in Plantin Light

Printed in Great Britain by
Clays Ltd, St Ives plc

The Orion Publishing Group Ltd
Orion House
5 Upper Saint Martin's Lane
London, WC2H 9EA

www.orionbooks.co.uk

This book is for Lobo,
who began as my pupil
and ended as my teacher

Acknowledgements

For help in reconstructing the Los Angeles of the 1940s, I'm indebted to David Wallace's *Lost Hollywood* and *Hollywoodland* and especially to Otto Friedrich for providing the social, cultural, and political context in his panoramic *City of Nets*. I drew on Joe Klein's engrossing *Woody Guthrie: A Life* for my portrait of the man, but I should add that the Guthrie in these pages also follows the rules of fiction. Robert Randisi and the Private Eye Writers of America gave me much-appreciated boost. My friend Alan Kessler was a helpful medical resource. Sincere thanks to the Crime Writers' Association of Great Britain, which must bear the guilt for having started me off on this particular writing path, and my agent, Jane Conway-Gordon, for keeping me on it. And I'm grateful for the editing expertise of Sara O'Keeffe, the guiding hand of Jane Wood, the friendly support of Juliet Ewers and Emma Noble, and the invaluable help given me from start to finish by my wife, Cathy.

1

Spotted over late-night scrambled eggs and onions at Schwab's Drugstore on the fabled Sunset Strip, none other than Clark Gable, one of our favorite leading men. Clark has earned a rest after his stellar performance in Homecoming *with the ever lovely Lana Turner. But what's this news about a romance involving a certain lady with a title? A real lady, that is? Clark, if you have secrets to reveal, you can always find us right here, broadcasting from the legendary Hollywood Alhambra Hotel.*

Turning to more serious news . . . All over Tinseltown, certain individuals are being summoned to appear at upcoming hearings in our nation's capital. Some say the documents showing up in mailboxes are salmon-colored. I call them pink, first cousin to red. And a very appropriate color, if you ask this reporter. These hearings will take a long-overdue look at the kind of motion pictures being produced by all the studios and the values of those people who work on them. Radio listeners, this is only the beginning. As the story unfolds, you will hear all about it on this program.

For now, this is Laura Lee Paisley saying . . . I love this town, I love all of you, and let's go to the movies!

'Are you afraid?' Davey Peake's easy grin took some of the sting out of the challenge, but not all.

'If that day ever comes, I'll be sure and let you know,' Maggie O'Dare shot back at him.

Her boyish husband speared a beef rib with the long-handled fork and flipped it over. 'I bet folks'd pay good money to see you do it,' he said, appearing to study his handiwork spread out on the sizzling barbecue grate. 'Bring back some old memories. You're not scared, are you?'

'I haven't got time for this,' Maggie said lightly. 'I've got to check the ice and the beer. You just keep cooking, you hear?'

As she brushed past him, John Ray Horn asked, 'What was that all about?'

'Just some damn fool craziness,' she replied.

The sounds of the afternoon party were all around, and the smell of fresh-cut grass mingled with the scent of barbecue. About three dozen people stood in small groups in the yard eating and drinking, many of them ranchers or growers from nearby. A few, somewhat better dressed, were from the sprawling city to the south. Under a big oak, a guitarist and fiddle player bounced through a variety of upbeat numbers in that curious hybrid known as western swing.

Horn watched Maggie as she walked away. In place of her customary dungarees, she had dressed for the party in tailored riding pants and a silk western-cut blouse, with a big-brimmed hat riding by its cord on her shoulders. She had the same long-legged horsewoman's stride that he had first noticed at Medallion Pictures years ago. Back then, his glances toward her would have carried more of a message. Now, over a decade later, he felt just simple appreciation of the sight of her, an auburn-haired, freckle-faced married lady in her late thirties, busy tending to her guests.

'That old boy is full of piss and vinegar, isn't he?' Joseph Mad Crow said to Horn when Maggie was out of earshot, glancing in the direction of Davey Peake. 'Always daring people to do things, then showing how he can do it better.' He made a dismissive sound. 'Rodeo riders.'

'Now wait a minute . . .'

'I know you used to be one of those idiots,' Mad Crow said. 'But something tells me you weren't quite so full of yourself.'

'Well, I thought I was hot stuff,' Horn said with a grin. 'That one good season I had—'

'Would you ask your wife to do something dangerous? If you had one, I mean?'

Answering Horn's quizzical look, Mad Crow went on, 'I heard him talking earlier. Said he was going to get her to do some Roman-style riding today.'

'*What?*'

'To entertain everybody. He knows Maggie used to be good at it, and he said he's never seen her do it.'

'Hell, it's been years since she's tried that.'

'I know. Wouldn't worry, though, she's got too much sense.'

Horn was in his usual well-worn sport jacket, slacks, and fedora, while Mad Crow wore party regalia – a fawn-colored gabardine suit tailored to accommodate his broad chest and shoulders, its slash pockets embroidered in an arrowhead motif. The outfit was completed by a matching Stetson and walnut-hued hand-tooled boots. His short ponytail showed just below the hat, and his Lakota blood showed in the bronze-toned planes and angles of his face.

They heard a distant, high-pitched yell above the party noise, and Mad

2

Crow pointed toward a nearby field. 'Looks like a fight.' Two boys were tussling out there, rolling on the ground, throwing fists.

'Maggie's busy,' Horn said. 'We better break it up.'

They loped over and each caught hold of a boy by the scruff of the neck and hauled him upright. They looked to be about ten and twelve, both spitting mad, the younger one with a bloody nose and close to tears.

'Break it up,' Horn said. 'What are you two doing?'

'Nothing,' said the older one, who was swallowed up in an army fatigue jacket with a 101st Airborne patch on the shoulder. 'Just playing war.'

'All right. Play war, but don't hit. That's why they call it play.'

'He wanted to be MacArthur,' said the smaller one resentfully. 'He said I had to be Stalin.'

'Doesn't sound right to me,' Horn said gravely. 'MacArthur never took on Uncle Joe Stalin. Why don't you be Hitler? Or Tojo?'

'He's gotta be Stalin,' said the larger one. ' 'Cause Stalin stinks. My dad says so.'

'Where's your folks?' Mad Crow asked the smaller one.

'They couldn't come,' he said, wiping his nose. 'But Maggie invited us. Said we could have barbecue and . . .' He trailed off, and it became obvious that both boys were staring, looking back and forth between the two men.

Mad Crow drew himself up, pleased. 'You know who we are?' he asked them. 'This old cowboy and me?' They nodded wordlessly. 'We always fight for the right side, don't we?' Another nod.

He grinned broadly, enjoying the moment. The older boy, his eyes now fixed on Horn, leaned over to his erstwhile enemy and whispered, 'Sierra Lane.' The younger boy, eyes wide, could only nod as he wiped his nose again.

'That's right,' Mad Crow said dramatically. 'Sierra Lane and his Indian companion. You seen a few of our movies?'

'Lots,' the older boy said. 'We seen lots.'

'Well, you know Sierra and me, we never wasted time fighting with our friends. We saved it for the bad men. You ought to do the same.'

Two more nods.

'White boys no make war,' Mad Crow said, lapsing into his old movie vernacular. 'Make peace. Go eat barbecue.' He slapped MacArthur on the rump, and both ran off.

'Your good deed,' Horn said.

'I love it when they recognize me,' Mad Crow said. 'Don't you? No, 'course you don't.'

Horn didn't answer. Although Mad Crow took pleasure in reliving his now-ended movie career, Horn's memories were much more ambivalent. The glory – if the life of a B-movie actor could be termed glorious – had

3

lasted only a few years. And what followed had given him no cause for pride.

Mad Crow shook his cuff up past his watch, a garish creation ringed by silver pounded into a miniature squash blossom design, and glanced at the dial. 'I need to go pretty soon.'

'Let me guess,' Horn said. 'The new lady friend?'

Mad Crow appeared mildly embarrassed. 'I promised to take her shopping before the stores close,' he said as they strolled back toward the party. 'She's discovered the wonders of the Bullock's out on Wilshire, where the models parade around in anything you want to see paraded and some gentleman is always available to carry your packages out to the car.'

'I bet it helps to drive up to the store with a carload of her daddy's Texas oil money.'

'Maybe so.'

Horn felt another comment on the way but held it back. Cissie Briar was not a totally comfortable subject. Mad Crow had met her a few weeks earlier when she and her father, in the course of a long visit to Los Angeles, had stopped by the Mad Crow Casino out in the northern San Fernando Valley, and he had been struck – 'pole-axed,' as he put it – by her striking looks and vivid personality. Since then he had pursued her with characteristic single-mindedness, even to the point of letting his business slide. This was of more than casual interest to Horn, since he worked occasionally for Mad Crow. Others might consider his tasks distasteful or dangerous or simply beneath them, but Horn could not afford to be discriminating. And when the Indian failed to tend to business, he had no work.

'Well, say hi for me and tell her not to buy out the store,' he said, and half-turned, looking to the range of hills several miles to the north that defined the outer edge of the San Fernando Valley. 'Smell that?' he said. 'That's not the barbecue.'

Mad Crow nodded. 'Brush fire,' he said. 'On the other side of the hills. I heard something about it on the radio this morning. Shouldn't be a problem unless the wind shifts and starts it headed this way.'

'The wind shifts a lot this time of year,' Horn said, feeling vaguely uneasy. 'It's almost time for the Santa Anas to start blowing.'

'I know, but fires don't usually make it down into the Valley. Hell, what do you care? You're over by the ocean. Maggie and me, we'll worry if we need to.' Mad Crow's own ranch was a few miles to the east, and his casino sat on a county road farther out, toward the foothills.

Maggie's O Bar D Ranch was a typical Valley spread – stables and corral, a grassy field for exercising the horses, and a small but comfortable house. On either side, the ranch's neighbors were barely visible through

4

the trees. A narrow blacktop road led straight south for miles toward the more civilized part of the Valley, where open land had given way to houses, shops, and neatly laid-out streets. And beyond that, just over the low-lying Santa Monica Mountains, lay the giant, pulsing city itself.

The two-man band had just swung into 'Take Me Back to Tulsa' when Horn looked off toward the road. 'Be damned,' he grunted in surprise. 'Looks like Cal Stoddard showed up.'

A long, dark-blue sedan came to a stop just off the dirt road that served as Maggie's driveway, dwarfing the other cars nearby. A tall, good-looking man got out and crossed the yard to where Maggie was tending to the drinks. His western outfit was even more elaborate than Mad Crow's, with a big-brimmed white hat and a fringed shirt in lavender and gold. It was the kind of outfit that not all men can get away with, but on Stoddard it seemed to fit. He hugged Maggie, chatted with Davey Peake for a minute, then came over to Horn and Mad Crow.

'Didn't you two use to chase bad guys together?' quipped Stoddard, shaking their hands. He stood somewhat stiffly, wearing a grin that flitted on and off his face as his eyes darted around the rest of the party. Some in the crowd had stopped to look in their direction; a few bent their heads together.

'Been weeks since I ran into you,' Stoddard said with forced joviality to Mad Crow, then turned to Horn. 'And you . . .' He stopped, searching for the words.

Horn returned Stoddard's look, as if daring him to say more. Seeing nothing in the other man's expression, he decided not to take offense and figured the elapsed time in his head. There was the year or so since he'd been back, and before that the time he'd spent in a cell up at Cold Creek. 'About three years for me, Cal,' he said. 'How you been?'

The question was largely rhetorical, for Cal Stoddard's success was obvious in the cut of his clothes, the shine of his car and, more broadly, the sale of tickets across the country every time one of his movies opened. In everything, in fact, save the wary, troubled look on his face.

'Just fine, John Ray. I've been lucky, I guess. Patty keeps telling me it's not going to last, so I should just be grateful for every day.' To Mad Crow he asked, 'How's business?'

'Not bad. I try to stay one step ahead of the tax collector and two steps ahead of the law.'

A girl of about fifteen came over and shyly asked for Stoddard's auto-graph. He obliged, appearing to relax a bit, and said to her, 'You be good now' as she left. The girl rejoined her parents, who regarded Stoddard with blank looks.

Silence descended on their group and Stoddard looked around, the unaccustomed awkwardness in his demeanor back again. Indicating the musicians, he said, 'I know those two characters who are making all that noise. Think I'll go say hello.'

As Stoddard walked away, Horn muttered, 'He's got guts, showing up here. Did you see that thing in the *Mirror* yesterday?'

Mad Crow nodded, his mouth slightly twisted, as if he tasted something sour. 'That crap?'

'You don't believe it?'

'Hell, no. Working on those two movies of his, I got to know him pretty well. Look, I don't care what kind of friends a guy has, or what kind of groups he joins. But Cal's got too much sense to . . .' He searched for the words.

'To sign his name on the wrong line?'

'That's right. He's got no politics that I know of. Does his work, goes home to his family. He's all right.' Mad Crow thought for a moment. 'The story didn't even use his name—'

'Didn't have to. It was pretty clear who they were talking about.'

'All right, but it didn't say he was on anybody's list, just that there was a rumor about him.' He looked at Horn sharply. 'Why? Do you believe it?'

When Horn didn't answer, Mad Crow looked disgusted. 'You believe it. All right, then. Well . . .' He made a show of looking at his watch again. 'Got to go. The fair Cissie doesn't like to be kept waiting.' He strode off without a goodbye.

Handled that really well, didn't you? Horn said to himself. He didn't like antagonizing his old friend, but Cal Stoddard was a touchy subject, just like Cissie Briar. And Horn was feeling edgy. Something about the hint of smoke that didn't belong in the air, the pockets of silence that fell on what should have been a boisterous party crowd. And the challenge thrown out all too casually by Maggie's husband, which stirred within Horn old protective feelings toward her, feelings that had been long dormant.

2

Horn listened to the music for a while from a distance. He watched as a car drove up and two more guests joined the party. The musicians, who had greeted Cal Stoddard with grins, wrapped up a tune with a fiddle flourish, and then the guitar player offered his instrument to Stoddard, who seated himself on the vacated chair and began to strum and sing. The song was 'San Antonio Rose', done this time as a ballad, and the man's pleasant tenor carried clearly over the yard. A few of the guests gathered around to listen, while others kept their distance.

Horn fetched another beer. Holding the long-necked bottle loosely between two fingers he headed over toward Maggie, but saw she was deep in conversation with the newly arrived couple, and paused. Spotting him, she beckoned him over.

'Let me introduce somebody,' she said to him. 'Owen and Lillian Bruder. This is my old friend John Ray Horn.'

Horn shook their hands. He guessed Bruder to be in his late fifties. The man was average height and solidly built, and his hand had once done heavy work. He had square features, a bulldog jaw, a lined face, and thinning, sandy hair. Except for his clothing, he could have been a laborer of some kind. His wife was prematurely gray, her hair done in a simple bun, but she showed traces of an elegant beauty. Both were well-dressed in a casual way. *They're not Valley people*, Horn thought. *Not ranch people. They're from over the hill.*

'I've been wanting you all to meet,' Maggie said. She seemed slightly tense. 'I think you might have some things to talk about,' she said to Horn, then took Lillian Bruder's arm and led her towards the food.

After a brief silence, which Owen Bruder showed no sign of filling, Horn said, 'Would you like a drink?'

'Sure. I'll have a beer.'

They stood at the beer bucket for a moment, listening to the music. Cal Stoddard was doing 'Goodbye Liza Jane', a crowd pleaser, and the audience had grown to include fully half of the party now. The front porch was populated with partygoers, but Horn spotted a couple of camp chairs set up at the side of the converted bunkhouse where Maggie had lived since she bought the ranch, even before she married Davey Peake. 'Want to sit for a while?' he asked.

'Fine.'

When they settled in, Bruder looked around at the ranch for a moment, then asked, 'You've known Margaret for a long time?'

'A little over ten years,' Horn said. 'We started out at Medallion Pictures around the same time. How about you?'

Bruder seemed slightly uncomfortable at the question. 'Quite a while, but not on a regular basis,' he said. His voice was gruff, almost a growl. Although he didn't seem unfriendly, he struck Horn as a man with little use for small talk.

'What kind of work do you do?'

'I've been a screenwriter,' the man said. 'At Global.'

Horn studied him anew. 'I may have heard of you. There was something—'

'In the papers?' Bruder's tone verged on sarcasm.

'That's right. Something—' Horn was interrupted by the sounds of a commotion over by the corral. Looking in that direction, he saw some of Maggie's ranch hands leading two mares through the gate. A crowd was starting to gather. Horn thought he knew why, and left his chair.

Walking over quickly, he saw that the mares, bridled but not saddled, stood side by side with Miguel, one of the hands, holding both sets of reins. Maggie had changed her silk blouse for a well-worn denim shirt. Now, as if struck by an afterthought, she sat in the dirt and began pulling off her boots, a determined look on her face.

'What are you doing?' Horn demanded.

'Nothing much,' she said, grunting as she pulled off the second boot. 'Just going to try something.'

Davey Peake stood nearby wearing a wide grin. 'You show 'em, girl,' he said.

'Come on, Maggie,' Horn said. 'Don't.'

She stood up, dusting off her rear, and handed the boots to Horn. Then, before anyone could say anything else, she grabbed a handful of mane on the nearest mare and swung up. 'Gimme,' she said to Miguel, who tossed her the reins. Swinging both horses around in a tight circle, she kicked her mount into motion, and both started off. Wasting no time, Maggie upped the pace to a gallop, then a faster gallop. After one turn around the corral, she braced her hands on the horse's back and jack-knifed her legs up until she crouched, feet firmly planted on the rump. Then, balancing delicately and timing her moves to the mare's rhythm, she slowly stood, hands grasping both horses' reins in a feather-touch. The crowd gasped almost in unison.

One more circuit, and then Maggie extended her right foot until it rested on the second mare's back. Davey Peake whooped in appreciation. She put more weight on it until she stood firmly atop both horses, her strong legs flexing and extending like springs.

Horn felt a yell forming in his throat, but suddenly it was all over. The mare on the right struck an uneven patch of ground with a foreleg, the great body lurched, Maggie's foot slipped. She plunged to the ground between the horses, striking the dirt with a thud and a muffled cry.

Horn was first over the fence. He found her sitting up, cursing.

'Are you all right?'

'I'm fine,' she gasped, out of breath. Her face was streaked with dirt, and she gripped her right wrist in her left hand. 'Think I sprained my wrist, though.'

'*Damn*, girl,' Davey Peake said as he arrived, still wearing his cook's apron. 'That was some show. Are you okay?'

'I said I'm fine.'

Horn helped her up. 'You shouldn't have prodded her into that,' he said to Peake.

'Well, hell,' the other man said, his smile exaggerated. 'She didn't have to do it.' To his wife he added, 'You sure looked good up there, honey.'

'Don't anybody make a fuss,' Maggie said, straightening up. 'I'll just put some ice on this.' She started off for the house, accompanied by one of her woman friends.

'Rodeo's over, folks,' Peake said to the guests. 'Who wants some more barbecue?'

When Horn returned to his seat, he found Owen Bruder standing up, a concerned look on his face. 'I saw what happened,' Bruder said. 'Is she hurt?'

'I don't think so,' Horn replied, his anger at Davey Peake still tightening his voice. 'But she could have been.'

'That was pretty amazing,' Bruder said. 'Must take a lot of guts to ride like that.'

'Well, that's her, all right. Never was much she wouldn't try. One time . . .' He smiled at the memory. 'In one of her first serials, she worked most of a day with a strained back, in a lot of pain. Nobody knew about it until later. She said she was worried that if she complained, they'd hire somebody else to do her job.'

Bruder shook his head, looking bemused, and Horn wondered just how well he knew Maggie.

'At Medallion, they called her the queen of the serials,' he said. 'You ever see any of them?'

'No. When I was a lot younger, I saw a few of the silent movie serials.

They called them chapter plays back then. Pearl White, that kind of thing. But these days, serials are . . .'

'I know,' Horn said. 'They're mostly for kids. They play along with double features, in the kind of theaters that don't show Cary Grant or Irene Dunne movies. Matter of fact, they play alongside the kind of movies I used to make.'

'I wasn't being condescending,' Bruder said brusquely.

'That's all right.'

'What was she doing, exactly?'

'Out there? It's called Roman-style riding. I don't know if the Romans did it or not, but that's the name the stunt riders gave it. There's no use for it except to show off. You see it in rodeos and sometimes in the movies, but there aren't many people around here who can do it, and hardly any women. Maggie used to be one of the best.'

'But she fell.'

'That's right. She's gotten rusty. Had no business trying it.'

'Why do you think—'

'I'm not sure. That husband of hers dared her to do it, but for a while there I thought she was too smart to take him up on it. Anyway . . .' He looked around, wondering how much more time he needed to spend with this somewhat distant man. Out on the lawn the light was softening and some of the guests were leaving. A man in a dark suit approached the musicians and spoke briefly with Stoddard, handed him something, and then walked to a car and drove away. Unmoving, Stoddard stood watching until the car was gone.

Horn realized Bruder had said something. 'Hmm?'

'Margaret's told me a little about your background and the work you do.'

'Uh-huh?'

'She thought you might be able to help me with something.'

'Uh-huh. What's that?'

Bruder shifted in his seat, unease written on his face. 'She said you were in prison.'

Horn gave the man a hard look 'What if I was?'

He became aware that Maggie and Bruder's wife had joined them, Maggie slowly rubbing her right wrist. Horn shot Maggie an accusatory look – *What are you doing talking about me?* – but she ignored it.

'I'd like to ask you about it.'

'Sorry,' Horn said, getting up. 'I know you're a friend of Maggie's and all, but I'm not going to be able to help you. If you want to write a movie about life in prison, go talk to somebody else. Or better yet, just make it up. Isn't that what you movie writers do anyway?'

'Tell him,' Lillian Bruder said quietly to her husband.

'Tell me what?'

Bruder took a deep breath. 'All right. I'm not writing anything. In fact, I suppose it's possible I may never write anything again. I'm asking you for myself.'

'I don't get it.'

Bruder sat there, looking like a man who wanted to talk but couldn't, a man who hurt somewhere.

His wife broke the silence. 'Owen may be going to prison, Mr Horn. Somehow, he needs to prepare for it. Will you help him?'

3

The leftover tang of barbecue lightly scented the twilight air with tomato, sugar, and vinegar. The fire in the grill was long extinguished, so the hint of smoke came from someplace farther off, Horn guessed.

The neighbors and the last of the guests had departed, and Maggie's ranch hands were feeding and watering and bedding down the horses. Finally at ease, Horn sat with her on the shallow front porch and talked. He could hear faint boyish cries from the field to the west, and saw the indefatigable MacArthur and Stalin, joined now in an uneasy alliance, assaulting an orange-crate fort defended by an invisible enemy.

'Davey hit the road almost before I noticed,' he said. 'I looked up and saw him and his buddies take off, hauling that big horse van.'

She laughed. 'He couldn't wait to get back to the life,' she said. 'When you marry a rodeo rider, you marry an old boy who's on the road a lot.'

She glanced at him quickly. 'What did you think of Owen?'

'Not much,' he said. 'I got the feeling he's smarter than everybody else and knows it. He's also a little bull-headed, and a little self-righteous . . .' He stole a look at her, noticing that her hair had been somewhat unkempt since her misadventure with the horses, and part of it draped the side of her face, like Veronica Lake. He decided he liked it. She had wrapped a dish towel in ice and held it to her right wrist.

'How is it?' he asked.

She appeared not to have heard. 'He's not as bad as he seems,' she said, a touch of defensiveness in her voice.

'How'd you meet him?'

'Oh, it was a long time ago,' she said vaguely. 'Not long after I came out here. I don't see much of him, but he's kind of an old friend.' She turned in his direction. 'Thanks.'

'For what?'

'For agreeing to go see him tomorrow night.'

He shrugged. 'I don't mind. But I'd appreciate it if you'd—'

'Tell you what it's all about?'

'Right. He acted embarrassed by the whole thing, having to ask me a favor.'

'I'm sure he's embarrassed,' she said. 'Worse than that. Ashamed.' She moved the ice pack to the other side of her wrist. 'They're saying he's a Communist.'

'I'll be damned,' he muttered. 'First Cal Stoddard, now him. What the hell's . . .' He stopped, remembering something. 'That's what it was. The thing in the paper. They're talking about a bunch of movie people who are Communists, or used to be. He's one of them.'

'Right.' She exhaled audibly, sounding tired. 'There's this congressman, J. Parnell Thomas. He's been in the news a lot; I've been reading up on him. He runs the House Un-American Activities Committee, and he's made up his mind that the movie business is full of Communists, especially writers, directors, actors.'

'Isn't he in town right now?'

'Uh-huh, has been for some time. He rented some rooms downtown at the Biltmore, and he's been calling in witnesses, kind of on the sly. Friendly witnesses, he calls them. They've been giving secret testimony, and what it amounts to is—'

'They've been handing him names.'

'That's right. And a few months ago somebody gave him Owen's name. And not long after that, Owen was mentioned on Laura Lee Paisley's radio show.'

'I've heard her. It's just gossip.'

'No, it's worse than that. It's poison, what she says about people. She has a lot of listeners. She tries to sound like she's just your gossipy big sister, but she's full of hate. For years she mostly talked about movie stars cheating on their wives, that kind of thing, and the studios were scared of her even then. Now she goes after anybody who doesn't fit her image of an American, and she's even more dangerous.'

Maggie took a breath, as if to calm herself. 'After she named him, the newspapers picked it up. And eventually he got a subpoena to go to Washington and testify in public. He's supposed to leave next week.'

Horn stretched his legs out on the porch. 'And he thinks he's going to prison?'

'It's complicated. I'll let him explain that part to you. But he might have to go.'

He started to speak, but she broke in. 'Something you need to know. He's not a Communist.'

'What? Then how—'

'He can explain that too. But he's not. All right?'

'All right.' Her tone puzzled him. So far, he had learned little about

Owen Bruder that made him seem likable, but Maggie clearly felt some kind of affection toward the man. And that puzzled Horn.

'You know, you don't seem to have anything in common with this guy. How'd you get to be friends?'

She sat quietly for a while, as if framing a difficult answer. He began to think she wasn't going to respond, when the phone rang and she went inside to answer it. He could hear concern in her voice as she spoke to the caller. Then she called out to him.

'It's Patty Stoddard, Cal's wife,' she said. 'She's looking for Joseph.'

'The Indian? He's out somewhere with the fair Cissie Briar,' he said. 'They were going shopping, and after that, who knows?'

She spoke for another minute, then returned. 'It sounds like Cal's off on a toot,' she said slowly, shaking her head.

'What? That's hard to believe.'

'I know. But . . . she says he and his band have got a thing at the Hitching Post tonight, and they went for dinner first. One of the guys in the band just called her from some eating joint, saying Cal's drunk as a skunk, and they can't talk him out of doing the show. She's looking for Joseph, because they're friends. Anyway . . . I told her I'd go over to the theater and see if I can get him to come home.' She took a step toward his chair. 'Do you want to go with me?'

When Horn hesitated, Maggie said, 'Come on, John Ray. They're good folks.'

'Oh, hell.'

With the canyon road behind them, Horn swung the black Ford left onto Hollywood Boulevard and headed east. He drove fast, looking out for black-and-whites.

'I thought he didn't drink.'

'He doesn't,' Maggie said. She rode with her injured wrist cradled in her lap. 'Not much, anyway. He didn't touch anything at the party. This doesn't sound right.'

A bell clanged, and the arm of a STOP sign flew up. He hit the brakes and waited impatiently for GO, then took off again.

'I know you don't like Cal much,' Maggie said, speaking up over the sound of the engine. 'Maybe no more than you like Owen. And I know why.'

'I guess that makes you pretty smart.'

'You don't like him because he's where you used to be.' Her voice nudged gently at him. Because of their history and his regard for her, Maggie could get away with saying things others could not. Sometimes, he thought, she came close to abusing the privilege.

'I saw one of his pictures,' Horn said, trying to keep it light. 'He wore a

14

white shirt with sequins, and he rode around singing and playing a guitar. Sitting on his horse, for crying out loud, playing a guitar.'

'I know,' she said, laughing. 'But that's the new style, and that's what they want. Look at Roy Rogers over at Republic. Same thing. All the movie cowboys get dressed up like Christmas trees now.'

'And they sing.'

'Well, some people enjoy that, especially the girls. And Cal can actually carry a tune, unlike some of those old boys. But the thing is . . .' She paused. 'What happened to you wasn't Cal's fault. He just happened to be there when you went away, and the studio needed somebody, and they picked him. You shouldn't hold it against him.'

'All right, I won't hold it against him.'

'Liar.'

After several blocks of homes and apartment buildings, the boulevard came to life with people and traffic and glowing theater marquees. Crossing Highland, they passed the giant pseudo-oriental facade of the Chinese, the movie palace built by Sid Grauman. After another half-mile, Vine was coming up, and Horn spotted the towering sign of the Pantages Theater on the left, and then, across the street, the smaller and homelier Hitching Post. The marquee read *Rogue Lawman* and *Guns of Snake River*, and below that, *Stage Show Tonight: Cal Stoddard and His Rhythm Wranglers*.

Horn pulled into the first lot he saw and parked the Ford. As they approached the theater, they saw a crowd milling about on the sidewalk around the familiar hitching post embedded in concrete. A few bicycles were tethered there, but no horses. Boys and girls, some wearing western outfits, stood around looking confused. A few parents were there as well. Some of the children were crying.

No one appeared to be selling or taking tickets, so they walked past the ticket booth, with its sign saying 'Check Your Six-Guns Here', and went inside. There was more confusion in the lobby but, beyond the swinging doors that led to the theater, Horn heard music. He pushed through.

The house lights were up full, and only a couple of dozen people remained in the seats. Up on stage, Cal Stoddard stood, hanging on to a microphone stand, talking, his voice amplified by the speakers. Behind him, his band played an up-tempo tune. Horn soon gathered that Stoddard and his band were in no way together. It appeared that he was trying to talk over the music, and they were trying to drown him out.

'. . . people you listen to,' he was saying, leaning into the mike, both hands holding on for support. 'You listen to your folks, 'cause they raised you and they got your welfare at heart. And your teachers, goddamn it, 'cause they're getting you ready to go out in the world. And your best friend, 'cause . . . I don't know, that's what best friends do.'

He paused and belched softly, the amplified sound carrying out into the auditorium.

Horn heard another voice nearby, looked around and saw a man in a suit and bow tie talking urgently to an usher.

'You the manager?'

'That's right.'

'How long's he been doing this?'

'A few minutes. He sang one song and then started talking like this. He's using profanity. The man's drunk. I've got to get the rest of these children out of here.'

'You do that. But first, where's the loudspeaker switch?'

'Uh, up in the projection booth.'

'Why don't you turn him off?'

The manager looked ridiculously grateful for the idea. He scurried away.

'But you don't listen to your government,' Stoddard went on, his words slurred. 'You know why? 'Cause they'll stick it to you, that's why. 'Cause they're a bunch of spineless, shit-eating . . .'

With an electric howl, the sound cut off. Stoddard stopped speaking and began thumping the microphone with his finger.

'Hey, Cal.'

Stoddard looked down, and it seemed to take some effort for him to focus his eyes on Horn. 'Well, I'll be,' he said slowly. 'John Ray Horn.' He wore an all-white outfit, complete with big hat and white leather boots. Even the handles of his pistols were inlaid with ivory.

'Your wife needs you at home, you know that?'.

Stoddard kept thumping. 'Got a few more things that need saying.'

'Your audience is gone. What say you come with me?'

Stoddard looked out and noticed that the auditorium was now empty. Sighing, he sat down heavily on the stage, legs over the side. The edge of the stage was littered with popcorn and boxes, apparently thrown by the audience.

'John Ray Horn,' Stoddard repeated, his eyes unfocused. 'They said you wouldn't like it if I . . . if I tried to . . .'

Take my job, Horn thought. *They were right.* 'Come on, Cal.' He helped him off the stage, up the aisle and through the doors. The lobby, packed with people, rumbled with discontent. A burly man pushed his way over and grabbed Stoddard by his bandanna.

'My kid worships you, you drunk son of a bitch,' he said in a low voice, his face almost chin to chin with the other man. 'You made him cry.' He drew back a fist.

Moving quickly, Horn ducked around behind the man and pinned both his arms, then swung him toward the wall, facing away from most of the

16

people. 'Let's not do this,' he said into one ear as the man struggled. 'Hear me? Not in front of your boy.'

After a moment's rigidity, the man exhaled loudly and was quiet. A minute later, Horn and Maggie had their white-clad charge out on the sidewalk, and soon they were in the car. 'I told the band we'll look after him,' Maggie said as Horn fired up the Ford and pulled out into the street.

'What the hell was that all about, Cal?' Horn asked.

'He's passed out,' Maggie said, peering into the back seat. 'I'd sure like to know what happened to him.'

After a forty-minute drive, Horn stopped in front of Cal Stoddard's well-appointed ranch house in the north San Fernando Valley. Fruit hung off a big orange tree in the yard, and beyond in the dark lay the low hills and lush acreage of his horse ranch. 'Is that Joseph's car?' Maggie asked as they got out and headed for the front door. 'Maybe she found him.'

Horn walked over to the white Cadillac, looked in the window at the showy pinto-hide upholstery, and nodded. 'No two cars like this one. Looks like a horse's rump in there.'

Patty Stoddard, accompanied by Mad Crow, came out to meet them, her face taut with worry. 'How is he?'

Horn was tempted to used the words *out cold*, but he said simply, 'Asleep.' He and Mad Crow wrestled the burden out of the car and into the house, where they laid him on a couch. 'We need to be quiet,' Patty said. 'The girls are sleeping.' Horn carefully put the big white Stetson on a table. Stoddard stank of booze, and one corner of his mouth was shiny with spit.

Mad Crow's brow was creased with the beginning of a question, but Horn merely shook his head. 'Tell you later,' he said quietly.

'Thank you both,' Stoddard's wife said to them. Horn didn't know Patty Stoddard any better than he knew her husband, but lately he had found small things to dislike about her. When Horn began his stretch in prison, Cal was starting his career as a leading man, and Patty was his co-star, soon to be his wife. She had a fresh-scrubbed look and a pleasant singing voice, and they made a good-looking couple. But as his star rose, she appeared to show a toughness that he lacked, and there were some who said she was the more ambitious of the two, that she pushed him. It seemed to Horn that she took too much obvious pleasure in being the wife and co-star of Medallion's biggest cowboy. Tonight, however, she seemed lost and bewildered by his condition, and it was hard to dislike her.

'I guess we'll be going,' Horn said.

'He never drinks,' she said suddenly.

'Then why—'

'It's this thing he got,' she said, going over to the fireplace mantle to pick up a piece of paper. 'Somebody gave it to him at the party today.'

She handed Horn what looked like a legal document, printed on paper that was an odd, pale shade of rose. *By authority of the House of Representatives of the Congress of the United States of America,* read the opening line.

'It's a subpoena,' she said, spitting out the word as if it were an obscenity. 'He has to go to Washington and tell them why he joined the Communist Party.'

Horn and Mad Crow exchanged looks. The rumor had been true.

'He never even told me,' she said, shaking her head. 'He didn't think it was important. He was twenty years old, living in Bakersfield. He got hired to play his guitar at some kind of rally, and afterward they were signing people up. He thought it was a good organization, doing the right thing for people, and he signed.'

'I'll be damned,' Horn said under his breath.

'He barely went to any meetings, and then he forgot about it for years, but they've got his signature. He said he isn't ashamed of it, and he'll admit to it,' she went on. 'But the studio's suspending him until all this is ironed out. He's got no more pictures coming. One of our girls starts school next month, and we've got no income.' Her voice rose with the last words.

'What about you?' Horn asked.

She looked away, her face hard. Mad Crow answered for her. 'No work for her either,' he said. 'I've heard how this works. It's called guilt by association. Am I right?'

She nodded silently. There was a noise from the couch. They went over.

'Cal, honey?' she said.

Her husband muttered something, and she and Horn bent over to listen.

'I know,' she said, her eyes moist. 'You hush now.' In a moment, he was softly snoring.

Later, as they stood on the porch, Mad Crow said, 'I'll stick around for a bit, make sure they're okay.'

'That's a good idea.'

'What did he say, just before we left?'

Horn paused, as if trying to decipher a riddle. 'He said he was scared.'

4

The headlights of the black Ford carved a meandering path down Laurel Canyon Boulevard. The passing cars and widely spaced street lights did little to illuminate the steep, narrow roads that climbed up from the canyon floor on either side. They looked dark and full of secrets.

The night air bore a slightly damp chill. As the road began to level off, Horn cranked up the driver's side window, both to warm the inside of the car and to allow himself another whiff of Maggie's perfume.

He glanced over at her, trying to recall the last time he had seen her this dressed up. Under her wool coat she wore a flowered print dress, and her shoulder-length auburn hair was unpinned. The spray of freckles across her nose and cheeks was concealed by makeup and her perfume smelled like sweet soap.

It was quite a transformation, and it prodded memories of scattered images from years ago. They passed across his mind quickly, like snap-shots – dinners together, hair brushed loose and free, a drive up the coast to a quiet cove one summer evening, when neither he nor Maggie had brought a bathing suit.

'We're almost there.' Her voice interrupted his thoughts. Once again she seemed a little nervous, just as she had when she introduced him to the Bruders. He had tried finding out more from her during the drive over the hill – how she had become friends with Bruder, why she was treating this evening as such a special occasion – but she had deflected his questions.

They reached the brighter lights and heavier traffic of Sunset Boulevard. 'That's it,' Maggie said, pointing, and he saw their destination diagonally across the street. He turned right, then quickly left into a driveway, past the sign that read Garden of Allah, and parked in front of a large two-story building with arched windows and a tiled roof.

Inside the lobby, they were met by Owen and Lillian Bruder, who took them into the rather cramped and ill-lit dining room. Their dinner was not relaxed. Bruder seemed distracted, speaking only in brief sentences, and

Maggie was quiet. Lillian managed to keep things going, smiling often and telling wry stories about the two of them. She had a low voice and a serene nature that seemed to come from an inner strength. Horn liked her looks and the minimum of fussiness with which she had put herself together – dark, well-fitted dress, little jewelry. Her graying hair was gathered almost severely at the back of her neck. He also liked the way she smoothed her husband's rough edges, sometimes reaching over to touch his hand when it seemed his temper might rear its head.

Some of the other diners looked their way from time to time, talking in lowered voices. Horn wondered when the Bruders would get to the point of the evening.

Finally dinner was over, and their hosts took them through the rear of the building and out the door. Maggie caught her breath. 'Isn't this pretty?' she said. 'I've heard of this place, but I never guessed . . .'

The grounds of the Garden of Allah stretched into the dark. Pathways led here and there, and small buildings in the same California-Spanish style as the hotel were just visible among the trees. Directly in front of where the four stood was a large, irregularly shaped swimming pool, glowing with underwater lights. Chairs were arranged on the grass around the pool, and in the near-dark Horn could see small groups of people and hear murmurs of conversation accented by bursts of laughter.

'The pool is a kind of social center,' Lillian said. 'Especially in the early evening. Around ten they turn off the underwater lights, and people go home.'

She led them along a path through the greenery to a bungalow with an entrance on the ground floor and an exterior stairway that led to another above. 'Here we are,' she said.

Entering at the ground floor, they found a cozy apartment, made even cozier by several large cartons against the living room wall. 'I hope you'll pardon us,' Lillian said. 'We're still unpacking. Who'd like a drink?'

A few minutes later, they were arranged comfortably near the open front windows, through which sounds carried faintly from the swimming pool. Near them, positioned to catch daylight from the windows, stood a small table bearing paints and brushes, and next to that an easel holding a nearly finished canvas. 'Did you do that?' Horn asked Lillian.

She nodded, smiling. 'I've found a gallery down in Laguna Beach whose owner is kind enough to sell my work. Do you like paintings?'

'I don't know anything about art,' he said. 'But every now and then I see something I like. It's usually a sunset or a horse and rider, something like that.'

'Cowboy art,' her husband said in a tone that sounded dismissive.

'Western themes,' Lillian said. 'Very popular, but I'm afraid I don't work in that genre.'

'I can see that,' Horn said, studying the canvas. The painting appeared to be a portrait of her husband, but the resemblance was overshadowed by the drama of the technique. The head was awash in deep crimsons and indigos, some of the paints applied liberally as if with a palette knife. On one side, Bruder's features were almost aflame in color, while the other became lost in the darkness of the background. It was a troubled face.

Horn decided not to comment. Instead he waited, drink in hand, studying his host. It occurred to him that he had not yet seen him smile. A man with a lot on his mind, he thought.

He tasted the good-quality scotch. 'So,' he said, hoping to nudge Bruder into the conversation that was the point of the evening.

Bruder, who had been staring out the window, stirred in his chair and turned his attention to Horn. 'Thanks for talking to me,' he said. 'This is Lillian's idea. No harm in it, I suppose. But it's a little awkward.' He sounded as if he were being pushed into something distasteful.

'Yesterday you mentioned prison.'

Bruder nodded slowly, then turned to Maggie. 'Did you tell him anything about me?'

'A little,' she said.

'The government's calling you a Red,' Horn said to him. 'She says you're not. How could they get it wrong?' He knew his words sounded cold, but he didn't feel that he owed Bruder any special handling.

Bruder visibly stiffened. 'People get things wrong all the time,' he said. 'And would it matter to you if I were?'

The question made Horn uncomfortable. 'Well, I don't know any Reds. But from what I've heard, I don't want to be buddies with any of them.'

Bruder nodded curtly at that, clearly unsatisfied by the answer. He took a deep breath and let it out. 'When I was young and hungry, I worked all over this country,' he said, sounding like a man beginning a story. 'Handled freight on the docks in Brooklyn, picked peaches out here in California, worked on the railroad a lot of places in between. When the Depression set in, I was writing plays in New York. By then almost everybody was poor, this country was in a lot of trouble, and some of us wanted to try to do something about it. So we wrote about the problems, and we put our ideas into our plays. Later I moved out here and began writing for the movies, but I still believed that writers had power to change things. And I wasn't alone.'

He must have noticed the doubt in Horn's expression. 'You're probably wondering if we made a difference? How the hell should I know? One thing's for sure, message movies usually don't make much money. As Sam Goldwyn once said, "If I want to send a message, I'll use Western Union."'

Horn thought Bruder was a strange combination of the tough guy and the schoolteacher. In the man's voice he could hear a faint echo of the words of his own father, the Reverend John Jacob Horn, in long-ago sermons to his small congregation in the hill country of northwest Arkansas. Horn had traveled a long way to escape the sound of that voice, and he was always uncomfortable around those who lectured or preached.

Lillian Bruder sat quietly, a faint smile on her face, and Horn guessed she'd heard this monologue before. She had picked up some knitting that lay by her chair, and she was focused on it now, her strong hands busy with the needles.

Maggie, meanwhile, listened intently. Horn wondered why this man apparently held such fascination for her.

'I made a lot of money writing for the movies,' Bruder continued. 'Some people thought I did good work.'

'You did,' Lillian said. For the others' benefit, she added, 'They gave him that.' She indicated a small cardboard box against the wall. Protruding from the top was a familiar gold-plated statuette.

'That was for *The Last Harvest*,' Bruder said. 'I'm damn proud of it, because it says people are capable of thinking about something bigger than themselves, bigger than their next meal. Did you see it?'

'No.'

'It doesn't matter,' Bruder said in a tone that suggested otherwise. 'That was years ago. No one's writing anything like that any more. Studios are terrified of anything that deals honestly with the poor, anything suggesting that it's not wonderful to be rich.'

Horn glanced at Maggie again and saw that she was openly staring at Bruder, seemingly mesmerized by his words.

Bruder drained his drink and refreshed their glasses. 'Anyway . . . No, I never joined the Communist Party. I knew some members, of course, and we agreed about a lot of things. But that all stopped for me in 1939, when that son of a bitch Stalin signed his treaty with Hitler and I realized that Russian-style communism was just as cynical as any other political movement. So I said to hell with all orthodoxies.'

'Then why—'

'Why is J. Parnell Thomas coming after me? It's simple, according to my lawyer. Someone named me.' He seemed slightly drunk, and Horn recalled that Bruder had had several drinks at dinner. And along with the signs of drinking was a growing anger.

'Why don't you just prove you're not a Red?' Horn asked him.

Bruder regarded him with a look that suggested equal measures of pity and contempt. 'Have you ever tried to prove a negative?' he asked. 'You can't.'

'Well . . .'

'I know what you're thinking. The truth always wins, right? Well, right now, the truth is being run out of town and replaced by lies, rumor, suspicion, innuendo, accusation. And let's not forget fear.'

'He's right,' Lillian said bitterly. 'All the time we've lived in this city, we've had wonderful friends, good people. At least we thought they were. Now it's almost as if we've become invisible. We don't hear from them. If we try to get in touch, they say they're too busy to see us.'

'Except for Wally,' Bruder said. 'He's still a friend.' He lifted his glass in a mock toast.

'What happens now?' Maggie asked him.

'Well, as you may know, I'm expected to go to Washington for the final act in the drama and confess in public,' Bruder said belligerently. 'Here's the way my lawyer explains it: If I refuse to answer their questions, they'll hold me in contempt of Congress and send me to jail. If I insist on telling the truth and contradicting their secret informant—'

'Wait a minute,' Horn broke in. 'Doesn't the law say you've got a right to face whoever's accusing you?'

'We've been over this with our lawyer,' Lillian answered. 'You have that right only in court, during a trial. This certainly will feel like a trial, but technically, it's just a hearing.'

'Yes,' her husband said. 'I'm sure you can see the joke here. If my testimony doesn't jibe with that of Mr Secret Informant, that could be interpreted as failure to cooperate. In other words, contempt. There's another thing: Even though it's rarely used, there's a law on the books saying it's illegal to advocate the overthrow of the government. Theoretically, anyone named as a Communist could be prosecuted under this law.'

Horn was silent. He was beginning to see what Bruder was up against.

'Finally,' Bruder said, 'if I take cover under my Fifth Amendment right against self-incrimination, I probably won't go to jail, but it's for damn sure I'll suddenly become unemployable.'

He spread his hands apart, as if acknowledging the irrationality of it all. 'The only way I could escape with a whole skin and make sure I go on working would be to falsely confess, name some of the others I know are Communists, and throw myself on the mercy of the committee.' He allowed himself a small, tight smile. 'When Hell freezes over.'

'What's wrong with naming a few Communists?' Horn asked. 'They're not on our side anyway.'

Bruder showed his disgust. 'Because some of them are friends, or at least used to be,' he said. 'And because it's just plain wrong. To name people, I mean. What's happening to me is wrong too, but that's no reason for me to take it out on people like myself. They're not the enemy.'

'That's not what I hear,' Horn said. 'We just finished fighting a war, and before we get to take a deep breath, we've got the Russians carving up parts of Europe and getting ready to take us on. If you ask me, anybody who tries to sell out this country shouldn't be working in the movies or anywhere else . . .'

He trailed off, a little surprised at his own vehemence. Horn rarely discussed politics. Communism, it was true, sounded like a threat to him, but he had never before felt passionate about the subject. He wondered if he was simply reacting to Bruder's sermonizing and trying to get under the man's skin.

If that was his intention, it worked. 'I keep forgetting where you come from,' Bruder said, his face beginning to redden. 'And how patriotic all you cowboys are. The dumb, unthinking kind of patriot.'

'Go to hell, Mr Bruder,' Horn replied quietly, ignoring a warning look from Maggie.

Bruder slammed his glass down on the table, the drink sloshing over the side. 'You're full of shit, young man,' he said. 'You've got a lot to learn about this world. Twenty years ago, I'd have just knocked you down a few times. Now, I suppose I'm a more patient man.'

'I'm not,' Horn said, getting up. 'And I don't like being preached to. Maggie, I think it's time we left.'

'Sit the hell down,' Bruder said.

'John Ray, please.' Maggie's voice was twisted with emotion. She started to say something else, but Bruder held up his hand. He appeared to be listening intently.

Then Horn heard it too. A small scuffing sound, possibly made by shoe leather on the brick walkway outside the front door. *Somebody just walking by*, he thought. But the apprehensive expression on Lillian's face suggested otherwise.

Bruder sprang to his feet, made it to the door in two seconds, and flung it open. 'Well, hello, boys,' he said in a booming voice, stepping outside.

5

Following him, Horn saw two men framed in the window light. One leaned nonchalantly against a tree near the path, arms crossed, regarding Bruder with a faint smile. The other, somewhat younger and noticeably bigger, had one foot propped up on the lip of a small stone fountain, apparently intent on tying a shoelace.

'Careful you don't trip over that,' Bruder said pugnaciously, taking a few steps closer to them. 'In the dark, you could fall and muss up your nice suit.'

The younger man nodded without looking up. He was fullback-size, with a thick neck, a military-style haircut, and a face devoid of expression.

'You hear what you need to hear?' Bruder asked.

'Don't know what you mean,' said the older man. 'We're just taking a walk.' He had an unusual face – round, with large eyes and prominent lips – stuck somewhere between handsome and ugly. He reminded Horn vaguely of a frog. Not a grumpy old bullfrog, more a vigorous frog, sleek, alert, and pleased with himself.

'On your way home, I guess,' Bruder went on.

'Maybe.'

The younger man, having retied his shoelace, now stood and squared his ample shoulders, glancing at his companion. He took off his hat and ran a hand through his hair.

'Where did you say you lived?' Bruder asked.

'Didn't say,' Frog Face replied.

'Oh. Of course not. You're probably not from around here.'

'We'll be going.' As the older man uncrossed his arms, Horn saw a small notebook in one hand.

Bruder stepped into his way. 'We don't like trespassers around here.'

The other man looked bored. 'Mr Bruder, don't you think you've got enough trouble as it is?'

Bruder looked oddly satisfied. 'So you know my name.'

The other man nodded. 'What I don't know,' he said, indicating Horn, 'is *his*.'

Horn said nothing.

'But since I've got his license plate, I'll have his name before long.' He turned to his companion. 'Let's go.' They headed down the path toward the front of the hotel.

'What the hell was that about?' Horn asked.

'That,' Bruder said grimly, 'is about my new life. And that is why you're here tonight.'

The four of them stood uneasily in the doorway. 'FBI, I'd imagine,' Bruder went on. 'Or maybe some of J. Parnell's people. J. Edgar's, J. Parnell's . . . doesn't matter, since they're all cut from the same cloth.'

'Have they been around before?' Maggie asked.

Bruder nodded. 'We're getting used to seeing them out there wherever we go – me on my walks, Lillian when she shops. But they usually keep their distance. Now, it looks like they're coming in closer, eavesdropping.' He made a rude snorting sound. 'Little white-collar pricks.

'Look,' he said to Horn, 'we got off to a bad start. Would you come back inside?'

Horn wanted nothing more than to leave, but Maggie spoke for him. 'Sure we will,' she said, and a moment later they were seated again.

'Back to the subject,' Bruder said, trying to find a comfortable position in his chair. 'Prison, as I suggested, is starting to look very likely.' He took a deep breath, making an effort to calm himself. 'Would you mind telling me about your experience?'

When Horn hesitated, Bruder pressed on. 'I know it's not a pleasant subject. I appreciate whatever information you can give me.'

'All right, then.' The answer came reluctantly.

'Margaret told me a little, and I asked around. It was assault, wasn't it?'

'That's right.'

'And how long were you—'

'Two years. In the state prison up in Cold Creek.'

'Margaret said what you did was justified, and you didn't deserve that much of a sentence.'

Horn smiled at her. 'Thanks, Maggie.' To Bruder he said, 'She knows the man I tangled with. He's not a very likable person. As for whether I deserved it or not, I'll just say I'm glad it's over.'

Bruder nodded. 'Can you tell me some of the things I need to know?'

'About stir? Sure. But first . . . if you get sent up, it'll be to a federal prison, won't it?'

'Yes.'

'Any idea where?'

'No.'

'Well, keep in mind that the folks in the federal pens are different. You'll meet some bank robbers for sure, maybe some kidnappers, but

26

most of the cons will be better behaved than the kind I mixed with. You know, the sort of people who cheat on their taxes. Not as many of the violent ones, the desperadoes.'

'So maybe if I'm lucky, I'll have an introverted little bank embezzler for a cellmate.'

'Maybe.' Horn paused while Lillian went around refreshing their drinks, then resumed.

'Anyway, what helps you in one kind of joint should help you in another. For starters, don't make friends too fast.'

'I don't usually do that anyway. But why not?'

'You'll need time to see who's who. Some people will want to be your friend because of something you can do for them. Maybe you're smart and they're dumb and they want to use your brains, maybe they figure you'll be getting regular money from the outside and they could use some of it. My advice is just to keep your head down and watch everybody. After a while, you'll get a feeling for who you want to be your friends. When that time comes, make as many as you can. You want friends who've got their heads on straight, who know how to do their time. You play chess?'

'A little.'

'It's a good way to pass the time. Better than cards, even.'

'Why?'

'Because it takes longer.'

'Oh. Of course.'

'A few chess-playing friends would be good to have. Another thing: They'll probably give you a job. If you have a choice, avoid the laundry and the chow line.'

'What's so bad about them?'

'They're boring, and boring jobs make the time go slower. Pick something that's got less routine. Some places make license plates, but those are mostly state pens. Others make manhole covers, but that's heavy work. Just pick the best job you can. If they let you.'

Lillian spoke up. 'How about the library?'

'Everybody wants the library. Usually it's the oldest cons who get it. But you can try.'

Horn paused, thinking. 'Cigarettes,' he said. 'You probably heard that cigarettes are like money in the joint. They're used for barter. So is candy and gum, but cigarettes are best. So always have a stock and you'll use them to get favors out of people. The best are the English kind, like Players, 'cause they're so hard to get and they're packed in boxes that hold up better. Have those shipped in and it's like having a roll of money.'

'I'll remember that,' Bruder said, glancing at his wife. She seemed to be lost in her own thoughts. Then she spoke up again.

27

'Is it going to be violent there?'

'Lillian . . .' he began.

'No, Owen, we need to know.' She looked at Horn expectantly.

Bruder exhaled deeply, audibly. 'All right.' He turned to Horn. 'Is it?'

A quick image passed through Horn's mind – words in the chow line, a flash of steel in a man's palm, and a con sagging to the floor, bleeding on the green linoleum as he screamed his lungs out. Horn still had occasional nightmares about it. Only in his dreams, he was the one on the floor, the one screaming.

'It can be violent,' he said. 'It will be, from time to time. You need to be aware of that and be ready for it. There are ways you can be ready.'

He stole a look at Lillian and quickly looked away, wanting to avoid the raw concern in her face. 'It's the young studs you need to watch out for, the ones who're always trying to prove they're tough, and when you're in the yard, it's a good idea to stay close to the wall until you know who's who. After a few days or weeks, you'll start getting the feel of the place.'

'All right.' Bruder's mouth was set in a grim line.

'One more thing: If a fight breaks out anywhere around you, sit down.'

'Sit down?'

'That's right. In the yard, showers, outside your cell, it doesn't matter. The guards will move in to break it up, and they'll use their clubs on anybody who looks like they're part of it. If you sit down and show your hands, you'll be telling them you're not dangerous.'

The room fell quiet, the silence broken faintly by the occasional bright sound of laughter from the pool.

'Time to change the subject?' Maggie asked with an uneasy laugh.

'Yes,' Bruder said emphatically. 'Okay, Mr Horn. You've been—'

'No!'

The word came out almost as a bark. Lillian sat forward on the sofa, hands clasped tightly, the hurt plainly written on her face. The other three stared at her.

'I'm sickened by this, all of this talk,' she said to her husband. Her sense of gentleness and calm had vanished, replaced by desperate concern for him. 'We need more from this man than just advice on how not to get killed in prison.'

'Lillian, we talked about this.'

'I know, but I'm not giving up so easily. And you're not either.'

'What the hell do you want me to do?'

'We haven't tried everything. I'm not going to let you walk into prison without a fight.'

To Horn she said, 'When all this started, the studio took his latest writing assignment away from him. They said they sympathized and they were sure it would all be resolved eventually, but he was put on suspension. It's the same as being fired, only it sounds more polite. That's why we're renting this place. We had to sell our house to pay the legal fees and get ready for who knows what else may be waiting for us – especially if he goes away.'

'I'm sorry,' Horn said.

'We hired an investigator to try to find out who secretly named Owen, but the man quit a week later. He wouldn't say why, but I think he was frightened of something.'

Horn studied her as she spoke. In the light from the table lamp, the bones of her cheek and brow and strong jaw stood out dramatically. As she talked and gestured with her graceful artist's hands, her graying hair was coming loose from the plain bun that held it at the nape of her neck, and a strand fell over her face. *She's one of those women who don't pay much attention to their clothes or their looks*, he thought. *But not long ago she was something.*

'A week after we moved in here, the FBI showed up,' she went on bitterly. 'First cousins to that pair we saw tonight. Two very clean-cut young men went around talking to the hotel management and then to all our neighbors, asking questions about us and making sure everybody knew who we were.'

'We're the new neighbors who wear the scarlet C on our chests,' her husband said with a straight face.

'I don't know how you can joke about it.' She turned to the others. 'We've gotten some letters. Anonymous. Full of hate. *Commies burn in Hell*, one of them said.'

Maggie reached out and touched her hand.

'Owen can't go to prison,' Lillian said quietly.

'Lillian . . .' he began.

'Don't try to stop me,' she said to him, her voice like a wire drawn taut. To the others, she said, 'He's sick. His heart. Prison would kill him. I know it.'

Maggie looked stricken. Bruder sat quietly, head lowered. Horn could find nothing to say, and all of them were quiet for a while.

Lillian turned to him. 'Margaret has told us about the kind of work you do,' she said. 'You work for a gambler.'

'A friend,' Horn said. 'Joseph Mad Crow. He runs a poker parlor. I help him keep his books straight.'

'When people owe him money, you're the one he sends to collect it,' Lillian said doggedly.

'If I have to.' He shot Maggie an accusing look.

'You were in the war. You got a Purple Heart, Margaret told us.'

'I was shot. That's what gets you a Purple Heart. Nothing else.' He wanted to change the subject. Memories of his time in the war always brought him shame.

'It means you were close enough to the enemy to get shot,' Lillian went on. 'Not all men have had experience with violence.'

'If you say so.' His tone now verged on rudeness. 'Why are we talking about this?'

'Because my husband and I want you to help us. We want to hire you to find out who named Owen, and we want you to confront this person and make him retract what he said. If he won't retract it, at least we'll be able to put a name to the lie, and maybe then we can fight it.'

'Lillian, I'm not the person to do this,' Horn said, putting down his drink as her husband listened silently. 'I've already got a job. I'm not a licensed investigator, and I've never gotten along with the police. You need somebody different—'

'We've tried someone different. Now we want you.'

'This is not the job for me,' he said emphatically. 'I'm very sorry.' He stood up and retrieved his fedora from a nearby table.

'We've got a long drive,' he said to Maggie.

'You told them a lot about me,' Horn said as he guided the Ford up the steep canyon road.

'Yeah, I did.' No apology in her tone.

He drove in silence for a while, still wondering about Maggie and Owen Bruder. He fiddled with the radio, looking for a station that could be heard in the canyon. After a while, he found a broadcast from the Cocoanut Grove nightclub in the Ambassador Hotel. Led by bandleader Freddy Martin's tenor sax, the orchestra launched into the grandiose, ersatz-Tchaikovsky strains of 'Tonight We Love'.

Maggie reached over and switched off the radio. In the dim dashboard light, her face was taut.

'Something on your mind?' Horn asked her.

'Damn right,' she said. 'You could have helped them.'

'Come on, Maggie. I'm sorry for them, but I'm not right for this. And I don't need a job anyway.'

'Hell you don't. Wasn't it just last week you were telling me how Joseph was spending so much time chasing this Cissie what's-her-name that he was letting things slide at the casino? When's the last time he gave you something to do?'

'I don't know. What difference does it make?'

'You could use the money.'

'Why do you care so much? What's this guy to you? I saw the way you were looking at him tonight. Is he an old boyfriend?'

'Oh, you're crazy.'

'Well, is he? That would explain a lot.'

As he spoke, he was surprised to feel a small nudge of jealousy. The idea of Maggie being with Owen Bruder stirred up in him a kind of resentment he had never felt toward Davey Peake.

She sat rigidly against the right-side door, absent-mindedly massaging her sore wrist with the other hand. 'Go to hell,' she said softly.

'How's your wrist?'

'It'll be all right.'

He drove in silence for a moment. Then: 'You know, I wondered why you got on those horses yesterday. Didn't make sense, because you'd just finished telling Davey what a damn fool idea it was. Next thing I knew, there you were, tearing around the corral like the queen of the serials. It was right around the time Owen and his wife showed up, wasn't it?'

When she didn't respond, he went on. 'It wasn't Davey. You did it to impress Owen, didn't you?' When he glanced to his right, he saw her staring at him, almost as if she were daring him to go on.

That's when the thought hit him. He braked suddenly and pulled the car over onto the narrow shoulder.

'Don't tell me he's your father. That would be . . .'

The look on her face told him everything. 'I'll be damned,' he breathed as a car swept by perilously close. 'Owen. He's your father.'

She nodded. 'Nobody's supposed to know,' she said. 'He wants it that way.'

'Because he's such a nice guy?'

'Don't make judgments. I'll tell you the whole story. But none of that's important right now.'

He knew what she meant. He waited for the next gap in traffic, then gunned the engine and twisted the wheel into a tight U-turn.

Ten minutes later he was knocking on the door of the Bruders' bungalow. Lillian opened it, still dressed, drink in hand. She looked tired and dejected.

'I've changed my mind,' he said.

6

One of Hollywood's longest-reigning queens, Joan Crawford, is set to step in front of the camera in the Michael Curtiz production of Flamingo Road, *and we predict that the role of a tough and sassy carnival girl may give new oomph to her career. Just how long has the ageless Joan been around? It would be rude to ask.*

And now, you know how I love it when a juicy rumor turns into a fact. The bosses at little Medallion Pictures are in a tizzy over the news that one of their most popular stars has been ordered to appear before the Thomas Committee and explain his membership in the Communist Party. We won't mention his name; we'll just say he's best known for riding a horse and playing a guitar. His hat, naturally, is white. But maybe it should be red.

This is Laura Lee Paisley signing off. Tune in tomorrow, and you'll find me here at the Hollywood Alhambra, same time, same station. I love all of you, I love this town . . . and pass the popcorn!

Horn and Maggie stood leaning back against his car's headlights, looking out over the vast basin of the city. Here at the crest of the Santa Monica Mountains, they felt a breeze borne up from the ocean. Maggie had buttoned her coat, and Horn had pulled up the collar of his sport jacket. Dark around all its edges, the basin was aglow with tiny lights, some faintly dispersed, others arranged in brighter strings that formed an irregular grid. Here and there the white lights were interrupted by richer colors – green, blue, red.

'Look down there,' Maggie said, pointing. 'Which one is that?'

'The tall blue one? I'm not sure,' Horn replied. 'I think it's the Roosevelt Hotel. Wait: Maybe it's the El Capitan Theater. Anyway, it's somewhere along Hollywood Boulevard.'

'I love neon,' she said. 'Didn't there used to be a lot more?'

'Uh-huh. You don't get over on this side of the hill much, do you? They turned 'em all off during the war. Afraid of Jap air raids. Now a few are coming back on. You know what I miss? The beacon on top of City Hall.'

'I knew there was something missing,' she said. 'You could see it for miles.'

They were still a long way from Maggie's place, but he had pulled over at a nearly deserted turnoff on Mulholland Drive, on the way back from the Garden of Allah, to give them a chance to talk. He pulled out his pouch of Bull Durham and his papers and began rolling a smoke.

'You never heard this story,' she said, still facing the broad display of distant lights. 'My mom was an adventurous girl. She left Arizona and went all the way to New York to find a job, and she worked as a secretary for some kind of theatrical agent. In his office she met my father. He was starting to write plays. She was pretty, he was good-looking and exciting to be around. They had a fling, very intense, for a few weeks. When she found out she was expecting and he didn't want to marry her, she realized she wasn't as adventurous as she'd thought, and she moved back to live with her parents on their ranch. And married her high school sweetheart.'

'Who was—'

'The man who raised me. Did a good job of it too. I thought he was my father until my mom told me the truth. I'd just turned twenty-three, and I was selling ladies' dresses at a store in Phoenix. A nice boy had asked me to marry him, but as soon as I heard that my real father's name was Owen Bruder and he wrote movies in Hollywood, I knew it was time for me to leave. I didn't hate my mother and father, or anything like that. I just knew I wasn't supposed to marry that nice boy or stay in Phoenix.

'My parents gave me the bus fare, and I came out here with my one suitcase and straw in my hair.' She laughed. 'Not really, but I must have looked that way. Your typical rancher's daughter.'

'Let me see,' he said. 'I think there's still a little bit stuck in there.' He reached for her hair, playfully fingering a lock of it. She brushed his hand aside with a grin.

'I looked up Owen and told him who I was. He had been married to Lillian for a year or so, and he wasn't happy to see me. My mother had written him about me, so it wasn't a total surprise. But he never really . . . owned up to being my father. Never said the words. He was polite, but that was all. Invited me in, gave me a cup of coffee, warned me that with the Depression on, it wouldn't be easy to get work around here. Didn't offer to help, either.'

'Great guy.'

'But I had my mind made up. I moved into a furnished room on Cahuenga, just off Hollywood Boulevard, down there somewhere—' She pointed. 'Six of us working girls in one furnished room with bunk beds and a hot plate, fifty cents a night apiece. He was right about jobs being scarce, but I had one thing in my favor: the movies were looking for women who could ride. And that's how I got my first job at Monogram, and then a little better one at Republic, and finally a decent one at Medallion, where you and I ran into each other.'

'And the queen of the serials was on her way.'

'Something like that. All that time, Owen and I were barely in touch. He knew where I was and I knew where he was, but we didn't do much about it. If anybody made an effort, I think it was Lillian. A really decent lady, and she didn't need to be. She was always the one who'd call me once a year or so, just to check in.'

'You know . . .' He took one last drag on the butt of his handmade, dropped it into the dirt, and ground it out with his heel. 'He's really kind of a son of a bitch, Maggie.'

'I know, but I've always been worried about what he might think of me. After a while, when I was starting to make good money at Medallion and people would come up to ask for my autograph, I was feeling like I'd made something out of myself. But the few times I'd see Owen, it was clear to me that he looked down his nose at the work I was doing. He was writing important movies for the likes of Henry Fonda and Joan Fontaine, and I was riding horses and getting my face dirty.'

'Then why—'

'Bother to help him? Well, I could say it's because he's my father, and I guess that's part of the answer. But I don't love him as much as I love the folks who raised me. No, I think it's mostly because . . .' She made a helpless gesture and tried again. 'Look, when the trouble started for them, that was when Lillian called me. I'm sure it was her idea, just like every other time, but this time it seemed different. I had the idea that he might really need something from me.'

She turned toward him, her face pale. 'Damn it, I want him to be proud of me. If this is the only way I can get him to be, then I'll settle for that.'

Horn couldn't see his wristwatch when he awoke, but he guessed it to be sometime after midnight. Something had tugged him awake, and he knew what it was. The new job.

He rolled out of the large couch that served as his bed, wrapped the blanket around him, went out to the front porch of the cabin and sat in the bentwood rocker. On nights like this, the rocker sometimes had the effect of the motion of a cradle, soothing him back into sleep.

In the near-total darkness, the muted night sounds of the canyon were all around him. He knew them well: the merest hint of wind through the trees, the skittering sound of a squirrel up in the branches. Coyote often ranged through the canyon, shadowy and hard to spot, haunting the night with their calls. One evening, as Horn had sat motionless, a doe and two fawns picked their way delicately across the ground a few yards below his porch. Catching his scent and then seeing him, they froze, motionless as lawn statuary, then bounded away up the slope behind the cabin.

The job felt wrong – a bad fit, like a pawnshop suit. He had no liking for Owen Bruder, only a grudging respect for his intellect, strong will, and bullheaded sense of rectitude.

As movie cowboy Sierra Lane, Horn had earned a lot of money for Medallion Pictures, riding a horse, mouthing his lines, and playing the hero. Since prison, though, he had found himself with few useful skills. In the sometimes touchy work he did for Mad Crow, he had developed a kind of simple, unpolished diplomacy in dealing with people, and he was usually able to keep a rein on his temper – the demon that had put him in prison. For the few cases in which diplomacy did not work, other methods usually did. Violence sometimes reared up, but he tried never to initiate it.

None of his crude skills seemed to be right for this job. He was doing it, he knew, for the money – and for Maggie. Horn had few friends, and even fewer good friends, but she, along with Mad Crow, was one. After their brief affair years ago, he had left her for the woman he eventually married. The marriage had not lasted. Maggie, even when hurt, had behaved decently toward him. He was grateful to have her friendship again and there was little he would not do for her.

The rocking chair did its work. Soon he was back on the couch, still wrapped in the blanket, and asleep.

In the morning, he drove into Santa Monica to have breakfast at a fish place out on the pier. As he ate, he looked through a day-old *Mirror* he had found on a bench. The lead story quoted Harry Truman's secretary of state as saying that the Russians, with the help of spies in America, were known to be working on an atomic bomb and might be ready to test it in a year or so. The FBI's J. Edgar Hoover said undercover Communist agents were the most dangerous threat to this country's internal security. There was a separate story on J. Parnell Thomas, the congressman whose investigative committee had taken aim at Owen Bruder. And, in the same story, a few references to Thomas' chief investigator, a man named Mitchell Cross.

Farther back in the paper he found a three-paragraph story saying that wildfires were burning at various locations in the Malibu hills and in the mountains to the north of the San Fernando Valley. They were not considered an immediate danger, county fire officials said, but a shift in the prevailing winds along with the usual dry conditions this time of year could change the picture overnight.

At ten, he walked to his bank and cashed Lillian Bruder's check, then he found a phone booth in a drugstore and called the investigator the Bruders had hired, but couldn't make it past the secretary. Another nickel got a friend at the *Times* who, for a fee, sometimes helped him dig up information on people . . .

The *Times* stood on the edge of a cluster of government structures, most of them vaguely classical in look. The newspaper building was squat, gray, and solid, resembling a mausoleum. Diagonally across from it loomed the tower of City Hall, pale and gracelessly monumental.

Horn parked in a lot nearby and soon he saw his young friend approaching at a sauntering gait.

'Hey,' Leonard said. He was probably still in his teens, coatless, his tie unknotted, his once-white shirt bearing stains that looked like ink.

'What did you find?'

Leonard handed over three business-size manila envelopes. 'Like usual, I got to ask you not to let anybody see you looking at these—'

'I'll just sit here in my car, all right?'

'Sure. They can't be out for more than an hour, so I'll have to come pick 'em up at noon The old lady who runs the morgue is a real hard case.'

'The morgue,' Horn said. 'Where old stories go when they die.' It was an old joke between them. 'You a reporter yet?'

Leonard shook his head. 'Still a copyboy.'

Horn handed him three dollars. 'This okay?'

'Fine.' Leonard folded the bills and crammed them in his pocket.

After Leonard was gone, Horn settled himself behind the wheel and studied the first envelope. Typed at the top were the words *J. Parnell Thomas, US Congressman*, and underneath that the line, stamped in red ink, *Property of LA Times Morgue; Please Return*.

Inside he found a small stack of articles clipped from the paper. He arranged them in chronological order and, removing a pocket notebook and pencil from his jacket, he began to read.

It was around five when Horn found the address, a tidy four-story building on the north side of Wilshire Boulevard, along a stretch of big-ticket addresses that included doctors, insurance companies and restaurants with menus in French. He drove through to a small, private parking area in the back and nosed the Ford into one of the empty spaces.

He adjusted the side mirror to give him a view of the rear entrance to the building, then pretended to look through the paper he'd picked up on the pier, his eyes never straying long from the mirror. After a little more than half an hour, he saw a man leave the building and walk toward a shiny sedan parked nearby. Horn got out and approached him.

'Mr Vance?'

The other man looked at him warily. 'I know you, sport?' He was sturdily built, good-looking, well-dressed, and carefully groomed. He reminded Horn more of a Cadillac salesman than the typical peeper, a trade that Horn sometimes encountered through his own work for Mad Crow. The Bruders had told him that Vance often did discreet work for those who could afford his fees, many of them in Hollywood, and had come highly recommended.

'Name's John Ray Horn. I called your office earlier today, trying to get an appointment.'

'Oh.' Vance showed no expression as he gave Horn the once-over, quickly noting the open-necked shirt under the sport jacket, the unshined Army-surplus oxfords, the slacks that had been worn a few too many times since their last pressing. 'My office is very busy right now.'

'Sure sounds that way.'

'How did you know me?'

'I didn't. But there are only two parking spaces marked A. Dixon Vance Investigations. One has an old Chevy, but that'd be your secretary's. You I'd figure for the nice new Buick.'

'All right.' Vance waited.

'Maybe I shouldn't have told your secretary I wanted to talk about Owen Bruder,' Horn went on. 'Soon as I said that, your calendar seemed to fill right up.'

'I don't discuss client business.' Vance's sport coat, single-breasted in the new style, was just this side of loud, a hound's-tooth in cream, brown and green.

'Way I hear it, he was your client for about five minutes,' Horn said. 'And I also believe his wife called your office to tell you it was all right to talk to me.'

'She may have,' Vance said. 'But that wouldn't matter to me, sport. It's a question of ethics.' He pulled car keys out of his pocket.

'Look,' Horn said with a grin. 'This was a long drive for me, coming to see you. We're kind of in the same business, you and me. Although going by your address and this nice car, you're a lot more successful at it than I am.'

'You're an investigator?' Vance asked.

'You could call it that. Whatever the job needs, I do.'

Vance tilted his head slightly, as if seeing Horn through fresh eyes. 'You look a little familiar,' he said. 'You weren't in the movies, were you?'

'For a while.'

'I've got a pretty good thing for names and faces,' Vance said slowly. 'Now I remember. John Ray Horn. Cowboy pictures, right? And some kind of trouble.' As the memories finally lined up in place, he looked pleased with himself. 'Now I've got it. You did some time.'

'That's right.'

'What's a guy like you doing working for Bruder?'

'Well, that's what I'd like to talk to you about. Can you spare me a few minutes?'

Vance looked at his watch. 'Oh, hell,' he said without much feeling. 'I suppose.'

A few minutes later they were settled in a plush booth in a bar a few doors from Vance's office. The place was cool and suitably dark, with the calculated look of an English pub, and the waitress called Vance by name as she took their order.

Horn took a few minutes to explain his involvement. 'So you're doing this as a favor?' Vance asked.

'No, I'm getting paid. But you could also say I have a personal connection.' He pulled at his beer. 'Now let me ask you a few things. For starters, why did you quit the job after a week?'

'For my own reasons,' Vance said evenly.

'Lillian Bruder told me you returned their whole retainer and kept only some expense money. Isn't that unusual for somebody in your line of work?'

Vance shrugged. 'It seemed the right thing to do. I wasn't able to help them.'

'Seems to me you didn't keep at it long enough to find out.'

Vance shrugged again, his face expressionless. *Bet he plays a good hand of poker*, Horn thought. 'Can you tell me anything you turned up? Anybody you talked to?'

'No, sorry. That's—'

'I know. Confidential.' Horn took a long swallow of his beer, thinking. 'A guy like you, who's obviously good at what he does, folds up his tent after just a few days and returns the client's money. That's like admitting failure, right? Just makes me wonder if you had another reason for quitting. Maybe you decided you didn't want to be mixed up with a Red or one of those – what do you call them? – fellow travelers. Maybe it wouldn't be good for your business.'

For the first time, Vance allowed himself a thin smile. 'Look around you, Mr Horn,' he said. 'There are about twenty people in this bar. Two of them are former clients of mine, and one of those owns some of the biggest buildings on this street. I've also done work for some well-known people in the movie business. I'm successful because I just may be the best in this town at what I do. I'll work for whoever I damn well please, good people and bad, and the clients will still show up at my door.'

'That's nice to know,' Horn said. 'But there are other possibilities. I just remembered something Mrs Bruder said, that you behaved a little bit like a man who'd had a scare thrown into him. And it occurred to me that her husband may have some pretty powerful enemies, going all the way up to the US Congress. Now I'm sure that if these people got it into their heads

38

to either strong-arm somebody or buy them off, they'd have very little trouble.'

Vance shook his head almost pityingly. 'I'm not going to be rude back to you, but I will try to give you some advice. You're a has-been actor who takes odd jobs. Now here you are, suddenly rolling dice with the big boys, and you don't have an idea of the size of the game you're in. I couldn't help Owen Bruder. You can't help him either. If you try, a bunch of people are going to step on you very hard. Try to be smart.'

Vance got up abruptly. 'I should go,' he said, pulling out his wallet. 'Enjoyed our talk. Good luck to you.'

'Put that away,' Horn said. 'I didn't expect any of this would be free.'

As he watched A. Dixon Vance nod pleasantly to several others on his way out, Horn wondered why a man would want to lead off his name with a lonely initial. J. Edgar Hoover. J. Parnell Thomas. A. Dixon Vance. And he found himself reminded of an old piece of advice from Mad Crow – delivered only partly in jest, it seemed at the time – *Never trust a man who parts his name on the side.*

7

The rough outline of Owen Bruder's life sprawled over two pages of a pocket notebook in Horn's inelegant scrawl. *Not much,* he thought, *but I guess it's a start.* What he had was the bare bones of a life as reported in the pages of the *LA Times,* the skeleton before the flesh is applied.

Bruder's earliest mention was in 1931, when the left-wing Group Theater in New York produced a play he had written. It was described as 'a song to the common man' and 'a celebration of working-class values.' It closed after two weeks.

Horn sat in a café on Wilshire, a no-frills place run by a Greek and known for good food at decent prices. While he waited for his pork chops, he went through the notes he'd quickly jotted down from the newspaper clippings, and tried to ignore the play-by-play coming from the portable radio behind the counter, the Yanks and the Indians back east.

His next note was dated 1935, when Magnum Arts Studios announced that Bruder had signed a three-year contract to write screenplays. A studio spokesman praised his talent for writing 'socially significant dramas.' In 1938 came his Academy Award for *The Last Harvest,* the story of a struggling couple out west trying to keep the family farm from being swallowed up by big business interests. The following year, Bruder was arrested in a group of demonstrators picketing a farmers' organization in the San Joaquin Valley on behalf of better wages for farm workers. After he spent a night in jail, the charges were dropped.

The clippings mentioned several more films over the years. Then came the item Horn had been looking for, dated just a few months ago. Under the headline *Prominent Hollywood Scribe Named as Red,* the article quoted sources on the House Un-American Activities Committee staff as saying an unnamed informant had testified to Bruder's membership in the Communist Party USA. Counting Bruder, the article noted, more than twenty writers, producers, directors, and actors had been named as members of the party, and all had been subpoenaed. Almost as an afterthought, the last sentence of the article noted Bruder's denial of membership.

He noticed one other thing: the news that Bruder had been named was first disclosed on 'the radio program of Laura Lee Paisley, whose well-sourced Hollywood gossip often strays into the field of politics.'

His dinner arrived, and he ate with one hand while paging through the notebook with the other. The clips on J. Parnell Thomas had been more extensive than those on Bruder. Horn ticked off the milestones: Mayor of Allendale, New Jersey, 1931. A year in the state legislature, where he began developing a reputation as a Communist hunter; elected to the US Congress in 1936, where he sponsored a bill calling for the public execution of kidnappers; a founding member of the House Committee on Un-American Activities, and eventually its chairman. A photo in one of the clippings, Horn recalled, had shown a broad, jowly, combative-looking Irish face leaning into a microphone, mouth open, his bald-topped head ringed by a fringe of white hair.

The rest of the pages dealt with Mitchell Cross, the committee's chief investigator, an ex-Marine lieutenant and war hero. Although not in the spotlight like his boss, he was instrumental in the committee's work, tirelessly digging up crucial information on individuals' pasts. 'He's like a bulldog,' said one committee staffer admiringly. 'He can get the goods on anybody.' Not even his boss hated Communists more than Cross, it was said. And a senator who was sympathetic to the committee's goals said that if Cross ever sought a career in electoral politics, 'we can use him.'

Horn's notes took him back to one particular article he had read closely while sitting in his car, an account of Cross' role in the battle for Okinawa. *Artillery and mortar fire all night long*, he read in his hasty scribble. *Waves of enemy attacks. All officers and noncoms wounded or dead. Lieutenant Cross took over, firing until barrel glowed red.*

In the morning, the article had continued, the ground in front of the trench was carpeted with Japanese bodies, and Mitchell Cross was slumped over the still-warm barrel of the gun, his mangled leg tucked underneath him. He returned from the war with a Silver Star and a permanent limp.

Horn knew about combat. Because of his doubts about his own courage, the notion of cowardice repelled him. But so did heroism, because it suggested an almost unattainable ideal. If he feared heroism because it was beyond most human capability, he feared cowardice because it was all too human, too attainable.

To Horn, the Mitchell Crosses of this world were bigger than life. Better, somehow, more trustworthy than most of humanity. Horn had signed on to defend Owen Bruder, who was accused of turning his back on his country. And Bruder's enemy, it said here in black and white, was one of the best and bravest of Americans. It seemed an unequal contest.

★

The next morning Horn was up early. He had work to do for his landlord. Putting on his heavy gloves, he carried a large canvas sack up the hill behind his cabin, walking steadily until he reached a broad plateau of several acres ringed by oak and eucalyptus. The plateau was grass and weeds, interrupted here and there by what might have been Roman ruins. But they were only painted plaster over wood frame, made all the sadder by a fire that had burned across the plateau about a decade earlier, leaving only foundations and a few scorched walls. This was the old Aguilar estate, a remnant of the time when the gods and goddesses of the silent screen built monuments to their own divinity. Now it was just a piece of property waiting to be sold, and Horn was its caretaker, living there rent-free in return for keeping it up.

He spent a couple of hours pulling weeds from around the tumbled-down remnants of the buildings. Then, after cleaning up and changing his clothes, he breakfasted at the diner down the road, where the canyon met the Pacific, then drove toward Hollywood, taking Sunset east. As he neared Vine, he saw it was almost ten. He pulled over, tuned in the radio and, at precisely ten o'clock, a smooth baritone announced, 'It's time for "Around and About Hollywood", with Laura Lee Paisley, brought to you by Silk, the beauty soap of the stars.' This was followed by the urgent, high-pitched *dit-dah-dit* of a simulated radio broadcast in Morse code. Then:

Hello, all, this is Laura Lee, with sixty seconds of Hollywood news, gossip, and secrets. The voice was girlish and well-modulated, with a sense of glee.

Let's get right to it, shall we? My spies tell me Robert Taylor and Ava Gardner are absolutely sizzling on the set of The Bribe. *The handsome Robert hasn't had a real hit since before the war, but maybe this one will be his ticket back. We all know he never should have made* Song of Russia, *MGM's misguided attempt to whitewash those people who called themselves our allies. But he owned up to his mistake, he did his patriotic duty during the war, and we wish him all good things.*

This is a perfect time for a Laura Lee bouquet in the direction of the Motion Picture Alliance for the Preservation of American Ideals, whose members are also doing their patriotic duty in protecting our way of life. Robert Taylor happens to be one of the founding members of this worthy organization, along with his lovely wife, Barbara Stanwyck. Memo to Barbara: Yes, it's true that Ava's divorce from Artie Shaw is now final, and she's back on the available list. But you shouldn't be concerned about those love scenes in The Bribe. *What's that they say? It's only a movie, dear.*

Now this is Laura Lee Paisley signing off. Tune in tomorrow, and you'll find me here at the Hollywood Alhambra, same time, same station. I love all of you, I love this town . . . and hurray for Hollywood!

42

Horn pulled back into traffic and took a left on Vine for a couple of blocks, parked across the street from the entrance to the Alhambra and walked over.

Although the Hollywood Alhambra was one of the oldest hotels in the city, Horn had never been inside. It was smaller and quieter than most of the others, and it seemed to belong to an earlier age, the infancy of Hollywood, before the movies learned to talk. He had heard that the hotel had become something of a refuge for old actors.

The two-story lobby was quiet and not very spacious. It was decorated in what passed for a Moorish motif, and had the slightly worn look of a place that was trying, with only modest success, to hold its own. The plush sofas and heavy drapes gave off the faintest smell of mildew. Giant urns flanked the base of the broad staircase. On the wall opposite the reception desk was a large, faded mural depicting a beautiful walled courtyard, populated by bearded men in robes and women in veils. Below the mural, a tiled fountain gave off a pleasant watery sound.

Horn signaled to a young bellhop, who came over. 'Yes, sir?'

'Laura Lee Paisley. She stay here?'

'Yes, sir. Got an office here too.'

'Point me there?' He flipped a quarter, George Raft-style, and the kid caught it expertly.

'Sure. It's on the mezzanine. Top of the stairs, to the right. Her name's on the door.'

'Thanks.' On his way to the stairs, he passed the dining room's open double doors. The room was in disarray. Some of the furniture was draped in sheets, and workmen were carrying a big table out another set of doors.

Upstairs, he found the name Laura Lee Paisley on a frosted-glass door. Inside was a small, windowless anteroom with just enough space for a desk, a chair and a young woman who was typing at a frantic pace, fingers flying.

'Miss Paisley in?'

'You making a delivery?' she asked without looking up.

'No, I'm bringing her some information.'

'She's up on the roof.'

'Where?'

The young woman looked up and took him in at a glance, her expression impatient. 'Every morning she works up on the roof garden,' she said, enunciating carefully. 'Take the elevator.'

'Well, thanks. You've been a big help.' The anteroom, he noticed, contained two doors, one bearing the Paisley name on an identical frosted-glass pane, the other made of solid wood and padlocked shut. 'I appreciate it.'

He took the rickety elevator from the mezzanine up to the roof garden and stepped out into bright sunshine. Looking around he saw much of Hollywood spread out below and, far off to the southeast, the tower of City Hall, tallest building of this horizontal town.

The roof garden was little more than a collection of potted palms, arranged in a big square in the center of which was a kind of pavilion – a garishly striped tent, open to the front – holding several lounge chairs and a table. He walked over. As he approached, he heard a voice.

'Get him,' the voice commanded. 'I don't care if he's in the crapper. Get him. Tell him it's me calling. And I know about the trip to Del Mar. And tell him I know it wasn't business.' A pause, then, 'All right. But if he doesn't want to be the star of my five o'clock show, I want a call from him in the next hour.'

Phone met cradle sharply. The voice was the one Horn had heard on the radio, and yet it was not. There was the same girlishness and music-ality, but this time it held an edge, a layer of menace.

The owner of the voice came into view. She reclined on a cushioned lounge chair, swathed in a brightly colored bathrobe, a matching turban covering most of her blonde hair, eyes hidden behind dark glasses. Although not tall, she was a large woman, and her face – fully made up, with blush on her cheeks and mouth the color of cherries – was round and soft-looking.

At a table next to the lounge chair sat a nondescript young woman in a plain dress, bent over a steno pad. At the rear of the tent, on a folding chair, sat a man of indeterminate age reading a magazine.

'Are you from Paramount?' the woman in the bathrobe demanded as Horn walked over. 'Did you bring the stills?'

'No, ma'am,' he replied.

'Well, who the hell are you?' The tone was neither hostile nor par-ticularly friendly.

'Name's John Ray Horn,' he said. 'I'm looking for Miss Paisley.'

'You've found her.' To get a better look at him, she lowered the dark glasses, showing off eyebrows with a pronounced, penciled arch. 'You're a long drink of water, aren't you?'

'Sorry to bother you,' he said. 'I'd just like a few minutes of your time.'

'About . . . ?'

'Owen Bruder.'

She reached for a pitcher of iced tea on the table, refreshed her glass and, taking her time, sipped at it, again hidden behind the glasses.

'You're not his lawyer,' she said. 'I know his lawyer. You're not the man he hired to snoop around. I know him too.'

'He quit. I guess I'm the new one he hired to snoop around.'

44

'Ah.' That seemed to satisfy her. 'Well, you don't dress as well as the last one.'

'No, ma'am.'

'You've got better manners, though. I don't get called ma'am very often. People usually kiss up to me or call me names.' She sighed theatrically. 'It's the curse of my profession.' Her manner turned brusque. 'I've got nothing to say to you about Bruder. I covered him in my broadcast, and he needs to be thinking about what he's going to say to J. Parnell Thomas.'

Horn was about to speak when the phone rang. The young woman answered it, listened for a moment, and said, 'It's Jack Warner.'

'Jack!' Laura Lee Paisley exclaimed into the phone, waving Horn away. 'I hear Errol is about to divorce his wife . . . What? A little birdie, that's who. I need to know if it's true.' She was silent for a moment. Then: 'Jack, you son of a bitch, don't try to con me. He's not the star he was ten years ago, what do *you* care if I pick this up . . . ?'

Since Hollywood gossip bored him, Horn wandered over to the edge of the roof, looked down, and saw men loading the dining room furniture into a big van. Turning, he again noticed the man reading in the rear of the tent and went over to him. He looked up and closed the magazine.

Horn recognized the cover. It was *Yank*. 'I didn't know they still put that out,' he said.

'They don't. This is an old one. I was just looking at it again.' He showed it to Horn. It was dated 1944, and the cover was on the Normandy invasion.

'You read *Yank*?' the man asked.

'Well, not for years. But I used to,' Horn said. 'Who's the pinup this time?'

The man flipped the magazine over and showed the back cover.

'Anne Gwynne,' Horn said. 'Wonder whatever happened to her.'

'I don't know,' the man said. 'But Laura Lee would. She knows what happens to everybody.'

Horn gave him a closer look. Something didn't sit quite right with the man. He was conventionally handsome, probably somewhere in his late thirties. His clothes were decent quality, but his shirt collar didn't fit snugly, his tie was slightly askew, and his razor had missed a couple of spots on his jaw. On the left side of his head, a patch of snow-white hair stood out amid the brown, like a poisoned place on the ground where no healthy grass would grow.

'She has a room next to her office,' the man went on, wearing a slight, fixed smile. 'It's all filing cabinets, all around the walls. She calls it her room of secrets. If you ever want to know what happened to somebody, I'll bet you it's—'

45

'George!' Laura Lee shouted. 'Don't bother the man.' She was off the phone.

'Thanks for letting me see the magazine,' Horn said.

'I've got more,' said the man.

Horn returned to the lounge chair. 'I'm afraid you're going to have to leave,' she said. 'I've still got three calls out—'

'What if I had some news for you about Mr Bruder?'

'All right. I'll bite.'

'He was never in the Communist Party.'

'Baloney.'

'It's true. Whoever said that about him—'

'Hey, my source is better than your source, buddy boy,' she said. 'Your client is lying to save his skin. If he can cut a deal in DC, he can stay out of prison. I'm through with him. I've moved on.' Then she smiled almost flirtatiously. 'Did you know that Errol Flynn is getting a divorce? It'll be on my five o'clock, but you heard it first.'

'Look, Miss Paisley, even if he stays out of jail, all this noise about him on the radio and in the papers has put him out of work.'

'What do you want me to do about it?'

'You could at least level with me about who told you.'

'That he was a Red? Uh-uh.' She shook her turbaned head. 'My sources are sacred.'

'Some of your sources lie to you. Don't you care?'

'I'm getting bored. There's the elevator. Remember what I said about those clothes of yours. I know a good haberdasher downtown on Sixth.'

'You're not a very nice person.'

'Don't make me call George over here. He'll send you down faster than the elevator.' Laura Lee had adopted a little girl's schoolyard voice. She seemed to be enjoying their repartee.

'What does George do for you? Just curious.'

'Anything I need. Goodbye, Mr Horn.'

As he headed for the elevator, he heard her say, almost to herself, 'I know you from someplace,' but he kept walking.

In the lobby, passing an elderly man asleep in one of the overstuffed chairs, he spotted the bellhop and gave him another wave. The boy trotted over.

'What's the deal with all the furniture moving?' he asked.

'You don't know? They sold the hotel.'

'Who to?'

'I don't know exactly, but word is, they're going to tear the place down. Everybody's got to be out of here in a couple of weeks.'

'Really? What happens to you?'

'I've got a job. At the Ambassador. My dad works there.'

'Good for you,' Horn said, flipping another quarter. 'You're going up in the world.' With a grin, the kid caught it overhanded this time.

On his way out the door, Horn thought, *I wonder if I'm somewhere in that room too. The one with the padlock.*

He stopped for supplies at the store on the way home, then drove the last few miles toward the point where Culebra Canyon, in some random quirk of geology, dead-ended in the Santa Monica Mountains. At the cabin, he changed back into his work clothes and spent the rest of the afternoon weeding around the grounds of the estate. The slow-moving brush fire in the hills of Malibu was a few miles up the coast. There was no wind, but he made a special effort to clear away dry brush, which could accelerate a wildfire almost as fast as gasoline.

The tennis court was overgrown with weeds, its net long gone. In the dead center of the court Horn noticed what was left of a coyote's fresh kill – a possum, perhaps. Somewhere in a magazine once, he had seen a photo taken at that very spot showing a group of doubles players on a long-ago sunny day. Radiant in tennis whites, he recalled, were Ricardo Aguilar, the beaming host, with shining teeth and gleaming, slicked-back hair; his partner, Gloria Swanson; and, on the other side of the net, William Randolph Hearst with his mistress, Marion Davies. They all looked impossibly rich, privileged, and happy.

I don't think you'd recognize your place now, Ricardo, Horn said silently.

Back at the cabin, he had just begun running a hot bath in the old claw-footed tub that took up most of the floor space in his tiny bathroom when the phone rang.

'Hello, John Ray. It's Cal Stoddard.' The voice sounded tentative. 'I hope I'm not interrupting your dinner.'

'Not at all.'

'I just called to, uh . . .' He paused. 'Patty told me what you and Maggie did the other night. How you brought me home and all. I called to thank you for it. And to apologize.'

'No need, Cal.'

'Kind of you to say that. But you know, I used to have to handle my daddy when he came home like that. My mama and me, we'd put him to bed. He was a sorry sight, and I was ashamed of him. Now I've behaved the same way, and even though she doesn't say so, I'm sure Patty's ashamed of me. If the girls had been awake and seen me, I don't even want to think . . .'

Your wife would have cut out your gizzard and it would serve you right, Horn thought, but searched for something appropriate to say. 'Don't

47

worry about it,' he said finally. 'You've got a few things on your mind these days.'

'I do indeed,' Stoddard said. 'It's good to have a friend when I need one.'

They hung up, and Horn turned off the bath water. It was hard not to take some secret pleasure in Cal Stoddard's misfortune, even though he felt guilty about it. One thing he had to admit, the man had character, and the guts to admit his mistakes.

He soaked in the tub for a while then, as it grew dark outside, he heated a can of beef stew, and took the bowl of food and a High Life out on his porch. After his meal, he looked for something to read.

Horn normally kept few books around, but there were some that he liked. One was *Huckleberry Finn*; and there was the Zane Grey trilogy about the settling of the Ohio River Valley in the late 1700s. He picked up the second volume, *Spirit of the Border*, and settled in with it, but the thoughts prowling around in his head wouldn't let him concentrate. He picked up the phone and dialed Maggie's number.

'Hi,' he said when she answered. 'It's me. Just calling to report that I've got nothing to report.'

'You sound discouraged.'

'I am. Nobody wants to talk to me. But I'm just starting to check off names on this list of mine, and I'm not going to give up. How are you doing?'

'All right, I guess,' she said, with little conviction. 'Davey called. He competed in Flagstaff yesterday.'

'How'd he do?'

'He finished in the money, so he's happy. But we had a bad connection, and there were a couple of women talking and laughing so loud, I couldn't hear him very well.'

'Was he in a bar?'

'Or his room. I wasn't sure.'

He hesitated, unsure if he should comment. Then he went ahead. 'Davey likes company, doesn't he?'

'Uh-huh. But I knew that when I married him.'

It seemed unwise to pursue the subject any further. 'Have you talked to Cal or Patty lately?'

'I talked to both of them today.' Maggie sounded angry. 'What the hell's going on, when decent people can get in this kind of trouble?'

'Yeah.' He felt the urge to comment that anyone foolish enough to join the Communist Party deserved what they got, but he kept silent. Finally he asked, 'You sure you're okay?'

'Hell, I'm fine. Main thing, if you'll just find a way to help out Owen—'

48

'I'll do my best.' Another pause. 'I guess he's not the kind of man you call Daddy, is he?'

'No.'

'Well, I'll see him again, to let him know what I've been up to. And to find out if he has anything else to tell me.'

'Thank you, John Ray. I mean it. Thanks for helping.'

'I'm doing it for you, not him. He's a little hard to like, in case you didn't notice.'

'Want to do me another favor? Try to like him. Just a little.'

Easy for you to say, he thought as he hung up the phone. A minute later he was dialing the Bruders' number at the Garden of Allah. Lillian answered.

'It's John Ray Horn,' he said. 'I was just wondering if I could come by sometime tomorrow.'

'Of course you can,' she answered. 'But what's wrong with tonight?'

'Well, it's a little late.'

'We're both night owls,' she said. 'If it's not your bedtime, you're welcome to come over now.'

He hesitated only a second. 'All right.'

8

A little over half an hour later he was parked by the Bruders' bungalow. Lillian answered his knock, holding a paintbrush in one hand. 'Owen's expecting you out by the pool,' she said with a smile. 'Why don't you join him? Then you can stop by here before you leave.'

It was after ten, the underwater lights had been turned off, and the pool area was dark. With no moon, the only illumination came from faint lights in the windows of bungalows glimpsed through the trees.

He heard Owen Bruder before he saw him. 'Over here,' the voice said. 'Off the pavement, on the grass. Watch your step.'

Bruder sat at a small table, and Horn seated himself on the other side. He heard the clink of a glass. 'Got ice, water, and something restorative,' the voice said. 'Interested?'

'Sure.'

Bruder filled a glass, added ice, and slid it toward Horn. 'We'll keep our voices down,' he said quietly. 'I promised myself I wouldn't alter my behavior because of those government shitbirds, but I'm not going to make it easy for them either.'

'Sure.' In the dark, Bruder's white shirt was the most visible thing about him. But gradually Horn began to make out his features.

'The old gal who built this place was a silent movie star named Alla Nazimova,' Bruder said. 'She was Russian, and they say her swimming pool is shaped like the Black Sea. It's not, really, but it makes a good story.'

'I wanted to talk to you,' Horn said.

'Shoot.'

'I'll be honest. I haven't done a thing yet to earn your money. I've talked to a few people and read up on some more, but I feel like I'm still in first gear.' He described his meeting with Vance and his impressions of the man in some detail, realizing as he spoke that conversation seemed to come easier in the dark. His drink tasted good, the night air felt good.

'This morning,' he went on, 'I looked up Laura Lee Paisley. She was no help either. For a while I thought she might have made up what she said about you, but she talks like she's got the straight gospel, and she believes it.'

'What do I care what she believes?' Bruder shot back. 'She's a twisted woman, and she trades in lies.'

'Maybe. But like you said the other night, it more likely came from somebody who talked to Parnell's committee. And this person almost has to be a party member. Right?'

'I suppose.' Bruder sounded sullen.

'Well, that's why I'm here tonight. I need to ask you: Who would hate you enough to do this? You said you turned against the party in '39. Maybe somebody still holds that against you.'

'Oh, hell.' Horn could hear the impatience in the other man's voice. 'Everybody's got enemies.'

'So who are yours?'

Bruder was silent.

'Come on, Owen. Don't hire me and then hold me back. Talk to me.'

The only sound was the hum of traffic from Sunset. Finally Bruder said, 'I'm not going to name anybody in the party.'

'Why the hell not?'

'Naming names is not what I do. Even to you.'

'How am I supposed to do my job?'

'Let me remind you that hiring you was my wife's idea, not mine.'

Horn lost his taste for the drink and put down his glass. 'I told Maggie the other night I thought you were a stiff-necked SOB. And now I'm saying it to you. I know you think you're being noble, but ask yourself how your wife and your daughter will take it if you go off to prison – maybe die there.'

He felt himself warming up to the subject. 'Your daughter, by the way, is worth two of you,' he said. 'She deserves a lot better than you've ever given her.' Once again, he realized, he had allowed Bruder's gruff obstinacy to get under his skin. But it was too late to turn back. He rose from his chair, the words *I quit* taking shape on his lips, when Bruder spoke.

'One thing,' he said, slowly and reluctantly. 'Marvin Felix. You know who he is?'

'He runs your studio, doesn't he?'

'Once he and I were good friends,' Bruder went on. 'We and our wives would have dinner together. A while ago that stopped. I don't know what happened, but we're no longer friends.'

'Does it have anything to do with politics?'

'No. He's not political. At least as far as I know. The only thing he believes in is turning out movies that make money.'

'When did the friendship stop?'

51

'Months ago.'

'Around the same time you first heard from the committee?'

'Could have been.'

'Well,' Horn said, 'after all, he did fire you, didn't he?'

'I'm sure he was forced to do that.'

'How do you know?'

More silence. 'It's not much, but at least it's something,' Horn said. 'Good night.'

He turned away, stepped carefully around the edge of the pool, and began heading for the bungalow when Bruder's voice stopped him. 'Just a minute.'

Horn stopped, looked back.

'I wonder if you'd mind doing me a favor. Not that you owe me one.'

'What is it?'

The ice tinkled faintly in the glass. Now Bruder was just a voice and a white shirt, pale and indistinct in the dark. 'If I should go away for a while, I'd feel better knowing that someone would be looking in on Lillian every now and then.'

'I wouldn't mind doing that,' Horn said. 'And I'm sure Maggie wouldn't either.'

Horn heard a sound that might have been a sigh. 'Thank you,' Bruder said, an unaccustomed warmth in his voice. 'I'd be grateful.'

Lillian opened the door to his knock, a brush and palette in her other hand.

'Come in.' She wore gray pants and what looked like a man's cotton sweater, loose-fitting and paint-stained. The room smelled pleasantly of oil paint. Two easels were set up now, one of them shrouded in cloth. A cigarette smoldered in an ashtray.

She pointed to the canvas on the nearest easel. 'I'm still trying to get this one right.'

The painting of Owen had become more intense, more troubled, the space around it even suggesting a gathering violence.

'Is there a name for this kind of painting?' Horn asked.

'I don't know. Expressionism, I suppose. Owen calls this his Dorian Gray face. But I think he secretly likes it.'

'I left him out there by the pool.'

'He enjoys it there. Says it's comfortable in the dark. He also walks a lot in the evening, It seems to be his way of dealing with everything that's going on. That and . . .'

'And?'

'He never drank much until all this started,' she said, her expression troubled.

'Well . . .'

'He's terrified of prison.'

'Anybody would be, but we don't know that he's going to prison.'

'No, but he's almost as terrified of never working again.'

'I can understand that.' He looked around the room. 'You wanted to talk to me?'

'Just for a few minutes.' She retrieved her cigarette and drew on it hungrily, as if for sustenance. 'May I get you a drink?'

'No, thanks.'

'A cup of coffee, then.'

'Sure.'

While she was busy in the kitchen, he studied the bookshelves. He saw histories, a few screenplays, art books, a biography of Leon Trotsky, and novels by John Steinbeck, Albert Camus and Andre Malraux. Most of the names were unfamiliar to him. He lifted the cloth covering the second easel and saw what appeared to be the beginning of a landscape. 'What's this?' he called to Lillian.

She looked out from the kitchen. 'Oh, nothing much. I'm trying something new. I keep it covered up while it's in the early stages, because I don't know if it's going to be any good.'

'How will you know?'

'I'm giving it to a friend. I'll know from the expression on his face.'

She came back in with two cups of coffee.

He took out his bag of Bull Durham. 'Do you mind?'

'Not at all, if you'll make me one too.'

Jerking open the bag, he began the deliberate process of rolling a cigarette. She studied him carefully. 'You're the only person I know who does that,' she said. 'Is it to save money?'

'Partly. It also slows me down, and I need that sometimes. I learned to do it in prison.'

Taking the paper and tobacco in both hands, he rolled it up deftly and ran his tongue across the edge, then sealed it and passed it to Lillian.

He started rolling his own, saying, 'I read up on J. Parnell Thomas and his right-hand man, a guy named Cross—'

'I hate him,' she broke in vehemently. 'Thomas, I mean. That red face and those squinty eyes. And when he's on the radio, you can hear the intolerance, the poison that comes out of that closed mind of his.' She moved the ashtray between them. 'Have you turned up anything?'

'No. I just finished telling Owen I feel like I'm taking your money under false pretenses.' He decided there was no reason to be diplomatic. 'Owen's no help to me. He doesn't want to tell me who might have it in for him.' His eyes met hers. 'Can you?'

'I would if I could,' she said. 'I honestly don't know.'

'He mentioned Marvin Felix, said you used to be friends with him and now you aren't.'

'That's true. But it's hard to think of Marvin . . .' She trailed off. 'So many friends have dropped by the wayside, the few we have left are precious. But I'm not sure Owen realizes it. Grover Jones has been calling the last few days—'

'The actor?'

She nodded. 'Owen wrote a couple of his pictures, and we knew him socially. Owen has been too depressed lately to take his calls, but I talked to him the other day, and he said he just wanted to give us his private support even though he couldn't do anything publicly.'

She picked at a flake of paint on a fingernail. 'You should talk to Wally – Wallace Roland. He's one of Owen's oldest friends. They wrote plays in New York, and he talked Owen into coming out here. For a while, they shared a writing office at the studio. He's a neighbor of ours here at the Garden. When we had to sell our house, he put in a good word with the owner and was able to get us moved to the front of the waiting list here.'

'Sounds like a good friend. Was he, uh . . .'

'In the party? Yes.' Her face turned grim. 'He's also been subpoenaed to testify in Washington. I think if you approach Wally carefully, he might be able to help you, at least point you in the right direction. You can tell him I sent you. Just don't mention this to Owen.'

'All right.'

'Wally goes even farther back with Owen than I do.'

'How long have you known your husband?'

'A little over fifteen years. When I met him, he was working in the New York theater. Like a lot of intellectuals back then, his politics were pretty radical.' She reached up and adjusted the two barrettes that held her gray-brown hair in back. In the light from the floor lamp, her face, free of make-up, was strong-boned and attractive. He wasn't sure why she had asked him in, but he was enjoying her company and in no hurry to leave.

'How did you come to marry him?'

'That's easy.' She smiled broadly, hands cradling her coffee cup. 'I grew up fairly well-to-do on Long Island, and I came out, like all the proper girls do—'

'Came out?'

'I'm sorry. That's shorthand for making your debut in society. I was a debutante. Very posh.' She smiled, self-deprecating.

'I see.'

'I studied art in Paris, then came home, and I was well on my way to marrying a stockbroker whose background was the male equivalent of my own.' She paused, remembering.

'So what happened?'

'I went to the theater one night, met Owen, saw one of his plays, and decided he had more passion for life in his little finger than all the boys I'd met at dancing school or college. And I married him.'

'And have you been happy?' For Horn, who usually considered prying to be rude, it was a presumptuous question, but somehow he knew she wouldn't mind.

'Yes,' she said. 'Owen can be difficult. And God knows this is the most difficult time of his life – of our life. He's better with ideas than with people; he can appear brusque and angry. But that's his surface. Underneath, he's a good and honorable man.'

Horn couldn't stop himself. 'How about the way he's treated Maggie? What's honorable about that?'

'He's beginning to feel some shame about that. With time, I think he'll be closer to her.'

'It's overdue.'

'I know.' A pause. 'He's very proud,' she said softly.

'I can tell.'

'He knows he should have been nicer to you when the two of you met the other day. He says he made some remark belittling the kind of work you used to do.'

'Cowboy movies,' he said. 'I hear that from a lot of people. I'm used to it.'

'Still, he knows he wasn't nice. It's just hard for him to apologize.'

'Then why don't I just take this as his apology?'

'All right.' She sounded distracted, and she appeared to be staring at his right hand. 'Come here.'

'What?'

'You're about to lose a button off your cuff. Let me fix it.'

'No, Lillian, really . . .'

'Don't be silly. It'll take me one minute.'

He suddenly felt awkward. She fetched a needle and thread, then knelt by his chair and pushed up the sleeve of his jacket. Soon she had the button off, the needle threaded, and was sewing it back on.

Studying the top of her head, watching her paint-smudged fingers at work, he reflected that it had been a long time since any woman had done this for him. And how lucky Owen Bruder was.

'There's one other thing,' she said without looking at him. 'The reason I wanted to talk to you tonight.'

'Uh-huh?'

'If it turns out that this is connected in some way to his problem, then I'll be glad I told you. If there's no connection, I'd like you to forget it.'

'So?'

'There's a woman . . .' she began. 'Owen's been in touch with a woman. Talking to her on the phone. Possibly even seeing her, I'm not sure.'

'How do you know?'

'Once, when we were in the old house, I picked up the phone, and a woman's voice asked for him. He was a little secretive, took the call in the bedroom. A couple more times, the phone rang, and when I answered the person hung up. And sometimes, when he comes back from his walks, he's wound up, distracted, almost as if he's been with someone.'

'Well . . .'

'I know,' she laughed. 'It's not up there in the same category as lipstick on his collar. I just have a sense that . . . You see, I know him very well, and I know when he's being secretive. What I don't know is what this represents. If it's connected with his troubles, then it's something you and I should know about. If it turns out to be something else—'

'Then what?'

She looked up, her eyes boring into his. 'Then let's say I just don't want to know. At least not right now. Not with all that's going on.'

'All right.' He had a new respect for her. 'I'll see what I can find out.'

She sewed in silence for a minute then, head bent. He felt something on his hand, looked down, and saw the tear.

'Oh, damn. I'm sorry.' She looked up at him, eyes glistening. 'I swore I wouldn't do this.' Angrily, she brushed at her eyes with the back of her hand. 'It's just that . . . I don't want to lose him. For years it was inconceivable, and now I can look out there and see it waiting for me. Life without him.'

He touched her shoulder awkwardly. 'Let's not get ahead of ourselves,' he said. 'I promise you I'll do what I can.'

'I know you will.' She smiled a little too brightly, ducked her head again, bit off the loose thread, and yanked his coat sleeve down. 'Good as new.'

'Thanks, Lillian.' They got up and walked to the door. As she opened it, he said, 'Maggie tells me you're the one who's done most of the work to make sure he stays in touch with her.'

She nodded, wiping her eyes one last time. 'Owen and I don't have any children. I think it's important that he has a daughter, and she's a good person. If he had to be dragged into the relationship, so be it.' She took a flashlight from a table. 'I should go find my husband and tell him it's bedtime.'

'I'll come with you, then I'll say good night.'

He took the light and led the way, shining it on the path through the trees to the big grassy area around the swimming pool. It was quiet there. 'Owen?' she called out.

'I think he's over there,' Horn said. The light fell on the table where they had sat. It still bore a bottle, two glasses, and a bowl of melting ice.

56

'Maybe he's gone for a walk,' she said, her voice suddenly uncertain. 'Although it's late . . .'

He could hear the water in the pool gently lapping at the sides, as if recently disturbed. He stepped over to the edge, saw dark stains on the concrete, something in the water. He swung the light quickly.

'Lillian, stay there, will you?'

Owen Bruder floated face down, head and torso just below the surface, legs trailing downward. White shirt stark in the light, trousers and suspenders dark. And dark red the tendrils that radiated outward from his head, undulating through the gently moving water in a graceful filigree.

9

The cold shock told Horn he was in the water. Surfacing and spitting, he swam noisily across the dark surface, arms reaching, until one hand grasped a shoe, then a pant leg. Seconds later he was on the far side, clambering up to the lip, then painfully heaving Owen Bruder's dead weight out of the water. As he pulled, he heard the gasps of his own breath and the almost otherworldly moans coming from Lillian.

She had the flashlight now and focused it shakily on her husband's face. Then she dropped it and came nearer, kneeling at Horn's side. He bent down, listening for breath. Nothing. He moved Bruder's head to one side, intending to feel for a pulse, and found that the right side of the head, just above the ear, was caved in, crushed as if by a mighty blow. Shards of skull, held together only by flesh and hair, moved beneath his fingers like broken crockery. His hand came away sticky with blood. Lillian took hold of her husband's shoulders and, with surprising strength, lifted them onto her lap where she knelt.

He had seen death, both in the war and afterward. The sight, the touch of it, always knotted his stomach. Almost as chilling was the knowledge that death had brushed near him, had spared him this time even as it took another. Sitting there in the dark, knowing that he and Lillian were vulnerable, his ears strained to pick up any unusual sounds. Whoever did this could still be close. But all was quiet, save Lillian's crying and his harsh breathing and the soft lapping of the water at pool's edge.

Then other sounds came, fresh voices, shouts, growing confusion. People gathered. Horn heard the word *police.* The underwater lights blazed suddenly, illuminating the onlookers as if by strong moonlight. The neighbors milled about, most of them in various kinds of night dress.

At first Owen Bruder's body, limp and soaked, drew their attention. But over time their eyes grew fixed on Lillian. She held her husband, rocking him gently, her moans so faint they might have been the notes of a lullaby. Horn knelt by her, one arm around her. A few people approached to offer help, but he waved them away.

Her moans became rasping breaths, in and out, and then the breaths took the shape of a word – 'No' – over and over. She raised her head to look up at the black void of the sky, her lips moving soundlessly now as her hands caressed her husband's ravaged head.

Finally the police arrived, two uniformed officers followed, minutes later, by two detectives. 'We have to talk to them,' Horn said to Lillian, gently disengaging her from the body. She leaned over, quickly kissed her husband's forehead, then rose to her feet.

One of the detectives, with the hotel manager's help, began cordoning off the pool area. The other went with Horn and Lillian to the bungalow. She walked like a blind woman, stumbling on the path as he steadied her. The detective accompanying them was the older of the two, solidly built, shoulders straining at his suit jacket. His name was Pitt, and his manner was respectful but authoritative.

Horn took a few minutes to tend to his wet clothes. In the bathroom he shucked off his jacket, shirt, tie, and shoes, then wrapped a bath towel around his shoulders and rejoined Lillian. When they were seated, the detective asked a few short questions before Horn described how he found the body. Then he asked for Lillian's account. She sat rigid, her hands – colored with paint and blood – clasped in her lap, a few smears of blood on her sweater where her husband's head had rested. She spoke in a low and measured voice, faltering only now and then. Midway through her story, she raised her eyes to Horn, pain written across all her features, and said simply, 'Margaret.'

He understood. Excusing himself, he went to the phone and dialed Maggie's number. He checked his wristwatch for the time, but the crystal was fogged with water from the pool. The phone rang several times before she answered, her voice murky with sleep. He stumbled through the words, heard her gasp once, then again. Then: 'I'm coming there.'

More talk with the detective, who took careful notes. Pitt's partner joined them, and they huddled for a few minutes, glancing toward him and Lillian. Then both men approached for more questions, and Horn sensed that the mood in the room had shifted. He suspected that the other detective had learned something of Owen Bruder's story.

'Mrs Bruder,' Pitt began, 'we understand your husband was going to Washington to testify in front of a government hearing. About the Reds.'

She nodded, waiting. Her eyes had regained some of their focus, and Horn felt her inner strength begin to re-emerge.

'He must have had some enemies.'

'Everyone has enemies,' she said. 'We've gotten some nasty letters lately. But do I know anyone who would have wanted to kill him? No.'

'How many letters?'

'Three or four, I think.'

'Do you still have them?'

'No. We threw them out as soon as they arrived.'

The man turned his attention to Horn. 'You a family friend, or what?'

'Yes,' he answered carefully. 'A friend.'

'What kind of work do you do?'

'I take care of some property in Culebra Canyon for the owner.' Not the whole truth, but true enough. He began to feel the discomfort, bordering on fear, that he always felt around policemen, so he pulled out his cigarette makings to give his hands something to do. 'There's something else. You'll find out, so I might as well tell you now. I've got a record.'

The two men swapped looks. 'Tell me,' said Pitt.

'Two years in Cold Creek. For assault.'

The younger one looked at him extra hard. 'Ever get your picture in the paper?'

'A few times.'

'I may have seen it.' Pitt's partner nodded, looking satisfied, as if he had turned a corner and could make out something up ahead. His gaze took in both of them. 'And how long have you two known each other?'

'Only a few days,' Horn replied. 'Why?' But he knew why, and he felt the knowledge turning to anger.

'Just wondered.'

'Your partner's got a wild imagination,' Horn said to Pitt. 'If you let him get started down this particular road, it'll turn into a waste of time, not to mention an insult to Mrs Bruder. I can't tell you how to do your job, but—'

'That's right, you can't,' Pitt said.

'But you ought to be looking elsewhere.'

'All right.' Pitt stood up, and his partner also. He handed each of them a card. 'If you think of anything else . . .'

'What happens to him?' Lillian asked suddenly.

'Him? Oh.' He turned to the younger one and asked quietly, 'The wagon show up?' The other man nodded.

'He'll be taken down to the morgue for an autopsy and coroner's inquest. Then the body will be released for burial. Most likely late tomorrow.' He looked at his watch and corrected himself. 'Today.'

'Thank you,' Lillian murmured. 'Please find who did this.'

'Yes, ma'am.' He touched the brim of his hat, and they left.

Lillian took a cigarette out of a pack on the table and tried to light it, but the match shook in her hand. Horn took the hand and steadied it until the tobacco glowed. 'What was that?' she asked. 'When you said to him—'

'It was just the young one jumping to conclusions. He's one of those who likes his answers neat and simple. When he heard I had a record, he started to figure me as the one who did it, then he thought he'd rope you into it to make it even neater. I didn't have the stomach to listen.'

'Oh,' she said. Her features sagged.

'There may be more of this,' he said, leaning in insistently. 'Anybody who might have hated Owen, and hated you for being with him, will be ready to believe the worst about you. Could be you'll hear some bad things. But you won't listen, you hear? You won't listen.' He heard the edge in his own voice and told himself, *Calm down.*

She nodded, but her look of exhaustion told him she might not have absorbed all of it. They sat for a while without speaking, listening to the absolute silence of the middle of the night. He wondered suddenly if the well-dressed government men who had been shadowing the Bruders knew what had happened. Maybe, maybe not – even J. Edgar's boys had to sleep. But if they didn't know, they soon would.

A tentative knock at the door: Maggie. She came in, sat down, and heard the story. Because of Lillian, Horn described it in a way that smoothed over some of the edges, but there was no avoiding the story's end. Her father was suddenly, violently dead.

As she listened, she appeared stunned at first. Then sorrow took over her face. Then something else: anger.

Maggie looked around the living room, still cluttered with Lillian's easels and the couple's unpacked boxes. She took in Lillian herself, then Horn. She appeared to be making a calculation.

'Any neighbors come by?' she asked.

Lillian shook her head. 'As we mentioned, most of the neighbors . . .'

Maggie got up. 'Anybody want some coffee?' She headed for the kitchen, stopped, turned. 'Wait. Let's make that a drink. Lillian?'

'Yes. Thank you.'

'John Ray?'

'Sure. Anything.'

When she came back from the kitchen, drinks in hand, she said, 'I'm sleeping here tonight.'

'Margaret, you really don't have to—'

'Please call me Maggie. Just about everybody does, if they know me well.'

'All right.'

'I'm staying here tonight. Just to look after you.'

'You're very kind.'

'I'm, uh, staying too,' Horn said, stirring his drink.

'Please,' Lillian said. 'It's not necessary.'

'I know,' he said lightly. 'But it's a long drive home, and I'm feeling lazy. I can sleep right here.' He patted the sofa cushion. There was more to it, of course. Lillian could be perfectly safe, but until things shook down a little, he wanted to keep an eye on her. On both of them, really.

'All right,' Lillian said with a shaky attempt at a laugh. 'I'm too tired to put up a fight.'

That was it, then. Twenty minutes later, feeling pummeled by the night's events, Horn fell asleep to the sound of lowered voices in the bedroom. He slept fitfully, brain swimming amid images of dark, cold water and a floating shape just up ahead. He didn't want to touch it, because he feared the sight of its face, but he knew he must. His hand reached out . . .

He awoke suddenly at first light, sitting up and throwing off the blanket. From behind the kitchen door came muted sounds and a pleasant, unmistakable aroma. Getting up and pulling on his pants, still damp, he opened the door to find Maggie eating a bowl of cereal at the small table. On the stove a coffee pot perked.

'Hi,' she said, unsmiling, with the air of someone with a mind full of business. 'Couldn't sleep any more. Help yourself to coffee.'

He did and took a seat in a small, uncomfortable chair. 'How is she?'

'Still asleep. Owen's doctor had given him some sleeping powder, since the trouble started. It's pretty strong. Last night I talked her into taking some along with her whiskey and she's still under.' She wore last night's clothes – a blouse and slacks; her hair was freshly brushed and fell over her shoulders, but her face was free of make-up, and the freckles ran riot over her nose and cheeks.

Horn, like most men, was not immune to the lure of powder and paint on a woman. His first wife, Iris, could do wonderful things with lipstick, eyebrow pencil, and all the other weapons in a woman's arsenal, but a long time ago he had been struck by the look of the unadorned Maggie O'Dare. Today, years later, he found to his surprise that he still was. He wondered if Davey Peake ever gazed at her across the breakfast table and gave thanks for her.

She pushed her cereal bowl aside and replenished her cup. 'Been thinking about something,' she said. 'Me and Lillian, we talked about it last night. Have you still got the money they gave you?'

'Sure, but I'll be—'

'I want you to keep that as a down payment. When that's used up, I'll start paying your expenses. Your fees, whatever else you need.'

'What are you talking about?'

'I want you to find out who killed him. She does too.'

His mouth fell open. 'I think that's up to the police, don't you?'

'Sure. That's their job. And maybe they'll find out, if it's real obvious,

62

and maybe they'll convict somebody, if it's convenient and it doesn't embarrass anybody.'

He thought he knew what she meant, but she went on. 'Everybody thinks he's . . . he was a Red. To them he wasn't a good American. Nobody's going to grieve over a man like that, and if it turns out he was killed because of politics, how hard do you think the cops will work on it?'

'How hard do you think I would work on it?' The instant the words were out, he regretted them. And yet they needed to be said.

'I know, you didn't like him much. I haven't forgotten that. But I've seen what you can do when you believe a thing needs to be done. I saw the way you went after Clea.'

It was true. Clea had been Iris' daughter from her first marriage. After Iris divorced him, Clea dropped out of his life. But when he learned that she was missing and was being hunted by a man who wanted her dead, Horn managed to find her and protect her.

'Well, she was my daughter,' he said. 'Stepdaughter.'

Maggie leaned toward him, both hands cradling her coffee cup.

'Do it for the money, if you want.' She noted his stubborn expression. 'Don't make a face like that. There's nothing wrong with doing a good job for pay. Do it for the money, and then go to the police with what you have.'

This time he rolled his eyes. 'There's another face,' Maggie went on. 'Can't you do anything this morning but make faces? I know, you don't like the police and they don't like you. But if you turn up something solid, they'll want to know it.'

She took a breath. 'Do it because it's the right thing, because even though Owen irritated people, he was a good man who was being stepped on by his own government, and we need to know why he died.'

'Maggie . . .'

'Do it because Lillian's a fine person. And you know she'd be indebted to you.'

She paused, and he thought he knew what was coming next.

'Or do it for me. Because I've never asked you for much, and I'm asking you to do this.'

He shook his head wearily, slumped back in the chair, raised his hands as if to fend off any more arguments. Finally he nodded and said, 'Okay.'

She got up, came around and kissed him roughly on the cheek. 'And I'll help,' she said as she began clearing the table.

'What?'

'You heard me. I wouldn't ask you to do anything I wouldn't do myself. Especially if it could be dangerous. I'm in on this too.'

'Sorry, lady.'

'Uh-uh.' For the first time since their conversation had begun, she sounded strangely content, almost happy. 'Sierra Lane and the queen of the serials. How the hell can they stop us?'

10

'You want to talk about what?'

Rusty Baird stopped figuring his angle on the five-ball and regarded Horn from underneath ginger-colored eyebrows.

'The time you were an organizer. Everything that went on back then.'

Baird laid his cue stick gently on the felt-topped table and straightened up, retrieving the cigarette that was balanced on the table edge. 'Cops sometimes come in here and ask me stuff like that,' he said, his expression unreadable. He had a pale complexion, a wiry build, and a face that could look boyish, but his eyes reflected years of hard-won experience. He was deaf in one ear and only partially sighted in one eye, the legacy of an old blow to the head.

They were at Baird's place, the Dust Bowl, located on a stretch of rural road in the Valley. It was still early evening, and they were the only occupants of the back room, which consisted of a pool table and a few small tables with chairs. Out in front, where the bar was located, they could hear the growing hum of conversation, clink of glasses, and the music of Bob Wills on the juke box, signaling a honkytonk coming to life. Horn liked the place. He and Mad Crow often could be found here, until the Indian began hanging out in more elegant haunts on the other side of town.

'Federal cops, I mean,' Baird went on. 'FBI, usually. Dark suits and fresh haircuts. And that way lawyers talk. In this place they stick out like tits on a bull.'

'What do you say to them?'

'I'm friendly. I tell 'em the usual things. It was a long time ago, I'm a respectable businessman now.'

'Do they ask you if you're a Red?'

'Hell, they know I'm not. Not a card-carrier, anyway.'

'Well, then, why do they bother you?'

Baird considered the question for a moment. 'I should get to work,' he said, motioning for Horn to follow. 'Let's get out front.'

Out in the main room, Baird took up his usual station behind the bar, where one of his employees was already filling drink orders. 'You never asked me much about any of that,' he said. 'How come now?'

Without mentioning Maggie, Horn began talking about Owen Bruder, starting with what he knew of the man's history, and ending with his violent death. 'I told his wife I'd try to find out who killed him,' he said. 'And I thought I'd start by looking for whoever lied about him. But I don't know anything about that world of his. That's why I'm talking to you.'

'Have you collected any money?' Baird asked.

'His wife wrote me a check.'

'Tear it up.'

'That's not funny.'

'Good, because it's not a joke. You signed up for a job nobody can do. Look at it this way: whether somebody lied or not, in the eyes of the *federales* he's a Commie. Today, all it takes is a few whispers, and you can find yourself out of work. Whoever you work for, he doesn't care if the whispers are true or not. He doesn't want the aggravation.'

He noticed a stain on the bar and began working at it with a rag. 'Maybe it makes more sense this way: Imagine one lone cowboy on one side and the whole town on the other. You're up against the US Congress and a good chunk of the government. Even in one of your rinky-dink movies, those are not good odds.'

'Come on, Rusty.'

'All right, look . . . You were getting ready to ask me why, if I never joined the party, the boys in the dark suits keep coming around. Their job is to build connections between people. Let's say they get me to name somebody I knew in the old days, a card-carrier, and they put the arm on that person, and he knuckles under and names a big fish. And finally they have a name they can use, one that looks good in the papers. It's all about intimidating people, getting them to finger others.

'I heard of your boy Owen,' Baird went on. 'He was a big fish, like a lot of other unlucky souls. If they could have nailed him – either sent him to jail or at least got him booted out of Hollywood for good – then the FBI and Mr J. Parnell Thomas would have called that a good day's work.'

Baird left for a moment and returned with a large burlap bag containing peanuts in the shell. He filled a half-dozen bowls scattered along the bar, depositing one in front of Horn.

'Tell me what it was like back then,' Horn said.

'The old days?' Baird shook his head, smiling faintly. 'I really felt alive back then. It was the worst time and the best, all rolled into one. I've never hated anything so much as I hated those people who were getting rich off our sweat. And I've never loved anything so much as I loved standing next to my friends, fighting for what we needed: a decent job, food on the table, some self-respect.'

Horn regarded him with some wonder. This Rusty Baird, speaking a kind of rough poetry, seemed new to him. And to Horn, the notion of getting involved in a cause bigger than himself was strange territory.

'I had a natural talent for organizing,' Baird continued. 'I could get up in front of people and stir them up, get them to do things. It's a scary talent, because you can use it for bad things. I tried not to. I like to think I helped a lot of people live better lives – get better working conditions, dig up more jobs. In '40 I was at the head of a rally on the docks in San Francisco. The cops and the strikebreakers moved in, and that's when I got knocked in the head.' He indicated a spot on his temple.

'What happened?' Horn asked. 'Exactly, I mean.'

Baird studied him for a moment, as if to determine how serious the question was. Then he grinned and his eyes seemed to focus on something in the distance. 'Like it was yesterday,' he began, his voice suddenly soft.

'There was a stiff wind off the bay, and I was wondering if I should've brought a heavier jacket. We had a speaker who was yelling into a microphone, and everybody was getting pretty worked up. Somebody started throwing oranges at the strikebreakers, and somebody said *Get 'em*, and they all came toward us. Every one of those guys had something to hit with. Clubs, shotgun butts, anything. I saw a few baseball bats. I was right in front, and – don't ask me how – but I saw the guy who was going to come for me when he was still twenty feet away. I locked eyes with him. Big guy, shirtsleeves rolled up, star on his shirt pocket.

'He came at me, I saw the club go up, saw how big his hands were. I was carrying a sign, and I tried to use it on him, but he just brushed it away. I ducked, but he was smart, and he knew which way I'd duck, and he was waiting. My head felt like it exploded. Next thing I knew, I was on the back of a flatbed, being hauled out of there along with all the other busted heads, and it was night time.'

Baird stopped, lit a fresh cigarette. Horn realized he had been holding his breath, just listening.

'After that I had trouble seeing, hearing, even keeping my balance. The war was just around the corner, jobs were finally starting to open up, and I guess I knew my organizing days were over.'

'And you went respectable.'

'Damn right.' The other bartender signaled that he needed help, and Baird moved down the bar to pour a couple of drinks. As Horn waited, he studied the framed pictures mounted behind the bar, what Baird called his Cowboy Wall of Fame. All of them were similar – strapping young men wearing big hats and gun belts, often posing with handsome horses – but Horn had no trouble differentiating between Rogers and Autry, Starrett and Steele, Boyd and La Rue. The last few times he'd been in, there was a gap in the lineup where his photo had once hung. Horn sometimes wondered if he'd been too impulsive in ordering Baird to take it down. No, he decided, he didn't belong there any more.

Tonight he noticed the gap was filled, and he recognized the face right away. Cal Stoddard, his smile bright and easy, was resplendent in white, with a spangled guitar slung over his neck. *Everybody likes the singing cowboys now*, he thought, his eyes straying to another of the photos. *You're to blame for that, Mr Gene Autry.*

Baird returned, having visited the jukebox and freshened his coffee cup. In place of Bob Wills, a simpler sound, guitar and harmonica, competed with the hum of the room.

Baird followed Horn's gaze to the pictures on the wall. 'Doesn't look good for him, does it?' he said, indicating Stoddard. 'I had him figured for the next Roy Rogers till this thing came along. Now . . .' He looked disgusted.

Horn was not in the mood to offer any sympathy for his replacement. 'I still need to know—' he began.

'Yeah. You need to know what to do now that you've promised the widow Bruder something impossible. Where to start.'

Horn shrugged. 'I've got no rule book here, Rusty. Right now, you're the only expert I know.'

'Then Lord help you.' Baird tipped his saucer, pouring off spilled coffee back into the cup. He appeared to be thinking hard.

'Somebody had it in for your boy,' he said finally. 'Somebody who was willing to ruin a man's life with a lie. I'd guess somebody in the party. Did they kill him too? Who knows? But I'd start sniffing around in Bruder's history, find his biggest enemy, and—'

'What if he doesn't have any enemies?'

'Everybody who's been active in leftist politics has enemies.' Noting Horn's look of incomprehension, he made a wry face. 'Good old John Ray. You think you live in a world where politics is just something in the newspaper. But you'll change your mind.' He turned his good ear toward the jukebox in the corner. 'Hear that?'

A man with a twang in his voice was singing about a soldier who fights a war in a uniform of dirty overalls, using weapons such as hoe and plow.

'He can explain things better than me,' Baird said. 'If you'd been in here one night last winter, you'd have run into him.'

'Who's that?'

'Woody Guthrie. Every time something important happened – a strike, or a lockout, or a march, or a lynching – he wrote a song about it. He was the one who told me I should call this place the Dust Bowl.'

'Is he a Red?'

Baird considered the question. 'I don't think so,' he said. 'But he might as well be, 'cause he sure behaves like one.'

'Maybe I'll meet him,' Horn said, unsure if the prospect really appealed to him.

'Could be. You never know when he's going to turn up. Last time I saw him, he'd just crossed the country on Greyhounds when he could afford it and flatcars when he couldn't. He walked into this place wearing five shirts, one on top of the other, and carrying just his guitar. 'Where's your bag?' I asked him. 'I'm wearing it,' he said.

Baird paused to wipe down a stretch of bar that was already clean. 'One thing you haven't told me,' he said, 'Why are you doing this? I know you, and you wouldn't sign on for a job like this without a reason. Don't tell me it's the money. You didn't think much of this Bruder character; I can tell by the way you talk about him. So why are you doing it?'

'It's just a favor for a friend,' Horn said casually.

'Well, you need a better reason than that.'

'It's good enough for me,' he said defensively.

'Here's what I mean: You've already got a better reason, and you don't even know it.'

'What are you talking about, Rusty?'

'Look.' Baird slung the damp towel over his shoulder and leaned almost pugnaciously on the bar. 'The Depression was bad enough, but at least most of us were hard up, and we felt like we were all in the same boat. And the government was on our side at least part of the time, trying to dig people out of the hole. Now, people are a lot better off and the government's decided that a small number of us are not good enough to walk the streets and ought to be tossed in jail. For what? Throwing bombs? Nope. For thinking and saying the wrong things.'

'What's your point?'

'Just this. It's not right. And people ought to say so. They come after Owen Bruder today, they could come after me tomorrow. And you the day after.'

'You, maybe,' Horn said. 'Not me.'

Baird just laughed.

11

'A Laura Lee note to the city fathers of Hollywood: One of our proudest symbols has been allowed to deteriorate shamelessly. In the hills above us, the old Hollywoodland sign once glowed brightly every night, a beacon for airplanes. But now its lights are broken and its letters in sad disrepair. Listeners, please contact the Hollywood Chamber of Commerce and demand that they restore this once-grand symbol to life.

Even here in Tinseltown, this reporter loves and supports live theater. But some plays have little to offer. The Coronet Theater soon will present a premiere of Galileo *starring Charles Laughton, who has mesmerized us in roles ranging from Captain Bligh to Quasimodo. Its author is a German-born playwright with known Marxist leanings, and its message is confused at best. Laura Lee's advice: Save your money for Laughton's next movie, the thriller* The Big Clock . . .

Horn spotted the place and parked the Ford on the east side of La Cienega, a broad street of shops and restaurants and furniture stores a few blocks east of Beverly Hills. The two-story building was of stucco, and unremarkable except for the tall marquee. He and Maggie walked down a passageway and through a small courtyard to the building's main entrance, but the big doors were locked. They soon found a side entrance that wasn't.

Inside, faint noises led them to the main auditorium. The theater was not large, holding only a few hundred seats, but it looked new and smelled strongly of fresh paint. The stage was occupied with casually dressed actors reading lines, while from backstage came the sounds of heavy objects being moved.

'I wonder if he's the one.' Maggie pointed to a lone figure seated near the back of the auditorium. Hearing her, the man turned, saw them, and waved them over.

He was portly, round-featured, with a sad baby's face, thinning hair, and steel-rimmed eyeglasses with Coke-bottle lenses. His jacket was draped over the seat to his left, and his shirt, tie, and even suspenders were dusted with cigarette ash. He squinted as he smiled at them.

'Pardon me if I don't get up,' he said in a reedy voice, gesturing to the open script and pile of photographs and memos spread out in his lap. His right hand held the nub of a lit cigarette, and as he waved it, more ash drifted onto the pages.

'I'm John Ray Horn. This is Maggie O'Dare.'

'Wallace Roland. Call me—'

'Wally!' The shout came from the stage, where they saw a hulking man wrapped in an enormous dressing gown. He stood on the lip of the stage, his fleshy features contorted in an expression of pained concern.

'Wally, if you must entertain visitors,' the man said in a rich, layered voice, 'kindly ask them not to distract those of us trying to—' He paused for dramatic effect. '— to *act* up here. If you please.'

'Of course, Charles.' He turned to them, lowering his voice. 'We'll speak quietly.' He transferred the inch of cigarette to his lips to shake their hands, then retrieved it. 'Would you like to sit?'

Maggie took the seat to his right, and Horn stood facing them, leaning back against the row of seats in front of them. Maggie continued to stare at the shambling figure on the stage, who by now had strode to a workbench bearing what appeared to be a primitive telescope, seated himself, and began working on it while reciting his lines to another actor who stood nearby.

'It's really him,' she said. 'The hunchback of Notre Dame.'

'Yes,' Roland said. 'In the flesh – to use *le mot juste*. Charles tells me that the only reason I agreed to work with him is because next to him, I look almost petite. He's an astonishing actor, and great company. But this play is an enormous challenge for him, for all of us, and he can be a little—'

'Temperamental?' she asked.

'You didn't hear it from me. I just sit here quietly going over the details' – he pointed to the papers in his lap – 'and allowing his genius to come out.'

Arranging the mass of papers in a slightly less untidy pile, Roland studied Horn, then Maggie, through his heavy glasses. 'Lillian told me a little about both of you,' he said. 'She said I could talk to you. Asked me to, really, which is the only reason I'm seeing you, since I'm absolutely buried in this production.'

'We appreciate it,' Maggie said. 'She told us you're the producer.'

'One of the producers,' Roland corrected her. 'A lesser one, but producer outranks writer in the usual pecking order, so I suppose I've come up in the world. I'm helping the formidable John Houseman put this thing on. Curtain goes up Saturday night. If we're all still lucid by then.'

'Problems?' she asked.

He gave her a squint-eyed grin. 'Lillian said the two of you have worked in films, so you know a few things about clashing egos. Well, here we have two of the biggest: Laughton and Brecht.'

'Brecht?'

'Bertolt Brecht, the German playwright. The Teutonic Terror. He sees his play a certain way, and Charles – no shrinking violet – sees himself playing it another way. Lightning and thunder every day, ladies and gentlemen, whenever the two are in the house.'

'Goody,' Maggie said.

'Unfortunately, the esteemed playwright is absent today, so I foresee a reasonably quiet rehearsal.'

'Too bad.'

'Anyway, the things Lillian said about both of you . . . well, if you rate that highly with her, I suppose talking to you is the least I could do for her. And for Owen.'

Maggie's expression lapsed briefly into the sadness that had gripped her for more than a day. 'She told us you were a good friend to them.'

Roland shrugged. 'It was nothing. They deserved more. When I heard what had happened, I felt like a fool. I'd come home after working here all day, had two stiff drinks and fell into bed. I must have slept through . . . what happened. I didn't learn about it until the next morning, when I went across the street to Schwab's and everyone there was talking about it. I ran back to the Garden to see Lillian – apparently you two had just left – and I spent the rest of the day with her.' His fingers felt the heat from his shrinking cigarette, and he dropped it on the floor, then fished in his shirt pocket for another. 'God damn whoever did this,' he finished under his breath.

'Do you have any idea?' Horn asked.

'Hmm?' Roland looked suddenly ill at ease. 'I don't know. How would I know? The man was just unwillingly inducted into the world's most unpopular fraternity. He was getting threats in the mail, horrid things. If I had to guess, any right-thinking, flag-waving American who hates Commies could have killed him.'

'Lillian told us you're a member of that fraternity,' Horn said.

Roland paused, looking Horn up and down. 'She did? Well, I was once, although I no longer am. It's common knowledge. And I'm not ashamed. In a few days, I'll be flying to Washington to make an appearance before that little New Jersey demagogue. I'll admit I once belonged to the party, then I'll give him a piece of my mind, probably be cited for contempt, and that'll be the end to my illustrious movie career. I suppose I'll have to learn to sell real estate, or maybe I'll take up the clarinet. I always wanted to be Benny Goodman. At least I don't have a family to support.'

'It's hard to believe,' Maggie said. 'I mean, that someone's career could be over, just like that, just for—'

'Believe it, dear lady. Owen's career was suddenly kaput, and all that talk about him and the party was just lies. As for me, I've been on suspension at my studio ever since my name first appeared on that mean-spirited radio show.'

'Laura Lee Paisley?' Horn asked.

'That's her. She gets everything straight from the horse's mouth. The horse being J. Parnell Thomas' people. Oh, normally she doesn't use names in her character assassinations. She doesn't have to. She simply describes the person well enough so that there's no question as to who she's talking about. So, when word about me got around, and the sub-poena followed a few days later, my goose was cooked. I was out on the street.'

'I'm sorry,' Maggie said.

'I'm hardly alone in this,' Roland said. 'We're a beleaguered little band of brothers, we are. Writers and directors and even a movie star or two. Christians plodding toward the lions. Except for the fact that a dis-proportionate number of us are Jewish. Which raises some interesting questions. Is the party a hotbed of Jews? Or is this anti-Communist crusade being used as an excuse for anti-Semitic behavior? There's a riddle for you. Maybe I'll ask J. Parnell Thomas that one when I find myself facing him.'

He turned his attention to Horn. 'You've been quiet,' he said. 'Do you have any opinion about any of this? Communists, for example?'

'I don't like what I've heard about them,' Horn said. 'Beyond that, I try to meet each person on even terms.'

'You seem an odd choice for someone to help Lillian,' Roland said. They heard fresh bustling on the stage. Laughton had again interrupted his line readings to confer with two men who now stood at the edge of the stage.

'That's John, our producer, on the right,' Roland said, indicating a tall, middle-aged man. 'I have a meeting with him in about ten minutes, and I'll have to leave you.'

Horn was about to frame a question, but Roland went on. 'John doesn't really need an assistant for this play,' he murmured. 'He just happens to be one of the good people on this planet. There are a few of them out there, you know. I'm out of work, and he offers his help. Owen Bruder could have used a few friends like him.'

'He had you,' Maggie said.

'I wasn't enough. Clearly, I wasn't enough.'

'What's the play about?'

Roland's face brightened. 'It's about Galileo, one of the greatest minds who ever lived. He had the audacity to declare that the earth revolved around the sun, rather than the opposite. The Vatican, naturally, decided to quibble with that interpretation.'

'Sounds interesting,' Maggie said. 'How does it end?'

'Why don't you come and find out?'

'Maybe we will,' Horn said, not sounding enthusiastic.

'You don't like the theater.'

'It's all right, I guess.'

'Would you like it more if we could find room for some horses on stage?'

Horn realized that Lillian had provided some details about his background, and also that Wally Roland's humor could carry an edge.

'I might like it more if every play had an honest, straightforward plot and every actor cared more about the story than about the sound of his own voice.'

Roland tilted his head slightly, as if to get a better look at Horn, then his face broke into a broad grin. 'Well, that makes pretty good sense, Mr Horn. Why don't we agree on that?'

'Fine with me.'

'I apologize for the sarcasm. I think I'm still reacting to the news about Owen. Forgive me.'

'Sure. But let me keep going with the questions. Lillian said you and Owen go way back. He was active in unions and political work. Were you involved in some of that too?'

'I certainly was. Owen and I worked together in the Group Theater in New York, then I came to Hollywood and found how easy it was for a talented writer to make money. I immediately wired Owen and said, "There are dollar bills hanging on the trees out here, and your only competition is a bunch of illiterates." He resisted for a while until I convinced him that he could still write about things he considered important.' He paused, and his eyes briefly lost their focus. 'That, of course, isn't possible anymore.'

'He was arrested once. Do you know anything about that?'

Roland looked slightly surprised. 'Yes, I do. I was there, in fact. Owen and I were between jobs, and the party – I was still a member then – had organized a march in some town out in the farm belt, in support of better wages for workers. You remember, a lot of farm workers came out here in the Depression, and only earned a pittance. Anyway, we decided to surprise the farm owners with a march, but they were waiting for us with an army of police and promptly arrested those of us who looked like leaders. We spent a night in jail and were released the next day.'

Roland noticed Horn's quizzical look. 'I know,' he said. 'I don't look the part. Well, I wasn't always dumpy and overweight. Once, I marched and protested. Once, I burned with the fire of the radical.' He gestured vaguely, making a little arc of cigarette smoke in the air. 'People age, I suppose. But down deep, there's a spark or two still left.'

Horn began to ask his next question, but something about Roland's expression stopped him.

'One of us didn't return from that particular march,' he said almost under his breath.

'Who was that?'

Roland stirred, as if awakening from a nap. 'Hmm? Oh, nothing. Nothing.'

'What do you mean he didn't return?'

The look on Roland's face was closed, almost hostile. 'I didn't mean anything.'

Horn decided to change the subject. 'The Bruders got some hate letters,' he said. 'Did you?'

'Yes, a few. I wasn't sure how seriously to take them. I turned them over to the police and promptly forgot them. The police probably did too.'

'I asked Owen about enemies,' Horn said. 'He didn't want to come up with any names, especially party members, but finally he mentioned Marvin Felix.'

'Ah, yes.' Roland shifted in his seat, looking ill at ease. 'They had some kind of a falling out. That's all I know.'

'But you know Felix?'

'Everyone who works in this twisted business of ours knows him,' Roland said. 'He's difficult, autocratic, sometimes petty. Since he let me go, I've no love for him. He was afraid of public opinion, the whispering, those voices on the radio and those words in the newspapers, but I imagine any other studio chief would have caved in just as he did. And he still runs one of the best studios in town, possibly the only one capable of turning out the kind of films that Owen and I could be proud of – like *The Last Harvest*.'

'Did Owen have any other enemies?' When Roland continued to look uncomfortable with the subject, Horn added, 'You can see how important this is. If you know anything—'

'Are you an investigator of some kind?' Roland asked abruptly. 'You sound like one.'

'No,' Horn replied. 'Maggie and I are just trying to help out Lillian. Any other enemies?'

'It's impossible to say for sure,' Roland muttered. 'Owen could be abrasive, and at any given moment he was likely to be involved in a spat with someone or other. But . . .' He paused, then went on. 'Well, some time ago, when we were still sharing an office, I overheard part of a phone conversation. It was heated, although I couldn't really hear the content, but after he hung up, he had some choice words about her.'

'Her?'

'Grace Stilwell. She's one of the other writers at Global. Very talented, I gather, although I don't know her very well. She came to the studio recently from Paramount. Anyway, Owen seemed about to let me in on what it was all about, but then he abruptly changed his mind. And the subject.'

'You knew him pretty well,' Horn said. 'Any chance he could have gotten himself involved with a woman? Grace Stilwell, maybe?'

Maggie's look of surprise, then reproach, told him this possibility was new to her.

'Where did you hear that?' Roland demanded.

Horn hesitated. There was no easy way to raise this. He could try to keep Lillian out of it, but without her involvement the question was just idle gossip. 'Lillian,' he said simply. 'She doesn't know anything for sure. But she's had some reason to wonder.'

'Well . . .' Roland's tone was defensive. 'Even if it could be true, what would that possibly have to do—'

'We don't know,' Horn broke in. 'I'm asking the questions for Lillian, so she doesn't have to. If it's true, and if it turns out to have any connection with his death, we'll be glad we asked.'

Roland gave him a steady look through the thick lenses, then shifted his eyes to the stage as if listening to the far-off voices. But he wasn't.

'There's not much I wouldn't do for Lillian,' he said finally, still looking straight ahead. 'I tried, in the gentlest possible way, to talk her out of marrying Owen, in the mistaken belief that I could have made her happier than he would. Later I realized how misguided I was. He was absolutely right for her, and he made her very happy, right up until this madness descended on all of us, and we saw our careers begin to melt before our eyes. That's when he began drinking, acting differently, and possibly made some terrible choices.'

He turned toward Horn. 'It's hard to accept that this information could be good for her, but, all right. I believe Owen *was* seeing someone else. I have no idea who. It's just based on little things he let slip from time to time.'

Horn glanced quickly at Maggie and thought he saw a look of anger pass quickly over her face. It could have been directed at him for framing the question, or at Roland for answering it. Or at Owen Bruder for not being the father she wanted.

'Nothing specific?' he asked Roland.

'No. Just hints. It's almost as if he didn't want me to know . . . but he did. Does that make sense?'

'I think so,' Maggie said tentatively. 'He needed to tell somebody.'

Roland looked at her with new interest. 'Were you very close to him?'

'No,' she said. 'Not as close as I would have liked to be.'

'At any rate,' Roland said, 'I can promise you it wasn't Grace. His comments about a lady friend occurred long before she came to work at Global. And besides, the unofficial word on this particular lady is that she leans in another direction, if you know what I mean.'

He began gathering up the pile of papers in his lap. 'And now, I'm afraid, I must go.'

'Thanks for talking to us,' Horn said.

'Lillian mentioned the movie work both of you did,' Roland said, pausing on his way down the aisle. 'Westerns, cowboy epics. I feel I should caution you—'

'What do you mean?'

'This is a very problematic time for us, here in this country,' Roland said, and his voice held no trace of its earlier flippancy. 'It's not easy to be an American right now, when one's own government has taken on the role of the oppressor. In the movies, especially the type you once made, issues seem so simple. Good has a face, and so does evil. That's not true in our world anymore, and it hasn't been ever since that glorious war we fought against Fascism.'

'I know that,' Horn said.

'Do you? All I'm saying is, things have become muddled. That kind of man you once portrayed, he may have had a kind of symbolic power, but he has no place here. The enemy is much stronger than he is.'

'Are you saying the government might have killed Owen?'

'I have no idea who killed him, but there are forces loose out there that none of us is strong enough individually to resist. So please keep your simple cowboy values packed up and put away. They'll do you no good.'

'I promise,' Horn said curtly, hearing a touch of condescension in the man's words.

'Your horse and guitar too,' Roland said with a smile.

'I never had a guitar.'

12

'Tell me what you thought about him.' Horn glanced sideways at Maggie as he steered the Ford northwest up the broad Cahuenga Pass Parkway. The windows were down, and the warm, rushing wind almost drowned out the sound of Tommy Dorsey's orchestra swinging through 'Marie' on the radio.

'I'm still trying to decide,' she said, thoughtfully. 'He seems decent enough. I can see why he was a friend of theirs. Real smart, but also sarcastic. And nervous.'

'Well, he's got a few things to worry about.'

'A lot of people do, all of a sudden,' she said. 'First Owen and Lillian, then Cal, and now Wally Roland. And others we don't even know.'

'Let's talk about what we need to do next. I'm going to try to get onto the Global lot and talk to Marvin Felix.'

'He's not an easy man to get to, especially if he doesn't want to see you.'

'Right. And there's this mysterious woman Owen apparently was seeing. We could use a line on her. Roland isn't much help, and neither is Lillian. I wonder if Owen might have left something behind – a note, a phone number, anything – that could point to her.'

When she didn't respond, he thought he knew why. Awkwardly, he asked, 'Were you surprised? To hear that he might have been sneaking around on Lillian?'

'Yeah, I was surprised,' she said, a little too loudly. 'So what? He was a man, and sometimes that's what men do. If it's true, it was a shitty thing to do to her, but let's not convict him until we know for sure, okay? Seems to me a lot of people were doing that to him before he died.'

'You're right.'

'So what are you thinking?'

'I think we should look through his stuff. Lillian may or may not like it, but it needs to be done.'

'All right. Maybe I can do that.'

'Good. And . . .'

'And what?'

'That thing about somebody who didn't come back from the march . . . Wally started to talk about it, then shut up. I wonder if there's anything to that.'

'Like what?'

'I don't know. But we're looking into Owen's past, and we want to know about anything that smells important. Here.' Steadying the wheel with his left hand, he reached into his shirt pocket, pulled out his small notebook, and handed it to her. 'You'll see some notes I made from a bunch of old newspaper stories. Near the top is something about Owen being arrested during a march out in the San Joaquin Valley. Do you see it?'

She was silent for a moment, running a finger down the first page, then the second.

'Here it is, the arrest. In a town called Pyrie.'

'Good,' he said. 'Just in case we need it.'

There was something else. His fingers drummed lightly on the steering wheel in time to the music. Finally he reached over and turned off the radio so he could think.

'J. Parnell Thomas,' he said under his breath.

'What about him?'

'Just thinking out loud. You know, a few days ago I was thinking that sooner or later I'd have to try to see him or his people, but now that Owen's dead, it could be there's no point. Unless . . .'

'Unless the government knows something.'

'Right. So maybe I need to see him after all.'

Maggie laughed. 'John Ray, you know you've got even less chance of busting in to see him than you do Marvin Felix.'

'I know. Like I say, just thinking out loud.'

They reached the crest of the Cahuenga Pass, leaving Hollywood behind, and started down toward the San Fernando Valley.

'Joseph wants me to come along tonight when his lady friend's daddy takes them out to dinner,' he said to her. 'Seafood. By the beach. Are you interested?'

When she hesitated, he thought he knew why. 'We won't call it a date,' he said. 'You can wear your wedding ring and get 'em really guessing about us.'

'All right,' she said. 'I admit I'm curious about this Cissie.'

'Pick you up at seven.' Horn saw an opening in the lane to his right, twisted the wheel and stepped on the gas. The small car leaped ahead.

'*Whoo!*' Maggie cried out, leaning her head into the wind and letting it play with her hair. 'This little thing is fast when it wants to be.' She looked out through the windshield. 'I think I know this car.'

'Sure you do. It's mine.'

'I mean I know it from before. Just never mentioned it to you. Didn't you say you got it from the guy who ran the motor pool at Medallion?'

'Uh-huh. Old Pete. He was a friend. This was one of his stunt cars for years. Many, many miles on it. When I got out of Cold Creek, the car had just got banged up shooting some scenes for a serial and Pete let me have it for a good price. How come you know it?'

'Because if you look past all the dust on the hood, you can see that the paint doesn't quite match the rest of the car. It's more blue than black.'

'That's right. It was a replacement hood, but it photographed black, so nobody cared.'

'Well, it just so happens that serial was called *The Green Mask*.'

'Ah,' he said. 'One of yours.'

'We were shooting chapter fourteen, and I was tussling with the Green Mask himself up on the roof of this jalopy just before it flew off the road and down into the canyon.'

'With you still on it?'

'It sure looked that way, but if you made it to the theater the next weekend, you discovered, lo and behold, that I managed to roll free just before this poor little car went flying.'

'Hallelujah.'

'So I have a special attachment to this beat-up Ford from . . . what year?'

'Thirty-nine. You can ride in it any time you like. Heck, you can drive it.'

She didn't speak while Horn drove west on Ventura and then cut north past open fields, nut groves and citrus orchards. Her ranch was less than a mile ahead.

After a long silence, she asked, 'Do you miss it?'

He understood the question and weighed his answer. 'Yeah,' he said finally. 'A lot of it. I miss the times we had when we were shooting, especially off in places like Vasquez Rocks. And Lone Pine in the spring—'

'The Alabama Hills, outside Lone Pine,' she said nodding. 'I worked there too.'

'In the early morning when we'd start, the air was nippy and those boulders would just be starting to warm up from the sun, and to the west you could see the slopes of the Eastern Sierra all lit up and still covered in snow. I liked making movies up there. Raincloud did too. Soon as we got him out of his trailer, he'd sniff the air and make fog with his breath and start pawing the ground, as if to say, "Let's get to work."'

She laughed. 'He was a fine horse. Smarter than some people I know.'

'And I liked being with good people, once I knew what I was doing and got over my camera fright, and . . .'

80

'And what?' she asked.

He turned off the road and pulled up in front of Maggie's place. 'Well, I liked it when some kid would come up and ask for my autograph. We'd be at a rodeo or some kind of thing over at Gilmore Field, you know. And sometimes his folks would be standing nearby, looking happy or maybe proud. I know it was just a job, but at times like that, it felt like it mattered.'

She gave him a curious look. 'Funny,' she said. 'Joseph tells me he can never get you to admit you enjoyed it.'

'I never said it out loud before. Even to him. When the Indian starts talking about the fine times we had, all I can think about is the way it ended, when everything went bad, and I usually change the subject.'

'Why don't you change the subject with me?'

'You're harder to fool.'

She reached over and covered his right hand with hers, patted it once. 'We should have worked together,' she said. 'One movie, maybe. It could have been fun. Sierra Lane and the queen of the serials,' she announced, piling on the drama. 'They would have lined the block.'

'We *are* working together,' he said.

She got out, closed the door, and leaned in the window. 'Took us long enough.'

He watched her walk away, the back of his hand retaining the feel of hers like a light breath of air from an open window.

The Sea Spray sat on a bluff that bulged slightly out into the Pacific. Like a lot of other oceanside eateries, it was a sprawling one-story with lots of glass, generous-size drinks, and jacked-up prices. The sun had just hidden itself at the point where coastline met water, and the light was going when he parked across Pacific Coast Highway, and they waited, smelling the salty breeze, until they saw Mad Crow's white Cadillac pull into the parking lot.

Horn said hello to his friend and to Cissie Briar. She was somewhere in her mid-thirties and solidly built, her hips filling out the low-cut navy blue dress. She wore twin strands of pearls and her dark hair was pageboy length, topped by a beret-style hat that matched the color of her dress. Her perfume was lush and direct – and she was pretty.

He introduced Maggie, who wore the same dress she had worn that first night at the Garden of Allah. Roy Earl Briar, who appeared to be in his mid-fifties, had a square, sun-darkened face and a no-nonsense haircut. He wore an ordinary dark suit and looked almost drab next to his daughter. He gripped Horn's hand with a firm shake. 'What say we eat?' he asked the group.

Inside, the restaurant was nearly full, and even those with reservations were waiting, but Briar thrust a wadded-up banknote of large denomination into the proper hand to ensure a window-side table. Obviously accustomed to being in charge, he commandeered a waitress to take their drink orders then turned his attention to Horn.

'I'll tell you something about me,' he said. 'I don't spend much on myself. Shoot, Cissie here'll tell you I still drive around Midland in the same old truck I've had for years. Bought this suit at Sears, and when it wears out I'll get the next one there. I only spend money on three things. One is my family, and now that my wife, rest her soul, is gone, that means my little girl here. Another is my business, which is doing just fine, thank you. And the other is getting the right people elected to office. That's how we'll make sure this country stays the pride of the world.'

'So when you got us this table—'

'I don't care where I eat. I got us this table because I knew it'd make her happy.'

'Daddy.' She leaned over and kissed him.

'So . . .' Briar opened his menu. 'They serve rare red meat at this place, or just stuff from the ocean?'

During their drinks and the dinner that followed, Cissie regaled her father with stories of her adventures in LA, especially the nightclubbing. 'We danced to Artie Shaw,' she said. 'I got Joseph to twirl me close to the bandstand, and I reached out and touched his leg.'

'He almost dropped his clarinet,' Mad Crow added. His infatuation for Cissie was written on his face. To Horn he said, 'Did you know she can fly a plane? We went out to the Van Nuys airport and picked up a little Piper that belongs to Roy Earl . . .'

They told more stories. Maggie and Cissie appeared to be hitting it off well. Every now and then, Cissie would erupt in laughter, unselfconsciously and from the gut, like a man. She was equally attentive to her escort and her father, and when she reached over to touch Mad Crow, her hand flashed a big, square-cut emerald ringed by tiny diamond companions.

Horn was struck by her vivid personality, a mixture of warmth and brittleness, sensitivity and toughness. He also began to understand that, like a lot of rich girls, she could be a handful, and he wondered if his old friend really knew what he was in for.

Over dessert and more drinks, a dialogue developed between Briar and Mad Crow, and the subject was Cissie. 'She tell you she's been married twice before?' Briar asked.

'Yes, sir.'

'Well, our two new friends haven't heard about it. First one was this old boy who worked for me. Good-looking and smart, but he married her for her money, no question about that. I saw it, and she wouldn't listen. I had to buy him off. After that was this Mexican from a well-off family—'

'Daddy, he was from Argentina. You know that.'

'All right. He played polo. Best I could figure, that's all he ever did. I have to say he was good with horses, but the man never worked a lick in his life. That one didn't last as long as the first. Less than a year. I didn't have to buy him off. He took on a girlfriend, and Cissie went looking for him with a .20-gauge—'

'I didn't shoot him,' she said quickly. 'I just divorced him.' She looked genuinely sad.

'Like I said, I want my little girl to be happy,' Briar said to Mad Crow. 'She's a grown woman, and she's got her own life to live. But I take a strong interest in her men, and I'm interested in you. She tells me you're self-made, and I respect you for that. I don't care if a man's a gambler or not. Hell, I got my start as a wildcatter, and a lot of people will tell you wildcatting's just gambling with an oil rig. What I care about is the man. You strike me as a stand-up kind of person. So am I, and I'm saying you treat her good, you hear?'

Mad Crow cleared his throat, about to speak, but Cissie broke in. 'Hell fire, Daddy, it's not like we're getting married or anything.'

'Married or not, that's my speech.' Briar turned to Horn. 'Cissie tells me you and Joe were in the movies together.'

'It's Joseph, Daddy,' his daughter interrupted. 'He likes to be called Joseph.'

'I forgot. Well, how about it?'

'That's right, sir,' Horn said. 'We made quite a few, starting before the war.'

'You quit the movies to go into business, like he did?'

Horn was grateful the man hadn't heard about the darker side of his life. That could mean Cissie didn't know, either, which was fine with him.

'He works for me part of the time,' Mad Crow broke in. 'Casino business. Anything my other people can't handle, John Ray takes care of it.'

'And the rest of the time?' Briar asked.

'I hire out for investigative work sometimes,' Horn said, omitting his caretaker duties. 'I just took on something new.' He looked to Maggie for permission, and she nodded. He began telling them about Owen Bruder, his life and his death. As he spoke, he saw surprise on Mad Crow's face.

When he was finished, the table was silent for a moment. Then Briar shook his head. 'Taking on a job like that, you must be pretty hard up,' he said with a half-grin, using a tone that could be taken as belligerent or joshing, depending on the listener's mood.

'Actually, I'm doing it as a favor for someone,' Horn replied without looking at Maggie.

'What I mean is, no disrespect to the dead, whether he was a Red or not, he was out there on the wrong side of politics,' Briar went on, and now there was no doubt as to his meaning.

'I don't want to get in an argument, sir,' Horn said. 'I'm just doing a job.'

'Nothing's just a job. You need to get on the right side of things,' Briar responded, signaling for the check. 'Make a choice. Time's running out.'

After they said their goodbyes outside the restaurant and prepared to cross the highway, Mad Crow left the others to join them. 'Damn, that was pretty awful,' he said. 'He's a wrongheaded old coot, isn't he? Sorry, buddy.'

'Don't worry about it. You got to get along with him. I don't. But as a matter of fact, I agree with him about a lot of things.'

'Then why—'

'I told you. I'm doing a favor for a friend.'

'It's all right. You can tell him,' Maggie said. She turned to Mad Crow. 'I'm the friend.'

He looked confused. When no explanation followed, he said to Horn, 'All right then. Just be careful. The world is full of Roy Earl Briars.'

When Horn turned in at the entrance to the O Bar D, lights were on in Maggie's small house, and they spotted a big sedan, with a horse van attached, parked by the stables. 'Is that Davey's rig?' he asked.

'Sure is,' she said. 'But . . .' She seemed uncertain.

'And is that him?' A man wearing a large hat was seated on one of the folding chairs outside the open front door, just beyond the patch of light.

'Guess so. Can you wait just a minute?' She got out and went over to her husband, bent and kissed him. They spoke for a minute, then she returned.

'He busted two ribs in Albuquerque and finished out of the money,' she said, and he thought he heard irritation in her tone. 'Didn't bother to call, but he's finished with this tour. And he's not in a good mood.'

'Anything I can do?'

'Probably wasn't a good idea for me to get all dolled up and go out with you tonight,' she said distractedly.

'Anything I can do?' he asked again.

'No. Just, uh, stay on the job. I'll call you tomorrow.'

The seated figure was staring in their direction. But under the Stetson, the face was lost in shadow, and Horn couldn't make out the expression.

84

13

The latest big name expected to appear before the Thomas committee in Washington is none other than that erstwhile little tramp known as Charlie Chaplin, and we doubt that his famous sense of humor will do him any good there. His last movie, Monsieur Verdoux, *a thinly veiled piece of pacifist propaganda, died a well-deserved death at the box office. We recall tongues wagging a few years ago when Chaplin took as his fourth wife Oona O'Neill, daughter of playwright Eugene O'Neill and thirty-six years younger than her gray-haired bridegroom. Memo to Congressman J. Parnell Thomas: Ask the little tramp why, after living in this country for decades and making a fortune here, he has never bothered to apply for US citizenship . . .*

Global Studios took up a few dozen acres on the south side of Sunset, deep in the heart of Old Hollywood. It was not as big as MGM or as classy as Paramount or as brassy as Columbia. It was a medium-size, scrappy studio, known equally well for its gritty dramas as for its fluffy comedies.

Horn had no contacts there, but he needed to get inside. Like all such places, it had sturdy gates and high walls, but a quick phone conversation with Wally Roland late the night before had given him an idea or two. Starting at eight in the morning, he waited around the main service gate in the rear for almost an hour before he saw what he wanted, a bakery truck making a delivery to the commissary. As the truck waited in line behind a couple of other vehicles, he stepped up to the passenger side and rested both hands on the window sill. A folded two-dollar bill peeked out from between two fingers of his right hand.

'Morning,' he said to the driver. 'I need to see a friend inside. All right?'

The driver, who was working furiously at a jawful of gum, peered ahead at the uniformed gate guard, then back at the deuce. Without a change of expression, he leaned over, neatly harvested the bill, and said, 'Climb aboard. Once we get inside—'

'I don't know you,' Horn finished.

'Right.'

He had little trouble following Roland's directions to the writers' area. It took up most of one wing of the main building, a big, four-story square enclosing a neat quadrangle laid out with grassy spots, benches, and palm trees.

At the entrance to the wing, he told a receptionist that he had a message for Grace Stilwell and was directed to an office down the hall. The office was messy, with two desks, a few chairs, and a well-used sofa. Windows looked out on the square.

At one of the desks a studious-looking young man was banging furiously on a typewriter, two-finger style. He looked up when Horn leaned in the door.

'Grace Stilwell?'

'She's at breakfast. In the commissary. Tell her not to forget the bagel.'

'Sure.'

The commissary was in a separate building next to the main offices. Inside he found a sprawling cafeteria almost filled with people seated at a couple of dozen round tables. He paused just inside the door. It had been three years since he'd set foot inside a similar place, the commissary at Medallion Pictures. The events of that day came back to him suddenly, a series of jerky images culminating in the bloody encounter just outside the building. The memory was so sharp, he could almost feel his knuckles ache, his stomach churn. *Everything changed that day*, he thought. *I changed it.*

He looked around, getting a feel for the geography of the room. To his left, near the front windows, were the secretaries, clerks, bit players. Farther back, probably the writers and the junior producers and directors. Next were the stars, some of them in costume. He spotted Zachary Scott, apparently on loan from Warners and garbed in what looked like a riverboat gambler's outfit. Finally, on a kind of platform against the rear wall, were the tables for the suit-clad senior producers and directors and the bosses.

In the cafeteria line, he drew a cup of coffee from the urn, then pointed to the sweet rolls and asked the counter girl, 'Any good?'

'Uh-huh, baked fresh this morning.'

'I know. I rode in with them.'

'Beg pardon?'

'I'll take one. You know Grace Stilwell?'

'Sure.'

'Do me a favor and point her out to me.'

'Hmm . . .' She took only a second. 'Third table this side of the wall.'

The table was full, seven men and a woman, and the noisiest in the place. He found a seat at a nearby table that gave him a view of the woman's profile and allowed him to eavesdrop as he ate. The high-pitched conversation was batted around the table like a badminton birdie.

The current topic, it seemed, was a producer with personal hygiene deficiencies. Then it shifted to a director whose casting couch was in a tiny room just behind his desk, furnished with a bed, a champagne bucket, and a framed nude photograph of Jean Harlow. Both anecdotes were met with loud laughter.

'I was having drinks with Budd Schulberg at Musso's the other night,' one writer said, 'and he told me the name of the guy who was the inspiration for *What Makes Sammy Run?*'

'And now you're going to tell us,' another prompted.

'No. He swore me to secrecy.'

Two of his companions pelted the offender with toast crumbs.

'I need help from some of you reprobates,' Grace Stilwell announced.

'What is it, Gracie darling?' one of them asked.

'I'm working on this Ann Sheridan thing, adapting it from the book—'

'*Laurel Drive*, right?'

'Right. They should call it *Lust on Laurel Drive*. In the book, she hooks up first with her husband's best friend and then with a cabana boy at the country club. Once in her cabana, once in the swimming pool after dark. The shallow end, naturally. Then she and the cabana boy put their heads together and slice up her boorish husband with a kitchen knife . . .'

On she went. Horn studied her surreptitiously as she spoke. Grace Stilwell was lean and fine-boned, with a knowing half-smile and light brown hair gathered casually in two barrettes before spilling onto her shoulders. She wore a loosely cut silk blouse and man-tailored gabardine trousers.

'What's the problem?' the man at her right asked.

'Well,' she drawled, 'you know me, I'm a romance-and-comedy girl. I've no idea why Marvin gave me this one—'

'Let me guess,' a bow-tied writer said with mock seriousness. 'It's because you graduated with honors from Vassar, and also because you have a natural proclivity toward illicit sex and violent acts.'

'I admit the thought of murdering our esteemed leader has crossed my mind,' she said coolly, refilling her glass from a pitcher of iced tea. 'But you see my problem – the Production Code. I banged out a first draft, but when the censors got through with it, Ann was just a bored housewife who eventually is forced to kill her cad of a husband because he's been using her for a punching bag.'

'Ah, the code,' said a writer across from her, who was filling his pipe as he spoke. 'It's like the Talmud, full of challenges to the intellect. We love it, because it makes us creative. Masters of the devious reference, the double entendre.'

'Well, I think it's arbitrary and silly,' Grace Stilwell said. 'And it makes me want to go back to romantic comedies.'

'You need a quick refresher course,' said the pipe smoker, pulling an index card from his vest pocket. He cleared his throat and began to read.

'"Excessive and lustful kissing, lustful embracing, are not to be shown . . . The sanctity of the institution of marriage shall be upheld."'

The one in the bow tie chuckled. 'It could be worse, Gracie. Imagine if the lady were a godless Communist.'

'You people are no help,' she said, getting up from her chair. 'I think I'll just rewrite this thing as a farce and call it *The Happy Housewife of Laurel Drive*. Goodbye, everyone. Thanks for the pep talk.'

Horn gave her a minute's head start and then followed. She walked with long strides, and he didn't catch up with her until she had passed through the wide portal in the side of the main building and was crossing the quad on her way to the writers' wing.

'Miss Stilwell?'

She turned and gave him a neutral once-over. With her long legs and elegant carriage, she reminded him of a thoroughbred he'd once been inspired to wager a sawbuck on at Santa Anita. And lost.

'My name's John Ray Horn,' he began, suddenly aware of the odds against this conversation. 'I'm a friend of Lillian Bruder, and I knew her husband.'

'Yes?' Her tone gave him no encouragement. She was wearing high heels, he noted, and her eyes were almost on a level with his. They were hazel.

'She naturally wants to know who killed him and why, and I'm trying to help out by talking to people here and there—'

'I'd think the police were taking care of that,' she said casually, looking him up and down, as if trying to pick up clues from his appearance.

'Yes, ma'am. Well . . . I suppose they are. Maybe they'll find out something, and maybe they won't.'

'And why wouldn't they?' She seemed only mildly curious, as if willing to pass the time of day with this stranger until someone more interesting came along.

'Owen was a very unpopular man the day he died,' Horn said. 'His own government had painted a big target on his back. But I suppose you know that.'

'Why are you talking to me?' All the wit and humor he'd heard her express during lunch had vanished. Her face was blank, and her tone bore an edge of hostility.

'I'd just like some of your time. A little conversation.'

'I barely knew Owen,' she said. 'I've only been here a few months, and I never worked with him. How did you get the idea—'

'Wally Roland,' he replied, deciding to add a little lie. 'He said he thought you two were friends.'

'He's wrong.'

Horn felt himself fast running out of gas. But he wasn't ready to give up. 'Wally Roland and Owen Bruder were in the same kind of fix,' he said. 'They lost their jobs because the people they worked for got scared and gave them up. Do you have any opinions about that?'

'You're pretty nervy,' she said with a half-smile. 'And I'm going back to work now. Before I do, I'll just say that getting involved in politics is dangerous these days. But I'm not political, so it's really not something that affects me.'

She turned abruptly and walked away. As he watched, he tried to think of anything that might stop her. 'Are you sorry Owen's dead?' he called after her.

Her stride faltered a tiny bit, but she recovered and went on without turning.

14

He stared after her for a moment, berating himself for not coming up with a better approach. *She needs careful handling,* he told himself. *Smooth talk, if you're up to it. Maybe you should have a look at one of her romantic comedies, pick up some ideas.*

He briefly considered following her to her office but decided it would gain him nothing. Taking a seat on a nearby bench, he rolled a smoke and looked around at the building's four walls and the windows that allowed glimpses of people at work. He was facing the wall opposite the writers' wing. The windows were larger, and the offices, from what he could see, more spacious. Must be the bosses' side, he thought.

On the top floor he saw a man standing motionless at a window, his face not quite visible. He appeared to be looking down at him. Horn returned the look for ten seconds until the man turned away.

He finished his cigarette and headed for the main gate, the only exit for those on foot. The departure line passed slowly through a narrow gate next to a guard station. Security at most studios, he recalled, was friendly but careful, aimed largely at keeping intruders out and pilferage down. When he drew abreast of the guard, he expected to be motioned through, but the man stopped him.

'Sir, would you mind showing me some identification?' the guard asked in a businesslike tone. 'Operator's license would be fine.' He was small and gray-haired, and his well-pressed uniform was complete with billed cap, Sam Browne belt, and holstered revolver. He had the look of a lifelong studio cop.

'Sure.' Horn pulled out his driver's license and showed it. The man studied it carefully.

'Mr Horn, could I ask you to step in here for just a minute?' He showed the way into the guard station.

'Anything wrong?' Horn considered making a joke about how much jail time he'd get for hitching a ride through the gate on a bakery truck. Or pestering a high-paid female screenwriter.

'Just have a seat.'

After a few minutes, the door opened and a man entered. He was somewhere in his mid-forties, big-shouldered, with a meaty, good-looking face, marred by a red-veined drinker's nose. He appeared rushed.

'Hi,' he said, extending a broad hand, which Horn took without getting up. 'Sidney Swain. You're Mr Horn?'

'That's right.'

'I appreciate your waiting for me.'

'I wasn't exactly waiting for you.'

'I know.' His smile was pained. 'But I'd like to ask you to come with me.'

'Is there a problem? You know, if I'm trespassing, I'd be glad to leave.'

'It's not that. I promise it won't take long.' He indicated the way out the door. 'Please.'

Horn shrugged and followed him. The studio was bustling, with groups of people, a few in costume and make-up, going to and from the gigantic sound stage buildings looming off in the distance. As they walked, Sidney Swain made small talk about the studio. He was big-voiced, pleasant and polite, and was obviously expert at showing people around, but he was too well-dressed in a pricey suit to be a simple tour guide.

Somehow, Horn was not surprised to see that their destination was the building with the quadrangle, although he had no idea why. Minutes later, after a trip to the top floor in a private, automated elevator, Swain was showing him down a carpeted hallway lined with large Oriental vases and blown-up glamour photos of various stars. At the end was a set of grand double doors, and beyond that a large anteroom holding a receptionist's desk and ringed with comfortable-looking but unoccupied sofas. Swain spoke briefly with the woman behind the desk, told Horn, 'It won't be long,' and departed.

It wasn't. He had barely taken a seat and begun to study the receptionist's elaborate hairdo and sculpted nails when the inner door opened and a woman came out. She was dark and thin, almost bony, and elegantly dressed in one of those outfits where everything is coordinated, from hat to shoes. Her face was familiar. She gave Horn a look that bordered on rudeness, then crossed to the outer door and left.

As the door closed, he matched the face with the name: Maris Felix, wife of the head of Global Studios. A fixture on the society pages, both with and without her husband.

A moment later, the receptionist looked his way and said musically, 'You may go in.'

The office was probably the largest he'd ever seen. Its size seemed designed to intimidate visitors. Almost everything – walls, ceiling, drapes, and deep carpet – was the color of cream. The gleaming antique desk near

91

the big windows rested on a platform, several inches high and also carpeted.

As he looked around the room for signs of life, Horn heard a shout from somewhere: 'Come on in and take a seat.'

He crossed the room and settled into a roomy love seat facing the desk. From an open door to his left he heard the sound of rushing water. Then a man emerged and seated himself behind the desk. 'Just a second.' The man grabbed a pen and wrote something down. 'I get ideas everywhere, even in the john,' he said.

Looking up at the man on the platform, Horn recognized him, but he would have known him anyway. In this particular universe, only Marvin Felix could rate such an office.

Felix was close to sixty, around medium height, and mostly bald, a fact that accentuated the dark, pencil-thin mustache that adorned his upper lip. His face was rather nondescript except for a strong jaw and the eyes, which were heavy-lidded and in constant motion. He wore a pearl-gray suit with the faintest pinstripe and a bold yellow necktie. Altogether, he presented something of a dandified figure, but Horn knew his reputation, and he knew better than to underestimate him.

'Secretary of mine, she's used to following me around with a notebook, taking things down,' Felix said, giving Horn an appraising look as he spoke. 'But that's one place she won't go.' He appeared to be waiting for a response.

'I got a look at her,' Horn said. 'She doesn't strike me as the type you'd invite in there.'

'Not her.' Felix looked amused. 'She's my receptionist. I hired her for her looks. She can barely find the telephone. No, my secretary hangs out in there—' He indicated a door on the other side of the office, opposite the bathroom. 'She's in her fifties, got a face like Wallace Beery's sister, and she's worth two of any producer on this lot.'

The next sentence came out as a bark. 'So what brings you to my studio?'

Horn considered his answer. He was facing one of the princes of Hollywood, a powerful man, part of the small group that had built the movie business with guts and ferocious cunning. During his years as an actor, he had come to know and respect the aura such men carried with them, but he had also learned that much of it was bluster. This man had the power to hire and fire and to spend obscene amounts of money. Horn, however, was no longer subject to the whims of such people. Felix's power was nothing compared to those who had sent Horn to prison. Horn still feared the police, but he was relieved to know that he had no fear of Marvin Felix, or any man like him.

He shrugged, putting his hat on the seat beside him and crossing his legs. 'Just having a look around.'

92

'You looked up one of my people, didn't you? Had a little talk with her.'

'I suppose I did.'

'No supposing about it.' Felix reached over to a humidor and extracted a fat cigar. Barely taking his eyes off Horn, he pulled an elaborate cutter out of a drawer, lopped off the end of the cigar, and fired it up. In seconds, his head was enveloped in smoke. 'No supposing about it,' he repeated through the haze.

Horn planned his next words. He counted himself fortunate to be sitting in the office of the very man he had wanted to meet, but something warned him not to show it. He knew that Marvin Felix and his kind, the men who ran things in this town, fed off other people's needs and weaknesses. Felix, he surmised, had summoned him because he needed something from him. Horn decided to play hard to get and see how much he could learn.

'If I'm not welcome at your studio, I'd be glad to leave.'

'You're not,' Felix responded. 'What I've heard, you're not welcome at any of them. In fact, maybe I ought to be grateful you haven't punched me in the nose already.' Since this was delivered with no change of expression, it took Horn a moment to realize that Felix was making a crude joke.

'What I've heard, that's the kind of thing you do. Go around punching people. Tough guy. I used to do some boxing, back when I was forty years younger and thirty pounds lighter. Might've taken you on then, see just how tough you are. Now, though, I've got people to do that for me.'

'Look, Mr Felix—'

The man held up a hand and threw him a look so dark that Horn could tell he was not used to being interrupted. Felix pulled heavily at the cigar, gathering his thoughts. 'So . . . no, you're not welcome here. But that's not what we're talking about right now.'

'What *are* we talking about?'

'Why you came here in the first place.'

Horn paused. He could see no good reason to lie to Marvin Felix, and possibly one or two reasons for telling him the truth.

'Fair enough,' he said. 'I came here looking for Grace Stilwell.'

'Because?'

'Because I hoped she might be able to help me find out who caved in Owen Bruder's head and dropped him in his swimming pool the other night.'

Felix did not blink. 'You sound like one of those private eyes in the movies,' he said. 'Is that what you are?'

'If you know a few things about me, then you know I'm not.'

Another long puff on the cigar, another cloud of aromatic smoke. 'I know you're somebody I wouldn't say hello to on the street, that's what I know,' Felix said deliberately. 'I've got janitors who dress better than you. Beyond that, I'm figuring whether you can do me any good.'

'You want something from me?'

'Maybe.' The telephone on the desk emitted a discreet ring. Felix punched one of its many buttons and answered, and for the next two minutes he listened, grunted, and made monosyllabic responses. Horn gazed past him out the window at the sprawl of Global Studios, the streets of Hollywood beyond and, in the distance, the tattered *Hollywoodland* sign high up in the hills.

Grunting a final time into the phone, Felix said, 'That's the way we'll do it. Let me know when it's set up.'

Hanging up briskly, he said to Horn, 'I just okayed three hundred grand-worth of movie.' He seemed pleased.

'Congratulations.'

Felix obviously thought Horn should have been more impressed. He glared at him then focused on his cigar, shaping its ash deliberately on the edge of a giant crystal ashtray. 'I've got a bunch of idiots writing movies here,' he said in an aggrieved tone. 'I can look out my window and see them across the way there, sitting with their feet up, playing catch, sailing paper airplanes at each other.'

'I don't see—'

'Stop interrupting me, goddammit. Grace Stilwell is not one of the idiots. She's one of the good ones. I don't want anybody bothering her.'

'I've explained why I talked to her. I don't enjoy bothering people. But I need to find out some things, and maybe she can help.'

'Who are you working for? Lillian Bruder?'

Once again, Horn saw no reason to lie. 'Uh-huh.'

'What kind of things do you need to know?'

That took Horn by surprise. Was Marvin Felix offering to help? He guessed it was something more complicated. But he decided to go along.

'I need to know about Owen's enemies, anybody who had anything against him. Personal or political.'

'That include me?' Felix's attention was again on his cigar, the ash now shaped into something artfully symmetrical.

'I think so. You used to be his friend, but you dropped him, and then you took his work away from him.'

'Who says?'

'Owen. He told me minutes before he was killed. Doesn't sound like friendship to me.'

Felix thumped the cigar on the edge of the ashtray, exposing the glowing end. He stared at it for a moment and then ground it out hard, almost as if trying to kill an insect. He leaned back in his chair. His eyes lost focus, and for the first time he looked tired. His lips formed around

94

a softly whispered obscenity, aimed not at Horn but at the air around them.

'I've never had a political bone in my body,' he said. 'Business and people, that's what it was always about for me. I'm a businessman, but I try to understand people, 'cause they buy the tickets. Never understood how anybody could put political ideas ahead of everything else. The Commies do it, they just love all those ideas. The people who are hunting them today, they worship ideas too, just different ones. Me, I don't take sides.'

The discreet bell sounded again. He picked up the phone, said, 'Give me a minute,' and hung up.

He rubbed his right eye with a knuckle, as if just awakening yet still tired. 'Right now I hate every goddam one of them, every fucking Red, every fucking Red-baiter. Country's going to hell, it's like a disease going around, and it's harder and harder to make movies. I'm losing people, good people, because they thought it was more fun to go out and march and carry signs than just do their job. I don't get it.' He looked genuinely confused.

Horn started to ask a question, but Felix made a warning motion. 'All those people headed to Washington to testify,' he went on. 'If any of them work around here again, I'll be surprised. Larry Parks, you know him?'

'The guy who played Al Jolson in the movie,' Horn said.

'Right. One of the biggest idiots. He had it made, you know. He goes from doing bit parts to playing Jolson, and he's a star overnight. Now they find out he's a Red, and he's on his way out. Harry Cohn over at Columbia, he's not going to lift a finger to save the guy. And that other guy, the cowboy . . .'

'Cal Stoddard.'

'Yeah. He's not as big a name as Parks, but still, he's big in horse operas, you know? And look at him now. You think Bernie Rome over at Medallion is going to stand by him? He's got maybe one chance. I hear he's thinking about giving them some names, like they want. If he's smart, he'll find himself with a job when all this is over.'

Horn was caught off guard by that, but he tried not to show it. 'What about Owen Bruder?' he asked. 'You must have believed what you heard about him, didn't you?'

'Damn right. I couldn't have him working here. I'm sorry as hell he's dead, but I'd do the same thing again.'

'Wally Roland too?'

Felix looked momentarily surprised, then lapsed into gloom again. 'You talked to him, I guess. Damn right I kicked him out. There's too much heat. The only people that are going to come out of this are the ones who have sense enough to admit their mistakes and get back to work—'

'That usually means naming names, doesn't it?'

'Hell, yes!' he roared, sweeping his arms wide. 'If that's what it takes. Name some names, and we could all get back to making movies.'

'Owen couldn't do that, and I don't think Wally can either.'

'Well, then they're damn fools, and I can't help any of them.'

'There's something else,' Horn said. 'Owen wasn't even in the party. Somebody lied about him. Made it all up.'

'What?' Felix looked at him with suspicion.

'That's right. It may not be too much of a stretch to say he'd still be alive today if it hadn't been for that lie.'

Felix turned that over in his head. 'How do you know?'

'Owen told me. I believed him.'

Felix shook his head several times. His voice sounded tired. 'You're wrong on this one. Like I said, I hate the government boys as much as I hate the dopes they're chasing, but I don't think they'd make a mistake on something like this.'

'Who turned him in to the committee?'

'I don't know. I wouldn't tell you even if I did, but I don't. It's all top secret. Hush-hush. They don't talk about where they get their stuff.'

'Don't bet on it,' Horn said. 'Laura Lee Paisley gets it from someplace, and I'd bet it's them.'

'Bitch.' Barely whispered, but audible enough. 'She's one of the worst of them all.'

'They say the studios are afraid of her.'

Felix stared at him, and Horn had the feeling he'd gone too far. 'Maybe some people are,' Felix said tonelessly. 'I just make sure I wash my hands whenever she's been around.'

Another ring, and he picked up the phone and listened for a few seconds. 'All right, tell them to wait a couple more minutes.'

He seemed suddenly embarrassed, a look that did not sit well on his face. 'I, uh, tried to call Lillian yesterday. She didn't want to talk. I don't blame her. The police came around, and I told them I'd try to help, but I couldn't think of anything.'

'Did they ask you if Owen had enemies here?'

'Sure they did. I'll tell you what I told them. He could be hard to get along with, just like me. But if anybody at this studio hated him, I'd be very surprised to hear it.'

'How did he and Grace Stilwell get along?'

Felix seemed surprised by the question. 'Far as I know, they barely knew each other. Why?'

'Just wondered. Was Owen especially close with any woman at the studio?'

Some of the old hardness returned to Felix's countenance. 'What the hell does that mean?'

'I think you know what it means. It's a question that needs to be asked.'

Felix took his time. 'The answer is no. And out of respect to Lillian, you might want to be careful about what you say to people.'

'You like her, do you?'

'I liked them both,' he said quietly. 'I'm sorry he's dead. I think the police will eventually find out who killed him. But if it makes her feel better to have you looking around, that's fine. You, uh . . .' The look of embarrassment returned. 'She may not have a lot of money to pay you,' he said. 'If so, I could chip in some.'

'You offering to hire me?' Horn was sure he showed his surprise.

'No. I don't want you working for me. Truth is, I don't think you're all that good. I just want to make sure Lillian doesn't go without anything she needs.'

'I think it's a little late for you to be worrying about her.' As soon as the words were out, he regretted them. He had no illusions about ever being friends with Marvin Felix, but there was no advantage in antagonizing him.

A few seconds passed. The room became so quiet, Horn could hear the muffled clatter of a typewriter in the secretary's office.

'I don't offer everybody favors,' Felix said slowly. His head was down, as if he were studying something on his desk, and Horn couldn't see his eyes. 'Those I do, they're usually smart enough not to throw them back in my face.' The voice had taken on an edge Horn had not heard before. It sounded like a file on metal. 'You can leave.'

On the way out the door, Horn met a collection of well-dressed men wearing anxious looks, waiting to file in. The receptionist said 'Goodbye' and picked up the phone as he left. Closing the outer door, he leaned against it for a moment, going over his talk with Marvin Felix. He didn't know if he'd just had a meaningful conversation with the man or had been taken on a ride. *The guy knew exactly what he was doing*, Horn thought to himself. *He learned at least as much about me as I learned about him.*

Exiting the building, he found Sidney Swain waiting for him, looking slightly tense. Swain gave off a scent of strong mouthwash that Horn had not noticed before.

'I'll walk you out,' the man said.

'Looks like you've been assigned escort duty,' Horn said to him. 'I hope I'm not too much trouble. If I start running for the commissary, would you have to call the guards?'

Swain waved the question away with a smile. 'You're no trouble at all.' They began walking toward the main gate. Swain noticed Horn looking at the veteran's insignia on the lapel of his sport coat. 'Army,' he said. 'I was a lieutenant in the MPs. No real combat. But after a day trying to control rowdy soldiers in a war zone and mean-as-hell POWs, I felt like I'd earned my pay.'

'I'm sure you did.'

'I hope you had a good talk,' Swain said. 'Marvin is sometimes hard on people, but he can also be an enormous help to someone when he has reason to be.'

Instead of responding to that, Horn said, 'Maybe you can help me with something. I'm wondering how I wound up in that office up on the top floor. How anybody even knew I was on the lot, and why they would have cared in the first place.'

Swain, looking straight ahead, ignored this, so Horn continued. 'After I scared off Grace Stilwell with my questions, I spotted somebody giving me the once-over from the same floor. A big man, about your size. If it was you, that would explain how I got stopped at the gate, wouldn't it?'

'Possibly.'

'It would explain how, but not why. Who cares if I sneak onto your big lot, have a conversation, and then leave? How would you and Marvin Felix even know my name and know that I've been asking questions about Owen Bruder? That's what I've been asking myself, and here's what I came up with. I remembered meeting a certain guy the other day, somebody who does a lot of what you might call back-door work for the country club and movie studio crowd, and gets paid to be discreet about it, and I'm just wondering if he might have picked up the phone and called one of his friends here at Global just to let him know that I'm snooping around.'

They arrived at the gate. 'And when I showed up here today, I bet that would have been a good chance for Marvin Felix to find out a little about me – how good I am, maybe even what I've turned up so far. Don't you think?'

'Interesting theory,' Swain said. 'You should be one of our writers.'

Horn nodded. 'Maybe so. I hear that with all the firings around here, there are jobs opening up.'

'Mr Felix has asked me to tell you that your name and description will be posted at all our gates and that you won't find it so easy to return,' Swain said without apparent malice. 'No offense, I hope.'

'Not at all. Maybe this is a good time for me to ask you exactly what you do around here.'

'I'm Marvin's assistant. I do whatever he needs.'

Horn recalled the slow-talking man who sat quietly reading *Yank* magazine on a hotel roof. 'It must be a popular kind of job these days,' he said.

★

In a drug store across the street from the gate he ordered a Coke with cherry syrup, then went to a phone booth in the corner and dialed Lillian Bruder's number. After a dozen rings he hung up, retrieved his nickel, and tried Maggie. Davey Peake answered and, after no pleasantries, put his wife on.

'How's the bronc buster doing?' he asked her.

'Not too well,' she said, her voice lowered. 'His ribs hurt, and he wishes he was out earning money.'

'How are you doing?'

'Good.' Her voice brightened immediately. 'I spent the morning over at Lillian's place, looking through Owen's papers. I found a few things and made some phone calls. Don't know exactly what this stuff means, and I've still got some calls to make, but . . .'

'Tell me.'

'I will. And when I've finished, I think you're going to want to take a little trip with me. How much gas have you got in that funny old car of yours?'

15

The sky to the east was just beginning to stand out from the horizon when he picked up Maggie. She came silently to his car carrying a large paper sack and a brown envelope. 'He's still asleep,' she said. 'Don't make too much noise leaving.'

An hour later, daylight now, they had left the flats and were climbing up into the Tehachapi Mountains, headed northwest on Highway 99. Along the way, Horn recounted his visit to Global Studios. They stopped at a turnout near the summit, where Maggie opened the bag and produced apples and deviled ham sandwiches. They washed the meal down with water from Horn's army-surplus canteen, then drove on. The road, which had been widened the year before, was now four lanes, allowing them to make good time as they threaded through the mountains and began the long, slow descent into the San Joaquin Valley.

It was harvest time through much of the region, and they passed countless trucks loaded with corn, snap beans, and melons headed for the markets of Los Angeles. They stopped for a meal in Bakersfield, biggest town in this part of the valley, and heard snatches of Spanish on the radio, a reflection of the population changes that had begun during the war when California growers, desperate for hands to pick the crops, opened their fields to Mexican workers. Then Maggie slid behind the wheel and put them back on 99.

Horn opened the envelope and began looking through what she had found. It wasn't much – a short and cryptic typewritten note; another note, this one handwritten, whose meaning was all too obvious; and a yellowed newspaper clipping. 'Read that,' Maggie said, indicating the clipping.

March Organizer Found Dead. The terse headline introduced a ten-paragraph news item from a 1939 Bakersfield newspaper. The report said a young man named Robert Nimm, one of the organizers of what the paper called the 'anti-farmers march' of the day before, had been found dead in his hotel room in Pyrie within hours of being released from police custody. Cause of death appeared to be a blow to the head. Blood had been found on the top edge of a steam radiator, suggesting an accidental death caused by a fall, but the county coroner would investigate.

The last paragraph was a list of those who had been arrested along with Nimm, then freed after trespassing charges were dropped. Owen Bruder's name was on the list, as was Wally Roland's and ten others.

Attached to the clipping with a rusty paper clip was a scrap of paper bearing a number written in pencil. 'What's this?' Horn asked.

'Phone number,' Maggie said. 'New York. I tried calling it, but it's been disconnected.'

On the radio, a voice droned its way through a recitation of weather conditions and forecasts for various parts of the region. Even though it was autumn, summer seemed to have blanketed the great San Joaquin Valley one last time. The air that roared past them and swept in the windows was uncomfortably warm, and Horn wiped sweat off his brow with his sleeve. On both sides, as far as they could see, lay rows and rows of just-ripened beets, celery, lettuce, and turnips, in fields swarming with pickers.

His eyes went over the two notes again, and he read the handwritten one aloud:

Your kind poisons the earth.
You would destroy our country, but you yourself will be destroyed.
We will act when you least expect it. You will not see our approach.
Enjoy those few days you have left.

'And it's signed *Order of Old Glory*.'

'Must be one of those good old patriotic groups,' Maggie said with unaccustomed sarcasm. 'Like the American Legion or the Boy Scouts.'

'Right. I thought they threw out all the hate mail.'

'Lillian thought so too. Owen apparently saved this one for some reason. She recognized it when I showed it to her. She said she had told Owen they should give the note to the police, but he had just cussed the police and made a joke about how this was the only note they'd gotten with the words spelled right.'

'Anyway, we get the drift,' he said, holding up the typewritten note. 'But what does this one mean?' He read it aloud:

I'm now sure it was W. I think I know why.
No more calls, no more meetings for now. Too risky.
I'll come to S. on Sunday at 9.

There was no name at the bottom. 'Any thoughts?' he asked.

'I don't know,' she said, chewing lightly on her lower lip. '*W* could stand for Wally. But we don't know that this note has anything to do with anything. It might be connected with Owen's death, but it could also be about . . .' She seemed reluctant to go on.

'A woman,' he finished for her. 'It could be about Owen sneaking around with a woman.'

'Maybe.' She sounded doubtful.

'If it is, would that change your mind about him?'

'What's there to change?' she said impatiently. 'He ignored me for most of my life. If it turns out he was doing something behind Lillian's back, I've got room in my mind for that. But let's not—'

'I know. Jump to conclusions. Did you show this to Lillian?'

'No. Nor the newspaper story. I'm not sure why. I thought we should talk about them first.'

'All right. Tell me about the calls you made.'

'Okay. Can I have some water?' He uncapped the canteen, which he had refilled in Bakersfield, and handed it to her. She took a healthy swig and passed it back to him. As he drank, she shifted position behind the wheel and leaned out the window for a few seconds to cool her face. 'I called the Bakersfield newspaper first, to see if they could tell me any more about the story. There was no reporter's name on it. I got sent back to somebody in the files, where—'

'The morgue,' he said. 'Where old stories go to die.'

'Right.' She laughed. 'Some nice girl back in the morgue, with time on her hands I guess, looked through the rest of the files on that story and said everything else was mostly a follow-up. A few days after this Robert Nimm died, the county coroner decided that he had fallen down and hit his head, and that was that.'

Horn made a gloomy sound.

'But that didn't stop the queen of the serials,' she continued. 'After asking the nice young girl for some advice, I called the city editor of the paper. Very gruff man. You could tell he's used to yelling at people instead of talking to them. He didn't have much patience for me, but I put on my little-girl voice and mentioned the article and asked him to draw on his years of experience and tell me who he would talk to if he wanted to know about something that happened in Pyrie almost ten years ago. He got a little flattered and calmed down and finally said the mayor. He even gave me the gentleman's name and phone number.'

'That was nice of him. Are you going to send him tickets to Davey's next rodeo?'

'Quiet, please. So I called the mayor. In Pyrie the mayor picks up his own phone, which also happens to be the chamber of commerce and the office of a lawyer. Who also happens to be the mayor. Anyway, he sounded like an agreeable sort, although a little self-important, like mayors can be. I told him I was looking into my family history and Robert Nimm was a distant relative, and I was curious about how he died. The mayor said he was around back then and could tell me a little about it. He started to go over the story real fast, but I asked him if I could come see him and take my time with the questions. He said he was awful busy, and that's when I kind of let slip that I used to work in the movies—'

'Smart.'

'And he talked for a minute about how he likes Deanna Durbin, and I said I met her once. Which is not exactly true. But he finally said if I wanted to come up and visit, he'd ask around and try to jog his own memory for any more details.'

'Well, I'm impressed,' Horn said. 'I know a slickster named A. Dixon Vance who couldn't do this better than you, but he'd charge a lot more.'

After another hour of driving, Horn spotted a sign reading *Pyrie, Pop. 8,100*, and they were there.

The town seemed to sag under the heat. The main drag – which was also Highway 99 – was a dusty, three-block row of stores and offices, a tractor dealer, a small hotel, and the occasional eating joint. They quickly found the law office of Mayor Kenneth Duke. The mayor had a small head and narrow shoulders but was a big man nonetheless, with most of his weight settled onto his hips and midsection. He greeted them in his shirtsleeves, then ushered them to his inner office.

'Well,' he began after the introductions. 'Long, hot drive for you.' He had a broad smile and, as Maggie had said, a mayoral manner. A fan perched atop a filing cabinet labored uselessly, moving warm air from one side of the room to the other. On one wall hung a calendar illustrated by color photos of trucks, tractors, and harvesters.

As if obligated to reward them for their effort in getting there, he began telling them about the town and its role in the valley's agriculture. He spoke in a big voice, using broad gestures, and Horn was reminded of how, as a boy back in Arkansas, he had accompanied his father to the town square to hear a candidate for the state legislature. The man had spoken from the back of a flatbed truck, and he had Kenneth Duke's voice and broad delivery. A politician, Horn thought, doesn't have conversations, he makes speeches.

Tiring of the town history, Maggie interrupted. 'Mr Mayor, we don't want to take up too much of your time,' she said. 'Could we talk about—'

'Robert Nimm. That's right. Your relative.' Duke adopted an exaggerated expression of embarrassment. 'Boy, I could have saved you some trouble.'

'Beg pardon?'

'I tried to call you early today – tried both the numbers you gave me.

103

You see, it's like this. I thought about it, and I asked around, talked to folks who've lived here about as long as me, and when I'd finished I said to myself, shoot, I don't know two cents' worth about that thing. I mean, I could have covered it all with you over the phone. Man gets arrested, gets released, goes back to his hotel room, starts packing – in a hurry, I guess – and falls and hits his head. It was all in the paper, and you said you saw the paper.' He spread his hands in a gesture of futility.

Maggie looked at Horn, then back at Duke. Her eyes narrowed. 'You told me there was more,' she said.

'I sure thought there was. More details, I mean. But it was a long time ago, and this old boy's brain must be getting soft. At least, that's what my wife tells me.'

'We came a long way.'

'I know you did, and I'm sorry as I can be.' He rolled his eyes upward, as if to invoke the deity. 'I sure am.'

'Well, I suppose we could stop off at the police station,' she said. 'They might—'

'That's your bad luck too,' he said with a grimace. 'The only full-time policeman in this town, the only one who's worked here a long time, is the chief, and he's away right now. Left today to go fishing in the Sierra. I suppose you could give him a call when he comes back in a couple of weeks, if that's any help.'

'What about his helpers?'

'The part-timers?' Duke made a dismissive sound. 'They're just boys. They wouldn't know anything.'

'Mr Mayor, you told us you asked around,' Horn said to him. 'Did anybody suggest to you that you shouldn't talk to us?'

Duke adopted a look of astonishment. 'Now why the heck would they do that?' An idea appeared to strike him. 'Tell you what,' he said. 'I've got to get back to work now, but what say you let me treat you to a meal over at Aunt Ray's? Fortify yourself for the trip back? It's just down the street. You can tell them it's on me.'

'Thank you, but no,' he said. 'We'll just be getting back.'

'It's a shame you drove all this way,' Duke said as he saw them out. 'A damn shame.'

They stood out on the sidewalk, smitten by the dusty heat. 'Damn shame you decided not to talk to us, Mr Mayor,' Horn muttered. He turned to Maggie. 'You suppose he's just an idiot, or did he have a reason for changing his mind?'

'Maybe somebody had a word with him,' she said. 'But who?' She looked down the street. 'Listen, what say we try Aunt Ray's? I could use something cold.'

As they passed a farmers' supply store, a teenage girl wearing overalls and a straw hat was heaving bags of fertilizer onto the back seat of an ancient car that might have carried Dust Bowl refugees all the way from Oklahoma. She glanced at them, then away, then back at them. She gaped at Maggie, and a bag slid to the sidewalk.

'Margaret O'Dare,' she whispered. 'Is it you?'

Maggie came out of her distracted state long enough to grin. 'I suppose it is,' she said.

'Oh, my, oh, my.' The girl approached her carefully, almost warily. 'I can't believe it's you, just walking along here. I seen every one of your movies and serials. Especially the serials. *Bandit Girl* was the best.'

'Why, thank you.'

'I got a picture of you on my wall, from *Photoplay*. You and your horse. You're the reason I wanted to ride. We got neighbors who . . . they let me ride their horse sometime.' She seemed out of breath. 'I'm not very good, but . . .'

'I'll bet you will be.'

'What's your next movie? I'll tell everybody about it.'

'Honey, I don't make movies anymore.' She said it gently.

'Oh. I'm sorry. Well . . .' She looked around again, patted her clothes. 'Can you wait just a minute? Please.' She ran into the store and was back in seconds, clutching a fountain pen. She whipped off her hat. 'Would you sign it?'

'Sure I would. Thank you for asking. What's your name?'

'Sue.'

'All right, Sue.' Maggie signed the band with a flourish. 'You stay on that horse now,' she said as they moved off.

Horn motioned for Maggie to wait. 'Ask you a question, Sue?'

The girl nodded dumbly, still transfixed by the encounter.

'Do you know anybody who's been around here a long time and would remember things that happened years ago?'

She thought briefly. 'Sure. There's Hazel, over at the hotel. Hazel Brownlee. My folks say she's been here longer than just about anybody.'

The Pyrie Hotel, a narrow three stories tall and built of faded brick, dominated one corner of the main street but probably held fewer than twenty rooms. Inside the small lobby, two old men sat silently in worn, overstuffed chairs, looking out at passers-by. 'Hazel Brownlee?' Horn asked one of them.

'Office behind the desk.'

Horn hit the bell on the counter, and Hazel Brownlee came out. She was sixtyish and well-upholstered, with a broad, open face. He introduced himself and Maggie and said, 'We met a young lady named Sue outside who told us you know this town pretty well. Could we take a few minutes of your time?'

105

'I suppose,' she said. 'What's it about?' She smelled faintly of talcum powder and regarded them wide-eyed behind her glasses.

'It's about a man who died in a hotel room back in thirty-nine,' he said. 'Maybe even this hotel.'

Now the eyes behind the glasses narrowed. 'You the folks came here to see the mayor?'

'Yes, ma'am.' *Word sure gets around.*

'What did he tell you?'

'To be honest, he wasn't much help.'

'What makes you think I know any more than he does?'

There was something about Hazel Brownlee, he decided. Maybe it was her steady gaze, the way she looked at him head-on. Maybe it was the talcum powder, like his mother once wore. She was asking the obvious questions, but not in a combative way. More like she really wanted answers. He had the notion that she was willing to talk if given the right reason.

Lies didn't work with the mayor, he reflected. Maybe the truth will work with her.

'Maggie's father was murdered recently in LA,' he said. 'Years ago, he was one of the people who marched here and got thrown in jail. We think there might be some connection between the two deaths. We just want to find out what we can. If you can help us, we'd appreciate it.'

More of that gaze, her mouth pursed a little. Fingers of both hands tapped lightly on the counter. Finally she said, 'You all like lemonade?'

A minute later they were settled in the back room, which was half office, half apartment. Through an open door Horn could see what looked like a tiny bedroom. Hazel Brownlee pulled a pitcher of lemonade from the fridge, cracked an ice tray, added the cubes, and poured them drinks. They sat around the table.

'What did the mayor say exactly?' she asked.

Horn told her.

She looked amused and irritated. 'He wants to be mayor for the rest of his life, and since we got nobody here who wants the job, he'll probably keep it. But he has to be careful.'

'What about the police chief?' Horn asked. 'Does he—'

'Have to be careful? Sure, since he's appointed by the mayor. I saw him over at Aunt Ray's having breakfast this morning. If he left on a fishing trip, it was pretty sudden. Or maybe he's just laying low until you two leave. Neither one of them old boys is worth two cents, you ask me.'

'Was the mayor in office in thirty-nine?'

'No, he ran his law office here. But I can guarantee he knew what was going on. If he says otherwise . . .' She grinned broadly.

'Ma'am, I have to ask,' Horn said. 'Why are you talking to us?'

'Maybe it's partly because I've got no use for our mayor or police chief.' She took a giant swig from her glass and gasped at the coldness of it. 'Tastes good, doesn't it? For years this town's been split in two. On one side you got the growers and their friends. They want what's good for the business. Anything that's not good for the business, like higher wages for pickers, they fight. The mayor's on their side.

'On the other side you got people who know that agriculture's important to us but who also believe in being fair. They'd like to see workers have better pay and clean water to drink, get a doctor when they're sick or have a baby, that kind of thing. I've always been on that side. My husband was, too, before he died. John was active in politics his whole life, he cared about this town. And I raised my kids to be the same way.'

'Yes, ma'am.'

'I don't want to bore you with our little town. I bet we're like a lot of places if you take a hard look at them. Anyway, here's what I remember. One day a whole bunch of people showed up downtown. They'd come in cars and trucks and even buses. It was pretty exciting, I can tell you. There was maybe a couple hundred of them, and they started down at the end of the main street, carrying signs and yelling, and headed for the farmer's coop building down at the other end. But they never made it, because a bunch of police cars pulled up in front of the coop and blocked the street, and as soon as the march got there, they broke it up. They arrested about a dozen people and scattered the others.'

'How many police cars does this town have, anyway?' Horn asked.

'I'll get to that. We don't have a jail here; nearest one's down in Bakersfield, so they just took the dozen men over to the hardware store and put some deputies to guard them. And they'd bring them out one at a time to the police headquarters and ask them questions. That went on all afternoon and evening. Meantime, my husband found out, the chief had talked to the county prosecutor, who told him they'd have trouble making anything stick. Chief could hold them for questioning, the prosecutor said, but he'd eventually have to let them go.'

She paused to refresh their drinks. 'Late that evening, there was some kind of ruckus over at the hardware store, and John went to see. He told me there was a lot of yelling, and the chief had his deputies go in and haul one of the men out of there and bring him over here to this place. John said he got the impression they were doing it for this guy's protection. They put him in a room. No guard or anything. He seemed all worked up, nervous, my husband said, and one of the cops left him a bottle. To calm him down, I guess.

'That was Robert Nimm. Next morning he was dead.'

'And the coroner called it an accident,' Maggie said.

'That's right. The bottle was empty, and there was a lot of alcohol in his system. My husband found the body, and it was pretty much like the papers described it. Blood on the radiator. Except for one thing. My husband said that along with the bad wound on the back of the man's head, there was a good-size bruise on his jaw that he hadn't had when they brought him in the night before. And he wondered how the man could have gotten that if he'd fallen backwards onto the radiator.'

'I wonder too,' Horn said.

'Other things were funny, little things that just make you wonder,' she said. 'Far as I know, nobody here knew this march was coming, so where did all the police come from? Must've been half a dozen patrol cars blocking that street, some of them county sheriff's cars from miles away. Why did they separate Robert Nimm from the others and put him over here? Why didn't they register him at the desk? And why did they put him in that particular room?'

'Which room?' Maggie asked.

'Number Eight. It's the room that the farmers' coop keeps year-round. They use it for visitors, sometimes for having parties, that kind of thing. Strange choice.'

They all sat silently around the table for a few moments. Then Maggie said, 'Thank you, Hazel.'

'Don't mention it.' She got up and carried the empty pitcher to the sink. 'Drive careful going home.'

As they said goodbye, the running water in the sink almost drowned out her words. 'Way I see it,' she said over her shoulder, 'it's not just this town that's split in two. It's the whole dang country.'

16

He gassed up at a place near the hotel, then headed south on 99.

'What do you think?' she asked as he drove.

'What do *you* think?'

'You know, any number of things could have happened in that town and that hotel room,' she began, 'but I don't need to hear them, because I think I know.'

'Tell me.'

'Understand, I don't know for sure. But everything is so fishy, and when you look at it, only one explanation seems to work.'

'So tell me.'

'I think the police were waiting because somebody tipped them off. And I think it was Robert Nimm, because he's the only name that makes sense. And who knows why he did it? Maybe we'll find out, maybe we won't. But I think he tipped them off, and all those others who got arrested found out about it later that day. Somehow. At the hardware store. They put it together, and they went after him. The police pulled him out of there to save his life, and they put him in the hotel to keep him safe, maybe to let the others leave town first. But somebody found out where he was and went to his room and killed him.' She paused, looking for his reaction.

'All right. I'm with you so far.'

'But none of this means anything to us unless it's connected with Owen being killed,' she said deliberately. 'And we don't know that. Yet.'

'We know he saved the newspaper story for years,' Horn said. 'Along with somebody's phone number. But that could just be because he was there and wanted to remember it.'

'It could be for other reasons too,' she said, almost to herself.

'Uh-huh. What's that you said about jumping to conclusions?'

'I remember,' she said with a small laugh. Then she turned serious. 'Do you think we should tell Lillian—'

'About what we found?' He paused, thinking for a few seconds. 'Yes, I do. She's one of the main reasons we're in this. We don't want to keep secrets from her. If she wants to tell us we're crazy and can go to hell, it's her privilege.'

'What's our next step?'

'A lot of little steps,' he said. 'I have an idea how to find out who had that phone number—'

'Wait,' she broke in. 'I just remembered. The phone number.'

'What about it?'

'The other thing I ran across in Owen's desk, another phone number. Didn't you find it in that envelope?'

'No.'

She plucked the envelope off the dashboard, dug into it, and pulled out a scrap of paper. 'It was down in the bottom.'

'Whose number is it?'

'I don't know. It was penciled inside the front cover of his address book, all by itself. The only number with no name next to it.'

'Let's call it, see what happens.'

'I did. A woman answered. I told her I thought I had a wrong number and asked her name, but she wouldn't give it.'

'What did she sound like?'

'I don't know. Young.'

'What's the exchange?'

'Hollywood.' She tossed the envelope back onto the dashboard. 'You were telling me about the things you plan to get done.'

'Right. The phone numbers. And I think we need to see Wally Roland again. I want to know what went on in that hardware store, and he was there. And . . .' He reached back in his memory. 'There's another friend of Owen's I should probably talk to. Grover Jones.'

'The actor?'

'Uh-huh. Lillian told me he'd been calling just before Owen was killed. She didn't say much about him. It sounded like he wanted to support them quietly but was nervous about doing anything in public.'

'A lot of people are nervous these days, aren't they?'

'I suppose.'

She thought for a moment. 'Don't you think the police need to see that Old Glory note?'

He didn't respond. 'I know you hate policemen,' she said forcefully. 'I would too, I guess. But we're trying to find out who killed my father, and I'd appreciate it if you'd keep your own likes and dislikes out of it. You know they need to see that note.'

'All right,' he said. 'I'll take care of it.'

'Thanks,' Maggie said. 'Then why don't you let me look up Mr Grover Jones?'

'Fine with me.'

'One more thing,' she said. 'When I went through Owen's desk, I turned up a note from that private detective, the one who didn't do them any good.'

'A. Dixon Vance. The man who drives a Roadmaster and parts his name on the side.'

'That's the one,' she said with a laugh. 'The note wasn't important, just something he sent when they first hired him, but Lillian and I got to talking about him. She told me he made a very good impression on her, and she was real disappointed when he decided to quit. Said she expected more from him.'

'I went over that with him,' Horn said. 'He got a little prissy about it, but I didn't learn anything.'

'I know. I just think it may be worth going at him one more time. I thought I'd—'

'Go right ahead.' He didn't want Maggie to waste her time, and he was also mildly irritated at her implying that he hadn't tried hard enough with Vance. But it wasn't worth an argument.

They stopped for supper in Bakersfield. As they ate, Horn browsed through a local paper and learned that the wildfires, it appeared, were still burning. Close to a dozen, large and small, were working their way along the slopes of the San Gabriel and Santa Susana ranges, mostly north of Los Angeles, and the Malibu Hills to the west. It was that time of year, he knew. After smoking up the air people breathed, the fires usually burned themselves out without threatening communities. Still, they made him edgy.

Maggie seemed tired and, an hour south of Bakersfield, he glanced over and saw that her head was back, wedged up against the door, eyes closed. The light was fading and the temperature was less oppressive, but her hair was still lightly damp from the heat. A tendril of it curled over her cheek and mouth. He reached over and gently hooked a finger under it and moved it away. Her hand came up slowly, brushed his own, then fell back. She could be asleep, he thought; some people move like that in their sleep. Or she might be awake and wanting to acknowledge his touch. For some reason, it seemed important for him to know.

Up ahead loomed the Tehachapis, and he felt the first gentle incline in the road that hinted at the climb ahead. To the right, the sun was going down over Pine Mountain, twenty miles to the west, but it was like no sun he'd ever seen. It looked furious. The molten red-orange ball seemed to be boiling the sky, and its color slashed across the entire horizon. Farther out from the sinking sun, the sky darkened to a dirty rust-brown.

Horn realized the angry sun was a creation of the wildfires. Wherever they burned, their smoke filtered the light in startling and sometimes frightening ways. He wondered how the Chumash Indians, who lived

111

here before the white man, had reacted when lightning brought the fire that scorched their mountains, darkened their skies, and stirred the anger of their sun.

It was dark when he pulled off the road, through the gate marked O Bar D, and came to a stop in front of the house. The lights were on inside. He touched Maggie's shoulder lightly to wake her. Sleepily, she got out and started for the house. The door opened, spilling light into the yard, and Davey Peake emerged, stumbling slightly on the steps. She stopped and spoke to him briefly, then went inside. Horn started the engine and put the car in gear, but then saw that Peake was coming over. He took note of the man's head-down, purposeful walk and decided he'd better get out of the car.

'Hey.' Peake thrust his chin almost in Horn's face, and the sour smell of booze came as no surprise.

'Hey there, Davey.'

'You and Maggie have yourselves a good time, wherever the hell you been all day?' His words had the slurred, knowing exaggeration of a drunk trying for both sarcasm and threat.

'I suppose so,' Horn said evenly. 'But it was mostly work, you know. A lot of driving, and a lot of conversation.'

'And nothing else, I suppose.'

'What do you mean?'

'You know exactly what I mean, piss-ant.' His breath was foul. 'You been trying to make time with my wife while I was gone?'

'No, sir, I haven't.' Horn knew a couple of relevant things about Davey Peake. He had two broken ribs. And he was tough as leather.

'No, sir, I haven't,' Peake mimicked, laying on the sarcasm. 'Well, sir, I think you're a liar. A broke-down, over-the-hill, fucking jailbird liar.' He bobbed his head and swung his shoulders back and forth in exaggerated gestures as he spoke, and Horn could sense the man coiling himself for a punch.

Out of the corner of his eye, he saw Maggie approach. 'Davey!' she yelled.

'Time I get through with you, you won't be sniffing around anybody's wife . . .' Peake took a step back, readying himself. Horn saw the muscles in his jaw clench.

'I'm not going to fight you, Davey,' Horn said, showing both his palms. 'You been hurt.'

'Chicken shit,' Peake said. 'I'm gonna—'

'Davey!' Maggie grabbed him by the arm, swung him around. 'Stop it. You hear? He didn't do anything.' He yanked his arm away from her, but she stepped up and grabbed it again. Horn feared he might strike her.

'We didn't do anything,' she said insistently. 'John Ray's just trying to

112

be helpful. What's wrong with you? I'm ashamed of you, acting like this.' She drew him away a couple of steps, and then suddenly he was down on one knee with a groan, bracing himself on the ground with one hand.

'Oh, no.' Maggie sank down beside him, still gripping his other arm. 'Now see, you're going to hurt yourself worse. Let me help you up.'

Cursing softly, he complied. Seconds later, to Horn's amazement, she was walking him to the door and inside the little house. A minute passed, then she came out.

'He'll be all right,' she said. 'He's got a temper, you know.'

'I'll say.' He had to ask. 'Maggie, has he ever hit you?'

She hesitated. 'I'm not sure that's any of your business, but I know you're asking for the right reasons. No, he hasn't. He knows what would happen if he did.'

'Fair enough. He doesn't handle the booze well, though, does he?'

'That's my problem, and I deal with it,' she said curtly. She put her hand on his arm. 'Good night. Thanks for everything you did today.'

'Sierra Lane and the queen of the serials ride again,' he said, trying to joke. But his heart wasn't in it.

The Dust Bowl was twenty minutes away, and he was hungry. When he arrived, he saw only about a dozen cars in the gravel parking lot, typical for early on a weeknight. Inside, the jukebox was going as usual, but otherwise the place looked almost sleepy, with few tables taken and all the bar stools unoccupied. The newly spread layer of sawdust on the floor gave off a fresh aroma.

'Rusty around?' he asked the bartender.

'He had to go downtown.'

'They make any chili back there in the kitchen?'

'Sure did.'

'I'll have me some.' He went over to the jukebox, selected 'Kentucky Waltz' by Bill Monroe and the Bluegrass Boys and 'East Virginia Blues No. 2' by the Carter Family, then took a seat at a nearby table. When his chili arrived, he made short work of it and ordered a second bowl and a High Life to go with it.

As he ate, the place began slowly filling with customers, mostly those who worked on ranches or farms nearby. Horn also saw a handful of Mexican pickers, who probably hired out by the day, and he recognized a Japanese man, who had come back from wartime internment at the Manzanar camp to resume work on his few acres of lemon trees.

Bill Monroe's high, nasal tenor, backed by banjo and fiddle, were familiar to Horn, but tonight he was not comforted by the music. He was considering another High Life when the front screen door closed with a slam behind Mad Crow. The Indian gave him a half-hearted wave and went to the bar for a Blue Ribbon, then came over.

'Evening, your lordship. Take it you don't mind a little company?'

Horn shook his head.

Mad Crow sat, killed several swallows of the beer, then sighed heavily. 'I'm not in a good mood,' he said.

Mad Crow indeed wore his stormy face, the look that in the old days had warned that a bar fight was about to break out. But he wasn't going to bust up anything tonight, Horn reflected, taking in his friend's expanding paunch and well-cut sport coat, along with the expensive-looking Stetson that now hung on the back of the chair.

'Me neither.'

'You neither, huh? Well, I got a nickel says I'm in a worse mood.'

Mad Crow groped a cigarette out of his jacket pocket, then reached into his pants for a bulky lighter, adorned with the same hammered-silver motif as his wristwatch. As he lit up, he shot Horn a sideways glance that, oddly, seemed almost embarrassed.

'Roy Earl,' he grunted.

'What about him?'

'Well, I might have mentioned that he owns something like three percent of all the oil wells in Texas. Now he's bought himself into the oil patch down in Long Beach.'

'Really? I didn't know that.'

'I just found out. Old Roy Earl is now one of the big dogs out here. His company's still based in Texas, but he's rented himself a whole floor in one of those big, shiny buildings out on Wilshire, and he's already had sit-downs with the mayor and some of the city councilmen and county commissioners.'

'Uh-huh. So what does all this have to do with anything?'

'He went to, uh . . .' Mad Crow cleared his throat and started over. 'He went downtown and looked up this congressman who's running the investigation of the Reds in Hollywood.'

Horn nodded, waiting.

'He gave him your name.'

'*What?*'

'He gave him your name. Not as a Red, understand. He told him you went to work for that guy Bruder before he was killed, and now you're working for his widow, trying to clear his name.'

'Why the hell would he do something like that?'

'Just doing his duty, he calls it. He says the congressman and his boys need to know about not just the Reds but people working for them. He says that's the way it's done. Just bookkeeping, he calls it. Fighting Communism is all about gathering information, he says.'

Horn gripped his beer bottle with both hands and cursed under his breath. 'How did you find out?' he asked.

'Cissie. The way she told it, Daddy's got his eye on some more oil leases in LA County, and the locals are starting to look at him as a rich, pushy Texan trying to horn into their business. He's trying to shine up his reputation around here as an old boy who's fighting on the right side. Good politics translates into good business, he thinks.'

Horn thought for a moment. Probably nothing to worry about, he told himself. I'm not breaking any laws. Still, he was coming to understand the power of whispers and rumors and secret lists, and he was not pleased to know that his own name was now written down somewhere.

Mad Crow was still speaking. '. . . so I went to see him, all worked up about it, and he looked at me like I was some kind of fool. "Just be glad they don't have your name too," he said, and he made it sound almost like a threat.'

The Indian shook his head. 'Sorry, bud,' he muttered. 'Some of this is my fault.'

'Tell you what's your fault,' Horn replied. 'Picking a girlfriend with the wrong daddy. A rich Texas peckerwood who's slippery as a snake.'

'I'll drink to that,' Mad Crow said, and went to the bar for fresh beers and an extra tumbler of rye for himself. 'So what put you in a bad mood?'

Horn told him about the drive northward, what he and Maggie had found out in Pyrie, and what had happened when he brought her home. As Davey Peake entered the story, a faint smile began to take over the corner of Mad Crow's mouth, but he said nothing.

'I think Owen Bruder got himself into something up there, something bad,' Horn said. 'At the very least, he knew about it. Don't know exactly what, or if any of it's provable, but it doesn't make me warm up to the guy any more than I did at first. Now that he's dead, I guess I'll never get to know him very well, but I'm already getting tired of him. And his politics.'

'You are, huh?' Mad Crow did not sound sympathetic.

'I think people like Bruder, and Wally Roland, who marched and carried signs and drew up petitions to save the farm workers or the Spanish peasants or whoever was in the news, were showing off. It was just dangerous enough to be exciting, so they did it. Now they're finding out that it's *really* dangerous – people are knocking on their doors, and they're losing their jobs and it's too late to change their minds.'

'It's really too late for Owen Bruder, isn't it?' Mad Crow said with one eyebrow up.

'Yeah. And he shouldn't have died, no matter who did it or for what reason. And I feel sorry for Mag—' He stopped himself. 'For Lillian, because I like her. But I'm tired of hearing about how the Communists and their friends are being persecuted. Somebody ought to tell them that they're being persecuted because they're on the wrong side.'

'I think they've heard that.' Mad Crow leaned back in his chair and swept his gaze around the room, now hazy with cigarette smoke and noisier with the growing crowd. On the jukebox, Gene Autry was singing 'That Silver-Haired Daddy of Mine', a song awash in sentiment that Horn had never liked, possibly because he couldn't imagine himself ever feeling sentimental about his own father.

Mad Crow was gazing toward the bar now, seemingly lost in thought. 'You ever take a good look at that picture?' he asked.

Horn turned around. 'Sure,' he said, focusing on the framed three-by-four-foot illustration that hung over the wide mirror behind the bar. 'Custer's Last Stand. It's a beer advertisement. What about it?'

'It's called *Custer's Last Fight*,' Mad Crow said patiently. 'I forget the artist's name, but it was painted in the 1880s, and Anheuser-Busch had it reproduced and turned into a Budweiser ad. You see it in bars everywhere.'

'I know,' Horn said. 'First time I saw it was in Little Rock, a long time ago.'

'One of my ancestors was in that fight,' Mad Crow went on. 'His name was Gall. I've seen pictures of him, and he was something. Built like me, but bigger.'

'I suppose you're going to tell me he was the one who killed Custer.'

'Nope,' Mad Crow said evenly. 'He always fought with a hatchet, and Custer was killed by bullets. We know that much, but we don't even know if it was a Lakota or a Cheyenne that killed him. You've probably heard me make jokes about that painting, the little things the artist got wrong. Like showing Custer with long hair, when he'd had his hair cut short for that campaign. And putting way too many war bonnets in the picture. Things like that.'

'Somebody's getting scalped, as I recall,' Horn said, squinting toward the illustration. 'Did he make that up?'

'Oh, no,' Mad Crow said. 'There was scalping, and worse. Much worse. Custer had no business taking cavalry into that part of the Montana Territory.'

'So what's the point of your story?' Horn asked with a grin.

'I'm taking a while to get there. It's something like this: When you look at the picture, you probably see a few heroic soldiers being massacred by a bunch of half-dressed redskins. I see what went before, and what came afterward – Wounded Knee. The Trail of Tears. Some American general saying "The only good Indians I ever saw were dead" – and the newspaper in North Dakota that told everybody it was okay to wipe out every tribe in the West because Americans needed their land to expand.'

Mad Crow was beginning to give off small signals that he was drunk. It's not one of the bad ones, Horn observed. It's one of those where he makes sour jokes and shakes his head a lot.

'I know about all that,' Horn said. 'I'm not proud of it.'

'Good for you,' Mad Crow said, lapsing into his old movie vernacular. 'White man not proud. White man ashamed.'

'Are you making fun of me?'

'No. Or maybe just a little. There's one other thing I remember. When I was six, I was taken away from my folks and sent to the reservation school run by this missionary couple. They put us in uniforms and gave us books. Some good things happened to me there. I learned how to read and speak English. I discovered Emerson and Wordsworth and the great language in the King James Bible. I was smart, and I learned how to get along in your world.'

Mad Crow covered a rumbling belch with a big hand. 'But every time I tried to speak Lakota to one of the other boys, Brother Prescott or his wife would slap me upside the head. The bigger I got, the harder they slapped, until I had all the Lakota slapped out of me. Years later, I came here to work, and I walked into an Indian bar on Alameda down by the rail yards and heard Lakota spoken for the first time in years. There they were, young men just like me, bellied up to the bar and speaking a language I'd been afraid to speak since I was six. I started blubbering, and I had to step out into the street so nobody would see.'

Horn was silent. This friend of his, this gruff, funny, sometimes fearsome friend, had a hidden side, he knew, a side where old wounds still throbbed, a side seldom held up to the light. Horn was getting a rare glimpse of it, and he was careful not to spoil the moment.

'So here it is,' Mad Crow said finally. 'This thing we've been knocking around for the last few days. It's not about whether it's a smart thing to be a Red, or whether we should all go out and hunt them down. It's not about whether they've got the answer to all the world's problems or whether that old snake Roy Earl does. It's not about whether the Commies are trying to steal our atomic bomb and sell us down the river – although if they are, I sure want to know it. It's not about . . .' He stopped, as if distracted, and drained the last of the rye in one gulp.

'What's it about, then?' Horn asked.

Mad Crow looked at him, eyes bleary. 'It's about which side you're on – the ones getting kicked, or the ones doing the kicking.'

'That's easy,' Horn said. 'I want—'

'I didn't say which side you *want* to be on, I said which side you *are* on,' Mad Crow broke in, clearly impatient. 'You got no choice. Like most people, we're little guys, because we don't have power, you know what I mean? The power to execute people, or make war, or put people in jail.

117

Remember how it was for you when they shipped you off to do two years at Cold Creek, and tell me how powerful you felt that day.'

'What's this got to do with the Reds?'

'Nothing. Which is my point. It's not about them. It's about a government that decides you can't speak the language you were born with, or decides you can't join a group with the wrong name.'

'All right,' Horn said, feeling the obstinacy in his own voice. 'But what about the SOBs who are after my bomb?'

'Throw their sorry asses in jail!' Mad Crow bellowed, causing heads at nearby tables to turn. 'If they're Americans, fry 'em, because that's treason. But don't send their friends to jail too, just for being friends. If people in Washington think they need to go after a man like Cal Stoddard just because he signed his name on some dotted line, then we ought to trade all of 'em in for a new bunch.'

Mad Crow slumped in his chair and let out a deep breath. 'End of sermon. Your daddy probably could have delivered a better one, but then he would've been sober.' He got up. 'I'm going home.'

'Me too.' As they walked out into the brisk air, lightly scented with smoke from far-off fires, Mad Crow said, 'Tomorrow's Patty Stoddard's birthday, and I asked her and Cal over for dinner. Nee Nee's doing a pot roast. Maggie said she and Davey'd show up. You want to come?'

'Thanks anyway, Indian.'

'Sure.' Mad Crow looked disappointed but said no more.

They stood by his gleaming white Cadillac. 'Still burning somewhere,' Horn said. 'Pray for no wind.'

'I'll have a talk with the Great Spirit.' Mad Crow tossed his keys up, caught them, apparently with something on his mind.

'I'm not too surprised to hear old Davey got in a lather over you and Maggie,' he said finally.

Horn waited, sensing there was more.

'Maybe he's been picking up things.'

'What things? There's nothing to pick up.'

'You don't think so?'

'Say what's on your mind, Indian.'

'All right.' Mad Crow tossed the keys up again, almost dropping them this time.

'I will. Everybody knew what was going on between you and Maggie back then.'

'So what? It's over.'

'To you, maybe. Not to her.'

'You're crazy.'

'Uh-uh. I'm smart, and I've got eyes. I see the two of you together every now and then, and I can read signs. Little things from her. You may have moved on, gotten a wife and a divorce, and she got herself a husband. But she never got over you.'

'Well, that's just—'

'Hey!'

They looked up to see Rusty Baird's old Chevy skidding to a stop on the gravel. He waved them over.

'Glad I caught you two,' Baird said, pointing to his passenger. 'I want you to meet a friend. Woodrow Wilson Guthrie.'

'Woody Guthrie?' Mad Crow said. '"Hard Traveling" Woody Guthrie? "Goin' Down the Road Feelin' Bad" Woody Guthrie?'

'He's the one.'

'Well, I'll be.' Mad Crow was clearly pleased. Then he looked closer. 'Is he asleep?'

A slightly built, bushy-haired man lay slumped in the passenger seat, head back, mouth open.

'He rode the bus all the way in from New York,' Baird said, 'and we decided to make a stop at this bar across from the Greyhound station. Guess we stayed longer than we planned to.'

'How long's he here?' Horn asked.

'I don't know. He never says. Just comes and goes. He, uh . . .' Baird looked uncomfortable. 'He's going to need a place to stay.'

'He's not staying with you?' Horn asked.

'Not this time. We've got my sister and her kids, and the place is overflowing. I don't suppose . . .' He looked at the two of them.

'Hell, I'll put him up,' Mad Crow said quickly. 'Maybe I'll hear some music while he's here.'

'I guarantee you will,' Baird said, pointing to a battered guitar in the back, covered with handwriting and various stickers. 'And a lot of conversation.'

'I think I've had enough conversation for one night,' Horn said, yawning. 'See you later.'

As he drove across the lot, he passed Baird's car and waved, then slowed to let a Dodge sedan leave ahead of him, but the man behind the wheel motioned him on. He headed south on the quiet country road, a citrus grove on his right, a field of soybeans on his left. Feeling drowsy, he rolled down his window to let the cool night air wash over him.

He had driven about a mile when he saw headlights appear in his rearview mirror. He was sure they hadn't been there seconds ago, which could only mean the car had been following him with lights off. His sleepy brain, instantly awake, went to work retrieving scattered bits of information. The Dodge in the parking lot. Not just a driver, but two men sitting in front. Both apparently well-dressed – better dressed, in fact, than anyone inside the Dust Bowl tonight. Passenger's face in shadow, but the driver's face vaguely familiar.

He cursed himself aloud for an inattentive fool just as the Dodge, with a burst of speed, pulled out and jumped abreast of him. The right-side window was down, and now he knew the passenger. The man with the face of the self-satisfied frog.

Frog Face leaned slightly out the window and motioned for Horn to pull over.

Not on your life. Not on a dark road. I don't care if you're J. Edgar Hoover himself. Not out here in the country, with nobody around to see what happens.

Jamming in the clutch, Horn down-shifted two gears. He heard the man shout to his driver, and he heard the surge of the other car's engine. Just as Horn let the clutch out, the Dodge jumped ahead farther and cut him off. Horn yelled and backed off the gas, but not before he raked the Dodge's right front fender with a prolonged scraping sound heard even over the noise of two engines. The next thing he knew, he had slammed into the ditch, the steering wheel jammed against his chest.

17

Pain seared his chest and ribs. Gritting his teeth, he pushed himself away from the steering wheel and wrenched open the door. As he clambered out, the two men approached, silhouetted figures in the beam from the other car's headlights. But he knew that the nearer one was Frog Face, and he surmised that the other was his younger companion, the one built like a fullback.

He did not know the size of the trouble to come, he could only try to ready himself. Taking a deep breath, he clenched both fists and went into a loose fighter's stance. But then he saw the glint of metal in Frog Face's right hand, the shape of the pistol, and relaxed his hands.

'You boys don't keep regular office hours, do you?' he asked them.

The gun made a small circular motion, its meaning clear. As Fullback walked up to him, Horn turned around, facing his car, and spread his jacket with both hands to allow a search.

But Fullback had a different intent. Horn heard a hissing intake of breath and just had time to clench his gut muscles before a fist exploded in his right kidney. The impact, like an electric shock, tore a loud groan from his throat and buckled his knees, sending him to the ground. Fighting nausea, he leaned against the car's fender, its metal cool on his cheek, as the other man deftly searched him from armpits down, not forgetting his pants legs.

'Nothing,' he said to his companion. Then he leaned in close. 'You should have pulled over like we asked you.'

'Let's get him in the car before someone comes along,' Frog Face said, his voice sounding far away.

Hands lifted him and half-dragged him to their car, where he was flung into the back and thrust down onto the floor. As Fullback got back behind the wheel and started off, Frog Face settled into the back seat, the soles of his shoes resting on Horn's back and shoulders. 'Stay right there.'

The fresher pain had now localized around his midsection. Kidney and bladder burned, and he felt as if he needed to pee, although he knew he did not. He also felt sick, and the motion of the car was no help.

Frog Face seemed to read his mind. 'Throw up in this car and you'll be sorry,' he said mildly.

They drove for miles, and Horn lost track of time and place. All he knew was that the car occasionally came to a stop and he continued to hear traffic sounds. This meant that they were most likely headed south, into the city. At least they're not taking me out to the desert, he thought, trying to find some comfort in that.

The two men talked as if he were not there. Their remarks were disconnected – work details that meant nothing to him, the upcoming World Series match-up between Cleveland and Boston, a little family trivia. Fullback was married, and complained about his wife's reluctance to shop for bargains, but his affection for her came through in his conversation. Frog Face sounded older and more worldly, and there was no mention of a family for him. Listening to them, Horn thought that an eavesdropper would have pegged them as a couple of educated, congenial white-collar types focused on their jobs, just a couple of the boys headed out for a drink after a long day in the office. Except they're carrying guns, and I'm here on the floor. He knew he should be worrying about his situation, but he wasn't yet ready to give himself permission.

After a while, the pain subsided into a dull ache. Surreptitiously, he began tensing and relaxing his arms and legs, making sure all were still in working order.

More time, more miles went by. 'This street's better,' Frog Face said to his driver. 'We can make some time now.' Horn twisted his neck and looked carefully up at the man. The passing streetlights carved deep shadows into his face. It looked confident. Not a bad-looking face, but the overall look was thrown off by the too-fleshy lips and the too-bright eyes.

The fire in his kidney had mostly cooled, but with the retreat of the pain came the first stirring of anger. The shoe soles were heavy on his back. Whatever the hell they've got in mind, he thought, I wish they'd just get to it. He decided to nurture his anger a little. It might serve him. It might, in fact, be all he had.

Then he heard it: the cry of a distant gull, and at almost the same instant he breathed in the first faint scent of salt air, and he knew they were headed for the ocean.

'Watch for that street,' Frog Face said. 'The one that goes . . .' Horn felt him shift position as he looked out the window. 'That's the one,' he said. 'Turn right.'

After more long minutes, the car went down an incline, and the smells of the harbor grew more distinct. Finally the car stopped, and the doors opened. Frog Face swung his feet out, leaned down, and tapped Horn lightly behind one ear with the gun barrel. 'End of the line.'

Horn got out slowly, waiting for feeling to seep back into his cramped limbs, and straightened up. They were at the head of a pier, looking out toward the ocean. A damp and chilly breeze came off the water. The pier was illuminated feebly by scattered lampposts, each one ringed by a corona of mist, and lined with motley fishing boats almost all the way out to the end. Beyond that, except for a bobbing buoy light here and there, all was gray-black, both ocean and sky.

'Why don't we take a stroll?' Frog Face said, again using the gun to emphasize the point. He seemed to be enjoying himself. They walked along the uneven planking that formed the pier until they came to the end, where no boats were moored.

Looking around, Horn could dimly make out other piers not far away, and he knew where he was. San Pedro. The fishing fleet harbor. He had come down here a couple of years ago to collect a debt for Mad Crow, and he had liked the feel of the place. Up until the war, much of it had been Japanese, built around a village of shacks where the fishermen and their families lived. But during the war the place was emptied, its residents sent off to internment camps, and the village fell under the bulldozers. Now a strange mixture of tongues could be heard among the fishing boats of San Pedro – Italian, Portuguese, even Croatian.

Horn breathed in the scents of the harbor – salt-encrusted pilings, fish guts, the slicks of gasoline and engine oil puddled on the surface of the water around the boats. He felt the fear building inside him, starting down where the fist had struck him and radiating outward like heat from a stove. He worked to hold it down, and to stoke the anger instead.

Horn turned to Frog Face. 'You going to shoot me?' he asked, and he was satisfied to hear that his voice was reasonably steady. The man, gun held loosely in his hand, took a step backward and now stood facing Horn with his back to the land. The younger man stood a few feet off to one side.

'Not unless you make me,' Frog Face said. 'But this is where we leave you, and you go for a swim.'

Horn stared at him.

'Jump in,' the other man said, as if coaching a child. 'Jump in, have yourself a nice bath. When you get out, we'll be gone, probably having some coffee and a Danish in that all-night diner we passed up the road. And while you're trying to dry off and hitch a ride all the way back, we hope you pause for a moment of reflection. Stick to what you do best, Mr Horn. Stick to your little odd jobs. Do not get involved in things that are bigger than you. Stay close to home, where you're safe. Leave politics to the big boys. If you don't, the next time could turn out much worse for you.' He made a small gesture with the gun. 'Time for your swim.'

Horn felt immense relief at knowing his life was not about to end, but this was followed by equally immense stubbornness. They were not going to humiliate him.

'Go to hell.'

'Not the right answer,' Frog Face said almost wearily. 'I've got no good reason to kill you, but if you're not in the water in the next five seconds, I've a perfectly good reason to put one of these in your kneecap.' He raised the gun. 'One . . . two . . .'

Horn made his decision. He was not going alone. Allowing his shoulders to slump as if in defeat, he quickly measured the angle between himself and Fullback to his left. Directly behind the man lay the bow of a fishing boat, but just six feet to the left was blackness. Nothing. And somewhere below – six, eight, maybe ten feet – lay the water.

'Three . . . four . . .'

Horn bent his knees, twisted to his left, and pushed hard off his right leg. His right shoulder caught Fullback at the waist, doubling him over. He felt the rocklike weight of the man, heard Frog Face's startled shout. Legs pumping hard, not slowing, Horn heard himself groan as he lifted the weight, and, an instant later, carried both of them, legs flailing, off the pier.

He had aimed at the blackness but misjudged, and he felt Fullback's shoulders slam into the bow of the boat, heard the man yell with the pain. Then, a split second later, they hit the water. The coldness of it gripped Horn like a new electric shock as they went under, but he grimly held on to Fullback's waist, feeling the man's fists striking at him, some of the blows landing hard on his face, his ears. Horn was a good swimmer. Vaguely, he thought of drowning the man, then swimming away in the dark.

Soon, though, the air in both their lungs brought them up to the surface. Horn heard a cacophony of sounds – loud splashing, their gasping breaths, yelling from above – all of it oddly magnified by echoes. They were under the pier. From a distance, he heard Frog Face shouting a name over and over: 'Danny! Danny!'

Horn felt the other man's hands at his face again, but now they were limp and without strength, flailing about, and he was making coughing, retching sounds. His head went under, emerged, then went under again. He couldn't swim.

Horn's vision was adjusting, and he could make out the outlines of the underside of the pier. He swam over to a piling and held on, gasping, listening to the sounds of the drowning man behind him, taking pleasure in them, remembering the feel of the fist in his kidney. The sounds of struggle grew fainter. Then the man let out the rest of his breath in a sighing moan of absolute despair, and his head sank one more time.

Horn clung to the piling for a few more seconds. Then he breathed the words *Well, hell* to no one in particular, pushed away from the piling, swam two strokes and ducked underwater. His grasping hands found the man's hair, then head, then shoulders. Gripping him by the collar, kicking furiously, he brought the dead weight to the surface. Soon he had the almost-limp form backed against the piling, his left arm wrapped around the damp wood, right arm steadying him. The piling was slick with moss and studded here and there with barnacles. The man gagged, coughed, and spit a few times, then appeared to be breathing all right. He had not inhaled any water.

'So you're Danny?' Horn said, still breathing hard. 'Danny Boy. A dumb name.' He fumbled his way around Danny's belt and chest until he located the snug holster under his left arm. He extracted a small pistol and jammed in into his own belt. Legs scissoring to keep himself afloat, he unknotted Danny's tie and awkwardly re-tied one end around his neck, then reached up and tied the other end around a crosspiece a couple of feet above the water. 'This'll keep your head out of the water. Better not move much, or you'll strangle yourself.'

Above, he heard renewed shouts and saw a jerky beam of light being played over the water near the edges of the pier. Apparently Frog Face had gone back to the car for a flashlight. 'Danny! Where are you?'

'Down here,' Danny gasped. 'He's—'

Steadying himself with his left hand on Danny's shoulder, Horn doubled up a fist and uncocked a short right to the man's face. He felt the nose cartilage buckle under his knuckles. A new cry of pain.

'Shut up,' he said. He waited, listening to the footsteps on the boards above. His rasping breaths mingling with Danny's as the sea water lapped softly at the pilings.

Soon Frog Face would find a way down here, and he had a gun. It was time to leave.

Horn leaned in close to Danny's face. 'Keep your voice down,' he said. 'Who sent you after me?'

The only answer was an obscenity. Horn touched the man's nose.

'*Ow!* Goddammit.'

'Answer me.'

A few seconds of panting breaths, then: 'Cross.'

Horn punched him in the gut as hard as he could manage underwater, taking what breath the man had left. He looked out at the beam of light, watched it move slowly around the head of the pier. When it was at the side farthest from him, he paddled away in the opposite direction, heading straight for the next pier, some fifty feet away. He kept arms and legs below the water to avoid splashing.

With each stroke he felt his strength going. Very soon he'd have nothing left. *It's just swimming*, he told himself. *Swimming's easy. Look at that big lunk Johnny Weissmuller.* A stray memory crossed his mind, a glimpse of a certain night years ago, when he and Maggie had waded into the surf, the moonlight turning her body into ivory . . .

His outstretched right arm brushed against wood. The hull of a boat. Seconds later he was behind it, reaching up for the gunwale, then hanging there, gasping. It took five minutes before he had the strength to hoist himself aboard. He heard faint voices from the direction he'd come and considered making his way onto the land, but instinct told him to hide and wait until they had left.

He found a tarpaulin covering the winch that pulled in the nets, dragged it down onto the deck and covered himself. He lay there shivering, his heart pounding, for an hour until his body heat gradually warmed the small space around him. Just before he dropped off to sleep, he saw Rusty Baird's face and heard his voice. What was it he had said? Something about how they could come for one man today and for you the next.

Funny thing, he said silently to Rusty. *I guess they just did.*

When he awoke he felt stiff and sore but somewhat rested. He heard low voices some distance away. Throwing off the tarpaulin, he could make out figures moving on the still-dark pier. The fishing crews were arriving.

Clothing still damp, he stepped off the boat and made his way onto land, drawing stares from some of the fishermen. He walked past pierside sheds and warehouses and shuttered bars, then uphill past ramshackle houses. After a few blocks he came to San Pedro's downtown and began to see cars and people on the street, either those up early or those at the tail end of a long night. Outside a darkened drugstore he spotted a phone booth and was glad to find that he still had change in his pockets. He considered calling Maggie but didn't want to stir up more trouble in her house, so asked the operator for a reverse charge call to another number. He saw the sky lightening to the east, a long bar of pale pink just visible beneath a low bank of marine clouds.

He heard Mad Crow's sleepy grumble as he spoke to the operator, then:

'John Ray? Where the hell are you?'

'She just told you. San Pedro.'

'San Pedro? What's going on?'

'Look, I'm sorry to wake you up. I need some favors, and I'll explain it all when I see you.'

'What's wrong with your voice?'

'I've got the shakes. My clothes are wet, and I'm cold. I'll tell you all about it. For now, though, just listen, all right?'

★

Two hours later they sat in big chairs across a heavy table before the fireplace in Mad Crow's living room. It was a large room with a beamed ceiling, Indian rugs, and antlers on the walls. The fire was going well, snapping and throwing off heat, and Horn's damp jacket and socks were spread out on the fire screen, his shoes propped up against it. He wore one of the Indian's bathrobes and sipped from a mug of hot coffee as he finished relating what had happened.

'Second time in the last few days I've taken a swim without wanting to,' he said. 'I think I see a pattern shaping up here.'

Mad Crow was about to comment when the phone rang. He spoke briefly, then returned. 'That was Slim,' he said, referring to one of his ranch hands. 'He and Paco found your car where you said. Lights left on, battery dead. There's a dent in the front bumper, otherwise it looks okay. Your key's still in the ignition, your hat's on the front seat.'

'Did you ask about—'

'That big envelope? It's sitting on the dashboard. They're going to jump the battery and bring the car over here.'

'Good. Have him stick it away somewhere, will you? I don't want anybody to see it here.'

'It'll go in the garage. What are you going to do now?'

'I don't want to be any trouble to you, but I'd appreciate it if I could hole up here for a day or so. I'd offer to sleep on the couch but' – he looked across the room – 'it seems that's already taken.' A body lay curled up under a blanket on the sofa, a mop of unruly hair visible on the pillow.

'You can have the spare room,' Mad Crow said. 'He said he'd rather have the couch. Said he's slept on a lot of them, even at home. When we got in last night, I made some coffee and we sat up for a while, talking. He's one of the fidgetiest men I ever met. Talks a blue streak, smokes like a chimney, can't sit still, loves to tell stories. When I gave out and had to turn in, he sat up a while longer. Said he had some ideas for a couple of songs and wanted to write them down while they were still fresh.' Mad Crow shook his head. 'He's not exactly what I expected, but he's quite a character.'

'What did you expect?'

'Oh, somebody bigger and tougher, more of a lumberjack, you know. Not this scrawny little runt.'

Nee Nee, Mad Crow's aunt, came out of the kitchen with a coffee pot and refilled their cups. Of substantial girth and indeterminate age, she functioned as his cook and housekeeper. One of several relatives he had brought out from the reservation in South Dakota, she had never bothered to learn much English and his Lakota was spotty, but they never seemed to have any trouble communicating.

She went back to the kitchen and Mad Crow pointed to the gun that sat on the table, its barrel gleaming in the firelight. 'You don't want to carry that around,' he said.

'Don't worry.' From time to time, they had discussed the dangers of an ex-convict being found within spitting distance of a firearm. 'I don't plan on hanging on to it for long. What time is it?'

Mad Crow looked at his watch. 'Almost nine.'

'Good. Use your phone?'

'Sure.'

Horn was back in a few minutes with his trousers and shirt, which Nee Nee had ironed for him. He went to the fireplace and touched the sleeve of his jacket. 'Dry enough. Since the Ford's not here yet, mind if I take your truck for a while?'

'Take the Caddie. I'm not going out till this afternoon.'

'The pickup's fine. I'd like to use your razor to shave and borrow one of your hats too.'

'Where you going?'

'Downtown. To see a certain congressman.'

'Bunch of crooks, all of 'em.' The voice, a soft Oklahoma drawl, came from across the room. Woody Guthrie, it appeared, was awake, but in the next moment, he shook out his blanket, fluffed his pillow, settled back in, and closed his eyes.

18

He went in through the towering glass and wrought iron entrance of the Biltmore and crossed the ornate Old World lobby to the reception desk, where he spoke to a clerk. As the man checked something behind the counter, Horn looked around at one of the city's grand spaces. Sunlight slanted in through the high door, warming the tiled floor, and the lobby smelled of furniture polish and freshly watered plants. Straightening up, the clerk directed him up a grand flight of marble stairs to a small, unobtrusive door off the lobby. It was a self-service elevator. Once inside the enclosure, he saw he had only one choice of button, and he punched it.

When the elevator stopped, he got out into a small corridor with a single large door at the end. Outside the door sat a young man in a gray suit, who stood and beckoned him over. Just as with Frog Face when he waved the gun, the man's gesture was unmistakable. Horn, who was holding the borrowed hat in his right hand, unbuttoned his jacket with his left and held his arms out wide. After the search, the man knocked once on the door and opened it.

Horn found himself in an elegant sitting room dotted with potted plants, small tables, comfortable chairs, and a pair of sofas. There were other, more unusual items – four filing cabinets against one wall and an assortment of wooden packing crates. The tables were piled high with books and files. Open doorways on both sides led to other rooms.

Two young men were quietly and busily filling the crates with material from the tables and filing cabinets. At a small desk a young woman, cigarette hanging off her lower lip, squinted through the smoke as she speedily worked a typewriter keyboard.

Horn noted that the heavy drapes, oddly, were closed and the room was in half-light, with the main illumination coming from two floor lamps, and smaller lamps atop the woman's desk and a larger desk near the windows.

As he began to frame a question, the man nearest him looked up from his work. 'Mr Horn? Come in.' The man spoke briefly to the typist, scooped up a pile of papers from beside her and carried them to the larger desk, noticeably favoring his right leg as he walked.

Sitting down and looking up, he noticed that Horn hadn't moved. 'Won't you have a seat?' He indicated a chair in front of the desk.

'I came here to see the congressman,' Horn said. 'You don't look like him.'

'I'm not.' The man, in shirtsleeves and suspenders, appeared about thirty, with a round face, full cheeks, and quick, intelligent eyes. He was well-groomed, with an already receding hairline adding to the acreage of his face.

'I called for an appointment, and I'd like to see him.'

'You spoke to Ellen there,' he said, indicating the typist. 'I told her to invite you.'

'What's the deal?' Horn was becoming angry.

'The congressman returned to Washington yesterday. Please have a seat. I promise I won't waste your time.'

After a moment, Horn complied. He stared at the man. 'My guess is you're Mitchell Cross.'

'You're a good guesser,' the man replied with a broad smile. 'And you're John Horn.'

'John Ray Horn. I use the middle name.'

'I'll remember that.' He leaned back in his chair and crossed his hands over his stomach. His cufflinks glinted in the dim light. 'And you came here to see Parnell and to let him know that two of his staff people have been . . . I guess you'd say operating outside the law.' He had a pleasant baritone, pitched a notch above normal volume, as if he knew there was an audience somewhere, listening.

'More than two, actually. But you've got the general idea.' Horn carefully laid the hat on the floor beside his chair. 'Since kidnapping is outside the law, last time I checked.'

'It is indeed.'

A discreet knock at the door Horn had entered, and a colored man in a white jacket rolled a room-service cart into the room.

'Set it up right here, if you don't mind,' Cross told him, clearing away several papers from his desk blotter. In a minute, a meal was spread in front of him, and he tucked a napkin into his collar.

'I don't want to be rude,' he said to Horn. 'But my hours are very irregular, and I eat whenever I'm hungry. That's the only way I can get my work done. My staff, bless them, have learned to put up with most of my eccentricities.' He lifted the cover off his hot dish and sniffed appreciatively. 'Beef stroganoff. They do it pretty well here. May I order something for you? It wouldn't be any trouble.'

'No, thanks.' Horn realized he was ravenously hungry, but he had no intention of eating this man's food.

'Nothing else, thank you very much,' Cross said to the waiter, and the man left. He turned to Horn. 'Then I hope you'll excuse me while I eat.'

As Cross dug into his food, Horn studied him. The man handled his knife and fork delicately, but his hands looked strong. Horn's thoughts immediately turned to the story of the Marine manning the machine gun. He tried to see the war hero sitting there, but all he saw was a youthful-looking, open-faced man with a forkful of stroganoff. What's a hero look like anyway, he wondered? Not a movie hero, but the genuine article. Aren't they supposed to glow like a radium dial on a wristwatch?

Cross appeared to notice Horn's stare. 'The presidential suite,' he said between bites, gesturing around the room. 'The congressman was installed here. Now that he's gone—'

'Is he coming back?'

'No, his work's finished here. The hearings begin in DC next week, and he needs to get ready for them. I'm doing clean-up chores here, and I'll join him soon. Anyway, I've inherited this nice suite of rooms for a few days. I hope you don't mind the low light. My eyes have taken a real beating lately, what with all the documents I've been going over. I find that it's easier on them if I can keep the shades drawn during the day. That's another one of my little quirks. Drives my people crazy.'

'I'm not that interested in your eyesight,' Horn said. 'Since I'm not going to meet the man I came here to see, why don't you just enjoy your meal, and I'll let you know what's on my mind.'

Cross' expression did not change. He took a forkful of food, then gestured for Horn to go ahead.

'Two of your boys forced me off the road last night,' Horn began.

Cross put down his fork. 'Ellen, Frank,' he said to the two workers. 'Would you mind moving to the other room for a while? Ellen, you can use the typewriter in there. I'd appreciate it.'

When they had left, closing the door to the room on the right, Horn continued.

'Ran me off the road. Stuck me in their car, drove down to San Pedro and pushed me off a pier. At least that was what they meant to do. The way it turned out, one of them went in with me.'

Cross' eyebrows went up, but he said nothing. In the next room, the muted sound of typing started up.

'Young man, burr cut, built like an athlete. Danny something or other. Looks like he might have played football in college. But he forgot all about the sportsmanship and fair play they're supposed to learn there. He likes to kidney punch a guy when his back's turned. Anyway, he wound up in the water with me, and I had to fish him out when he was going down for the third time.'

'That's not exactly the way I heard it.'

'I'm sure you didn't. But your boys are a little embarrassed, aren't they? You send them out to intimidate me, and they botch the job.'

'Can you prove they did any of this?'

'No, 'course not. If I went to the police, they'd laugh at me. Accusing two federal government employees of picking on a private citizen. Who ever heard of such a thing? But, uh . . .'

'But what?'

'But you know it's true, don't you? Hell, you sent them.'

Cross picked up his fork and resumed eating, eyes on his plate.

Horn allowed himself a small laugh. 'If I were you, I wouldn't answer either. You're a lawyer, right? You know better than to incriminate yourself. But you know what happened, and so do I. My only question is, why? Why am I so important to you?'

Cross studiously buttered a roll. 'Mr Horn, I allow my men a good deal of latitude. It's possible that, from time to time, they might misunderstand my wishes. If that's what happened last night, I regret it. One of them came out of the encounter with a broken nose and a bruised ego. Naturally he wants another chance to prove himself.'

'And you're going to make sure he gets it, right?'

Cross took a sip of coffee and wiped his chin carefully with the snow-white napkin. 'Not necessarily. The reason I invited you up here today was to get a look at you and see how much of a nuisance I thought you might be. If you give me the right answers, I'll send you home safely. You can get back to your job, forget everything that happened, and just stay out of our way.'

'That's what Danny Boy and his friend – what's his name . . . ?'

When Cross didn't respond, Horn went on. 'Never mind. I'll just call him Frog Face.'

'He wouldn't like that.'

'Anyway, that's what he told me I should do. Be smart. Walk away and quit pestering the US government. Now you want me to be smart too. The thing is, though, I'm feeling really dumb today. And I've decided I'm not leaving this great big hotel suite without some news.'

Cross seemed faintly amused. 'Why should I tell you anything?'

'Well . . .' Horn reached down to the floor and picked up the hat. 'How about a peace offering?'

Turning the fedora over in his lap, he grasped something inside the crown. There was a tearing noise, and he laid a revolver on the desk, its grip, cylinder and barrel covered with a broad strip of adhesive tape.

Cross stared at it. 'How did you—'

'Get it past the man at the door? I just took off my hat and held out my arms. He didn't think of looking inside.'

132

Expressionless, Cross reached for the gun. 'He will next time.' He tore off the tape, broke the cylinder and spun it.

'I threw away the bullets,' Horn said. 'If your police dog outside had been better at his job, he would have found an unloaded gun. I'd appreciate it if you'd return it to Danny Boy, and tell him that if I ever see him again, I hope it's a friendlier meeting.'

Cross compressed his lips in a thin line. 'Wilbur!' he called out. The door opened, and the guard entered. In appearance, he could have been Danny's older brother, Horn thought.

'This belongs to Dan,' Cross said to him, holding out the gun. His voice was abrupt. 'See that he gets it. I'll tell him later just how I came in possession of it.'

The man seemed to understand. Eyes darting between Cross and Horn, he took the gun, muttered an acknowledgment and left.

Cross started on his dessert. It was cherry pie, and to Horn it looked delicious. 'You're an interesting man,' Cross said between bites. 'Maybe you're not quite as slow as you seem. But how do you know I won't send someone after you again?'

'You could,' Horn said. 'And for a while there, I thought you government boys just might be capable of the worst sort of behavior. After all, it was Owen Bruder's murder that started me asking questions and got me in your hair. I already knew you hated him, because you seem to hate everybody like him. So I thought you or J. Parnell Thomas or somebody like you might have had Owen done away with.'

'Be careful what you say.' Cross didn't sound overly concerned.

'Oh, I'm careful, all right. Sure, you were already wrecking his life with all the rumors and accusations. But maybe you got impatient with all that and decided, Hell, let's get rid of the guy.'

'That's quite a theory.'

'But if that's so, then what's to stop you feds from wiping out anybody who gets in your way? Including me? Last night your boys could have put a bullet in me, tossed me in the drink, and gone for that midnight snack they talked about. Instead they tried to pull some silly-ass college-boy practical joke on me.'

Cross was listening intently. He no longer looked boyish. Maybe it was the subtle web of crow's feet that framed both eyes. Or the stubborn set to his ample jaw. Horn revised his estimate of the man's age. Mid-thirties, he thought.

'I don't have any respect for the way you do business, Cross – you or your boys. I think your behavior stinks. I think you work best in the dark, just like this room. You sneak around getting the goods on people, then you smear their names without waiting for judge or jury. Some of the

133

people you go after are spies and traitors. That's fine with me, since somebody should. But I think you ought to do it in broad daylight.'

Horn took a deep breath. 'I'm getting off the track. What I started to say is, I think you smell to high heaven, all of you, but I haven't yet seen any evidence that you kill people.'

'Fair enough,' Cross said wryly. 'Let the record show we're not murderers.' He finished the last bite of pie and pushed the plate aside. 'You asked why you're so important to me. Let me assure you you're not. You're just a mosquito buzzing around my ear. Now that Owen Bruder is dead, I consider him a closed chapter, and I'm mildly curious as to why you're looking so energetically into his death, since you don't do that sort of a thing for a living.'

'You know what I do for a living?'

'Oh, yes. I know as much as I want to know about anyone. That's what the federal government pays me to do these days. I accumulate information about people, and I use it in the most effective way. But let's get back to you and your work. You're a one-time movie actor who now collects bad debts for a gambler, and takes care of a remote piece of property up the coast. That's about it. So why are you now trying to behave like a poor man's Sam Spade, poking around, going for long drives up to the middle of nowhere, devoting so much of your time to the question of who killed a Communist screenwriter?'

'He wasn't a Communist.'

'Pardon me?'

'You heard me. I don't know where you and your buddy J. Parnell got your information, but whoever told you lied. And when you passed it on to Laura Lee Paisley so she could tell the world about it . . . well, it was still a lie. Owen Bruder was somewhere out there on the left, but he never joined the Communist Party. Whoever told you otherwise wrecked Owen's career and may even have gotten him killed. And when I find this person, he's going to answer to Owen's widow.'

Cross was silent, his eyes fixed hard on Horn.

'You want to tell me who it was?' Horn said quietly.

For the first time, Cross laughed out loud. 'No, I don't want to tell you,' he said, shaking his head.

Raising his voice, he called out, 'Ellen, would you have them bring up another pot of coffee, with an extra cup? And another piece of pie.' Horn heard the click of the telephone receiver and the woman's voice asking for room service.

Cross turned back to him. 'We protect our sources. I don't expect you to understand all the reasons, but it's very important that we do. They know they can tell us something in confidence without fear of reprisals from anyone they name—'

'Seems to me you should be more worried about trouble from the other direction,' Horn broke in. 'From the ones who sent Owen Bruder and his wife all that hate mail, and the one who actually killed him.'

'That was tragic,' Cross said. 'All murder is. I hope the police find out who did it. I had no wish to see him harmed.'

'Just ruined,' Horn said. 'And jailed.'

'That would have been up to the House committee, and would have depended on how he testified.' Cross fiddled with a fountain pen on the blotter. It was not a relaxed gesture. Horn wondered if he was beginning to get past the man's outer shell. He hoped so.

There was a knock, and the door to the next room opened. 'It's almost ten,' the young woman said. 'You wanted me to remind you.' She withdrew.

'Oh, yes.' Cross got up and, limping noticeably, went over to a tabletop radio by one of the sofas. He turned it on, waited for it to warm up, and dialed a station.

'We can take a short break for some morning entertainment,' he said to Horn. 'This might interest you too.'

The announcer was breathlessly touting the virtues of Silk, the beauty soap of the stars. A few seconds later, Horn heard a familiar voice.

Crusading Congressman J. Parnell Thomas has just wrapped up his informal hearings here in Los Angeles and moved to Washington, where the curtain will go up on the big show next week in the House of Representatives office building. All of Hollywood is holding its breath to see if the public hearings will surpass the drama of the private disclosures made to Thomas' committee here recently. We predict the hearings will produce both heroes and villains. The heroes will win laurels, and the villains will get their just deserts. This is America, and we play fair, but we play rough against those who would sell us out to the Kremlin.

This is Laura Lee saying forget Jack Benny, forget The Shadow, forget Gangbusters. This station will carry the hearings live all week long, and you'll find all the entertainment you want right here on your radio dial . . .

Cross turned it off with a sharp click and returned to his desk. 'She's something, isn't she?'

'Sounds like it's going to be one great big circus,' Horn said. 'With elephants and cotton candy and clowns and everything. Especially clowns.'

'I like to think of it more in terms of lions and Christians,' Cross said.

19

'I'm curious about this sweetheart on the radio,' Horn said. 'It's pretty clear that she has an exclusive pipeline that runs from you and your boss all the way to her microphone. So—'

'I won't have anything to say about that,' Cross said quickly.

''Course you won't. But does it work the other way too? Does she feed you information from that secret room of hers? It would make sense to me, since she shares your politics. One hand washing the other. Very cozy.'

Cross affected a look of boredom. 'No comment.'

Since Cross appeared to be getting little out of the conversation, Horn wondered why he hadn't ordered young Wilbur to throw him out. Fearing he may have little time left, he plowed ahead.

'I understand you've gotten yourself a new informer,' he said casually. 'Man named Roy Earl Briar. Must make you feel good to have a pillar of the community, a rich Texas oilman, on the payroll, so to speak. Although I'm sure you don't have to pay him anything. He probably does it for the love of his country. Just like Laura Lee. Have you introduced the two of them? I bet they'd like each other.'

Horn remembered something else. 'And as for my long drive up to the middle of nowhere, just who clued you in on that? Wouldn't have been some small-town mayor, would it? You must have a lot of friends, Mr Cross.'

A knock on the door, and the same waiter entered, carrying a tray. 'Right here, please,' Cross said to him. 'We'll both take coffee, and the pie is for my guest.'

'Not for me, thanks.' Horn stared at the slice of pie, which was still hot, with cherries and filling oozing out from under a flaky crust. His stomach growled. But, even as he acknowledged the childishness of the feeling, he was determined not to place himself in Mitchell Cross' debt, even for a piece of pie.

The waiter left, taking the lunch dishes with him. 'Are you sure you won't have any?' Cross asked.

'I'm sure. But back to Roy Earl.'

'I know Mr Briar,' Cross said. 'He's an estimable person, with a lovely daughter. He and I have had some good conversations.'

'I bet you have. About me, among other things.' Horn leaned back in his chair, attempting to escape the aroma of the pie, and crossed his legs. 'What about Cal Stoddard? Why in the world would you want to go after a man like that?'

Cross thought for a moment. 'I'm sure he thinks his motives are good,' he said carefully. 'But in a way he's one of the most dangerous individuals, because children look to him as an example—'

'What the hell are you talking about?' Horn shot back. 'He's a good man. He signed his name on a goddam line years ago. And because of that, you're going to ruin him? You're the dangerous one, Cross. You and all the others like you. I don't know yet if you had anything to do with Owen Bruder's death, but even if you didn't, you and your friends came along and laid the foundation for it.'

Horn stopped and took a breath. The vehemence of his support for Cal Stoddard, a man he had little reason to like, surprised him. He got up, grabbed the plate off the desk and carried it over to the typist's desk, where he deposited it with a clatter.

'You don't respond well to temptation, do you?' Cross asked.

For an instant, Horn hated the man. But he knew that hate could get in his way, and he tried to control it. 'You don't have anything I want.'

'Are you sure?' Cross looked at him appraisingly for several long seconds. Then: 'We don't really need to be on opposite sides of the fence, when you think about it.'

'I like it fine over here.'

Cross nodded. 'I'm not trying to convert you. I'm just saying if you want to visit on this side of the fence from time to time, it won't hurt you and might even do you some good.'

'I always appreciate it when people talk plain English to me.'

For the second time Cross laughed, and his original youthful look returned. Once again Horn found himself trying to imagine this rosy-cheeked young man finding the supreme courage to face a small army of Japanese on a faraway island. He wondered why the question was so important. But of course he knew why.

'Have you turned up anything on the Owen Bruder murder?' Cross asked abruptly.

'No,' Horn said. 'But I'm pretty sure I will.'

'How do you know?'

'I'm good at this,' he said with a shrug. 'I'm not trained at it, and I can't explain it. But I'm good.'

Cross tilted his head slightly, as if trying to get a different perspective on his guest. 'I'm interested in the same question.'

'Mind telling me why?'

'Let's just say that if he was killed for political reasons, it could complicate things for a lot of people.'

Horn nodded. 'Especially if one of your right-wing buddies turned out to have done it. Could be very messy, couldn't it?'

'Maybe. But regardless, I'm interested in the question. If you should turn up the answer, I imagine you'll go to the police. If you could see your way to sharing the information with me, possibly before you talk to the police, I'd be very grateful.'

'How grateful?'

Cross straightened the edge of his blotter. It wasn't far out of line. 'We're being cute with each other,' he said impatiently. 'If you can't see that I could be useful to you, then you have very little imagination.'

'You want to tell me who fingered Owen Bruder?'

Cross' expression turned hard. 'No.'

'Then I'm afraid we've run out of things to talk about.' He reached for his hat.

'Wait, please.' Cross opened one of the lower drawers in the desk, pulled something out of it, and laid it on the blotter. It was a thin manila file, resembling many of those stacked in great numbers around the room. 'Before you go, I think you'd be interested in hearing some of this.' He opened the file and began to read aloud.

'John Ray Horn. Born November 20th, 1909, in Green Springs, Arkansas, firstborn son of the Reverend John Jacob and Edith Horn—' He looked up briefly to ensure that he had Horn's attention.

'Sounds pretty boring to me,' Horn said.

'It gets better.' Cross resumed reading. 'Left home before finishing high school. Worked as a dishwasher and ranch hand in Oklahoma and Texas for the next several years, then joined the rodeo, where he competed in bull riding until injuries forced him to quit. During the Depression he traveled to California, where he picked fruit, washed more dishes, pumped gas, and worked on a horse ranch in the San Fernando Valley.' Cross was reading the words as a prosecutor might read a charge sheet, with no emotion.

'Hired as a wrangler at Medallion Pictures and soon found himself acting in western movies. By the late 1930s, under the name Sierra Lane, he was one of the studio's biggest attractions. Married Iris Brand, who had a daughter, Clea. Served in the Army during the war, Italian theater, after which he went back to work at the studio.'

He paused briefly. 'According to this, though, it all ended when he attacked and severely beat one Bernard Rome Junior, leaving him with a broken jaw. Sentenced to two years in the California State Prison at Cold Creek. While he was there, his wife divorced him. He was released a year ago, and since then has worked for one Harry Flye, a real estate speculator, living rent-free on one of Flye's properties in return for performing caretaker duties. Also works for one Joseph Mad Crow, a full-blooded Sioux Indian who once played Sierra Lane's companion in more than two dozen movies. Mr Mad Crow now operates a small gambling casino in an unincorported part of the northern San Fernando Valley that, although technically illegal, appears to be tolerated.'

He looked up. 'Correct so far?'

Horn shrugged. 'I suppose.' He wondered what might be coming next.

'I'm wondering,' Cross said. 'Two years seems excessive for what I believe was a first offense.'

'People have said that. Only thing is, the guy I beat up was the son of Bernie Rome Senior, who ran Medallion. Because of that, there weren't many people ready to step up and testify for me. Just Joseph and a couple of others. It didn't do any good. That was the same reason why there were no jobs waiting for me in the movies when I got out. Not just at Medallion, but anywhere.' Horn wasn't used to telling the story, and the words came awkwardly.

'There's nothing in here about why you did it.'

'Simple,' Horn said. 'He crippled my horse.'

'How did he—'

'He was showing off for a girl while I was away from the studio. Put a saddle on the horse and rode him into a fence, broke one of his forelegs. Horse had to be put down.'

'I see.' Cross looked at him appraisingly for a moment. 'That's a big price to pay for a moment of vengeance.'

'Maybe.'

'Would you do it again, knowing the consequences?'

'I don't know.' It was true. And it was a question Horn had already asked himself, many times.

He shifted position in the chair. 'You about finished? There's not much in there that people haven't heard before. Lot of it's even been in the papers.'

'I know,' Cross said. 'But not this part.' He picked up the file again.

'May 3rd, 1944, wounded in the battle of Monte Cassino, southeast of Rome. Sent to a field hospital, where certain complications developed. Shipped stateside and admitted to Mason General Hospital, Long Island, New York. The, uh . . .' He appeared to be looking for the term. 'The psychoneurotic wing.'

Horn reached for his pouch of Bull Durham and his papers. It seemed important to give his hands something to do. But then he remembered that his cigarette makings had not survived his swim the night before. He crossed his arms in front of his chest, waiting.

'Doctors determined that the patient was suffering from what some call battle neurosis, caused by his wound, by the deaths of his friends, and by the extreme conditions of combat in the Italian mountains. In his case, the condition was marked by withdrawal and non-communication for long periods of time. Treatment included sodium amytal, hypnosis, and consultative therapy. After ten weeks, patient was granted an honorable discharge for medical reasons and returned to civilian life.'

Cross closed the file. 'I read somewhere that about twenty percent of all the battle casualties in the war were labeled "psychoneurotic." Nothing was really wrong with them. Except in the head.'

Now Horn knew where all this had been leading. His eyes met the other man's. 'I may have heard that somewhere too.'

'Of course, there's still a stigma attached to it,' Cross went on. 'Don't you agree? It's only natural, when you hear that someone caved in during combat, you tend to think of him as less than a man. I'd imagine that if this got out –' he patted the file '– it wouldn't do your reputation much good.'

'You mean, for example, if Laura Lee Paisley got hold of it?' Horn said. 'How important do you think I am, anyway? I'm nobody, and nobodies don't make it onto her show.'

'You are pretty close to a nobody,' Cross said. 'But Sierra Lane, the man you used to be? He was somebody, just like your friend Cal Stoddard still is. A heroic figure, at least to children. And if this ever makes its way onto the radio or into the papers, the reason will be Sierra Lane, not John Ray Horn. And just how do you think your legion of young admirers will feel about you then?'

He knew that Mitchell Cross had the power to do everything he said. Considering the lives and reputations he had wrecked thus far, Horn knew Cross wouldn't hesitate to add him to the list. He would smear him, and then he would move on to the next target. Horn felt hatred for this man, and his kind, bubble up in him. He felt it so strongly he knew it must show on his face. 'Say what you mean,' he told him.

'I think we understand each other,' Cross responded. 'If you don't make things difficult for me, I'll return the favor.' He got up from his chair with a slight wince. 'They tell me I need to keep this leg of mine from getting too stiff.' He began to pace slowly around the room, talking. But his words didn't appear to be addressed to anyone in particular.

'You were raised in a Bible-reading household, just as I was,' he said. 'Although, considering your father's calling, you doubtless got more of it than I did. Remember the story of the cleansing of the temple?'

Horn shrugged, then nodded, not eager to admit religion into the conversation.

'Jesus found that the moneychangers had turned the temple into a marketplace, so he went in and overturned their tables and cast them out.'

'I know the story.'

'There's another cleansing coming,' Cross said quietly, still pacing. 'It's going to affect this whole country. And when it's over, we'll be a cleaner nation because of it. Straighter. Better. And more suited to lead the rest of the world through this century.'

'Is that because all the bad people will be in jail?'

'Some of them will be,' Cross replied. 'Some of them will be out of work, others will simply be exposed for what they are.'

'And it all starts here,' Horn said wryly. 'Here in this second-rate town and its movie business.'

'It makes sense when you think about it,' Cross said. 'Motion pictures say a lot about us as a people. They tell us who we are and who we want to be. When they're in the hands of subversives, the message they deliver is going to be tainted. We can't allow that.'

'People are talking about a blacklist,' Horn said. 'They say it's coming. And if somebody's name is on it—'

'They won't work? Oh, there'll be a list, all right. Just like in the Last Judgment. You could ask your father about that. Except that instead of being a list of the saved, this will be a list of the damned.' He smiled, nodding his head as if in agreement with himself.

Horn grabbed his hat and got up.

'Enough of this Bible talk for me,' he said. 'Do what you want to with that file. And good luck with your cleansing.'

He was almost at the door when Cross' voice stopped him. 'You think you're on the side of the angels, don't you?'

'Not at all,' Horn said. 'I don't think the angels have a monopoly on either side.'

'Then you might at least consider—'

'Joining up with you? No. It's anybody's guess where the angels are. But there's no doubt in my mind where the little men with the pitchforks are. And so I guess you could say I've picked my side. Or maybe it picked me.'

He opened the door and looked back. 'You really could use some more light in here.'

20

Outside the hotel, he crossed Pershing Square to a cigar store on South Hill, where he bought tobacco and rolling paper. At a café three doors away, he found a seat at the counter, ordered a Denver omelette and toast, and told the waitress to keep the coffee coming. He was tired to the bone, but first he needed food, and then he still had things to do this day. The omelette failed to kill his appetite so, with Mitchell Cross' tantalizing dessert still on his mind, he pointed to a piece of apple pie displayed under glass, and asked the waitress to add a slice of cheese. He rolled a smoke and alternated drags with bites of the pie.

Mitchell Cross' face swam in and out of his vision. *Now you know what a real, live hero looks like,* Horn thought. *Like the milkman. Like that short-order cook I can see behind the counter. Like me. Like anyone, everyone.*

Still, he noted, the face was different from others in one key respect: it shone with absolute certitude about life's important issues. Where do you get that kind of conviction? he wondered. Clean living? The Good Book? Politics? It must be nice to go through life knowing you're on the side of the angels. Armed with that belief, it becomes easy to mow down all those who are marching behind the wrong banner, like so many Japs in front of your machine gun.

A real hero and a genuine rattlesnake, he thought wonderingly. *And both of them wrapped up inside the same skin.*

After lunch, he walked along Hill until he found a phone booth. He called the homicide detective bureau at the Hall of Justice and asked for Pitt but was told that he and his partner were out. Horn told the voice he'd be bringing something over for the two men later in the day.

He dialed Maggie's number but got no answer. He used the same nickel for a different number. 'Douglas? It's John Ray. I've got a couple of phone numbers for you.' Douglas Greenleaf was a nephew of Mad Crow, young and smart and only a few years off the reservation. He had an LA cop for a brother-in-law and a friend in the Department of Motor Vehicles and, while studying for his private detective's license, earned a few extra dollars from his uncle by helping Horn chase down those who owed Mad Crow money.

'If we get bingo on both numbers, you're ten bucks richer,' Horn told him.

'Better pull out your wallet.'

'Not so fast. One of 'em's New York City, and it's been disconnected. I need to know who it used to belong to, and where I can find them now.' He read out the numbers.

'How did you manage to catch all those bad guys in the movies without my help?' the young man joked.

'Well, you see, Douglas, we hadn't invented the telephone yet, so you wouldn't have done me much good,' replied Horn in similar vein.

Next, he tried Lillian Bruder's number. She sounded glad to hear from him. 'Maggie told me about your trip,' she said. 'I'm not sure about all the conclusions to be drawn—'

'We're not either, Lillian.'

'But if it brings us closer to finding out who murdered Owen, then you've spent your time well, and I'm grateful.'

'Good. And speaking of Maggie, I had a hunch she might be with you today.'

'It's a good hunch. I'll put her on.'

'Hi,' she said. 'I tried to call you this morning.'

'I've been off on an adventure,' he said. 'Remember those two snoops Owen caught outside his place? I had a run-in with them last night.'

'Are you all right?' Her voice was low and tense.

'I'm fine. My car got a little banged up, is all. They tried to rattle me, and they did a great job, but I think we all understand each other now. We have one of those uneasy truces you read about but, more important, I found out they're not exactly G-Men. They work for Mitchell Cross, J. Parnell Thomas' right hand, and, what's more, I just came from a long talk with Cross himself. Have you got a minute?'

'I'm listening.'

He gave her an abbreviated version of his conversation. When he was finished, she let out a long breath into the phone. 'So . . .'

'So I wouldn't rule out anything yet, Maggie. Right now, I don't think Owen's murder was paid for by our tax-payer dollars, but I still think Washington has some scary people running around, people who are capable of almost anything. Let's just concentrate on what happened up there in Pyrie all those years ago. And . . . let's see what we can find out about the woman.'

'All right.' Her voice brightened. 'Maybe I'll have some news for you before long. I'm going to see that detective Vance in about an hour. And I

143

got Lillian to call Grover Jones, and he agreed to see me tomorrow afternoon.'

'Good. Can I come along?'

'Sure.'

'How's Lillian?'

'Not too bad.' She lowered her voice. 'I mean . . . it's clear that she's still grieving. She's hardly seen anybody since it happened, but this seems to be her way of handling it. She paints and she reads, and every now and then Wally comes over, and he's good company for her – though he seems pretty depressed himself, what with the hearings coming up. You can tell he's dreading going to Washington.'

'How are things with Davey? Does he mind how much time you're spending with Lillian?'

'No. Listen, John Ray . . . I feel bad about last night, and I think he does too. When we woke up this morning, I decided I needed to tell him everything, about me and Owen and how important this is to me, finding out why he was killed.'

'So he knows Owen was your father?'

'He does now. So does Joseph. I'm tired of keeping it a secret. The only reason I did was because Owen seemed ashamed of it, and it made me feel that way too. Well, to hell with that. He had faults, but he was still a big man, and I'm proud he was my father, and I don't care who knows it.'

'He was a fool, Maggie, not to do better by you.'

'He *was* a fool, wasn't he?' she said with a laugh. 'Most men'd be proud to have me for a daughter. Well, I'll show him, and everybody else. I'll find out who killed him.'

'This sounds a little familiar,' he said, kidding her now. 'Didn't you do one called *Vengeance Trail*, around the time I first met you?'

'Damn right,' she said, ignoring his tone. 'Anyway, Davey's trying to be better about all this. He knows that you and I are just doing a job together. Only thing is, when he drinks . . .'

'You don't have to tell me. I'll keep my distance.'

'That's smart of you. Joseph tells me you're not coming for Patty's birthday tonight?'

'I told him I couldn't make it.'

'Is it because of her, or Cal?'

'I don't know. Cal's all right, I guess, but she's not one of my favorites.'

'I've heard that from other people too,' Maggie said. 'How she pushes him too hard, that kind of thing.'

When he didn't respond, she said, 'So why don't you just do it for Cal? You know he needs friends right now. They both do.'

As always, it was hard to say no to Maggie. He paused for only a moment. 'You're right,' he said. 'I'll be there. Tell Davey to hold his fire.'

144

He drove to Mad Crow's place. In her halting English, Nee Nee told him her nephew had gone over to the casino to get some paperwork done. She invited him in for coffee, which he declined, but left Mad Crow a note: *I won't need the room. Looks like I'm not a fugitive from justice after all. But I will be here for dinner tonight.*

Then he retrieved his car, checking to make sure the envelope containing Maggie's discoveries was intact. He drove back downtown, stopping at the Hall of Justice where he found that Pitt and his partner were still out. He left the threatening letter signed by the Order of Old Glory for them, appending a handwritten note of his own explaining where the letter had been found and adding his own phone number.

On the way home, he stopped at a pawnshop in Santa Monica where he paid seven dollars for a used Hamilton with a leather band and a sweep second hand. The crystal was slightly scratched, but the watch seemed to keep good time. Inscribed on the back were the words *To Bill, Love Forever From Eileen.*

Bill had died, he supposed. Or he and Eileen had run out of money. Or some punk with fast hands had made off with the watch and hocked it. Or any number of things, all of them unhappy. All Horn knew for sure was that for Bill and Eileen, forever had come and gone, and the Hamilton was now ticking on another man's wrist.

He drove to his place in Culebra Canyon. There was no real mail in the box, only a note from his landlord, Harry Flye, stating that he intended to bring a prospective buyer to view the property over the weekend and reminding Horn to clean up around the pool and tennis court.

Inside the cabin, he shucked off his shoes and jacket, poured and downed three fingers of Evan Williams, took the phone off the hook, folded himself into a blanket on the couch and slept.

He woke suddenly to a sound he knew: the quiet crunch of tires on gravel. Rolling off the couch, he steadied himself with one hand on the floor, then straightened up and went to the front window. The light outside was filtered through the trees, and a glance at Bill's old wristwatch told him it was a little past five.

Shaking his head to clear away the sleep, he wondered if he were about to get a return bout with Cross' men, and his stomach knotted at the prospect. He parted the curtain and looked out at an angle, past his parked Ford to the low stone and cement wall and the locked gate, and beyond that saw the glitter of a shiny car. It was aquamarine, with four distinctive, chrome-edged decorative holes in the side, above the white-wall tire – a new Buick Roadmaster.

He pulled on slacks and shoes and tucked in his shirt, then opened the door. A. Dixon Vance stood by the car, examining his surroundings. Horn went down and unlocked the gate.

'Hello, sport.' Vance wore the same loud jacket, accompanied this time with fawn-colored slacks, spectator shoes, and a cream-colored sports shirt. 'I was just admiring your place. You're really out in the woods here, aren't you?'

'I suppose I am.'

'I tried calling you before I came over—'

'I had the phone off the hook for a while.'

'Oh. You're probably wondering how I found you.' Vance was holding an ordinary file folder, and he seemed to be in a good mood.

'Well, you're a detective.'

'That's right, I am. I didn't have to put in any work on this, though. I got your location from Margaret O'Dare.'

'She said she was going over to see you—'

'She did indeed see me. We had a nice talk. She's quite a gal. Married, I guess, from the ring?'

Horn nodded.

'Happily?' Vance grinned boyishly, something he seemed good at.

'As far as I know.'

'Well,' Vance said. 'She's not really my type. I like the cocktails and dancing type, you know. God knows I've spent enough on them. I went out with Dottie Lamour once, back when I was a young investigator for a big law firm and she was a new girl at Paramount . . .' He smiled at the memory. 'But every now and then I wonder what it would be like to be with a woman who always says just what's on her mind, who doesn't play any of the usual games. You know the kind of gal I mean.'

'Like Maggie.'

'You've got it, sport. She's one of those, I can tell.' He sighed dramatically. 'A woman like that would see right through me, though, that's the bad part . . .' His voice trailed off.

'So what brings you here?' Horn asked. Then, not wanting to sound rude, he added, 'You want to come up to the porch and have something to drink?'

'That sounds fine. Nothing alcoholic, though, I've a dinner date in about an hour and a half, over near MacArthur Park.'

'There's a pitcher of orange juice in the fridge. Fresh-squeezed.'

'Perfect.'

Minutes later, Vance was installed in Horn's rocker, the only chair on the porch, while Horn leaned against a railing. Sipping at his drink, Vance made small talk for a minute, touching on the remote life of canyon dwellers, the silent movie career of Ramon Aguilar, and speculations about Aguilar's death. Horn waited for the man to get to the point of his visit.

146

Finally he did. 'She told me she's Owen Bruder's daughter, which knocked me over,' he said, shaking his head slightly. 'Then it made sense, because you can see similarities – the integrity and the feeling she gives off that she wouldn't take any shit. But she was nice to me. She asked me very nicely to let you know if I'd turned up anything at all while I was working for the Bruders.

'Thing is, I didn't turn up much in the time I had, and what little I found . . . well, it's interesting, but it's anybody's guess as to how much it relates to his murder. So when I returned their money, I didn't feel obligated to pass on the information. I sat on it, like I sometimes do. A thing like this goes into the files, and you never know when it might prove useful.'

He picked up the folder from the planking where he'd laid it a minute earlier and placed it on his lap. 'Might surprise you if you knew how much stuff I've dug up on people that I've decided not to use, for one reason or another. Sometimes it's for the simple reason that I don't want to see someone get hurt. That might surprise you too.'

When Horn didn't answer, he went on. 'That wasn't a consideration in this case. I don't really care if this person gets hurt or not, you know what I mean?'

'I'm not sure.'

'You will when you look at this.' He passed over the folder. 'You didn't get it from me.'

Horn opened it and thumbed through its meager contents. He extracted an official-looking document printed on heavy photo paper and scanned it. A second sheet was a duplicate of the first. Then he pulled out a smaller sheet of the same weight, containing two photographs, and looked them over. The last item was another copy of the photos. His eyes darted back and forth between the two items. He looked up at Vance. 'Is this what I think it is? And who I think it is?'

The other man grinned lightly, and with a touch of devilment. 'It is.'

Vance spoke for about three minutes as Horn listened intently, eyes dropping occasionally to what he held in his hand. Then the detective put down his glass, got to his feet, and descended the uneven stone steps without shaking Horn's hand. He paused on the gravel of the driveway.

'As you can tell, I'm no particular friend of yours,' he said evenly. 'I'm doing this partly for Lillian Bruder, who's all right in my book, and mostly for Margaret O'Dare, who has nice hands and who doesn't color her nails. She told me she used to make movies like you did.'

'That's right.'

'Sorry I missed them. Bet she was a firecracker.'

Vance looked off toward the opposite crest of the canyon. 'A blackmailer could clean up with that thing I gave you. I'm no blackmailer.'

'I'm not either,' Horn said. 'But I'll use it if I need to. Tell me something: who got you to quit the Bruders? Was it Mitchell Cross?'

Vance gave him a snappy salute and got in his car. 'See you, sport.'

After locking the gate, Horn resumed his seat in the rocker and once again studied the items Vance had left. The light was noticeably dimmer now, and the porch was in heavy shade. He found himself straining his eyes over the fuzzy lettering of the photocopy.

After days of frustration, when he had felt as if he were wandering through a strange house where all the lights were out and all the doors locked, he now thought he could see one door slightly ajar, and a glimmer of light beyond.

This isn't really the answer to anything, he thought, but it could be a tool to finding an answer. His eyes went back to the photos, and his tense mouth eased into a smile as he almost said out loud: Hurray for Hollywood.

21

When dinner was over and Nee Nee praised for her pot roast and squash and home-baked bread, the guests moved out into Mad Crow's spacious living room, where oak and sycamore logs burned in the fireplace. Nee Nee and Cissie Briar went back to the kitchen and returned with ice cream, and a birthday cake that was cut with due ceremony as they all sang 'Happy Birthday' to Patty Stoddard. Two voices stood out, her husband's familiar tenor and the more ragged but enthusiastic baritone of Woody Guthrie.

While Cal looked uncharacteristically somber in a dark suit, Patty wore a gay, full-skirted party dress, white with gold piping. Both had been determinedly upbeat over dinner, talking about their girls, joking about the last movie they made together, and in general betraying none of the tension of the past few days. No one had mentioned Cal's upcoming testimony in Washington, although the subject seemed to flavor the dinner with a sour, melancholy taste.

Cissie filled the role of hostess enthusiastically. After dessert, she and Mad Crow took orders for highballs, and a more subdued mood settled in, with people breaking off into smaller groups for conversation. Horn, not always comfortable at parties, was making an effort on the Stoddards' behalf. For a few minutes he found himself sitting with Maggie and her husband. Davey Peake had greeted him without expression, but otherwise seemed to be on good behavior, showing none of his recent animosity.

Patty Stoddard joined them, holding a fresh drink. Her eyes were bright and her cheeks slightly flushed. 'We should probably leave soon,' she said. 'We've got a neighbor looking after the girls, and we always try to get home before their bedtime.'

'You're lucky to have such wonderful girls,' Maggie said.

'Aren't we?' Patty took a big swig from her glass. 'We're lucky in a lot of ways. At least we were until all this . . . this *shit* started coming down on us. Pardon my French.'

'I know,' Maggie said.

'Cal and I've hardly slept for days. We leave for Washington next week,

149

and it's bound to get even worse then, until it's over. Then maybe we can get back to our old lives . . .' She gave a big sigh and stared out the window.

'Patty, people are talking about some kind of blacklist,' Maggie said. 'If Cal winds up on it—'

'Cal's not going to be on any list,' Patty responded quickly. 'I can promise you that.'

'But how can you—'

'He'll do what he has to do.' Her sudden smile had no warmth in it. 'He'll do what any good husband and father would do.'

Horn and Maggie looked at each other in silence, their expressions framing the question in their minds.

He moved across the room to where Stoddard sat with Mad Crow's house guest. The evening had provided Horn with his first good look at Woody Guthrie. The man appeared slight, almost delicate, but with an expansive brow that tapered down to a sharp chin, and his face topped by a head of untamed, Brillo Pad hair. He wore the same denim shirt and khaki trousers in which he'd first arrived, now washed and ironed, courtesy of Nee Nee. Over dinner, Horn had noticed that Guthrie had an eye for both Maggie and Cissie and engaged both of them in conversation whenever possible. 'A ladies' man, no doubt about it,' Maggie had whispered to him.

Wearing a habitual half-smile and squinting through the smoke of a Camel loosely held in his mouth, Guthrie strummed on his guitar, stopping every now and then to provide Stoddard with a running commentary. 'Way I keep this baby tuned, when you hit all the strings, you get a G chord.'

'Never heard of that,' Stoddard said.

'It's easier that way,' Guthrie said. 'Especially for a half-baked guitar player like me. I never learned how to pick and finger very good. Mostly I just strum. I always thought the words were a lot more important than the music anyway. Hell, if I hear a tune that sounds good—' He shifted melodies suddenly and slowed the tempo.

'Like this one,' Guthrie continued, nodding at Horn as he took a seat nearby. 'Well, then, I'll just borrow it and think up some words of my own. Way back, this was a song called "Pretty Polly". A few years ago I was up in the Northwest, where a lot of Okies traveled from California, and I found a lot of them living in government camps, looking for farm work. So I sat down and came up with some words, and "Pretty Polly" turned into this.' His voice rose as he sang:

I've worked in your orchards of peaches and prunes,
Slept on the ground in the light of the moon,

On the edge of your city you've seen us and then,
We come with the dust and we go with the wind.

Horn noticed that Guthrie's speaking voice changed when he sang, from a soft drawl to a rough-edged twang, as if he felt the need to underscore the harshness of his songs' messages.

'I like that,' Stoddard said. 'It makes most of the stuff I sing sound pretty unimportant.'

Horn pointed to Guthrie's guitar. 'What's that say?'

'This?' Guthrie raised his right arm to uncover the sounding board, where the words 'This Machine Kills Fascists' were written in bold, black script.

'Seems to me words like that could get somebody in trouble these days,' Horn told him.

'I suppose,' Guthrie said. 'I heard about what's going on out here, how they're looking for Communists under every orange tree. And I've heard about Cal here and what he's got himself into. But wasn't so long ago that everybody was talking about killing Fascists. It was our duty, right?'

He laughed loudly and went into a long story about the war, when he was in the Merchant Marine and his ship was torpedoed. 'We thought we were going to sink any minute. I was so damn mad, I stood there on the deck and hollered out, "God bless the Red Army! They'll finish off the fascist bastards!"'

'Did you join the party?' Horn asked.

'Nope,' Guthrie replied. 'But I might as well have. I went to rallies, played and sang. I even wrote a column for the *People's World* called "Woody Sez." I did everything 'cept sign my name on the membership list. Maybe that's why they haven't come after me yet.'

His voice turned confidential. 'You got to be careful, though. If you make the wrong noises, it gets harder to find work. I was on a radio show once, and the sponsor decided they didn't like some of the things I talked about. Told me to tone it down.'

'Did you?' Stoddard asked, as Maggie joined the little group.

Guthrie bent over his guitar, picking out slow chords. 'Sure,' he said casually. 'I had a wife and a kid. Man's got to work, doesn't he?'

'How much longer are you out here?' Maggie asked him.

'For a while yet,' Guthrie said. 'Joseph's gonna let me borrow his truck. I got some business over at Capitol Records, and I want to spend some time with Rusty Baird. I was going to stop by and see my cousin Jack and his family over in Glendale, but they're out of town. I used to do a radio show out here years ago, playing hillbilly music, and I still know some folks at the station, so I'll see them for a while. And Jack and me, we used to play at another station down in Mexico and I might head there for a while. Then I need to get back to New York, find a way to scare up some money.'

'Any ideas?' Mad Crow asked.

'Oh, I don't know,' Guthrie responded vaguely.

Horn saw it was almost ten and beckoned to Maggie. 'Let's listen to the radio for a minute.' They went over to Mad Crow's fancy floor-model Motorola radio-phonograph; he turned it on and dialed Laura Lee Paisley's station as it warmed up, careful to keep the volume low. After the end of a dance-band number and the commercial for Silk, beauty soap of the stars, the voice – girlish yet mocking – came over the air. She began with a plug for 'the fabulous chili and mouth-watering hobo steak' at Dave Chasen's restaurant in Beverly Hills, then got down to business:

We've learned that some well-meaning but misguided Hollywood personalities are flying to Washington, where they hope to distract the public's attention from the House Un-American Activities Committee hearings. Among the left-leaning celebrities are Danny Kaye, who was born Daniel Kaminsky; Edward G. Robinson, whose real name is Emmanuel Goldenberg; and John Garfield, formerly known as Julius Garfinkle. Others lending their support are Humphrey Bogart, Lauren Bacall, and Gene Kelly. A word to the wise from this reporter: Whatever name you might use, be very careful not to stand in the way of a righteous Congress and an angry American people. This country defeated Fascism, and it will just as surely defeat Communism . . .

Horn heard a low whistle and looked up to see that Woody Guthrie had joined them.

'Ain't she something?' Guthrie exclaimed. 'Sounds scary as hell, that woman. Is she good-looking?'

'Maybe,' Horn said. 'If you like a lot of meat on the bone.'

'Sometimes I do,' Guthrie said, looking meaningfully across the room at where Cissie sat with Mad Crow and Davey Peake. 'But she still sounds scary.' He wandered back into the kitchen.

Horn switched off the radio. Keeping his voice low, he told Maggie what A. Dixon Vance had brought him. Her eyes grew wide. 'What are you going to do with it?'

'I'm going to use it,' he said. 'Don't know what good it'll do, but I'm definitely going to use it.'

Still looking into his eyes, she laid her hand lightly on his arm. He couldn't tell if the gesture was affectionate or cautionary, or both, but she kept it there for several seconds. Then she got up to rejoin her husband.

Horn went out to the front porch, which was easily twice the size of his own and which held several comfortable chairs. He sat, looking out over the dark lawn and the old oak that dominated it. The evening air, he noted idly, had still not cooled.

After a while, Guthrie joined him, carrying a couple of High Lifes in one hand and his guitar in the other. He handed a bottle to Horn. 'Last two in the fridge,' he announced.

His bony features lit eerily by the harsh light from inside, Guthrie took a long swig from the bottle. 'Joseph's told me a little bit about you,' he said. 'How you did movies together, and why you went to jail for a while. I always said a man who likes horses can't be all bad. Joseph also told me you aren't from around here.'

'Arkansas.'

'Thought I heard something like that in the way you talk,' Guthrie said. 'Did you come out here during hard times, like everybody else?'

'That's right. I didn't feel welcome, though. They sent cops from LA all the way to the state line to block the roads, keep the Okies and Arkies and all the others from coming in. If you didn't have any money in your pocket, they turned you around.'

'The Bum Blockade,' Guthrie said with a chuckle. 'I remember it well. It was a miserable time for a lot of people. Funny thing, though: I got a lot of good songs out of it. In a way, it was one of the best times of my life.'

'Rusty Baird told me the same thing just the other day,' Horn said. 'The time he felt the most alive. That's how he put it.'

Guthrie was silent for a while. Horn heard a creak as the man settled back in his chair, then soft strumming sounds.

'Songs I write now are all about real things,' he said as he played. 'I like to say the best music is about what's wrong and how to fix it. But when I was growing up in Okemah, Oklahoma, I used to love cowboy songs, the kind Cal plays. All about falling in love and riding the range and living a dangerous life. Very romantic, but not very real.' He laughed. 'I miss those songs. Especially the real sad ones that they call laments. Do you know any of them?'

'Sure,' Horn said. 'All about death and dying.'

'Uh-huh. Here's my favorite.' Slowly and deliberately, his right hand picked out a string of familiar notes.

' "Streets of Laredo",' Horn said, nodding.

'Right. Beautiful song. It has another title: "Cowboy's Lament". Somebody stole the melody from an old Irish tune. But did you ever hear anything sadder? Young man makes one mistake and now he's dying, nothing ahead of him, hardly anything behind him.'

Guthrie picked out the last few mournful notes. 'You know how I was talking about needing to get back to New York to make some money?' he said. 'You see, a long time ago back in Oklahoma I wrote a song called "So Long, It's Been Good to Know You"—'

'I know it,' Horn said.

'It was about the Dust Bowl and people losing their homes and having to move on. Well, when I was doing that radio show in New York, the

153

sponsors liked the song so much, they wanted me to write some new words so they could use it as a kind of jingle. For pipe tobacco. So I did.' He took a swig of beer.

'Now . . . well, people must like that song an awful lot, 'cause I been asked to come up with some new words, turn it into a kind of love song.'

'Really?'

'Yep. I been working with this arranger, he's gonna record it with a big orchestra and chorus.' He emptied the bottle and put it down on the porch. 'A man doesn't lose his ideals, not really,' he said. 'It's just that when he's got a family and needs to put food on the table, things kind of . . .' He trailed off.

Horn searched for a response. Finally, he said, 'Well, it's your song. I guess you can do anything you want to with it.' He noticed that only the back of Woody's wild head of hair was illuminated; his face was in shadow. Horn was reminded of his conversation with Owen Bruder out by the pool at the Garden of Allah. *You can talk about almost anything*, he thought, *if you can't see the other man's face.*

Maggie opened the screen door. 'Joseph's showing Davey and Cissie his gun collection,' she said. 'I thought I'd join you boys for some dirty jokes.'

'We're fresh out, darlin',' Guthrie told her. 'Now we're talking about people who sell their ideals for cold, hard cash. But join us anyway.'

She took a seat on the top step of the porch. 'Sell their ideals?'

'Never mind,' Guthrie said. 'I'd rather talk about that lady on the radio with the little girl's voice and the evil mind. Why do y'all go to the trouble to listen to her?'

Neither one answered for a while. Then Maggie spoke up. 'We'll tell you, if you've got a few minutes.'

Guthrie shifted position and stretched out both legs, resting his heels on the porch railing. 'Shoot,' he said.

'You tell it,' Horn said to her.

She did, omitting a few details but not her relationship with Owen Bruder. Halfway through the story, they heard a whinny from the stables, as if one of the horses was listening. Otherwise all was still.

'Damnation,' Guthrie said softly, when she'd finished. 'That's a story, all right. Somebody needs to write a song about it.'

'Maybe later,' Horn said. 'When it has an ending.'

'Only one thing bothers me.'

'What's that?'

'I don't think anybody killed your daddy over politics.'

'How do you know?'

'I don't. It just doesn't feel that way. Oh, people get killed over politics all the time. But not like this.'

'Sorry, but you're not making much sense,' Horn said, trying to make his tone friendly. He didn't want to offend Guthrie, but the man sounded as if he had put away too many beers.

'Maybe you're right,' Guthrie said, stifling a belch. 'I'm just a broken-down songwriter. Don't pay any attention to me.'

'We need to be going,' Maggie said. She went in to get her husband. A minute later, all of them stood on the porch saying goodnight. Maggie and Cissie kissed. 'You're taking pretty good care of this old boy,' Maggie told her.

'Well, he's a handful,' Cissie said with a grin.

Mad Crow started to make a joke, but stopped and looked off across his property. Then he went down the steps and paced over toward the side of the house. Horn followed.

'What is it?' But as soon as they reached the corner and felt the breeze from the north, he knew. 'The wind's shifted.'

'You can really smell the smoke now,' Mad Crow muttered.

They walked back to the others. 'Santa Ana's blowing,' Mad Crow said to Maggie and her husband.

'I've heard people talk about that,' Guthrie said, 'but what is it?'

'Wind from up north. Sometimes in winter, the wind gets reversed, and it blows down from off the desert. When it does, it gets funneled through the mountain canyons, picks up speed, and can rattle the windows down here. No trouble, usually, except when there's already fires burning on the other side of the range. Then, it can bring 'em down, sweep 'em right over you.'

He turned back to Maggie and her husband. 'I got nothing but mountains at my back here, but you got that little canyon a couple of miles north of you.'

'Las Cruces,' Davey Peake said.

'Right. That'll funnel the wind right down toward you.'

'There's nothing burning up above Las Cruces right now,' Peake said.

'You better pray it stays that way.'

22

The next morning he made a pot of coffee, drank one cup, and filled his army canteen with the rest. Then he put on his work clothes, hooked the canteen onto his belt, loaded a shovel and a stubbly, long-handled janitor's broom onto his wheelbarrow, and wheeled it up the cracked asphalt drive to the ruins on the plateau.

The warm, dry, northerly winds had scoured the air and swept the haze and light marine moisture out to sea. Everything seemed in sharp focus, even a point of land far up the coast, even the red-tailed hawk that rode the currents a hundred feet up. Horn's throat was dry. He sniffed the air but found no trace of smoke in it this morning. What fires may be burning were miles to the north and over two ranges of mountains.

He worked steadily for close to an hour down in the concrete shell of Ricardo Aguilar's swimming pool, shoveling and sweeping ashes, charred wood, and other debris onto the wheelbarrow. He turned up a few tin cans that had once held stew, beans, and fruit.

By the time he finished, he had made two trips over the crest of the hill to a small dump site among the trees, where he emptied the wheelbarrow and shoveled fresh dirt over the debris. Then he remembered the remains of the coyote's kill on the tennis court, swept that up, and added it to the burial site.

There you go, Ricardo, he said to the ghost of the departed owner. *All nice and neat. Maybe we can sell your place to somebody who'll bring it back to glory.*

Back at the cabin, he took a bath, shaved, dressed, and drove to the café on Pacific Coast Highway, where he sat at the counter and had flapjacks and sausage. Behind him, outside the open door, the ocean was strangely silent, as if waiting for something. On the portable radio that sat behind the counter, a voice announced with gravity that an American physicist was accused of passing atom bomb secrets to the Russians, then returned listeners to a program of rumba music.

During his second cup of coffee, he laid a nickel on a pile of papers that sat by the front window and slid a *Times* out of the stack. The main story on the front page bore the headline *Panel Begins Probe of Red Influence*.

Under a Washington dateline, the story described the opening of formal testimony before the Thomas committee. The first witness to appear was Jack Warner, head of Warner Bros. Studios, who denounced the Reds' attempts to influence the content of American films. In front of a bank of microphones and newsreel cameras, Warner told the committee that 'ideological termites have burrowed into many American industries,' and added, 'I say let us dig them out and get rid of them.'

He had been followed by Marvin Felix, who said he had already taken steps to purge Communists from the writers' ranks at Global Studios. 'They have no place on my back lot or in this country,' he declared.

Other sympathetic witnesses expected to appear were Gary Cooper, Robert Taylor, and Louis B. Mayer.

Reading through the rest of the report, Horn could see what was taking shape in Washington. The first days of formal testimony would echo those disclosures made in secret in the suite at the Biltmore. J. Parnell Thomas was first calling on his allies in Hollywood to denounce the subversives at the studios. By the time the accused writers, directors and actors were summoned to the stand, they would find no sympathy in the room.

Putting aside the paper, Horn wondered if Owen Bruder's secret accuser was one of those who would speak. Could it have been Marvin Felix himself?

He drove into the city under a blinding sun and parked across the street from the Hollywood Alhambra, noting signs of change in the old hotel, even since his last visit. Although a few guests lounged on the peach-stucco veranda, workmen were erecting a chain-link fence across the front, where the narrow lawn bordered the sidewalk. Up on the top floor, a single window screen hung slightly askew, a stray eyelash on a still-attractive but aging face.

The lobby appeared normal, if a bit quieter. Only one guest was ensconced among the jumble of comfortable love seats and potted plants. The room clerk looked bored. Up on the mezzanine, Horn spotted more workmen carrying boxes.

He heard a young voice. 'Help you, sir?' It was the chipper bellboy from his last visit.

'You still here?' Horn asked. 'Thought you had a new job at the Ambassador.'

'Next week,' the kid said, grinning. 'That's when we close the doors here.'

'And they start tearing it down?'

'That's right.'

'Any word on what's going to replace it?'

'Uh-uh.' The kid didn't seem overly concerned. He had his new job lined up. And the tips would be better at the Ambassador.

'Laura Lee Paisley,' he said. 'Has she moved out already?'

'Nope. I heard her yelling at the manager the other day. Said they're going to have to drag her out.'

He felt relieved. 'Good.' He flipped a quarter, and the kid caught it waist-high, almost without looking. A pro. 'Thanks.'

On the mezzanine, he walked past boxes of goods stacked here and there. He heard typing inside the Paisley office, opened the door, and looked in.

'Good morning,' he said to the receptionist. 'Is she here or up on the roof?'

'Neither,' she replied, looking up from the typewriter. She put on a polite smile but narrowed her eyes, trying to place him.

'I was here the other day,' he reminded her. 'Had a nice talk with Laura Lee up there. Can you tell me—'

'She's out,' the receptionist said brusquely, apparently having decided that he was of little importance. Just another supplicant begging for some kind of publicity. 'At Columbia. Lunch with Mr Cohn.'

'Ah.' He nodded. 'I need to see her, and it's kind of important. Would it be okay if I waited?'

'You wouldn't want to,' she said, enjoying the chance at sarcasm. 'After that she has an interview.'

'Where? Maybe I can catch her.'

'In a private home in Bel-Air. She won't be back until late this after-noon.'

He looked at his watch and thought quickly. He didn't have time to chase Laura Lee Paisley around town today, but he wanted her to see what he had brought.

'Mind if I leave something for her?' Before she had a chance to respond, he stepped back to a small table behind her and plucked a large white envelope off a stack. In the upper left corner was a garish illustration of a microphone emitting radio waves and the words *Laura Lee Paisley, The Voice of Hollywood*.

'Certainly not,' she said, sounding unutterably bored.

Opening the file folder he had brought, he withdrew two of the sheets of photo paper and put them in the envelope. He sealed it closed, wrote briefly on the front, and handed it to the receptionist.

'I'd sure appreciate it if you'd give this to her when she comes in,' he said, smiling as ingratiatingly as he could. 'She'll want to see it. Tell her that's my phone number there.'

The woman nodded, already engrossed in her typing again. She was very fast.

In the lobby, he walked past an elderly couple at the front desk, flanked

158

by a battered assortment of luggage. They looked like refugees on their way to an uncertain future. But his thoughts were elsewhere.

I lied, he thought. *She won't want to see it. But she's sure going to need that phone number.*

Horn found Grover Jones' home on a quiet street in Beverly Hills, a street of lush lawns, well-tended palms and assorted architectural styles. The Jones residence resembled an overblown English cottage, with a thatched roof and leaded windows. Every detail of the place looked lovingly cared for.

He pulled up behind Maggie's nondescript Chevrolet and rang the bell. A uniformed maid took him through to a spacious room, with a low, beamed ceiling, which looked out on a lavish garden. Horn could see a young man tending to the plants. Maggie and her host were seated by the window with tall glasses and a pitcher of iced tea on a table between them.

'Mr Horn,' Jones exclaimed, getting quickly to his feet and coming over. He extended his hand and gave Horn a hearty shake. 'Please come join us.'

'I hope you'll call me John Ray.'

'Most pleased to. Maggie and I are already on a first-name basis. I'm Grover.'

They sat, and Jones resumed a history of his long career, which had begun in the silent era. He was an entertaining storyteller. 'I looked young for my age,' he said. 'So I could play teen-agers well into my twenties. I was usually the kid brother or the boy down the street, somebody for the ingenue to fall in love with. I spent an inordinate amount of time running around in bathing suits and tennis outfits.'

Horn studied him as he spoke. Jones was dressed casually but elegantly. He was somewhere in his late forties but could pass for younger. His face was unlined, and his grin could still be called boyish. The only thing that gave away his age was a full head of almost shockingly white hair.

'Later on, when sound came in, I did all right,' he went on. 'I had the voice for it, and I was well suited for the best friend, the madcap playboy, you know. And I have to say it's been fun. This business has been very good to me. I just pray I've got another twenty years in me.'

He caught Horn looking at his hair. 'Aha,' he said, pointing to it. 'This happened almost overnight, sometime in my thirties,' he said. 'I got it from my mother, who was a great beauty but who was also prematurely gray. I don't mind it, because it's easy to fix. Whenever they tell me it's time to get back in harness, I just hop over to the studio hair stylist, and . . . presto! God forbid we should look our age. In this town, that's one of the cardinal sins, along with a few others I could name.'

159

They heard the front door open, and a moment later a woman looked into the room from the hallway. 'Hello,' she said.

'Hi, sweetheart,' Jones called out.

'Don't let me interrupt.'

'No, not at all.' He introduced his guests as Horn stood up. 'My wife, Frances.'

The woman smiled politely. Her face was elongated and rather plain, and she was nicely dressed in a tartan sweater and a pleated tweed skirt. 'I picked this up at the studio,' she said to her husband, gesturing with what looked like a screenplay. 'I'll start reading it tonight.'

'Larry's pruning the acacia tree with his usual heavy hand,' Jones said to her. 'Would you ask him to be careful?'

'Why don't you ask him?' she replied. 'I need to get back to the bookkeeping.' She nodded to the others. 'Please excuse me. Nice to meet you both.' She went off down the hall.

'Oh, well,' Jones said with an exaggerated grumble. 'Let me take care of this.' He went through a set of French doors into the garden. Through the branches of the acacia, Horn glimpsed him as he explained what he wanted. The young man was bare-chested, and Jones stood close to him, at one point placing his hand on the other's shoulder to make a point.

In a minute he was back. 'Don't know what I'd do without Frances,' he said as he took his seat. 'She's a combination agent, manager, and I don't know what all. She was over at Global to get a look at the next one they want me to do, something called *The McFarlanes*. A comedy. Not a big part, but a good one, I hear.'

'Think you'll do it?' Horn asked.

'You once worked in this business, I understand,' Jones said.

'That's right.'

'Did you ever turn down a movie?'

'Nope.'

'Well, there you are. Olivia de Havilland, bless her little turned-up nose, went up against Jack Warner and beat him in court, but generally it's hard to fight the studio. As I said, this business has been good to me. I've made a career out of giving them what they want, and they've rewarded me beyond most people's dreams. If the script doesn't have me kissing a monkey, I'm sure Frances will recommend that I take it, and I almost always follow her advice.'

'Your home is beautiful,' Maggie said, looking around. 'Did she decorate it?'

'Well, that just happens to be one of my talents,' Jones said with a self-effacing smile. 'I was an art and design major before I fell into this insane business.'

'Grover, we appreciate you spending time with us,' Maggie said. 'We just wanted to talk to you about my father.'

'Yes,' he said, refreshing her glass of tea from the pitcher. 'Lord, I was so amazed when you told me that earlier. Owen's daughter. So naturally you're interested in finding out why he . . .' He stopped, as if unwilling to finish the thought. 'Such a horrible thing. And so awful for Lillian too. How's she doing?'

'All right, I suppose. Trying to get her life back to normal. We're doing what we can for her, along with friends like Wally Roland.'

'Ah, yes.' Jones looked back and forth between them. 'They were once close, I understand. Wally and Lillian.'

'I think so,' Horn said. 'He mentioned that he told Lillian she shouldn't marry Owen, but that didn't stop him from being friends with both of them later on.'

'Yes. Well, Wally's a very talented man. With what he's facing now, he'll need all his talent . . .' He appeared to lose the thought. Through the French doors came the faint snip, snip of the gardener's shears.

'I hate all this nonsense that's going on now,' Jones said quietly. 'This persecution. I despise it.'

'Lillian appreciated your calling after Owen's death,' Maggie said. 'Were you very close to them?'

'Not really. Owen wrote two of the movies I worked on. And I knew them socially. Now it's too late for me to know him any better. Maybe I can help her in some way.'

'Just stay in touch,' Maggie said. 'And maybe you can help me and John Ray with what we're doing.'

'If I can,' he said.

'Do you know if Owen had any serious enemies?'

'I've been racking my brain ever since you called,' Jones said, his face troubled. 'I had a feeling you'd ask that. And I can think of absolutely no one who could have hated him that much. Oh, he had the reputation of being prickly from time to time, and he had a way of putting anyone in his place. But worse than that? No.'

Horn found himself studying Jones' mannerisms. When the subject of Owen Bruder first came up, Jones had run his hand through his white hair, fingers spread, combing it, and he was now repeating the gesture every minute or so. Maybe it meant nothing, Horn thought, but it certainly suggested nervousness.

'Who were his good friends at the studio?' Maggie asked.

'Beyond Wally Roland, you mean? No one else, no one I knew of.'

'How did he get on with Marvin Felix?' Horn asked.

Again the hand swept through the hair. Jones seemed oblivious to the gesture. He smiled faintly. 'Not well, I suppose. Like most of us. Marvin is a brilliant man, in his way, but he's a terrible leader. He alienates people. Uses them, manipulates them. I don't think he'd hesitate to crush . . .'

He looked uncomfortable. 'Listen to me go on. If Marvin heard me talking about him like that, he'd boot me right out the door.'

No one spoke for a while. Jones stared out the French doors. The gardener was nowhere to be seen.

'This is awkward,' Maggie began. 'But we need to ask you if you know anything about my father and a woman—'

'I don't know anything about a woman,' he said quickly, without turning to look at her.

'He may have been seeing a woman,' Maggie pressed on. 'Maybe it had something to do with his death, maybe not. I don't even like asking the question, but it's important.'

Jones shook his head emphatically. 'I don't know anything about a woman.' He looked pointedly at his wristwatch. 'Oh, my. I've let the time get away from me, and there are a few things I need to attend to. Would you excuse me?' He stood up. 'It's been a pleasure to meet you both. I'll see you out.'

Twenty minutes later, Horn pulled into a slot in front of Simon's Drive-In on Wilshire. In his rear-view, he saw Maggie park her Chevy on the street. She walked over and got in beside him. Before they had time to talk, a snappy-looking carhop, blonde ringlets erupting from under her jaunty cap, bustled over, clamped a tray onto the door on Horn's side and took their order.

Simon's was all curves and glass and shiny metal and neon, like something out of a Flash Gordon serial. The place was ringed with cars, and the air reeked, not unpleasantly, of a mixture of barbecue and automobile exhaust.

'Grover Jones,' Horn said, watching the waitress' trim slacks-clad figure disappear into the eatery. He repeated the name as if it were a piece of food he was trying to dislodge from his teeth. 'Grover Jones. Nice guy. But he gave us the bum's rush.'

'I'll say. Do you think he knows something?'

'Sure looks like it. He got very twitchy when we asked about the woman. And there's something else, too: wife or no wife, Grover Jones is a member of the boys' club.'

'I could tell as soon as I sat down with him,' she said, nodding. 'But so is half of Hollywood, and who cares? Do you?'

'No, but . . . I'm not sure what I'm trying to say. Bear with me for a minute.' The carhop was back with their drinks, a strawberry shake for Maggie and a chocolate malt for him.

'Remember when Owen talked about the old days, marching and picketing and fighting for causes? It was all out in the open then. Later it changed, and now people who joined the wrong groups have gone underground, trying to keep their secrets.'

'Uh-huh. So?'

'Well, all of us know some members of the boys' – and girls' – clubs. They've gotten along pretty well in Hollywood, mostly by keeping their lives separate from their jobs. In other words, keeping secrets. If the secrets ever came out – even just rumors of secrets – they'd have a rough time of it, just like Owen and Wally and Cal and all the others.'

'I'm not sure what the connection is, John Ray.'

'Me neither. I'm just saying that it's not a good time to be hiding a secret. And Grover Jones is carrying at least one around with him.'

The carhop brought their barbecue sandwiches and French fries, and they were occupied with eating for the next few minutes. Horn turned on the radio to Laura Lee Paisley's station, but it was too early for her second show of the day. Instead they heard a male voice, awash in profundity, intone, 'Now we present once again "Backstage Wife," the story of Mary Noble, a little Iowa girl who married one of America's most handsome actors . . .'

'I'd almost rather listen to Laura Lee,' Maggie said wryly. 'The woman who's scary as hell, according to Woody.'

He turned the radio off. 'I have a feeling we'll be having a conversation real soon, the scary woman and me,' he said.

Maggie dug into her purse. 'Just remembered,' she said. She pulled out two theater tickets. 'Lillian got these from Wally Roland. Tonight's the opening night of that play he's working on. She's not sure she feels ready to go out yet, and she thought you and I might want to see it. I thought about it for a while, but I really need to stay close to Davey.'

'Take him.'

'He's not up to snuff yet. But even if he felt all right, you know Davey.' She laughed. 'Him and some play about a guy who lived hundreds of years ago? He'd snore all the way through it. Here, you use them. And take Lillian.'

'You said she—'

'I know. But I think she really *is* ready to go out, needs to go out, and just doesn't know it.'

'It's kind of late.'

'She'd appreciate it. Go on, call her.'

He thought. 'Okay, I'll see what she says. And maybe I can corner Wally there. I've got a lot of questions for him.'

Maggie finished her food and dug into her purse again.

'My treat,' he said to her.

'No.'

'Yes. I want to.' He hunted for the right words. 'I enjoy our meals together. Our meals on the run.'

'Well, so do I.' She looked at him with great seriousness. 'Thanks for doing what you're doing.'

'Say hi to Davey,' he said as she got out.

After he had watched her drive away, he worked the dial until it came to rest on Frances Langford singing 'Harbor Lights'. Then he finished his meal slowly. He tried to focus on Grover Jones, but every few seconds he found himself distracted by thoughts of Maggie. He felt like a schoolboy with a new crush.

Grow up, he told himself. *You had your chance, a long time ago.*

23

Finishing up, he laid everything on the tray and flashed his lights for the carhop. 'Your date decide to walk home?' she asked. It came out like a soft wisecrack, something just between the two of them. He paid up, and tipped her extra because she was funny.

Before leaving, he went inside to the pay phone. The first number he dialed was for the police detective, Pitt.

'This is John Ray Horn,' he said to the cop. 'Occurs to me I keep calling you by your last name only. You got a first one?'

'It's Vernon. But that doesn't mean we're suddenly on a first-name basis.'

'I understand. Just thought I'd ask you if you got that note.'

'From the Order of Old Glory? Yes, I did. Thanks for dropping it off. Matter of fact, I know the gentleman.'

'Who?'

'The character who signs his letters that way. He's a familiar name around here.'

'And what *is* his name?'

'I don't think I'll tell you that,' Pitt replied with no evident hostility. 'All you need to know is that he's not our guy. He's a disabled vet from the First War, likes to talk about how he fought with Black Jack Pershing. Lives with his sister in Echo Park, and he spends most of his time sending out mail to people he reads about in the paper, people who aren't patriotic enough to suit him.'

'Making threats.'

'That's right. But he couldn't follow through with his threats even if he wanted to, because he's in a wheelchair. Every time we find one of his little notes, we go over and slap his wrist. His sister makes coffee for us, he promises to be a good boy, and we leave.'

'So . . .'

'He's not our guy. But thanks for trying.' Pitt's tone softened a little. 'We're pretty sure you're not our guy either, just in case you were wondering.'

'I thought your partner was chewing over the idea that I was in cahoots with Lillian Bruder.'

'Oh, maybe he was for a while. You don't exactly have a spotless record. But then we asked around and got a better look at you. Bruder's daughter, for one, turned out to be a pretty good character witness for you.'

Maggie told the police she was his daughter, Horn thought. *Next thing, she'll be taking out an ad in the paper.*

'So you're still looking for the guy,' he said to Pitt. 'Any new ideas?'

'No offense, but if I had any, I'm not sure I'd share them with civilians.'

'Can you at least tell me exactly what killed him?'

'Bruder? A blow to the right side of the head with an unknown blunt object. Coroner said it was consistent with the size and shape, and maybe the weight, of a piece of pipe. It crushed the skull, and he was close to dead when he hit the water.'

'Would it have taken a strong man?'

'Hard to say. A piece of steel pipe can do a lot of damage. You don't have to be Ted Williams, but a good arm would certainly help.'

'Did you talk to the neighbors?' he asked.

'Sure we did,' Pitt replied with obvious impatience. 'All of them. Nobody saw anything. A couple of them thought they might have heard two men talking out there for a while, but nothing more.'

Pitt paused for a moment, then: 'Sounds to me like you're doing some work on this yourself.'

'Just as a friend of the family,' Horn said. 'I'm asking around, trying to be helpful.'

'And if you find out anything, will you be helpful to me too?'

'Yes.'

'Make sure you do.'

Horn's next call was to Douglas Greenleaf. 'Been trying to reach you,' the young man said to him in his usual gee-whiz voice. 'Like I told you, pull out your wallet. Bingo on both numbers.'

'Tell me.'

'The New York number was disconnected about a year ago. Before that, it belonged to a Mr and Mrs Raymond Santini. They moved to a new address a few blocks away in Little Italy.'

'You have the new number?'

'Well, natch. What do you take me for?'

'Douglas, every time we talk, you sound more like Mickey Rooney.'

'I was trying for Sam Spade.' He read out the new number, and Horn wrote it down.

'Now, that Hollywood number . . .' Horn heard the crinkle of paper. 'It's an address in the hills. Got the name too.' He began reading. 'Do you want me to spell that?'

'No.' Horn underlined the name. 'I know how to spell it.' A grim smile crossed his face, and he found himself nodding his head.

'Thanks, Douglas. I owe you ten.'

His last call was to Lillian. As it turned out, Maggie was right.

The small theater buzzed with the energy of the first-night crowd. The final curtain had been rung down, and the cast had taken its bows to loud and sustained applause. Now the curtain was up again, and the stage was filled with costumed actors, backstage crew, and well-wishers from the audience. At stage center, near a big glass bowl full of punch and vaporous dry ice, stood Charles Laughton, his damp hair in disarray, his obese figure swaddled in what looked like a monk's robe. With his wife, Elsa Lanchester, at his side, he held court among a constantly shifting crowd of admirers.

'He was very good, wasn't he?' Lillian said to Horn. They had remained in their seats, content to watch the crowd. 'I think Owen would have enjoyed writing for him,' she continued.

'Do you know him?'

'Not well, but he and Elsa used to live at the Garden of Allah years ago. They have one of those unusual marriages we see a lot of in Hollywood.'

'I think I've heard,' Horn said, thinking of Grover Jones and his wife.

'Wally tells us that when Charles was shooting *The Hunchback of Notre Dame*, he'd come home from a long, hot day at the studio and head straight for the pool. The neighbors would see him paddling around there in the evening with the big hump still strapped to his back.'

'There's a sight I'd pay admission to see.'

'Me too. I'd much rather think of the sight of Charles swimming in our pool than . . .' She stopped, unable to go on.

'I know, Lillian.' Looking around him, he noted that it was a typical Hollywood crowd: a few instantly recognizable faces along with many more of the near-famous – producers, directors, and some of those actors whose names had never adorned a marquee.

Standing near the back of the auditorium was a group composed of Marvin Felix and his wife, with Sidney Swain and Grace Stilwell. All four were elegantly dressed, the men in dark suits cut in the new single-breasted style and the women in off-the-shoulder evening dresses. From that distance, the conversation looked lively.

'You came.' Horn felt an unsteady hand on his shoulder and looked around to find Wally Roland leaning in close. 'Both of you. How nice.'

'Wally.' Lillian greeted him with a smile. Like all her recent smiles, it was tinged with sadness. 'It was a wonderful play. You can be proud of it.'

'What little I had to do with it.' Roland was in tuxedo and stiff shirt, his bow tie askew. It was clear he had been drinking, and Horn suspected it wasn't the punch.

Roland aimed a kiss at Lillian's cheek and seated himself heavily behind their row. He pointed to a stocky figure standing on the stage next to Laughton, wearing a rumpled suit and big horn rims. 'Bertolt Brecht, the playwright,' he said. 'Charles worked with him to come up with this translation.' He turned his attention to Horn. 'And how did you like it, sir?' he asked. 'Enough action for you?'

'I thought it was fine.'

'And what did it demonstrate to you, if anything?'

Horn thought for a moment. 'That the government's not always right. That a man alone doesn't stand a chance against them. And that no matter how smart you are, no matter how much you might have done to make people's lives better, it can all be taken away from you.'

'Bravo.' Roland clapped soundlessly. 'We should continue this. There's much to be said about the lone hero standing against the forces of repression, armed only with his Winchester and his flair for *bons mots*. Would you two care to stop off with me for drinks somewhere on the Strip?'

'I'm afraid I'm too tired,' Lillian said. 'But maybe John Ray can join you later.'

'No drinks for me,' Horn said, wanting to keep Roland away from any more alcohol tonight. 'I wouldn't mind something to eat, though.'

'Then why don't you meet me at Schwab's after you see Lillian home?'

'Sounds good.' Horn looked around again. 'Would you excuse me for a minute?' he said to Lillian. As he got up, she rose to join Roland in the row behind. Glancing back, he saw her look of concern as she sat next to him.

As Horn approached Marvin Felix and his party, Felix spoke quickly to Sidney Swain, who intercepted Horn with a broad smile and a firm handshake. 'Good to see you again,' he said. 'Some play, huh? Marvin and I are like a lot of movie people, we think every story can be told better with a camera. But Maris—' He indicated Felix's wife, who was staring at Horn much as she had the time he saw her leaving her husband's office. 'She loves the theater. Gets back to New York every chance she gets, to shop and see all the plays.'

'How about Grace Stilwell?'

'Hmm?'

'She like the theater too?'

'Well, I suppose she does.'

'I think I'll ask her myself.'

'Oh, that's probably not a good idea.' Swain shifted position slightly until he was planted in front of Horn, blocking his way.

168

'Am I going to have to walk around you?' Horn kept his tone light. When he got no answer, he stepped to the side, but Swain took hold of his left arm above the elbow.

'Marvin doesn't want your company tonight,' he said quietly, smile still in place. His grip was strong, his gaze unblinking, and Horn suddenly saw the man in a new light. Sidney Swain, he thought, is not just a well-cut suit. He knew he was going to have to do something about the hand on his arm, and soon.

'Sidney!' It was Marvin Felix. 'It's all right. Let's not spoil the man's evening.'

Swain released his grip and stepped back. Horn approached the others. 'Hello,' he said, nodding to them.

'Well,' Marvin Felix said heartily. 'Mr Horn, the man who came around unannounced the other day. My wife, Maris. I believe you know Miss Stilwell.'

'Pleased to meet you,' Horn said to Maris Felix. She was somewhere around forty, with dark, angular looks and deep-set eyes. Not a beauty, Horn thought, but a woman you'll remember. She wore a chinchilla stole draped casually over one shoulder like a serape. She nodded coldly and wordlessly.

'Enjoy the play?' he asked them.

'It was okay,' Felix answered. 'But don't look for it at your local movie house. The audience would be on their way out before the end of the first reel.'

'Maybe we could turn it into a musical, Marvin,' Grace Stilwell said. 'You know, write a few songs, add a few jokes . . .'

'Huh? Oh, I get it.' He turned to Horn. 'She thinks I got no class, just because I started out in the junk business. Well, this old junk man knows a few things about selling tickets.'

'I was hoping I could borrow Miss Stilwell for a minute,' Horn said, looking at her. 'Since we didn't have much time to talk the other day.'

She looked vaguely amused. 'Oh, I suppose,' she said. 'Just for a minute, then we all have to leave.'

The two of them stepped away a short distance. 'You're a little friendlier tonight,' he said.

'Just marginally so,' she said, 'because I happen to be enjoying myself, and you're not interrupting me at work to ask rude questions. But you're on probation.'

'I have some more questions for you,' he said. 'But I'm not going to interrupt your evening out. What I'd like to do is ask you to set aside some time for me.'

Her head tilted slightly. 'I don't think so.' She said it in an absolutely unruffled manner, which appealed to him. Much about her appealed to him, he reflected, including her midnight blue dress topped with a light cashmere shawl and a single strand of pearls, her discreet make-up, and her neatly swept-up hair. She smelled like the first orange blossom on the tree.

He tried a different approach. 'Did you like the play?'

'Yes,' she said, 'but it was hard to watch. For a lot of people in this town, it hits too close to home.'

'I thought people like Marvin Felix would avoid being seen at a play like this, where you can hear unpopular opinions.'

'It's not that simple,' she said with a shrug. 'If anyone has anything to be afraid about, then yes, they wouldn't want to be seen at a play by Brecht, but the Marvin Felixes don't feel that kind of fear. They're more likely to make other people afraid.' She sounded almost sad.

'What about you?'

She knew what he meant. 'I'm with him tonight, so I suppose some of his immunity rubs off on me. And besides, everyone knows I don't have any politics.'

'Must be convenient these days,' he said. A subtle change of expression told him she didn't appreciate that comment. He knew he should be careful.

'Wally Roland's been working on the play,' he said, pointing over to where Roland and Lillian sat, deep in conversation. 'After getting bounced from his job, he's lucky to find anything, don't you think?'

She did not respond. Her look was hard and appraising.

'From what I've heard, working at Global – hell, working at just about any studio – is pretty risky. You must feel lucky just to have a job there.'

She seemed about to answer, stopped, and looked back at her companions. *Have I pushed her too hard again?* he wondered, but she turned back to him and said, 'I need a cigarette.' Reaching in her purse, she headed for the main exit. He followed, and in seconds they stood in the tiny courtyard, their backs to a wall amid a noisy crowd of people.

With practiced gestures, she pulled a cigarette from a slim case, tapped it on the cover, and slid it between her lips. He lit it for her, and she took a deep drag, then exhaled the smoke upward into the air between them. She seemed in no hurry to speak, and there was no warmth in her expression, but he was encouraged by the simple fact that she was standing there with him.

'You might have seen that I was sitting with Lillian—' he began.

'How is she?' she asked quickly. 'Mrs Bruder.'

'Well, she's doing all right, I suppose, for a woman who's just lost her husband in the worst way you can imagine. It'll take a while, but she'll come out of it. Do you know her?'

170

She shook her head. 'We've never met. But people say good things about her.'

'They're right. But you know Wally Roland, don't you?'

'Just to say hello. At the studio.'

'And Owen? You didn't know him?'

Her eyes narrowed, and she allowed herself to smile briefly. 'Ah, you're trying to trick me, aren't you? It seems to me I answered that question just the other day.'

'Right.' He found himself studying her. She was probably the most attractive woman within eyesight: not only well dressed, but also cool and wry and ironic. Just the kind of woman who, against all reason, sometimes attracted him, with disastrous results. The Maggies of this world, he thought, they're the ones I feel most at home with. Why do I sometimes go for the others, those with the glamorous looks and the icy manners and the smart mouths?

She took another long drag and dropped her cigarette to the pavement. 'I should go back,' she said. 'The others—'

'Sure. When can I see you?'

'Pardon me?'

'That talk we need to have. Somewhere in private, without Marvin Felix and his wife looking over your shoulder.'

'You misunderstand. I came out here for a little air. We're not going to have any talk, now or ever. If you contact me again, I'm going to have to tell the police about it. They won't want to hear that a man with a prison record has been bothering me.'

'You checked up on me.'

'I asked around.' She looked slightly uncomfortable.

'Well, I'm flattered. The way you brushed me off the other day, I didn't realize I'd made such an impression.'

'Don't flatter yourself.' She made as if to move past him.

'If you decide to call the police, I can point you in the right direction,' he said. 'Fellow named Pitt. The same one who's looking into Owen Bruder's murder. He'd be glad to hear from you, because he's running out of ideas, and he might want you to explain why your phone number was sitting all alone inside Owen's address book.'

She stopped, not looking at him.

'He'd probably ask you why you lied when you told me you didn't know Owen. You see, we're pretty sure Owen had been seeing a woman before he was killed. If that woman turned out to be you, I don't see how you could keep it a secret once the cops start turning over rocks the way they do. I'm just an amateur, but they're the real pros when it comes to finding things out, catching people in lies. I mean, it's one thing to sneak

171

around with another woman's husband, but when the husband winds up dead . . .'

He decided to stop. She hadn't moved, but stood motionless amid the chattering crowd, which was now beginning to thin out.

'Grace!' It was Sidney Swain's voice, coming from inside the big open door.

'They're looking for you,' Horn said. 'Make up your mind.'

She stepped right up to him. As he had noticed that day at the studio, in high heels her eyes almost met his. The look in them was so full of enmity, he almost blinked.

'You son of a bitch,' she said quietly. Then she said it again.

'What's it going to be?'

The look disappeared, replaced by one of indecision. 'I'll be at home tomorrow night,' she said. 'My address is—'

'I know it,' he said.

When he rejoined Lillian and Roland, their heads were still bent together, and his hand was clasped in hers. She looked up at Horn and smiled another sad smile.

'Shall we go?' She gave him a second look. 'John Ray, if I didn't know you better, I'd say you looked almost happy.'

'Must be the company,' he said.

24

Schwab's, which bustled with noise and energy in the daytime, was quieter in the late evening. Horn and Roland sat at the end of the counter near the back of the big, high-ceilinged drugstore, Horn with a bowl of soup and his companion with a tall glass of milk. Horn's plan to get the other man sobered up for conversation had already hit a snag. As soon as the milk had arrived, Roland extracted a flask from inside his tuxedo jacket and poured a quick measure into it.

'Ulcer,' he said.

'Which is for the ulcer?'

'The milk,' Roland said with elaborate seriousness. 'And the other . . . is for everything else.' He swigged most of the glass, wiped his mouth, and motioned to the soda jerk. 'Oh, Lester.'

'Mr Roland?'

'Another drink, barkeep. The same.'

'Yes, sir.' The sandy-haired young man, in bow tie and white shirt with rolled-up sleeves, brought him another milk.

'Lester here's going to be a movie star,' Roland said to Horn as he dosed the second glass with amber liquid. 'Aren't you, Lester?'

'No, sir. That's Al, on the day shift. I'm going to be a screenwriter.'

'Of course you are. Just be sure to write exactly what they tell you, and you'll be a happy screenwriter, with a bungalow in the hills and a swimming pool in your backyard.'

'Yes, sir.'

'Everybody comes to Schwab's,' he said to Horn when Lester had moved down the counter. 'Now more than ever, since that apocryphal tale about Lana Turner having been discovered while perched on one of these very seats, sipping a soda.'

'Not true?'

'No, but who cares? In this town it's the mythology that counts.'

He stirred his milk slowly with a long spoon. 'I like this place because it's the screenwriters' second home. The famous, the infamous, the Oscar boys, the has-beens. The nice thing is, they continue to like you here even when you're out of work.'

'That's good,' Horn said. 'I saw your old boss at the theater tonight.'

Roland nodded. He was bent over his milk, clasping the glass with both hands, studying it. 'As did I. We didn't exchange greetings.'

'Sidney Swain and Grace Stilwell were with him. Are they some kind of a couple?'

'Could be,' Roland said. 'But if so, I doubt if it's permanent. Sidney's quite the ladies' man. He bounces around from one starlet to another. That's one of the great benefits he derives from his family connection.'

'What connection?'

'You didn't know? Maris Felix is his sister.'

'Hmm. No, I didn't know. So he's the boss' brother-in-law.'

'Exactly. When he was younger, he tried various jobs and business ventures, all of them failures. He was fond of the bottle, and all he was ever really good at was living beyond his means. The big brother-in-law got tired of bailing him out of debt and various troubles, so Sidney finally gave up, went to work for Marvin, and discovered what he was born to do.'

'And what was that?'

'Doing another man's dirty work while keeping a smile on his face.'

'Doesn't sound like much of a job.'

'It is and it isn't. One of the more onerous tasks assigned to him is to watch over his sister.'

'Why?'

'Maris is a troubled soul. She has an arrogant side, enjoys being the lady of the manor. Marvin's assistants run when they see her coming, but she's also very fragile. Once or twice a year she goes through a kind of nervous collapse, and it's Sidney's task to pack her off to Old McDonald's Farm.'

Seeing Horn's quizzical grin, he added, 'That's just what the wags call it. It's a place somewhere up the coast where the studio hides its high-priced talent when they run into problems with the bottle or the needle or just about anything. Very hush-hush.' He grinned. 'But old Sidney's job definitely has its compensations. Marvin has been his ticket to the good life – starlets, clothes, the house in Beverly Hills, the polo ponies—'

'He plays polo?' Horn remembered the man's powerful grip on his arm. 'Well, a man who hangs around horses can't be all bad.'

'He's not all bad, old Sidney. He's just come to terms with life, and he pays the price.'

'How about you, Wally?'

'Me?' Roland took another long swig of doctored milk and made an exaggerated lugubrious face. 'I was once one of the hotshots. Now I'm just Wally Roland, out of work and soon to be infamous.'

Horn leaned in close. 'I know you're going to Washington soon.'

'Washington,' Roland intoned. 'Going tomorrow, in fact. Where I will take a stand for artistic freedom. Where I will give them a piece of my poor, pickled mind.'

'I appreciate you spending time with me.'

'Lillian asked me to. And if I weren't here carousing with you and Lester, I'd be at home packing my bags and contemplating my mortality.'

'Before you leave, I need to know a few things.'

'Well, of course.' Roland regarded him with tired eyes. 'But I told you—'

'For starters, I need to know what happened in Pyrie.'

'Pyrie.' Roland looked surprised. 'Of course. That's the place. How could I have forgotten the name?'

'I don't know, but you were the one who got me interested in finding out about it. I went there.'

'That was very enterprising of you, sir.'

'I found out about Robert Nimm, the man who died.'

'Robert Nimm. Of course.' Again that look, as if confronted with something long buried. Horn was beginning to feel irritated. He wondered how much Roland had truly forgotten and how much of this was pretense.

'I think somebody killed him, Wally. Somebody in your group. And if it was Owen who did it, then I can't help but think—'

'Think what?' Roland's look was one of growing astonishment, eyes wide. 'Wait a minute. Wait just a minute.' He looked around the drugstore, as if searching for someone else to listen to Horn's theory.

'I think I see.' He hiccuped, pulled a handkerchief from the breast pocket of his tuxedo jacket, and wiped his glasses. He put them back on and laid a hand on Horn's arm.

'My friend,' he said. 'I understand you're trying to help Lillian and Margaret. That's admirable. I also want the answers to Owen's death, and I hope you or the police succeed in finding them. But I can assure you that you won't find them in Pyrie.'

'Why is that?' Horn asked, not trying to hide his impatience.

'Let me just tell you what happened.' Roland uncapped his flask, poured the remnants into the tall glass, and stirred the contents.

'I've never told anyone. I always feared that Lillian would find out, and I was especially careful . . . But with Owen gone, I suppose it's all right.'

He took a drink, neglecting to wipe away the trace of milk. It gave him the look of a pudgy little boy with an inattentive mother.

'I've tried not to think about this for a long time, and now it's all coming

175

back to me. I suppose I have you to thank for that, although it's not much of a gift.' He shook the flask lightly, then slid it into his inside jacket pocket.

'Owen was responsible for the death of Robert Nimm,' he said, exhaling the words quickly as if to get them out there in the air. 'I don't want to say *murdered* because it was more complicated, but he was responsible.'

Across the room someone fed a nickel into the drugstore's pinball machine and began playing. It was a sound that Horn usually enjoyed, one that spoke of happy times. But tonight it sounded tinny and raucous.

'Robert sold us out. We never found out if it was for money or something harder to define, but he let the police know about the march. We lost the element of surprise, and it was a disaster. A humiliating failure. We went there to help the workers, and we wound up looking like fools.'

'How did you find out about Robert?'

'It was easy. All of us were under enormous stress that night, and our little makeshift prison, the hardware store, was like a pressure cooker. Owen led the investigation into what had happened, and it took very little time to identify Robert. He was not a very strong person, and he folded up, admitted everything. Some of the men started to beat him, but Owen stopped them, and that's when the police came and took him away.'

'To the hotel.'

'Yes. To protect him. You know what Owen was like. Well, back then he was even more so. Impassioned, unstoppable. He couldn't rest until he got Robert to tell him everything, especially the reason why.

'The hotel where they put Robert was just down the street, and not long after they took him away, we saw a light go on in one of the rooms. It was late, and we put two and two together. Later, when Owen and I were talking quietly in the rear of the store, we found a window in the bathroom that we were able to force open, and Owen climbed out as quietly as he could. He came back an hour later, pale and silent. It was a long time before he told me exactly what happened.'

Roland paused in his story. A couple had entered the drugstore and headed for the display of liquor bottles against the wall, where they engaged in noisy discussion.

'Where was I?' said Roland, after a long sigh. 'Oh, yes. The next day, all hell broke loose. Robert was dead, but it looked like an accident, a drunken fall, and everyone seemed eager to close the books. Owen and I surmised later that if they had labeled it murder, they would be admitting that someone – the government, the farm owners, who knows? – had informants planted in the various union organizations.'

'What happened in the room?'

176

'It was after midnight, and the hotel was quiet. Owen found the room and knocked lightly on the door. Robert was up, pacing the floor, and quite drunk – drunk enough to open the door without checking first. Owen demanded to know why he had sold us out, but Robert was frightened and belligerent and threatened to wake the hotel. Owen lost control and hit him. It was just a simple blow, delivered in anger, but Robert's head hit the radiator, and he was dead in a second.'

'All right,' Horn said. 'Suppose it happened that way. Then why—'

'Why couldn't Owen's death be connected with what happened in that little town all those years ago? Simple. Because no one knows what he did. No one except myself. And now you.'

Horn looked doubtful.

'Owen was tormented by what he did. We never talked about it again, but I could see what it did to him. He was a man with a strong moral code, and that code had no place for murder in it. Maybe Robert didn't deserve to die, but Owen paid the price for what he did, many times over.'

'All right.'

'Let this rest. And please don't tell Lillian. She has enough to deal with.'

'You like her a lot, don't you?'

Roland assumed a look of goggle-eyed comedy. 'That's the way you'd put it in one of your cowboy movies, I imagine. "You know, Tex, I like that new schoolteacher a lot." Well, yes, you could say I like Lillian Bruder a whole lot. In another life, she might have married me. But then she would have missed out on being married to Owen, who was twice the man I am.'

He got up, weaving slightly. 'And now to bed.'

'Good luck in Washington. Give 'em hell.'

'Hell will definitely be given, in one direction or another.' Roland fumbled with some change, put it on the counter. He appeared to be thinking about something.

'Did you notice, in tonight's play, how Galileo came to betray everything he once stood for? Science, reason, the trust of mankind?'

'He was afraid,' Horn said.

'Do you remember what he said, what he feared?'

'He didn't want to be tortured.'

Roland nodded. 'They didn't torture him, because they didn't have to. All it took for him to deny that the Earth revolved around the sun was to threaten him.'

Roland seemed to be almost in pain. ' "They showed me the instruments," Galileo told his friends. And we all understood, didn't we?' He walked away.

'Good night,' Horn said.

177

He finished the last spoonful of soup, put some money on the counter, and started to get up, but something stopped him. A few words adrift in his mind.

Everybody comes to Schwab's, Roland had said. No surprise there. But it was another set of words Horn was trying to retrieve, words on a typewritten note found in Owen Bruder's desk. He pulled the note from his inside jacket pocket, where he had carried it for days.

I'm now sure it was W. I think I know why.
No more calls, no more meetings for now. Too risky.
I'll come to S. on Sunday at 9.

He motioned the soda jerk over. 'Lester, you work weekends?'

'Yes, sir. Nights.'

'Did you know Owen Bruder, who lived over at the Garden of Allah?'

'Yes, sir. He was a neighbor of Mr Roland's.'

'That's right.' Horn pulled out his wallet, peeled off a single, and laid it on the counter. 'I'm doing a job for his wife, Lillian, and Mr Roland is helping me. Did you talk to Mr Bruder much?'

'Yeah, sometimes. I showed him a screenplay I've been working on.'

'What did he say about it?'

'He said it was crap.'

'Oh.'

'But when he gave it back to me, it was covered with notes. And he sat here for . . . I don't know, about twenty minutes late one night, telling me why it was crap. So I've been rewriting it, and now I think it's better.'

'Lester, I need some help. I'd like you to try to remember anybody you ever saw here with Owen, anybody he spent time talking to.'

'Hmm.' Lester gathered up the used crockery and cutlery and deposited it in the sink. Then he picked up the change left by the two men without touching the dollar.

'He was here a few times with his wife. Sometimes for a late supper, or just coffee. I got the idea that they didn't like the dining room at the Garden. Too gloomy, they called it.'

'All right.' Horn laid another dollar on the counter.

'Mr Roland, of course. A lot of times.'

'Uh-huh.' Another dollar.

'One time, when his name had been in the paper, a guy sat down next to him at the counter and said he was a reporter and started asking him questions. Mr Bruder called the night manager over and said, "What kind of a dump is this, when a man can't eat in private?" or words like that. And the manager made the guy leave him alone.'

'Okay.' Another dollar.

'I think that's about it. He was kind of private, you know? Not joking around with anybody who happened to be here, like some people.'

'I know.'

'Oh, one time . . . I think it was a couple of weeks ago . . . I saw him standing over there by the cigar counter with a woman. They talked for quite a while. At first I wondered why they didn't take a seat over here, but sometimes you can tell when people want privacy.'

'Did you know the woman?'

'She looked familiar, so I guess she's been in here before. Don't know her name, though.'

'Can you describe her?'

'Nice-looking. Tall. Long brown hair – not worn fancy, just long. I don't remember what she was wearing, but I remember thinking she looked good in her clothes.'

'Could it have been a Sunday night?'

'Yeah, maybe. Yeah. It was.'

One last dollar joined the others. 'Thanks, Lester.'

He let the car take him home. His thoughts were on other things. He wondered if Grace Stilwell had been having an affair with Owen Bruder. If so, the implications were interesting. Horn had assumed that the wave of hate and suspicion washing over the country – this thing people were calling the Red Scare – had in some way brought about Bruder's death. But what if the answer were much simpler?

Love, he knew, could sometimes turn violent. There were memories from his marriage to Iris – memories of drinking, screaming, and worse – that still had the power to repel and sicken him. Horn hoped he would never be that man again, but he knew that life held few guarantees. Had Owen Bruder died for one of the oldest reasons of all – a love gone sour? To Woody Guthrie, something about Bruder's death didn't feel right. *People get killed over politics all the time*, he said. *But not like this.* What did he mean?

And since the subject of love and its destructiveness was on the table, his thoughts turned to the complicated, tormented Wally Roland. How much, he wondered, did Roland care for Lillian Bruder, and what might he have been driven to do about it?

Questions only, no answers. But Laura Lee Paisley would no doubt have opened the envelope by now, and Grace Stilwell would open her door to him tomorrow night. Maybe some of the answers were not far off.

He was in darkened Culebra Canyon now, away from the lights and the smells of the city. As his car followed the familiar thread of the canyon

179

road, he tuned the radio to a local news broadcast. Dry weather, said an announcer, combined with winds sweeping off the desert had spread the wild fires across the northern slopes of the San Gabriels. Some of the smaller blazes had merged into greater ones, and firefighting crews had been recruited from San Diego and San Bernardino to work around the clock. Three people were dead, lost when flames descended on their ragged community of shacks on a remote hillside. Although the fires had not yet crossed over the range into the San Fernando Valley, the alert was out to its northern residents.

Maggie and the Indian, Horn thought. They'd better—

The outer edge of his headlight beam fell on shiny metal. The car sat facing him about fifty feet ahead, parked just off the road beyond his turnoff. He thought of Mitchell Cross' wayward boys and touched the brake, ready to twist the wheel.

But the other car flashed its headlights. At least he's not looking to surprise me, Horn thought. He slowed and turned left onto the road that led toward his cabin, passing in front of the other car. He pulled up just short of the gate and got out.

The other man was out too, standing by his door. In the dim light from the car's interior, Horn made out the splash of white hair, like the blaze on a horse's forehead. It was George, the slow-talking man who did Laura Lee Paisley's bidding.

'Hello, George,' Horn called out. 'You're out late, aren't you?'

'Laura Lee wants to see you,' George said. 'She wants me to bring you.'

'Bring me where?'

'To a house. She said to say it's not far. Fifteen minutes.'

Horn walked over. 'A Chrysler limo. Nice car.'

'Yes,' George said. 'It's a Crown Imperial. Eight people can ride in it, but it's usually just Laura Lee in the back seat.'

'Somebody's been taking very good care of it,' Horn said.

'I polish it almost every day. She likes it to look good when we go to the studios.'

'Bet she does. I'd like to ride in it sometime. But I don't think I'll ride with you tonight, if it's all the same.'

'She said to bring you.' George's voice bore a childish insistence.

'I know. Tell you what: You show me the way, and I'll follow in my car. How's that?'

George hesitated. This was obviously not included in his instructions. But finally he said, 'All right.'

'One other thing,' Horn said, walking over to him. 'No offense, but I need to see if you're carrying anything. Would you mind raising your arms?'

When George didn't respond, Horn held up his own hands to demonstrate. 'Like this.'

George's eyes widened. 'You want to frisk me,' he said as the notion sank in. He seemed quietly delighted. 'Like in the movies.'

'That's right.'

25

He trailed the big car down the canyon road, and left onto Pacific Coast Highway. They drove until they reached Santa Monica, with the Palisades looming over them to the left and the black gulf of the ocean to the right. Just off the road on the ocean side was a row of beach houses crammed together. Although their owners had money, the places looked thrown together and temporary, done in wood and concrete and worked over by the beach sun and the salt air.

The Chrysler pulled over in front of a small place with a facade of worn redwood beams and glass blocks. A sagging fisherman's net was strung between two of the beams in an effort to lend a nautical air to the house. Horn parked behind George and followed him to the heavy wooden front door. George rang the bell and, without waiting for an answer, unlocked the door and let Horn precede him inside.

The building was narrow, modern, and clean, with high ceilings, more redwood, a dolphin carved out of driftwood over the fireplace, and low lighting. The furniture was mostly bamboo and rattan, the popular South Seas look. Much of the far wall was glass, with sliding glass doors open to let in the hiss and rush of the invisible ocean.

Laura Lee Paisley sat in a comfortable-looking chair, head down, apparently writing by the light of a table lamp. Without looking up, she said, 'George, why don't you fix yourself something to eat?'

George went into the small kitchen visible beyond a counter, opened the refrigerator and began rummaging around.

Horn approached her. The room smelled musty and vaguely sour, like any place near the ocean that had been shut up for a while. 'Nice place,' he said. 'Yours?'

'No,' she said without looking up. She was writing on a stationery pad. 'Darryl Zanuck's. He comes here whenever he wants to get away, maybe with a special friend. He lets me use it from time to time.'

'That's good of him,' Horn said. 'Is it because he likes you or because you've never had anything to say about him coming here with his special friends?'

She put the pad and pen aside and looked at him for the first time. 'You probably wonder why I told you that about Darryl. Some people could use that against him, but I'm not afraid of you, and I'm sure he's not either. You don't carry enough weight in this town for anyone to worry about you.'

He looked around the room. 'Why are we here?'

'Simple. A public place wouldn't be appropriate. I don't like having conversations in parked cars, and I wasn't about to—'

'Invite me over to your house, where I'd dirty up the rugs.'

'Exactly.' He knew the conversation was not going to be easy.

Her hair was done in elaborate curls the color of corn and she wore a shapeless caftan adorned with big tropical flowers. Her feet were tucked up underneath her legs. She might have been settling in for the night to read a Daphne du Maurier novel or listen to Guy Lombardo.

'You mind if I sit down?' he asked, settling himself a few feet away from her.

'You know what happens to blackmailers?' she asked.

He shrugged. 'Sometimes they get caught, and they go to jail. Sometimes they don't, and they walk away rich.'

She stared at him, the fierceness of her glare in comic contrast to her golden ringlets. She looked like a demented Mary Pickford. 'I know about you,' she said. 'Jailbird. Ex-con. Ex-actor, but small-time.'

'I suppose you've got a file on me.'

'Bet your ass. Sad-sack cowboy with horseshit on his boots. No steady job. No connections. You think I'm afraid of you?'

'No,' he said. 'I know you're not afraid of me. I've heard too much lately about people being afraid, and I don't want to get into that with you. I just want to do some business and be on my way.'

She appeared to have no ready answer to that, but continued glaring. 'First thing I need to know is how you got hold of this.' She indicated the envelope Horn had left for her that morning, which lay on the table, its contents alongside it.

'No dice.' He shook his head. 'You don't need to know anything about that. All you need to know is that when we make our deal, you get to keep this stuff.'

'Along with the copies. Rats like you always make copies, don't you?'

'Sure we do, rats like me. You get the copies.'

He walked over to the table and picked up the two stiff sheets of paper. He looked at the young brunette woman in the booking photos, shown full-face and in profile. She was in her twenties, and if you didn't mind the slight fleshiness of the features, she was very pretty, with large, expressive eyes and a shapely mouth.

He turned his attention to the second photocopied sheet, with the

183

booking information. 'You were Lily Rae Smallwood back then,' he said. 'This was your first arrest—'

'My only arrest,' she said in a harsh voice.

'Your first arrest,' he repeated, 'but it says here the St Louis PD had observed you for days, approaching men in the train station—'

'That's right.' Her laugh was more of a cackle. 'They called it solicitation. Hell. It was the Depression, I had a two-year-old kid, no husband, and no job, and I'd been in town for less than a week. I was hungry. My little girl was hungry. I was just looking for—'

George came out of the kitchen carrying a sandwich on a plate and a bottle of beer. He went into another room and closed the door. A moment later, Horn heard radio music.

Her eyes had followed George. Now she turned back to Horn, but it was a moment before she spoke.

'They called it solicitation,' she finally said. 'It was just plain begging, that's what it was. Anyone who's ever had a kid would understand. I started talking to one old guy, and he got the wrong idea. Next thing I knew . . .'

'It says you got a suspended sentence.'

'The judge had a soft heart, I guess.' Horn couldn't tell if she sounded grateful or sarcastic. 'They told me to get out of town. Hell, I was ready. The next day, some church lady staked me to a train ticket, and we were on our way to California. That's where I'd been meaning to go all along.'

'And you became Laura Lee Paisley.' He thought of Maggie bunking with other girls in a rented room, long before she became the queen of the serials. All those girls, he said to himself, must have come from someplace else, all must have had some kind of dream.

'And why the hell not?' she said loudly. 'Isn't that why everyone comes out here? Isn't that why you came?'

'What happened to your daughter?'

'Not that it's any of your business, but she's in finishing school back east. I've just been writing a letter to her. She's going to have it a lot easier than I did.' She gave him a knowing look. 'You've had a kid of your own, haven't you? A stepdaughter?'

So that's in the file too, he thought. *I shouldn't be surprised.*

'That's not what I'm here to talk about.'

'Oh, right. Let me guess. You want to see how much you can milk me for.'

'Something like that.'

'Suppose I tell you that you've wasted your time bringing me this. I didn't kill anybody, I didn't rob any bank. If this got in the papers, I think people would understand.'

Horn was ready. 'Maybe they would. But it would depend on how they got the news, don't you think?'

'What does that mean?' But her expression told him she had already guessed.

'Well, if the newspapers got it, it would be one thing. But what if I delivered it first to Hedda and Louella and the studios? Those two old gals would love to bring you down a notch or two, just for making them compete with you for gossip in this town. And the studios would make a meal out of you, for all the times you've thrown their dirty laundry out there for the world to see. By the time it was over, I don't think anybody would care about your hard times or your little girl or anything else. They'd be calling you Laura Lee Hooker. You'd be a joke. And how do you think your daughter would feel about that?'

Even though he'd rehearsed these words, he was surprised by their meanness when spoken aloud. Her face told him how hard they had struck her.

She cursed him then, quietly and efficiently and at some length. Horn, no slouch himself, was surprised at her creativity. In a contest with this woman, he concluded, Grace Stilwell would find herself heavily out-matched.

'Well,' she said finally. 'You want to play rough. That could be a mistake. I can get rough too.'

He wondered if she knew as much about him as Mitchell Cross did. Did it matter? He had been over this in his mind, and he had decided to push forward, no matter what.

She made a vague gesture toward the papers he was holding, and her heavy bracelet glittered in the light from the lamp. 'But what the hell. It's not worth my time to make an issue out of this. How much do you want for those?' Her voice was overly casual.

Horn pretended to think. 'Ten thousand dollars.'

'That's a lot for a small-timer like you,' she said. 'I'll bet if I offered you five thousand, you'd take it and run.'

'Actually, I wouldn't take the ten.'

'What?'

George came out of the other room carrying his plate and empty bottle. 'I finished my sandwich,' he said.

'Uh, that's fine,' she said distractedly. 'We'll be going soon.'

'I'll wait in the car,' he said.

When he had left, Horn asked, 'How long have you been married?'

Her composure slipped noticeably. 'George? How did you know?'

'The same way I know the other things about you,' he said, recalling his front-porch conversation with A. Dixon Vance.

'It doesn't matter,' she said quickly. 'George has always been in the background, but some people have known about him. What do you care?'

'I don't,' he said. 'I'm only interested in things I can use against you, the way you use information against other people. From what I hear, George isn't anything to be ashamed of.'

'Oh, spare me.' She plucked a cigarette out of a bowl next to the lamp and lit it with a table lighter. The smoke from her lungs clouded her words. 'Don't be so fucking polite to me.'

'All right. But I'm the curious type. How long have you been married?'

She sighed loudly. 'Is there some reason we're making idle chitchat?'

'I don't know. If you're polite to me, maybe I'll give you a break when it comes time to negotiate.'

Another angry stare. He was getting used to them. Finally she said, 'In thirty-five, not long after I came out here, I got a job as a secretary at a publicity firm where George was a messenger. We were both poor, but we both wanted to make something of ourselves. He liked my little girl. It was an easy decision. Later, when I found what I was good at, he didn't mind letting me be the main breadwinner.'

'And then the war came,' he prompted her.

'The war,' she repeated, and for the first time he saw something resembling sorrow cross her face.

'I hear he was a Ranger, one of the guys who took the cliffs at Normandy.'

She nodded. 'He was a hero. One of the bravest of the brave.'

'How did he happen to wind up—'

'George's unit lost so many men, he was transferred to the First Army, and he went into Germany with it. That was where it happened.'

He knew the outline of the story, but he waited for her to tell it.

'They reached a town called Torgau on the Elbe River, and there was the Russian army on the other side of the river. A historic moment, the two armies coming together there. Everybody was happy, and there was a lot of celebration, but when George was on his way back to his unit that night, he passed a group of Russian soldiers who were raping a German woman. He tried to stop them. They hit him with their rifle butts and crushed his skull. He came home . . . *different*. With a metal plate in his head. He's not George any more, but he is.'

'I'm sorry,' Horn said, and he meant it.

'Russians,' she said, the word injected with poison. 'They were our allies then, but I knew better. Animals. As people, they're scum. As a country, they're the same.'

'Does he hate them as much as you do?'

'He doesn't even remember them,' she said wonderingly. 'Little things

186

bother him, though. He doesn't like anyone to know about the metal plate, so I've told very few people. George seems to like you, though, so . . .'

She gripped the arms of the chair and sat up straighter. 'Don't you think we've talked long enough? Let's get to the point, and you can leave. What did you mean when you said you wouldn't take ten thousand?'

'I don't want money.'

'Then what do you want?'

'I want to know who killed Owen Bruder and why.'

'Oh, for God's sake. Is that what this is about? I don't know who killed him!' She fairly shouted it.

'Then tell me where you got the word that he was a Red.'

She twisted her mouth into something ugly. 'Mitchell Cross,' she muttered.

'I thought so. And where did he get it?'

'I don't know.'

'If this is all the help I'm going to get from you—'

'Look, I don't know. He's not going to tell me his sources. They're secret. Why the hell are you doing this, anyway?'

'I'm the curious type.'

'You're going to get yourself in trouble.'

'Blackmailers get in trouble too. You said so.'

'This is bigger.'

'Shut up and listen for a minute,' he said. 'You started this thing. I'm just following it through. You started it when you decided to pick on Owen Bruder, put him on your radio show and turn him into a target. I know you and Cross think you're on the side of the angels, but if you hadn't named Owen, he'd still be alive today. Think about that.'

He stopped, surprised to find he was breathing heavily. Something in his face had caused her almost to shrink from him.

'Help me out, or I'm leaving. And I'm taking those with me,' he said, glancing toward the papers on the table.

'Cross didn't tell me who his source was,' she said quietly. 'But I know Bruder wasn't the one he went after at first.'

'What does that mean?'

A sheen of sweat stood out in the light from the lamp, visible through the powder on her cheeks. 'At first he told me he was going to have something I could use. A few days went by, and then he called with the information about Owen Bruder, how he'd been named in secret by someone who talked to the Thomas committee. But I knew Bruder wasn't the person he'd called me about earlier.'

'How could you tell?'

'Because in the first phone call, he was talking about a woman. Without naming anyone, he used the word *she*. "She'll make a good story for you," he said.'

'She,' Horn said thoughtfully. 'Did he say anything else? Tell you where she worked?'

'No. There are a lot of women who write for the studios.'

But only one at Global, he thought. *Now I have an even better reason to see her tomorrow night.*

'This isn't enough,' he said. 'Not nearly.'

'I've told you what I know.'

'Do you think I'm kidding about this?' he said, raising his voice to her for the first time. 'As long as I sit here, you've got a chance to keep your secret. But if I walk out that door unhappy, I'm going to—'

'No need for any of that.' She appeared to be thinking about something. 'I could let you in on a few things,' she said with a weak smile.

'What are you talking about?'

'Things I have on people. Whoever gets their hands on certain information could make some money from it. I know you said you're not interested in money, but I'm talking about a lot.'

'Blackmail, right? The kind of thing you accused me of when I walked in here.'

'I call it using information as leverage, and I'm an expert. I've been collecting secrets on people for years. I know things. I've been very selective about what I've used, though, and not for selfish reasons.'

'Did I hear you right?'

'Not for selfish reasons,' she said forcefully. 'Only to expose people who deserved it. But here's my point: A lot of valuable material is still sitting in the files, secrets that, for one reason or another, I may never use. I could pull out some things for you, and you could set yourself up in business. Nobody would even know where you got it. We could help each other.'

'Hmm.' He pretended to consider it. 'Sounds pretty juicy. If I were interested, that is. But I want more.'

'What?'

'I want you to let me into all of your files, let me see whatever I want.'

She shook her head. 'Nobody looks through my files. They're my bread and butter. And if word ever got out—'

He leaned forward. 'Nobody will ever know,' he said. 'I won't take anything. I'll just spend some time there, that's all. And when I'm through,' he said, pointing to the items on the table, 'I'll leave the copies of those behind. And our deal will be done.'

She sat very still for almost a minute, with myriad emotions shifting over her face – hatred, defiance, indecision, despair. And, finally, defeat.

She nodded. 'You can just go in and look around,' she said. 'Don't try to double-cross me.'

'When can I do it?' he asked.

She exhaled heavily. 'Not right away,' she said. 'There's still too much activity at the hotel, packing up, coming and going. All the residents and guests are gone except for me. They're allowing me extra time to move. The last of the staff leaves in a couple of days, and the place will be deserted. That will be the best time.' She picked up the writing pad and pen.

'Why are you still there?'

'George,' she said, wincing slightly. 'He's not comfortable in new surroundings, and he's been terrified of the idea of moving. I've put it off as long as possible. But I've found a new place at the Roosevelt Hotel. My two secretaries have relocated there. Next we move the office, including the files.'

'You're making the right decision. About me, I mean.' He got up. 'I'll leave those things with you. Call me when I can come over. And make it soon. You already know I'm the curious type. I'm also very impatient.'

As he reached the door, she said in almost a conversational tone, 'I didn't know anything was going to happen to him.'

'I'll tell his widow,' he said. 'She'll be happy to hear.'

Outside he saw George sitting behind the wheel of the big Chrysler, and he walked over to him. George was smoking a cigarette and listening to Fibber McGee and Molly with a smile on his face. Horn could hear the audience laughing loudly at the jokes. George nodded to him.

'Do you remember Normandy?' Horn asked him.

'A little,' George said, nodding vigorously, as if he were asked the question every day.

'What, exactly?'

'Climbing, a lot of climbing,' he said. 'And noise, and screaming . . . I try sometimes, but that's about all I can remember.'

'Must have taken a lot of guts to do what you did.'

'That's what Laura Lee says. I don't know. Were you in the war?'

'No.' Horn started for his car. 'I'll be seeing you.'

26

When the telephone jarred him awake he saw it was barely first light, and knew that the call could mean nothing good.

'It's me.' Mad Crow's voice was hurried. 'Fire came down Las Cruces during the night, and it's spreading out in the Valley. Maggie can see it coming. I'm heading there now. Can you—'

He slammed down the phone, got dressed, and was firing up the Ford inside of a minute. Instead of unlocking the gate that would let him down onto the canyon road, he pulled out onto the rutted asphalt driveway and headed up the steep road that led to the ruined estate. By the usual circuitous route, Maggie's place was thirty miles away. Too far. But in the past year, forestry workers had cut a new access from the western ridge of Culebra Canyon, just north of the Aguilar place. It was gravel and dirt, barely graded, and not open to regular traffic, but it could shave ten miles off the distance.

Reaching the top, Horn found the road and floored the accelerator. Sending up plumes of dust, the Ford tore along, Horn gripping the wheel hard, working gas, brake, and clutch to get every ounce of speed possible without skidding off the road.

In twenty minutes he had crossed the dirt road that traced the east-west crest of the Santa Monicas and was speeding downhill with the Valley spread out below him. Almost ten miles to the north he could make out the flat, ugly brown cloud that showed where the fire had poured through the notch in the mountains.

He passed a crew of road workers who yelled furiously at him. Five minutes later the rough road gave way to paving, then a divided street as houses rose up on either side. The road bottomed out at Ventura Boulevard, and from then on it was due north toward the slab of brown covering the lower sky, past miles of stores and houses before the land opened up for farms and ranches.

Mad Crow, the gentleman rancher, kept only a few horses, for recreation and to remind himself of his time as a western actor. But for Maggie, her ranch was her livelihood. She had bought it even before she married Davey Peake, and built it into a good business, a place where an owner might stable his own horse or where weekend riders could rent horses by the hour or day. Movie studios had found the O Bar D a reliable place to lease horses for westerns. If Maggie lost her ranch, she lost everything.

The air grew thick, visibility lessened, sirens wailed in the distance. Horn coughed, rolled his window up. A mile this side of Maggie's place a lone cottage stood in a scorched yard, its roof beginning to burn as a dozen people tried to quench the flames with hoses and buckets. Up ahead he saw the O Bar D sign, and his stomach knotted. The stables were on fire.

He left the Ford next to Mad Crow's soot-covered Caddy just inside the gate and ran past the still-intact house. Davey Peake, holding his side in pain, was aiming a hose at the roof of the little structure, but the flow of water was little more than a leak. At the stables, Maggie waved him over. 'We're getting the horses out!'

Her two ranch hands, Luis and Miguel, both coughing, were wrestling one of the horses out the open doors. Inside, the big building boiled with clouds of smoke. For now, the fire was concentrated on the far side, and Horn could hear the burning eaves and roof shingles crackle under the flames.

Mad Crow, a bandanna around his face, emerged leading another horse. He followed Luis and Miguel over to the corral, where a half-dozen or so nervous animals were already penned and where the flames were not likely to follow.

'How many more?' Horn yelled to Maggie.

'Eighteen,' she said. 'They're all at this end, but it's moving fast.' She tossed him a twelve-foot length of rope and started into the building. He followed.

He found Doodle Bug, a docile mare, in a stall on the right. Making a quick loop in the rope, he tossed it over the horse's head and, without much difficulty, led it out and over to the corral.

Over and over, as the heat and smoke intensified, the five of them worked their way through the remaining horses. The animals were now whinnying in fear and kicking the sides of their stalls. With a few horses still left, visibility inside was now almost zero, and the rescuers had to do their work while trying to hold their breath.

Horn and Mad Crow found another horse so panicked that it would not be led out until Horn stripped off his shirt and used it as a blindfold for the animal. Once outside, he recognized the horse he was leading. It was Bonnie, a mare that had foaled months earlier. He bent over, struggling for air.

Maggie came back from the corral at a run. 'We don't have Sierra,' she

191

said. 'He's in one of the far stalls. We must have missed him.' She cursed loudly, eyes wide in desperation.

Sierra was Bonnie's colt, and Horn had been present at the birth. Maggie, in a whimsical touch, had named the newborn after his movie character.

'Which stall?' Horn asked her.

'Next to the end on the left. Oh, Lord.' Her voice sounded defeated. 'We can't get in there.'

Horn knew that if he gave himself time to think, he could freeze with fear. He dashed over to a horse trough full of murky water, dipped his shirt in it, wrapped the wet garment around his head so that only his eyes showed, and ran for the door.

Maggie's scream followed him through the smoke. Inside, his eyes instantly began to burn. Holding his breath, he felt his way along the stalls on his left, counting posts with his hand. The wood felt hot. Two stalls, three, then four. Heat from the burning roof seared the top of his head. At the fifth stall, he swung open the door. Inside was all blackness and the feel of straw underfoot. He was almost out of breath. He worked his way around the inner walls by feel and found the colt, silent but quivering, in the rear corner.

Horn dived down to the straw for the cleanest air he could find, sucked up a lungful, coughed and gagged, stood up, whipped the damp shirt off his head, and wrapped it clumsily over the colt's eyes. Then, holding his breath again, he gripped a handful of mane and led the frightened animal out of the stall and toward the door.

Finally he saw sunlight, then they were out. He fell to his knees, gasping and retching. He felt Maggie and Mad Crow grab him, lift him up. 'Damn fool,' Maggie said breathlessly. 'Damn fool.' He liked the way she said it.

'We better step back and let this building burn,' said Davey Peake, his face twisted in pain.

All of them dunked hands and faces in the horse trough to wash off most of the soot, then they retreated to the house thirty yards away. There, Miguel had relieved Maggie's husband of the hose and continued wetting down the roof with a pitiably small stream of water.

As the fire took over the rest of the stables, Horn asked, 'Why did you wait to get the horses out?'

Maggie shook her head ruefully. 'The wind died for a while, and the fire stopped about a mile away. To be safe, we carried some valuable things from the house out to the car, but all the time we thought the fire department would get here. Didn't know they'd headed over to a boys' camp a few miles away to get all the kids out first. Then the wind kicked up real fierce, and embers started landing on the roof of the stables, and it

192

caught. The tack room went first. All the saddles and gear and everything. Then the rest . . .'

'I'm sorry,' he said. He looked up at the smoke from the stables. Instead of being whipped around by the wind, as before, it billowed straight up. 'The wind's died again,' he said. 'Maybe your house will get lucky.'

For an hour they stood by, waiting. In the ensuing huge bonfire, the stables burned to the ground, pockets of sap in the flaming wood exploded from time to time, sounding almost as loud as gunfire, and the air stank of charred wood – but the wind did not resume. By mid-afternoon, the stables were reduced to blackened, smoking remnants, with only a stray flame here and there. For miles around the O Bar D, tiny flames were visible in the distance, but they were mostly grass fires and were burning at a slower pace. Finally a fire truck pulled up, and firemen rigged up a big hose to quell what was left of the stable fire.

'I don't know about you boys and girls,' Mad Crow said, looking around at his companions, 'but I need a drink.'

Leaving Luis and Miguel behind to stand fire watch, they rode to the Dust Bowl in Mad Crow's convertible, their faces still faintly streaked with soot. During the drive, Horn told the others about his talks with Wally Roland and Laura Lee Paisley and his plans to inspect the room of secrets at the Hollywood Alhambra.

Davey Peake looked interested. 'Let me know what you find on Errol Flynn,' he said, sitting in the back seat with his good arm around Maggie.

'Bet he's got a file an inch thick,' Maggie said.

'And eight inches long,' her husband said with a leer.

'You be quiet.'

'I don't think I'll have time to browse,' Horn said.

He was relieved that Peake seemed to have adjusted to the notion that he and Maggie were working on a serious job together, though he still had no love for the man.

At the Dust Bowl, they took a table and ordered drinks, and Mad Crow called Cissie Briar to let her know about the fire. 'She's coming over,' he announced to the others. Usually quiet during the day, the honky-tonk had been converted into an impromptu rest station, with firefighters and others constantly coming and going, stopping in for something cool before going back out to chase the latest flare-up. Rusty Baird was busy filling orders at the bar.

Maggie said to Horn, 'You've got enough to do in the next few days. Why don't you give me that New York phone number? I'll call it and see if I can find out how Owen knew them.'

He fished around in the pocket of the shirt he had hastily put on that morning and found the slip of paper, along with the notes he had taken from his talk with Douglas Greenleaf. 'I'd appreciate that,' he said.

They ordered another round, and after a while Cissie showed up.

'Sweet pea,' she said with concern, touching Mad Crow's cheek. 'Oh, my goodness, look at all of you.'

'It's all right, darlin',' Mad Crow said. 'We just look awful, that's all. Maggie lost her stables, but we're all alive, including the horses. Oh, and Davey here didn't do his busted ribs any good with all that activity. He's going to have the doc look at them.'

'Oh, no.' She made a sympathetic face at Peake, who was pale but who managed a grin.

'Well, the least I can do is buy all of you a drink.' Cissie took orders and headed for the bar.

'A woman who likes to buy drinks?' Peake said with mock astonishment. 'You better hang onto her.'

'Ain't she something?' Mad Crow said. 'Good looks and money, *and* she can drink me under the table. Too bad she comes loaded down with the wrong daddy.'

Horn got up and dropped a couple of nickels in the juke box. Soon Woody Guthrie's rough-edged voice filled the bar.

'That's my recent house guest,' Mad Crow said.

'Recent?' Horn asked.

'He pulled up stakes, moved in with his cousin and family for a while. Funny guy.'

'How so?'

'Oh, I don't know. I had him figured for lazy, because he spent so much time on my couch. Then I found out he's up all night writing in his notebooks – songs, letters, ideas for a book he's working on. Also found out he's managed to sing some of his songs at a couple of union rallies – one for fruit pickers up in Bakersfield, one for dockworkers down in Long Beach. Each time, he just asked to borrow my truck and drove off.' He cocked an ear, listening to the music. 'What's this one?'

'It's called "So Long, It's Been Good to Know You",' Horn said. 'It's about people who lost their homes and farms in the Dust Bowl. The original Dust Bowl. He told me somebody in New York's asked him to change the words and turn it into a love song.'

'Sounds like a dumb idea to me,' Peake said.

'Says he could use the money.'

Cissie returned with a shot of whiskey for Mad Crow and another pitcher of beer for the others. She wore a simple but smart dress with a large gold brooch pinned to one breast. Sitting with that bedraggled group, she stood out like a flamingo among crows.

The jukebox shifted gears and started up another song. At a nearby

194

table, a group of firemen, their faces blackened, stopped talking to listen to the words.

'This one is my favorite,' Maggie said, and began softly singing along: *'This land was made for you and me.'*

'Late one night,' Mad Crow said, 'when I was turning in and he was just getting up, he told me about this one. He said it's gotten watered down, and now you only hear the happy verses, but when he first wrote it, he was sick of songs like "God Bless America" that try to pretend there's no dirt and misery in this country. So he wrote an angry song, about looking around this country and seeing the bad as well as the good.'

Over at the bar, Rusty Baird and his bartender huddled near the radio, listening. After a while, Baird waved to Mad Crow and called out to him.

'I'll go see what he wants.' The Indian stood at the bar for a minute or two, listening to his friend. When Baird got back to work, Mad Crow spoke to the bartender and then returned to the table with a shot of whiskey in each hand. He sat down with a face that could have been carved from wood. The others waited.

'Heard a story,' he said before downing one of the shots. 'Seems big, bad Laura Lee Paisley just finished talking about somebody we know. Two people we know, as a matter of fact. The way she puts it, if you had any doubts that Cal Stoddard is a Russia-loving, America-hating son of a bitch, you should have seen him the other night, when he sat down with the notorious Woody Guthrie—'

'What?' Horn burst out.

'—and took lessons from him on how to deliver this country to the Russkies. Spreading lies, propaganda music, that kind of thing.'

'That's crazy.'

'You think so?' Mad Crow stared at Horn. 'Hell, Rusty just heard it on the radio. How many people you think won't believe it?' He downed the second shot and brought the glass down loudly on the table.

'How would she even know about the other night?' Maggie asked.

'Good question.' He looked around at the others, finally fixing his gaze on Cissie. 'How about you, Sugar? Any idea how she'd have found out what went on at my house?'

Cissie's eyes were on the table. When she spoke, her voice was steady. 'I told Daddy,' she said. 'I knew he would tell the story to other people, and I knew who the other people were.'

'Why?' Mad Crow's voice was soft, his right hand curled tightly around the shot glass.

'Because,' she said, her eyes meeting his, 'it was the right thing to do. Because I don't trust Cal Stoddard, and because I think Woody Guthrie is a dirty-minded little man.'

'They're my friends.'

'I kept you out of it,' she said, her voice rising. 'I made Daddy promise that nobody would mention your name. Or any of your names,' she added, looking at the others. 'Just those two.'

'You made a mistake,' Mad Crow said.

This is the old Mad Crow, Horn thought, the dangerous one. The one who, with a few drinks in him, could turn a room inside out, could turn into the wrath of God. Or the Devil. He kept his eyes on the hand that held the glass. Its knuckles were white.

'Oh, come on,' Cissie replied, regaining some of her spirit. 'Somebody had to. You don't want to be seen with people like that.' She put her hand on his arm. 'Daddy likes you, but he thinks you can do better for yourself. He can help set you up in the right kind of business, help you get to know the right people—'

'And help me drop the wrong kind of people.'

'Don't be so sarcastic. You know I'm right—'

The sound of breaking glass was like a pistol shot. Mad Crow dropped the fragments of the shot glass and stared at his right hand, from which blood was starting to seep and spot the table. Maggie and Cissie both sprang up, but it was Maggie to whom he held out the hand, letting her wrap a handkerchief around it.

'Well, then.' Mad Crow seemed to have reached a decision. He got up and stood behind Cissie's chair. 'Time you went home to Daddy, Sugar.'

She suddenly seemed to understand, and she looked so sad and stricken that Horn almost felt sorry for her. He wondered if Mad Crow, along with the two worthless ex-husbands, would someday become another of Roy Earl Briar's stories.

She allowed him to pull back her chair. With a tiny smile, she looked at him searchingly, said, 'Goodbye, Joseph,' and left.

Mad Crow sat down and looked at his hand. The handkerchief was fast turning crimson. 'Davey,' he said, 'you mind if I go along with you to see that doc?'

Before driving Peake to the doctor, Mad Crow dropped off Horn and Maggie at her place. 'I'm sorry about Cissie,' she said to Mad Crow.

'Maybe I've been spending too much time around paleface women,' Mad Crow said with forced geniality, holding his injured hand aloft to slow the bleeding. 'Maybe I should go looking for a raven-haired Indian maiden.'

'With a few oil wells,' Horn put in.

'There's a thought.' He gunned the Caddy. 'Hi-yo, Silver.'

'It's been a sad day all around,' Horn said to Maggie, looking at the smoldering stables, where Luis and Miguel were inspecting the ruins. 'Can I help out here?'

'No, thanks. We'll dig around a little to see if we can salvage anything. Then tomorrow we'll take stock and . . .' She seemed to lose the thought. 'Anyway, you've got work to do, starting with Grace Stilwell tonight. You never told me if she's pretty.'

'Why?'

'Just wondered.'

'Well, I'd be lying if I said she wasn't.'

'Then it shouldn't be hard work.' She snapped her fingers. 'I need to give Lillian a call. I was going to have lunch with her today, and she'll be wondering what happened to me.'

Horn said goodbye and headed for his car. He had barely pulled out of the gate when he heard Maggie yell and saw her in his rear-view mirror running out of the house. He put the car in reverse and backed up quickly. What could it be now?

She stumbled and almost fell, catching herself on the car door. Her mouth was agape, as if she'd been punched in the stomach.

'Maggie, what's wrong? Is it Lillian?'

She shook her head wonderingly and took a breath. She seemed to be weighing her words even as she spoke them.

'It's Wally.'

27

'I knew he was leaving for the airport early this morning, so I didn't expect to see him. I thought we'd talk later, when it was all over. Maybe he'd call from Washington, and . . .'

Lillian sat on her sofa, wearing a plain housecoat and slippers. Her graying hair fell about her shoulders, lank and unbrushed. She looked beaten down.

'But around nine I heard noises out on the grounds, voices,' she went on. 'I went out, and there were neighbors and the manager, and the same two policemen who talked to us the other night. And men in white jackets, carrying him away.' The faintest smile crossed her lips. 'It reminded me of the night Owen died. I know the police must have thought it was strange – two deaths at the same place, two men who were good friends. But they spoke to me for a minute, and they seemed convinced right away that this was not another murder.'

'How do they know?' Horn asked, anger in his voice. This was too much of a coincidence, and he did not trust the police to make the right judgment. 'How do they know?' he asked again, then regretted it, because Lillian seemed to shrink from his words.

'I think I know,' she said quietly.

'How?' Maggie asked. She sat next to Lillian, a protective arm around her. Maggie also looked worn out, Horn thought, but she had pulled herself together to come here.

'When I returned, I noticed that an envelope had been slipped partly under the doormat. It's addressed to me.' She swallowed. 'It's in Wally's handwriting.'

'Oh, Lillian. What did it say?'

'I haven't been able to open it. I just can't.' Her eyes were dull. 'Would you read it?'

Maggie looked at Horn, who nodded. 'Sure we will,' he said.

The envelope sat on an easel by the window, propped against a painting that was hidden by a piece of drop cloth. Horn wondered idly if that was the painting she had been working on and, if so, what it would turn out to be; he noticed, too, that the same unpacked boxes cluttered the living room. The world has killed off two people close to her, he reflected. Maybe it has decided not to go easy on her either, to sentence her to a kind of exile, never allowing her to settle in one place.

Lillian brought the envelope to the couch. 'You read it,' Horn said to Maggie.

She tore it open, separated the two sheets of paper. 'It's got a lot of words crossed out,' she said.

'Do the best you can.'

Hesitantly, she read:

My Dear Lillian,

Well, this is a fine mess I've gotten myself into, to paraphrase the immortal Oliver Hardy. In two days I'm expected to appear before a jury of my inferiors and abandon that thing I love most in life – writing down one word after another until they add up to something comic or tragic or simply entertaining. Up until tonight I believe I was prepared to face my accusers, throw their charges back into their faces, and walk out, head held high, to prison.

Now, I suddenly find I cannot. Without my work, I am nothing – just a pudgy, opinionated wordsmith who has let most of life's chances pass him by. Further, I am haunted by the thought that, once before the committee, I might be tempted by their offer of leniency into giving them the names of others. Sadly, I fear I am capable of that. And yet it would shame me beyond words.

No one needed to show me the instruments . . .

Maggie looked up. 'I wonder what that means.'

'I think I know,' Lillian said. 'Please go on.'

No one needed to show me the instruments. I know them already. On the one hand, the barrenness of a life without my work. On the other, the humiliation of being branded a coward. Both choices are unacceptable. My old friend Owen would have taken the first road and somehow found a life with you beyond the loss of his work. I wish I were capable of that.

So I take this third alternative. I pray I won't leave too much of a mess. As I write this, I can dimly see a small light across the grounds through the trees, and I comfort myself in thinking that it's your light. I wish things had worked out differently. I'm very tired.

I can discern some of . . .

Maggie's voice caught. Then she went on.

I can discern some of Owen's better qualities in Maggie, and I'm glad that he, in his rough way, managed to bring the two of you together.

Try to think well of me . . . Wally.

Lillian wiped her eyes. 'His maid found him. They said he took a sedative, filled the bathtub, got in, and cut his wrists. Damn it. It's such a waste. Why couldn't he . . .'

She stopped herself, and her face twisted into something ugly. 'No, I'm not going to blame him. All right, maybe he wasn't brave. Well, who can be, when half the world is lined up against you? No, I blame the others, the ones who pushed him into a corner.'

She got up. 'I feel helpless, and I hate the feeling,' she said. 'I'm going to make a big pot of coffee.' She looked at the note in Maggie's lap. 'I suppose the police are going to want to see that.'

'We'll take care of it with a phone call,' Horn said. 'And as for feeling helpless, maybe we can't handle all of that, but we can find out who killed Owen.'

'Can we?' she asked, making no attempt to hide the doubt in her voice.

'Yes,' he said, not altogether confident. 'I have a feeling we're getting close. I'm working on something tonight.'

'If you need to go, it's all right,' Maggie said. 'I'll stay with Lillian for a while. I can take care of calling the police. And one of the hands can pick me up later.'

'Thank you. I could use the company,' Lillian said. 'Oh, I just remembered – the wildfires. They're on the radio. Have they been getting close to you?'

'Close enough,' Maggie said, shooting Horn a warning glance. 'We're keeping an eye on things.'

At his cabin, Horn stripped off his odorous clothes and dropped them in a corner. He drew a bath, making the water as hot as he could stand, and scrubbed himself until he had erased the smells of sweat and smoke that clung to his skin. He shaved, then opened a can of beef stew and heated it on the stove, flavoring it with a splash of bourbon. He stood at the kitchen counter and ate his supper out of the pot. He liked to take his meals in a leisurely manner, but tonight he was in a hurry.

Dressed in clean clothes, he carefully locked up, and drove away. As he steered the Ford down the winding canyon road, his mind was busy with the questions he wanted to ask Grace Stilwell.

Were you and Owen lovers? An obvious question. *And why was it so urgent to meet him that night at Schwab's? And what did you talk about, standing over there by the cigars? Who is the man or woman with the initial W? And by the way, do you know who murdered Owen? Was it W?*

200

Or were you the one?

I'll go in, ask my questions, she'll give me the answers she's rehearsed, and I'll add up the score, he told himself. I'll either shake some answers loose from her, or I'll find out absolutely nothing. He wasn't particularly hopeful about the outcome.

Once in the Hollywood Hills, it took him a while to find her address, but that was no surprise. Throughout these hills, nothing ran in a straight line. Some streets were the length of a stone's throw; others ran for a mile or more, but like serpents twisting back on themselves, forming loops, hairpins, corkscrews. A good address for someone who likes privacy.

The days of the big estates up in these hills were over. Now, space was at a premium, and a good-sized front yard was a luxury. Some houses sat on reasonably level lots, others hung out into space, supported on timbers that looked perilously frail. All the stilt houses, Horn knew, had been built since the last big earthquake, the one off Long Beach in thirty-three. They wouldn't have survived that shaker, and they probably won't survive the next big one. Whenever it comes.

But who needs quakes when you've already got wildfires that can consume entire hillsides in the time it takes to unwrap a stick of gum? And don't forget the mudslides that always accompany the heavy rains of winter, slides that start by picking off your neighbor's house just up the hill and, gathering steam, pick up your house next and then pile both of you onto your downhill neighbor in one muddy heap of broken timbers, split shingles, and doll-house furniture.

As he digested that thought, he found her house. It sat on the downhill side of the street, behind a neat flowering hedge. The place was medium-size and one-story, with a gabled roof and a vaguely Swiss chalet look. He parked and went down the brick walkway to the front door. The house was dark, shades drawn.

He rang the bell once, twice, and got no answer. He knocked loudly; no response. He walked around to the back by way of another brick walkway that took him along a narrow passageway between house and garage. The garage door was closed but unlocked. He lifted it and saw a new Studebaker convertible inside.

The walkway led to steep steps, where the hill dropped off, and he saw that in the rear the house became a two-story, with the lower part not on stilts but clinging to the hillside. At the bottom he found a patio with wood furniture and a big striped umbrella. On the lower level of the house, French doors broke up a row of windows. As above, the shades were drawn and the interior dark. He knocked several times on a door pane, waited. Nothing.

Then he noticed that one of the windows was pushed fully up. He parted the curtain and called out, 'Hello.'

Going back to the door, he tried the knob and found it unlocked.

Something wasn't right. He pushed the door slowly open. 'Miss Stilwell?' he called out. 'It's John Ray Horn.' The house was silent. He let his eyes get used to the dark until he could make out bedroom furniture. He walked slowly and quietly on deep carpet through the room, found the wall switch and turned on the light, then went past other doorways to a bathroom and a smaller bedroom, turning on lights as he went. No one was there, and nothing seemed to be out of place.

A quick thought passed through his mind, an image of someone – not Grace Stilwell – waiting for him upstairs. Right about now, Sierra Lane would coolly unlimber the Peacemaker he wore strapped to his side and proceed fearlessly up the stairs. John Ray Horn, unarmed and not without fear, had to show more caution.

But he had come this far, and he wasn't about to give up now. Watchfully mounting the stairs, he turned on the next light switch and found himself in a hallway that branched off into various spaces – living room in the front, kitchen and dining area in the rear and, in between, a guest bathroom and a small study.

Turning on more lights, he inspected each room. Nobody was in the house. It was as if its owner had just stepped out to buy cigarettes and the evening paper and would be right back.

He gave the living room a quick going-over, then moved to the study, where Grace obviously spent more time. The room was a work space, with floor-to-ceiling shelves stocked with books and screenplays and a table with an upright Underwood and a stack of more bound screenplays. Judging by the sheet of paper in the typewriter and the pages beside it, she was working on something called 'The Fisherman's Daughter'.

Most of the books on the shelves, he saw, were plays. Shakespeare, Ibsen, Shaw, Miller. Some were in French. On a shelf at floor level behind a chair, he spotted two titles, *Das Kapital* and *Ten Days That Shook the World*. Horn had not read either, but he knew enough about them to think them odd reading for a woman who professed to have no politics.

He looked quickly through some of the screenplays on the table. They appeared to be shooting scripts for films that had been produced, all written by Grace Stilwell. Only one title was familiar, *Under One Roof*. He had seen it not long ago, when he had spent an afternoon with Iris, Clea, and one of Clea's friends from high school. The girls had wanted to see it, and he had taken them to a matinee in Westwood.

On the cover of the shooting script, someone had written a note in a bold hand:

To Grace – Thank you for putting those wonderful words in my mouth. I couldn't have said it better! With affection, Whitey.

Thumbing through the pages, he retraced the plot in his mind. It was a big, sprawling comedy about a group of misfits who shared a residential hotel in New York. Lots of colorful characters, fast one-liners, heart-tugging situations. And at the center was the hotel's manager, a kindly man with problems of his own who somehow was able to help out all the others . . . The actor, he remembered, had been widely praised for his performance.

Grover Jones, with the snow-white hair.

Whitey.

Could he have been the name behind the initial in Grace Stilwell's note to Owen Bruder? The reason for their urgent, late-night meeting?

I'm now sure it was W, the note had said. *I think I know why.*

Are you the one, Whitey? Horn asked silently. *If so, what did you do? And why?*

He looked quickly through the kitchen and dining room, then checked the upstairs closet, which held several pieces of luggage. One large space on the floor was clear, and some of the luggage looked as if it had been piled there carelessly.

Downstairs, the guest bedroom looked unused. In the main bedroom, the bed was mostly made, but the spread was missing. In some of the dresser drawers, small piles of clothes looked as if they had been moved around, disarranged.

The only thing he noted in the bathroom was an extra toothbrush. Since none of the closets appeared to hold any clothes not belonging to Grace Stilwell, he ruled out a roommate and guessed that the lady had an occasional visitor.

He started to leave the room, then remembered to check the bathtub. He pulled the shower curtain aside. Everything looked normal, except that a bottle of shampoo had been knocked into the tub and shattered, leaving shards of glass and a pool of thick green liquid around the drain.

He got down on one knee. There was more. A faint pink smudge on the bottom of the tub. He rubbed a finger over it, and it came off – waxy, lightly perfumed. Lipstick.

Still more. About a foot to the right of the smudge were two tiny, perfect pearls of clear liquid. Too viscous to be water. He touched them with a different fingertip and sniffed, then tasted. Something medicinal.

He knelt there, trying to absorb all this, then heard a sound. The front door opening. Heels walking lightly on the hardwood floor above. A woman's heels.

He went through the bedroom and started up the stairs, preparing himself for her angry response to his snooping. As he reached the top, he saw her in the living room, standing motionless. 'Hello,' he called out. 'For a while, I—'

Then he saw that it wasn't Grace Stilwell. And then he saw the gun in her hand, pointed at him. And then he saw the little spurt of flame and heard the shot.

28

His gut clenched as he grabbed the stair railing and ducked behind the corner of the entryway. For a second, he was ready to lunge down the stairs and find a way out the back. But then he heard sounds – frantic whimperings – from the living room. He peeked around the corner and saw the woman, her jaw agape in fear or consternation or both, fumbling with the mechanism of a small gun.

Now or never. He pushed off the railing and ran straight for her, collided with her, and drove her back into the front door. He wrenched the weapon from her with both his hands.

She yelped in pain, then stood there, emitting little gasps. Horn stepped back, took a deep breath, and saw that she was angular and well-dressed. The gun he held in his hand was an oddity – a two-barrel derringer, a modern version of a gun once considered a gambler's weapon, easy to conceal. It was no larger than his palm. After inspecting it for a moment, he figured out how to break it open and checked the two chambers, tapping a bullet into his open hand, followed by an empty shell.

He recognized the woman then. 'Why did you try to shoot me?'

Her face was pale. In her left hand she clutched a small purse, apparently the source of the pistol.

'I, ah . . . I didn't mean to,' she said, sounding out of breath. 'You startled me, coming up the stairs like that.'

'Like what? That's the way I always come up the stairs.' Now that the pounding of his heart was subsiding, he was getting angry. 'What are you doing here, anyway?'

'I could ask you the same thing. Where's Grace?'

'Lady, you're the one shooting off guns. Wait a minute.' He stepped into the hall and, after a brief search, found the spot where the slug had torn into the wood molding. Then he walked past her to the front door, opened it, and listened for a while.

'If anybody heard that, they might be calling the police right now. I kind of doubt it, because that popgun of yours doesn't make a lot of noise. But if they show up, we need to be ready to leave fast. I'd suggest the back way.'

'I asked you about Grace.'

'She's not here.'

'Why the hell should I believe you?'

Her voice was taut, on the edge of cracking. A gunshot was bad enough, he thought; a hysterical woman could complicate things even more.

'Don't believe me,' he said. 'Have a look around.' He stepped away from her.

After a moment's hesitation, she began looking through the house. She covered the main floor first, then the lower level. When she came back upstairs, she looked worried but somewhat more settled.

'Let's have a talk,' he said. 'Why don't we step in there?' He lightly took her arm and led her to the dining room, where he helped her into a chair. 'Drink?' He went to a sideboard and took the stopper out of a decanter, sniffing the contents.

'I believe that's scotch,' she said. 'And yes, I will.'

He poured both of them a drink and sat down. 'What's the wife of the top dog at Global Studios doing waving a gun around in somebody else's house?'

'So you know me,' Maris Felix said. 'I recognize you too, but I don't remember your name.'

'John Ray Horn,' he said. 'Last night at the theater wasn't the first time we've seen each other. Several days ago you saw me waiting outside your husband's office.'

'Why are you here?' she asked. 'Are you a friend of hers?'

'Me first,' he said. 'I'm the guy who got shot at, and I'm the guy now holding the gun. I get to ask the questions. What brings you here?'

He saw anger and defiance in her look. This was clearly a woman who was not used to taking orders. Then the look passed. She took a sip from her glass, and some of the color returned to her cheeks. 'I tried to call her,' she said simply. 'About half an hour ago. I couldn't get through, and the operator told me her phone's out of order—'

'Hold on.' Horn went out to the hall, where he found the telephone inside a wall niche. It was dead.

'I'd spoken to her earlier in the day, at the studio, and she told me something was bothering her. She wasn't specific, but I got the impression she felt someone was watching her, maybe even following her. When I couldn't get through to her tonight, I thought I'd better come over.'

'And brought the popgun.'

'I always carry it,' she said. 'My husband gave it to me for protection. Every now and then, when there are labor problems, someone makes a threat against the studio executives. Marvin said he hoped I'd never have to use it, but . . .' She shrugged. 'Until tonight, I never have.'

'Scared the hell out of me,' he said. 'But you should know it's not much of a weapon. Unless you hit somebody in the heart or face or private parts, a .22-caliber slug is probably not going to stop them from getting at you. You'll need to get in close before you pull the trigger.' He noted that she was wearing fine leather gloves. 'Also,' he said, 'if you took those off, it would be easier to get your finger inside the trigger guard. That's just in case you ever plan to do any more shooting.'

'I don't,' she said. 'Guns frighten me, and I hope I never fire it again as long as I live. But thank you for the advice.' The last was delivered with a touch of sarcasm, and he knew she was regaining her equilibrium.

He handed the tiny pistol back to her, minus the shells. 'You'll want to wrap that in something,' he said. 'Otherwise it's going to smell up your purse.'

She nodded, wrapping the gun inside a monogrammed handkerchief and putting it away. While in the purse, she fished out a silver cigarette case and slim silver lighter, both adorned with the same monogram, and went through the motions of lighting up.

He watched her. Her movements were small and precise, almost bird-like. First she manipulated the cigarette out of the case, making it look easy even with her gloves on. Then she snapped the case shut with a flourish and tapped the cigarette on its silver face, once, twice, three times. Then she flipped the cigarette into smoking position between second and third fingers, clicked a flame to life with the lighter, held it carefully to the tip, drew on the cigarette once to get it going, replaced case and lighter in her purse, then took a fresh drag, this one serious, filling her lungs. She exhaled a thin, audible stream of smoke just over his shoulder.

It was quite a show. Horn would rather watch a woman with a cigarette than a man any day. A man made it look like the only point was to get smoke into the lungs, but some women turned every step, every pre-paration, into a graceful ritual. Maris Felix was one of those.

'How did you get in the front door?' he asked her abruptly.

'I have a key. I told you, we're friends.'

'Does she have a key to your house?'

'You're starting to sound presumptuous now.'

'I'm not finished yet. I noticed a spare toothbrush in the bathroom downstairs. You know anything about it?'

'I think this is about enough.' She started to push her chair back.

'Don't you want to know what happened to her?'

She stopped. 'Of course I do.' He heard a tiny bit of emotion in her voice, enough to suggest that she might be telling the truth.

'Then stick around for a while. Please. Maybe we can come up with something.'

She sighed, settled back in her chair, and stared hard at him. 'I think it's my turn for some questions,' she said. 'Why did you come here tonight? Are you a friend of hers?'

He took their glasses to the sideboard for refills and returned. It gave him a few seconds to think. If Maris Felix was on the up-and-up, he needed to level with her. If, on the other hand, she was one of the shadowy figures behind what was going on, then chances were good she already had an idea of what he was up to. Either way, he could see no reason not to talk to her. But he couldn't forget that, as the wife of one of the most powerful men in Hollywood, she would be no stranger to intrigue. He decided to tell her just enough.

'She invited me over. I had some questions for her. Whatever happened here, I didn't have anything to do with it.'

'And what happened?'

'That's what I'm trying to decide.'

'What kind of questions did you have for her?'

'You know who Owen Bruder was,' he said.

'Of course.'

'I'm working for Lillian, his widow, to try to find out who killed him. As I looked around, Grace Stilwell's name came up, and I wanted to ask her if she knew anything that could help me.'

'Such as?'

'Well, for starters, I think she and Owen may have been involved—'

'That's ridiculous.' She bit off the words.

'Maybe so, but I had to ask.'

'Ridiculous,' she repeated. 'I know Grace, and I'd know if that were true.'

'You want to tell me how you'd know?'

She didn't answer, just gave him a level, emotionless stare. *Maybe we can get back to that one later*, he thought.

'And then there's Grover Jones,' he went on.

'Don't tell me he was involved with her too,' she said. 'This is getting more and more outlandish.'

'No, I don't think he was,' Horn said. 'But I think he may be one of those who know something about Owen. The connections are all pretty feeble at this point, but they all happen to involve people at your husband's studio. Even poor Wally Roland. I'm sure you know what happened to him.'

She nodded.

'Little bit of a coincidence, don't you think, that Owen Bruder and

Wally Roland both get tossed out by your husband and both wind up dead?'

Her eyes narrowed. 'I knew them both. It's tragic that they're dead. I hope you're not trying to joke about it.'

'It wasn't supposed to sound like a joke, but that's what brought me here tonight. I was hoping your friend Grace could give me something I could hang my hat on. Instead . . .' He gestured vaguely.

'Do you have any idea where Grace is?' she asked. 'Or what happened to her?'

'I do have an idea I've been putting together,' he said. 'It's not pretty. I think somebody cut her phone line, broke in through a downstairs window, and grabbed her. They wound up in the bathroom, where something got broken. I think they bent her over the side of the tub and shot her up with something. Then they wrapped her in a bedspread, took her out the back door, and drove off with her.'

Through his description, her expression froze into something grave and unreadable. Her cigarette burned untended in the ashtray.

'Was it because she was going to talk to me? I don't know,' he said. 'Is she alive somewhere? I think so. From the looks of things, they packed up some of her clothes to take with them.'

Maris Felix shook her head, as if to clear it. She looked as if she'd awakened from an ugly dream. 'I have to go,' she said.

'Is there anything you can tell me that might help?' he asked urgently.

'I have to go,' she repeated. 'I have to think.'

'Somebody should call the police about this,' he said. 'Why don't you—'

'I'm not sure that's a good idea.' .

'Why not?' When she didn't answer, a thought struck him. 'Why didn't you call the police when you couldn't get through on the phone?' Still no answer. 'Is it because you think you know who's behind this?'

She got up. 'I'm leaving,' she said, tucking her purse under her arm. 'Don't try to stop me.'

'I've had all the rough stuff I can handle for one evening,' he said. As she went out the door, he called after her, 'If you decide there's anything you want to tell me, I'm in the phone book. Or try the Mad Crow Casino.' A minute later, he heard a car engine start up.

After washing and drying the whiskey glasses, he methodically went through the house, wiping down any surfaces he might have touched, then left the way he had come.

Coming down out of the hills, he decided to stop at a familiar bar on Vine, just off Hollywood Boulevard. It was another of those places that try to look English, with brass-studded leather chairs and a portrait of the king and some pretty decent ales and stouts. He and Mad Crow had seen David Niven and Basil Rathbone in there once. Sitting at the bar, nursing a bourbon and water, he thought about Grace Stilwell and Maris Felix and Wally Roland and all the others. The bartender was fiddling with the radio. It had been pulling in a live dance band broadcast from the Allerton Hotel in Chicago, but then static began competing with the music, and he twirled the dial, looking for a clear signal. He paused on one station for a few seconds, and voices came over the air.

'Just answer the question.'

'Congressman, I'm trying to tell you—'

'You're not answering the question.'

'Sir, I'm doing my best.'

Then the bartender twisted the dial again, resuming his search. 'Hey, friend,' Horn said, 'would you mind going back to that last one for a minute?'

The voices resumed, and Horn knew one of them. He guessed that the first – aggressive, pugnacious – was that of J. Parnell Thomas; the other – softer, almost diffident – was Cal Stoddard's.

'Let me go back to this date, August 12th, 1933,' the congressman began again. 'In Bakersfield, California. You have stated that you performed at a rally for farm workers on that date. Is that correct?'

'Yes, sir.'

'And the rally was sponsored by the so-called Farm Workers Alliance. Is that correct?'

'I think so,' Stoddard replied. 'Me and my band, we were just there to play.'

'Well, we have it in our files,' the congressman said in a professorial tone. 'And the Farm Workers Alliance is a well-known front for the American Communist Party. Did you know that?'

'No, sir.'

'You sound almost too innocent to me, Mr Stoddard. But let's proceed. After your performance, a member of the FWA spoke and then circulated a sign-up sheet for those interested in joining the American Communist Party. Do you recall signing that sheet?'

'Yes, sir, I do.'

Horn knew what was coming. He felt angry and depressed over Cal Stoddard's predicament, and he didn't want to hear the man abase himself before his questioners. But he knew that Stoddard had little choice if he wanted to keep working.

'You did, in fact, sign the sheet. And you joined the American Communist Party.'

'Yes, sir. I knew some of the boys who'd already joined, and they told me it was a good organization, and it was looking out for—'

'Never mind that. And you never resigned your membership in the party.'

'Well, I never went to any meetings either.' Subdued laughter in the background. It sounded like a large and restless crowd.

'Just answer the question.'

'Yes, sir. I never paid any attention to my membership after that. They tried to get me to come to meetings; I was just too busy. But no, I never did resign.'

'And do you recall the others who signed up for membership that day? Is it not true that all the members of your band signed, individuals who later went on to work with you in motion pictures?'

'I believe so, yes, sir.'

'Please give us their names now.'

Here it comes, Horn thought. A long silence followed, punctuated by the stirrings and murmurings of the crowd. Finally he heard Stoddard's soft reply.

'I don't think I can do that.'

'Repeat that, please.'

'I said I don't think I can do that.'

The murmurings grew louder. Horn leaned forward to hear. 'You will provide the names.' The chairman's voice was harsh. Horn could almost see Thomas' face begin to redden. Something tells me this is not the way the rehearsal went, he thought.

'No, sir. I mean I could, but . . .' Stoddard's voice seemed to be finding its footing. 'Look, Mr Chairman, I can read the newspaper as good as anybody, and it seems to me that the Russians are not exactly our friends today. But they were our friends just a few years ago. Back when I signed that sheet of paper, nobody told me that one day they'd be lined up against us. And I really believed the party was out to help people, and that's why I joined. If I had a chance to go back to that day in Bakersfield, maybe I'd handle things differently, knowing what I know now.'

'Is the witness going to respond to the question?'

'I'm trying. If you want to hold me responsible for what I did, then I reckon I'll take what's coming to me. But you want me to turn in my friends, I can't do that. If they want to name themselves, that's fine. But I won't name them.'

The murmurings swelled into sounds of surprise, even outrage. The crack of the chairman's gavel sounded sharp over the air. 'Order,' he barked. 'You refuse to provide the names?'

'Mr Chairman, I know what's waiting for me back home if I don't answer your questions.' Stoddard's voice rang out. 'But I've also got a wife and two little girls waiting for me, and—'

The gavel cracked over and over. 'The witness is excused,' Thomas said loudly.

'And I don't know how I can look them in the eye if I—'

A continuous banging now. 'The witness will step away. The witness will step away.' Thomas was shouting, the noise of the crowd sounded like radio static, and Stoddard's voice was lost.

A moment later, an announcer cut in. 'You have been listening to today's hearings of the House Un-American Activities Committee in Washington, transcribed from an earlier live broadcast. We now pause for station identification.'

'You mind if I get some music now?' the bartender asked.

'No,' Horn said. 'Thanks.'

Cal Stoddard, you son of a bitch, he said silently, admiringly. *Say goodbye to the movie business.*

He wondered if Mad Crow had heard the broadcast. The bar had a phone booth, and he shut himself in it to call the Indian. He dialed the casino and spoke to Lula, Mad Crow's assistant.

'He left about an hour ago,' she said. 'He got a call from the police.'

'What about?'

'I don't know,' she said. 'I picked up the phone, and that's who they said they were. Then he talked to them and ran out without saying anything.'

Horn dialed Mad Crow's home number, and Nee Nee came on the line. Horn groaned. She answered the phone only when her nephew wasn't there, and talking to her was always a challenge. To further complicate things, she sounded under great stress. Horn questioned her as patiently as he could, but the only words he could understand were *police* and *Maggie.*

Maggie. Had the fire come back? He doubted it. Scattered fires still burned the other side of the San Gabriels, but those in the San Fernando Valley had been quelled. If not fire, then what?

Finding another nickel, he dialed Maggie's number, but it rang endlessly.

He had to know, and he didn't pause to consider whether it made sense to drive all the way out there to find out. Back in the car, he took the Cahuenga Parkway over into the Valley, and twenty minutes' fast driving brought him to Maggie's place. It was close to eleven when he pulled through the gates of the O Bar D. The porch light was on, the little house still stood, and the stables still reeked of charred wood.

He walked towards the small porch, but even before he reached it he knew no one was there. Something had blown a jagged hole in one of the front windows, and splinters of wood and glass littered the floor planks. And there was more – dark patches of crimson, spotted and smeared over some of the planks on the porch and on one of the supporting posts: blood, barely dried.

He felt sick. The front door was unlocked, and he went in, turning on the light in the small living room. Some furniture was disarranged, and there was more blood on the floor.

Looking around as if for guidance, his eyes lit on the phone by the sofa. Then it hit him: Call the police, you idiot. He got the operator to ring the number of the nearest Valley station. He spoke to a desk sergeant, then a detective. After a few minutes that seemed like an eternity, he had what he needed to know, and he was back in the car. Fifteen minutes later he walked in the door of a hospital in Van Nuys. He asked directions, found his way to the second floor, and spotted Mad Crow sitting in the corridor. The Indian got up.

'She's alive,' he said. 'Davey's dead.'

29

M ad Crow led him down the hall to a long room that held about a dozen beds separated by cloth partitions.

'Before we go in, let me tell you,' Mad Crow said, putting a hand on his arm. 'They just moved her up here from emergency. Her left arm's broken in about three places, along with her collarbone. She also took a bad hit on the head. It tore the scalp open, and she bled a lot before they got to her. They took over a dozen stitches. Just want you to know she looks bad, but they tell me she's going to be all right.'

'Who did it?'

'We don't know. Yet.'

'I want to see her.'

They went in, and Mad Crow took him to Maggie's bed. Her head, left arm, and most of her left side were swathed in muslin bandages. What he could see of her face appeared undamaged except for some bruises. Her eyes fluttered, then focused on the two of them.

'Hey, there,' she said.

'Maggie.' Horn bent over her. 'Maggie.'

'They told me Davey's dead.' Her voice was little more than a whisper. She winced as she spoke.

'Don't talk if it hurts to,' he said.

'Hurts like the dickens,' she said. Then: 'Davey's dead.'

'I'm so sorry, Maggie.'

'He's the reason I'm alive.' A tear formed in a corner of one eye and rested there.

Horn could think of nothing to say. He felt a rage building in him. He knew he must control it or it would take him over.

A doctor materialized at the bedside. 'You two shouldn't be here,' he said.

'Just another minute,' Horn said.

'I need to give her a shot,' the doctor said. 'I'd appreciate it if you'd step outside.'

'No,' Maggie almost shouted. Her face twisted with the effort of speaking. 'Not yet.'

'It's for the pain,' the doctor said patiently.

'I've had broken bones before,' she said. 'I don't want to go to sleep yet. I need to talk to them first. Come back later.' She coughed, and her face twisted again. 'Please.'

The doctor looked at the two men with hostility. 'Five minutes,' he said, and left.

They stood close by her bedside, leaning over to hear every painful word, asking occasional questions. In bits and pieces, her story took shape.

After an exhausting day spent digging through the wreckage of their stables, caring for the horses, and confirming that the fires had receded from their corner of the Valley, Maggie and her husband had cleaned up, eaten supper, and settled into chairs on their front porch, almost ready for bed. The air was smoky and pungent, but every now and then a light breeze would clear the sky to reveal a bright display of stars overhead. They turned off the living room light to give them a better view.

Then they heard a loud sound from the stables, behind the house, as if some of the burned timbers were settling. Davey said he would have a look. Maggie remained there, feeling drowsy. The last thing she remembered clearly was tilting her head back to get a better look at the Big Dipper.

After that, she said, everything was a jumble.

A footfall to her left as someone climbed over the side railing to get on the porch. The sight of a figure bearing down on her, arm raised. She managed to shout Davey's name once, threw up her left arm, felt a crushing blow that shattered the bone above her elbow. Then another blow on the same arm, breaking bone again and throwing her off her chair. She screamed as another blow fell, this one on her chest. She couldn't breathe. The figure swung again, at her head this time, but misjudged, and the blow raked along her skull. At this point everything went black.

Out of breath, she interrupted her story and asked for a drink of water. Horn fetched some for her in a paper cup. Then she went on.

Later – it must have been only seconds – she heard Davey's voice, screaming at her to get inside, to get the shotgun. She opened her eyes and dimly saw two figures grappling out on the grass.

Half-blinded by the blood in her eyes, she got to her feet and staggered inside, where Davey's 30-30 hunting rifle and double-barreled 12-gauge shotgun hung over the fireplace. Even in the dark, she found it. The shotgun, she knew, was always loaded, just in case. Her left arm was useless, but she managed to wrestle the big gun off the wall with her right.

As she cradled it under her arm, trying to cock one of the hammers, she heard a gunshot outside, followed by a loud groan. Davey's voice. Then another shot. Then footsteps on the porch, and an indistinct figure approaching the doorway.

No time. She managed to cock the hammer on the right, swing the barrel up, and pull the trigger. The mule-like kick threw her aim off, and the deafening blast took out most of the window just to the left of the door. But it was enough. The figure was gone.

And Davey, out on the grass, was dying.

As she finished the story, Maggie's head sagged back onto her pillow, her face shiny with sweat. 'I didn't even see his face,' she said bitterly, as if that was the worst of all. 'I missed him with the 12-gauge, and I didn't even see him.'

'We'll see him when we catch up with him,' Horn said.

'Davey's got family in Houston. His parents and—'

'We know. We'll take care of all that. Right now you just rest.'

The doctor returned. 'Time's up,' he said brusquely.

Out in the hallway, Mad Crow looked closely at his friend. 'Are you all right?'

'Why are you asking me that?'

'Because you've got the look of a man who's ready to put his fist through a window. Or maybe a door.'

'Maybe I am.'

'Well, don't go off half-cocked, that's all I'm saying.'

Horn looked at him. Mad Crow's worried expression did not fit with his clothes. He was in his casino regalia, a chocolate-brown suit with amber piping on the lapels, a white silk shirt and a bolo tie with a hammered silver clasp. During Mad Crow's hard-drinking days, Horn had hauled his friend out of many an ugly scene. Now, it seemed that they had reversed the roles. Mad Crow knew that Maggie's brush with death had pushed Horn close to some kind of edge.

'Don't worry. If I had somebody to go after right now, I would. Believe me. But I don't.' He leaned against the wall next to a cigarette receptacle filled with sand. 'Can I have one of your Luckies?'

'Sure.'

They lit up. 'How did you hear?' Horn asked.

'Hmm? Oh, when they brought her in, she gave the police two names. Yours and mine. They said they tried to reach you.'

'I wasn't home.'

'There was a cop here, name of Pitt. Says he knows you. He heard about what happened and recognized Maggie's name and decided he'd see if there was any connection to her daddy.'

'Good for him. At least he's using his head. Did you tell him anything?'

216

'I told him there sure as hell was a connection, and he looked like he just might agree.'

Horn flicked ashes in the general direction of the sand. He was thinking hard. 'This is the same guy. Has to be. He caved in Owen Bruder's skull with something, and he went after Maggie the same way. But when he tangled with Davey—'

'He pulled out a gun. What does that tell you?'

'I don't know. Maybe he likes to beat people to death, and he just carries a sidearm for insurance, in case he needs it.'

'Maybe he's crazy.'

Horn nodded.

'Maybe we'll work him over with an ax handle when we catch him,' Mad Crow said reflectively. 'You ever hit anybody with a stick?'

'No, I don't think so.'

'It's kind of satisfying.'

'I'll take your word for it.' He studied the lit end of his cigarette. 'She told me she wanted to work on this with me. I didn't know anybody would come after her.'

'It's not your fault.'

'He might try again. One of us should be here.'

'I been thinking the same thing,' Mad Crow said. He looked at his watch. 'It's almost midnight. Why don't I stay here tonight? You can get some sleep and come by in the morning. Even better, why don't you sleep at my place? It's a lot closer.'

'Thanks, Indian.'

He drove to Mad Crow's house, where he did his best to calm Nee Nee and informed her, through words and gestures, that he would spend the night there and that her nephew would stay at the hospital. *I'll leave it to Joseph to break the worst of the news to her*, he thought. It took a great effort to remain awake while she put fresh sheets on the guest room bed. As soon as the bed was made, he pulled the covers up over himself and was soon asleep.

He did not rest easily. His sleeping brain took him into Grace Stilwell's house, where a faceless individual stalked him through dark rooms. Gradually the rooms shifted their shape and became the house by the ocean where he had met Laura Lee Paisley. And the faceless individual began to take on many faces, one after the other, like someone trying on and discarding so many Halloween masks.

As he stumbled from room to room in his dream, looking fearfully over his shoulder, he saw George, with his impassive gaze and white shock of hair, coming steadily after him. Then the patch of white bloomed over the entire head, and George had become Grover Jones, wearing a fierce look

217

Horn had never seen. Then Grover grinned and became Sidney Swain, who was reaching out to grab his arm. As Horn shook off the man's grip, the face became that of Marvin Felix, saying, 'Why are you talking to my wife?'

And then, from a bathroom somewhere, he heard a scream, first in Grace Stilwell's voice and then, excruciatingly, in Maggie's. The sound tore through his head and awakened him.

It was a long time before he got back to sleep.

In the morning, he borrowed Mad Crow's razor for a shave, and Nee Nee fixed him a good breakfast of bacon, eggs, and fried potatoes. Before leaving for the hospital, he reminded himself to make a couple of phone calls. First he called the Roosevelt Hotel and asked the switchboard to connect him with Laura Lee Paisley's office. One of her secretaries answered the phone.

'This is John Ray Horn,' he said. 'I left my home phone number with Miss Paisley—'

'Sir, she's not here,' the young woman interrupted, sounding frazzled.

'I know you're moving, and everybody's busy,' he said. 'But I have a new number to leave for her, in case she can't reach me at the first. It's very important, because she's going to be calling me soon.'

'Who are you with?'

'Nobody. Would you take this down?'

'All right,' she said brusquely. 'What is it?'

He recited Mad Crow's number, repeated his own name, and asked her to repeat everything. She did so grudgingly, and he hung up.

Next he went to Nee Nee and tried to get some information out of her. After several tries, her face brightened, and she showed him a pad of paper by the telephone where Mad Crow had written some names and numbers, including the one he wanted. He dialed the number of Guthrie's cousin in Glendale, and when a woman answered, he asked for Woody.

'He's not here,' she said. 'He and my husband have gone down to Mexico, to visit the radio station where they used to play.'

'Any idea when he's coming back?'

'You know him very well?'

'Not very well.'

'If you did, you wouldn't ask that question.'

'Yes, ma'am. Well, when he comes back, I'd appreciate it if you'd ask him to give me a call.' He left his number and Mad Crow's.

He drove to the hospital, where he found a groggy Mad Crow keeping his vigil by Maggie's bed. Maggie was awake but silent and preoccupied.

He and Mad Crow spoke briefly about their plans, and the Indian left. Soon a nurse came for Maggie and wheeled her to a nearby room, where doctors worked to immobilize her broken bones. When they brought her back, her upper torso was encased in plaster. Another cast immobilized her upper left arm, which was held away from her side by a strut. Her face was haggard. Her head was no longer wrapped in bandages but had a large oblong patch applied to the scalp on the upper left side. And most of her hair was gone.

'I had them chop it off,' she said angrily. 'I figured if they were going to shave it off on this side, might as well even it up. I'll wear it short and start over.'

'On you it looks good.'

'Shut up.'

'How are you feeling?'

'How do you think? Let's get out of here.'

Horn helped her check out and eased her into his car. She held a bottle of pills. 'They gave me this for the pain,' she said. 'I think it's just a big fat aspirin. At least I'm not doped up any more.'

'Joseph said he'd call Davey's folks as soon as he got home,' he said. 'He's probably done it by now.'

'Good. Some of them may want to come out from Houston.' She sighed. 'If only I'd seen his face . . .'

'Don't think about it, Maggie.'

'I just want to sleep now,' she said. 'For a long time.'

'That's what you should do. Joseph and I talked about it, and he wants you to come stay with him for a while. If you don't mind, I'll take you there right now. Later I can pick up some things from your place.'

She didn't respond, and they drove a mile or so in silence. Then she said, 'Do you know how we met?'

He knew who she meant. 'No,' he said. 'How?'

'I went to the Coliseum Rodeo with some friends. We were sitting down close, and I saw this good-looking young man in the chute, getting ready to come out. And he looked over at me, bold as you please, and said, "If you'll give me something, I'll ride this one for you." So I untied my bandanna and handed it to him, and he wrapped it around his upper arm and took off. Well, you should have seen that man ride. You know how I am about a guy who looks good on a horse. When I saw him out there wearing my bandanna . . . Anyway, that's how Davey and I started out.'

'You and your young stud.'

'One night we went out for a drive over in Griffith Park, and he parked the car and said, "You want to take a chance on a cowboy? I'm not the steadiest old boy who ever lived, but I sure do love you." And that's when I knew I was getting married.'

'That sounds like Davey, all right.'

'Maybe he wasn't the most dependable husband around, but he was my Davey.'

219

'I know.'

'I'm tired. I just want to sleep.'

When they reached the house, Mad Crow was asleep in his room. Nee Nee greeted Maggie with hand-wringing and contorted expressions of sympathy, and soon had her installed in the bed Horn had left just a few hours before.

'I want to tell you something I just remembered,' Maggie said to him.

'You sure it can't wait?'

'Just listen. I called that number in New York yesterday. Mrs – uh – Ray Santini. Turns out she was Robert Nimm's sister. His only living relative. Owen had called her about a year ago, said he'd known Robert. They were friends, he said. Told her how sorry he was about Robert's death, and said he'd just found out about some kind of union insurance policy Robert had. With a death benefit.'

She shifted uncomfortably in the bed, then continued. 'He didn't give her any details, just said she'd be getting some money. A week later, a cashier's check showed up in her mailbox. A thousand dollars, drawn from a California bank and signed by Owen.'

They looked at each other for a minute. 'I guess there's nothing more we need to know about that, is there?' he said finally.

'No.' She closed her eyes. 'I'm going to sleep for a while now.'

He drove over to her place. Luis and Miguel, both grim-faced, had been contacted by the police and knew in general terms what had happened. They told Horn they would continue to look after the horses and property until they heard from Maggie. He loaded up the car with some of her clothes and other things he thought she might need. The police had apparently taken the 12-gauge. He lifted the hunting rifle off the wall pegs and put it in the car, along with a .38-caliber revolver he found in the bedroom and ammunition for both.

When he returned to Mad Crow's place, his friend had gotten up and was in robe and slippers, having coffee in the living room. 'I'm going to let Lula run things at the casino for a few days,' he said. 'While I was squiring the fair Cissie around, I learned that they could get along without me if they had to. I don't have to be there all the time. Somebody should keep an eye on Maggie, and maybe you and me—'

'That's fine,' Horn said. 'I'll bunk here, and we'll split things up.'

'You mind taking the couch?'

'If it's good enough for hard-travelin' Woody Guthrie, it's good enough for me.'

'Okay. And if we need more help watching the place, I'll ask Billy to come over. I don't think he'd mind a little guard duty.'

Billy Looks Ahead, seven years off the reservation, was Mad Crow's most formidable nephew and one of his mainstays at the casino. He had fought with the Marines in the Pacific. Horn had vivid memories of a terror-filled night among the ruins of the Aguilar estate, when men with guns had come for him and Clea, and Billy showed that he had forgotten none of the deadly lessons he learned during the war.

'Fine. It'll be like Fort Apache, with the good guys holding off the Indians.'

'I would have made that movie differently,' Mad Crow said.

Horn found Maggie sitting up in bed, sipping a cup of tea Nee Nee had brewed for her. She looked irritable. 'How are you feeling?' he asked her.

'Oh, just fine, except for a few broken bones and the worst headache God ever gave man or woman.'

He went to the bathroom, wet down a washcloth, and applied it to her forehead. 'Better?'

'Hmm.'

'Can we talk a little?'

'Sure. I'm not going anywhere.'

Not wanting to tire her out, keeping it as brief as possible, he told her what he'd found out in the past few days – his talks with Laura Lee Paisley and Maris Felix, the disappearance of Grace Stilwell.

'We've got to find her,' she said. Then, looking down at the heavy casts encasing her, she corrected herself. 'You've got to find her, John Ray. She's smack dab in the middle of this.'

'I know.'

'And Grover . . . He's the one in the note, isn't he?'

'Well, we don't have any proof. It's just the initial *W*.'

'Sure. It could be Woodrow Wilson. Or Woody Woodpecker. To hell with the proof. What do you think?'

'I think he's the one in the note.'

'Well, then.'

'Well, then, I should go see him, shouldn't I?' He got up.

'Just a minute. Ever since you came to the hospital, you've had that look. You know the kind I mean.'

He nodded. 'Joseph mentioned it.'

'So don't do anything to get yourself in trouble. If you do, we'll lose you, and . . .' She shook her head. Her eyes glistened, and she blinked fiercely, denying herself the right to cry. He didn't know who the tears were for, but it didn't matter. She had any number of reasons for them.

'You've lost enough,' he said. 'You won't lose me too.'

31

He parked in the driveway of Grover Jones' house, raised the big wrought-iron knocker, and let it fall. He waited a minute, then knocked again. Finally Frances Jones opened the door, wearing shorts and a blouse and a wide-brimmed hat, as if she had just come in from the garden.

'John Ray Horn, Mrs Jones,' he said with a smile. 'I met you the other day. I'd appreciate it if I could see your husband.'

'I'm sorry,' she said, not returning the smile. 'I'm afraid he's not here.'

'Can you tell me where I could find him?'

'Ah, no, I can't. He's just . . . out. Would you like to leave a message for him? Maybe he could call you later.'

'I need to see him today. It's real important.'

She took a small step forward, as if to speed his exit. 'Well, I don't know if that's possible. If you had called first, you might have saved yourself some trouble, Mr . . . Horn?'

'Yes, ma'am.' Some instinct told him she was lying, and he decided to drop the pretense of politeness. 'I guess I will leave a message, then. Tell him I just came from seeing a friend who was attacked and almost beaten to death last night. It's Maggie O'Dare, who was here with me when I met you. Her husband wasn't as lucky. He's dead.'

She put her hand to her throat but said nothing.

'So, I guess you can tell him that Owen Bruder was only the beginning. Now it's two people dead, most likely killed by the same person, and somehow Global Studios is right in the middle of the whole mess and I'm pretty sure your husband knows something about it. Oh, yes, please tell him the police are working very hard on this, and I'm going to have to mention his name to them sooner or later. But if he'd rather talk to me first—'

'It's all right, Frances.' Horn recognized the voice. The door opened wider, and Grover Jones stepped into view. He was also wearing shorts, with sandals and a white polo shirt. He looked tired. 'What do you want?' he asked Horn.

'Just some answers.'

'Come in, then.' The voice was flat. The genial, ingratiating actor was gone, at least for the moment.

'Grover—' his wife began.

'No, it's all right.'

'I'm not so sure.' Her face was grim. 'I don't trust him.'

'Well . . .' He tried to smile. 'Isn't it exhausting, not trusting anyone?' He led Horn into the living room, and she followed them. 'Sweetheart, you don't have to bother with this,' he said to her.

She seemed to have reached a decision. 'Yes, I do.' As if suddenly remembering her manners, she said to Horn, 'We can sit here.' She indicated a furniture arrangement in the center of the living room, a flowered-print sofa and two big matching chairs flanking a long, recently polished coffee table. Horn took one of the chairs, and they sat side by side on the sofa, facing him.

'I'm very sorry to hear about Maggie's husband,' Jones said. 'Is she going to recover?'

'I think so,' Horn replied. 'At least from her injuries. I don't know how somebody recovers from losing her husband and her father to the same killer.'

Jones nodded. He sat forward on the edge of the sofa, unwilling or unable to relax in it. 'You already asked me some questions,' he said. 'There are more?'

Horn nodded. 'When Maggie and I were here, we talked about a number of things, but we never got a chance to get to the real reason we came. As I recall, you cut the visit a little short.'

He needed a smoke, but when he looked around for an ashtray, he saw none.

'What we wanted to talk about was the thing that kicked off all of Owen Bruder's troubles. The thing that happened before he was murdered, and even before the government cracked down on him. I'm talking about the time somebody went to see J. Parnell Thomas and his people down at the Biltmore Hotel and told them that Owen was a Red. That started the ball rolling, and it hasn't stopped yet.'

Frances Jones removed her big straw hat, laying it carefully on the table. Sitting in their shorts, the couple almost looked like a pair of serious children, a brother and sister who had just come in from their playtime and were waiting to be told what to do next.

'For the record, he wasn't a Red. You may or may not know that; I'm just telling you, because we need to get that out of the way. That person, whoever he or she was, wrecked Owen's life and career. I also think the lie got him killed, but I don't have any proof of that yet.'

Jones had not moved, not even blinked.

'Maggie and I tried to ask you about whether Owen may have been seeing a woman. That's when you ushered us out the door. The woman was Grace Stilwell. You know her pretty well – well enough to send her a note thanking her for doing such a good job writing that big movie of yours. I got my hands on another note, one she sent to Owen not long before he was killed. She talked about you—' Here he was on shakier ground, but he decided to stretch the truth a little, on the chance that he was right. '—And she referred to something you had done. It sounded like something very secret and very important. And she met Owen later at Schwab's Drugstore on a Sunday night to talk about you. And soon after that he was dead.'

The words were coming easier for him now. He didn't know how they were going to respond to his story. He just wanted to get it all out.

'Grace Stilwell. It's starting to sound like she's the key to this, don't you think? And she finally agreed to talk to me about it. There was only one problem. When I showed up at her house last night, she was gone. Not just gone. Somebody had taken her.'

Jones' mouth opened slightly, as if to help him breathe better. His wife glanced at him, then turned back to Horn.

'I feel like I'm racing against some kind of deadline, and if I don't get to the finish in time, she's going to wind up dead too. Too many dead already, don't you think? And all because of one puny lie whispered about a good man.'

He finally allowed himself to relax in the soft chair, and found his back and shoulder muscles were taut with tension.

All three were silent for a while, but Horn was aware of Grover Jones breathing audibly – deep breaths, in and out.

Finally Jones spoke. 'I, uh, I have a lawyer. I don't use him very often, but he seems to be very good. I think I should call him.'

'You should do that,' Horn said, 'but you don't need him with me. I'm not a policeman, and whatever you tell me here is just conversation. Don't you think it's time you had that conversation with somebody?'

Jones didn't respond. Horn, sensing an advantage, pressed on. 'I think you know that eventually the police are going to find out the whole story – not only who murdered Owen but why, and how it all came about. Whoever knows something should speak up now, before the cops come and drag it out of them.'

He leaned forward. 'Owen Bruder didn't get a fair deal,' he said forcefully. 'And now it's too late for him. Don't you think it's time we—'

'I didn't know,' Jones said in a voice so low Horn almost missed it.

'Didn't know what?'

'That any of this would happen. To begin with, just about everyone knew that Owen held strong socialist beliefs. Whether he was an outright

224

Communist or not seemed to me only a technicality. I also knew enough about him to know how strong he was. I thought this would be no more than an annoyance to him. I thought he would easily prove his innocence. I couldn't imagine that a transparent lie like that would stand. How could it? How could a lie stand against the truth?'

'I guess it depends on who spreads the lie and how good they are at it,' Horn said slowly, absorbing what Jones had just told him. He wanted to grab the man and shake the rest of it out of him, but he knew enough to tread softly. It's coming, he thought. Don't push. Let it come.

'So tell me how it happened,' he prompted Jones.

'I was told to call up the Thomas committee investigators and say I had some information for them about someone at Global,' Jones said in a hushed voice, like someone telling a bedtime story. 'I was assured that whatever I told them would be absolutely confidential. I would not be required to testify in public, and my identity would be protected.'

Horn noticed that Frances Jones had laid her hand on her husband's bare knee, palm up. As he continued to speak, he rested his hand in hers, and their fingers intertwined.

'I, ah, I told them, as I had been instructed, that Owen once confided in me that he had joined the Communist Party while in New York, that he had never resigned, and that he still subscribed to all their goals, including the dismantling of our society. They asked me if I knew the names of any other party members. I said no. They thanked me, they, uh' – he cleared his throat – 'they called me a good American. They excused me, and I left.'

He cleared his throat again, more loudly this time. 'When it hit the newspapers and the radio, I wasn't too surprised. I gathered that had been the point. Naturally I felt terrible about what I'd done, but I guessed that once Owen was called to testify, he would get himself a talented lawyer and easily clear himself. Then I heard he was dead. Oh, Lord . . .'

His voice faltered, and he stopped. His wife's hand gripped his own so hard their knuckles were white.

'So you decided not to tell the truth when Maggie and I came over,' Horn said.

'Of course,' Jones said. 'Of course I did. To protect myself. And when you mentioned a woman—'

'Did you know it was probably Grace Stilwell?'

'I guessed as much.'

'Why?'

'Because I knew she had an affair with Owen.'

Another piece in place, Horn thought. Good. Let's keep going.

'How did you know?'

'She told me. Grace and I are good friends. I felt protective toward her.

Also, the affair was brief and long ago, before she came to work at Global. By the time she joined the studio, it was over. That's why I doubted that it was a factor in his death.'

'Are you sure it was over?'

'Yes. Again, because she told me so, and I believed her. Grace is a complicated person, with a complicated set of values, but I'd never doubt her honesty with me. I may be the only person who knows that she . . .' His voice trailed off.

'That she what?'

'I doubt that this is relevant to your investigation,' Jones said, but the expression on Horn's face made him go on. 'She has been having an affair with Marvin Felix,' he said in a barely audible voice.

'What?' Horn exclaimed. Then he said wonderingly, 'Busy gal, isn't she?' His opinion of Grace Stilwell had just plummeted

'As I said, she's complicated. And you don't know the half of it.'

'Well, I'm glad she tells the truth to somebody,' Horn said. 'When she talked to me, she lied through her teeth.'

'She has things to protect,' Jones said vaguely.

'Like what? An old affair with Owen? And a new one with Marvin?'

'Maybe more than that,' he muttered. He drew himself up straighter on the sofa. 'This conversation should be about me. I'm not going to say anything that might get her in trouble.'

'Sorry, but we can't limit this to you,' Horn said. 'For example, you haven't even told me yet—'

'I know,' Jones said bitterly. 'I haven't told you who sent me to the committee. I'm not trying to protect him. He doesn't deserve my protection.'

Horn waited.

'It was Marvin Felix.'

Now we're getting somewhere.

'And why did he do it?'

'I don't know why.'

'Sure you do. You must.'

'I truly don't. He made it clear what I was to do, and, uh . . . and what would happen . . .'

Horn suspected what was coming next. He waited, but Jones failed to continue.

'How did he pressure you?' Horn prompted.

'He, uh . . . Let's say he threatened to reveal something about me that would not reflect well on me. In fact, it would probably mean the loss of my job. My career.'

His wife placed her other hand on top of their clasped hands. Her eyes were riveted on his face.

'I can guess,' Horn said. 'But it's hard to believe. He'd be cutting off his own nose, to throw out one of his biggest stars—'

Jones laughed. 'Thank you, Mr Horn. I'm proud of my work, but I've also tried to keep a level head about it. I'm no movie star. I'm a reliable character actor. If Marvin Felix lost my services, he'd just go over to Paramount or MGM and hire some reasonably competent replacement. He's a ruthless individual, and I knew he wouldn't hesitate to follow through on his threat unless I cooperated. I was afraid of losing all this.' His gesture took in the room. 'Of losing this life that Frances and I have made together. I was a coward.'

His wife spoke up. 'Grover is a good man,' she said to Horn. 'A good, decent man. Ask anyone who knows him.'

'Yes, ma'am.' He got up. 'Thank you for talking to me and for being honest with me. I'll stay in touch.'

A good, decent man, Horn said to himself as he drove away. *I guess maybe he is. I believe Owen Bruder was, too. And Wally Roland. If the good, decent men can't stop this world from skidding down to hell, then no wonder the Marvin Felixes and Mitchell Crosses and Laura Lee Paisleys are taking over.*

Maybe Woody Guthrie should write a song about it.

He got to the cabin in the middle of the afternoon, intending to pack up some of his clothes and carry them over to Mad Crow's place. Once there, however, he felt the need to slow down, to take stock of the things he had learned over the last couple of days. As he often did, he decided to free his mind by working with his hands. He changed into his work clothes and began looking for simple things to do around the estate.

So Marvin Felix started the ball rolling, he thought, as he pulled weeds near what was left of the main house. He's the one who painted the target on Owen Bruder's chest. But why? When they talked in his ornate office, Felix described himself to Horn as a man without politics, and Horn tended to see him that way. The emperors of Hollywood – the Mayers, Warners, Felixes – were men of petty spites and grudges, it was true, but what drove them was the dollar, the search for moviegoers to fill the seats in their theaters, not some abstract ideal. Whatever drove Felix to destroy Owen Bruder, Horn had trouble believing that it was politics.

After two hours, he had a tarpaulin piled high with weeds. Clumsily taking hold of two corners, he dragged the tarp and its contents over the hill to the makeshift dump, where he had accumulated months' worth of weeds, fallen branches, and palm fronds. He would let it all dry out, and once the fire season was safely past, he would burn it.

He soaked for a long time in the tub. As he got out and was beginning to dry off, the phone rang.

'Howdy-do,' the voice said. 'I heard you wanted to talk.'

'Hello, Woody.' He was glad to hear the little man's voice. He knew they needed to talk about unpleasant topics, but he wanted to put it off for a moment. 'How was Mexico?'

'Oh, pretty good.' Guthrie seemed surprised at such a casual question. 'We went down to Tiawanny just for fun.' Horn guessed he meant Tijuana. 'Back in thirty-eight, my cousin and me and some other friends and relatives worked at this radio station down there, XELO.'

'I've heard that station,' Horn said. 'They play a lot of hillbilly music.'

'That's right. Got a signal so strong, they cover the whole South and West, blast those American stations right off the air. So, how you been?'

'Not so good. Some things have happened here.'

'I know. Guess I didn't have to ask how you been. I talked to Joseph a while ago, and he told me about Davey. And Maggie. A crying shame. You got any idea who done it?'

'The same person who killed Maggie's father. And that's why I called you, because you and I talked about that a little bit when we all got together for dinner. You remember?'

'Uh . . .'

'Maggie and I told you about her father and why he might have been killed. You said you didn't think it had anything to do with politics. People get killed over politics, you said, but not like this. I thought that sounded pretty crazy, and I didn't give you a chance to say any more about it.'

'Now I remember.' Horn heard a slow strumming sound, fingers on strings, and he knew Guthrie must be hunched over his guitar, idly playing as he talked. And he probably had a drink in front of him and a cigarette hanging out of his mouth and a pencil behind his ear, just in case some song lyrics occurred to him.

'So what did you mean, Woody?'

'I guess I was thinking something like this: I know people get stirred up over politics. Sometimes they get killed over it, but not like this. They get shot, or lynched; not quiet-like, at night, in the dark. Politics is all crowds, and noise, and big emotions – lies and the truth – but all of it out where you can see it and hear it.'

'I know,' Horn said, 'but still—'

'You think somebody killed him because they didn't like what he believed. I'd look in another direction.'

'Where?'

'Someplace . . . *smaller*. I know Maggie'd feel better if her daddy was killed for a big, important reason. But I don't see it that way. When one man murders another, he does it 'cause somebody's messing with his wife, or he wants the money in the cash register, or he's sitting at a bar drinking and some fool says the wrong thing. It's hard for me to see one man killing another because they disagree about how to save the world. See what I mean?'

'I suppose.' Horn exhaled loudly into the phone. 'I still don't know if I can agree with you, but . . . thanks.'

'Don't mention it.'

'Did you hear about Cal?'

'No. What happened to him?'

'He showed up in front of that committee in Washington yesterday and, basically, he told them to stick it where the sun don't shine.'

Guthrie emitted a soft, low whistle. 'Well, I'll be damned. Good for him. I didn't really expect that.'

'None of us did.'

'I imagine he's in trouble, isn't he?'

'I don't think any studio in town will hire him now. It's going to be hard on his family.'

More strumming, followed by the soft exhalation of cigarette smoke. 'Sometimes I think this country ain't ever going to get it right, you know? Maybe it's time to pack up and leave.'

'Where to? Mexico? Russia?'

'The Big Rock Candy Mountains.'

Horn laughed. 'You mean . . .'

'I mean where it's sunny every day, and you sleep out every night, and they got the lemonade springs where the bluebird sings, and, uh, there's a lake of stew and whisky too . . . You ever heard of that place?'

He laughed again. 'Sure. Don't tell me you wrote that one.'

'Nope. An old boy named Harry McClintock, back in the twenties when every miserable hobo and Okie and boxcar rider out there knew the words. We all wanted to go there someday. It sounded like Heaven.'

Horn thought of Laura Lee Paisley's simpering voice on the radio, of Mitchell Cross collecting names in his shadowy hotel room, of Wally Roland taking his last, lonely bath. 'I don't think there's any such place, Woody.'

'Something tells me you're right. Well, I probably won't see Cal again, so you give him my best.'

'Off for New York?'

'In a couple of days. Got to go jump through some hoops for those advertising idiots.'

'Okay, Woody. Thanks – and take care of yourself.'

'So long,' Guthrie sang in his trademark twang. 'It's been good to know you . . .'

Horn dressed, took a couple of pork chops out of the fridge and fried them while he boiled some grits. When the chops were done, he made gravy, opened a High Life, and carried his supper out to the porch.

If the boss of Global Studios was the man behind the lie, he thought as he ate, did this mean that he was also behind Owen's murder? And the attack on Maggie and Davey? And the apparent taking of Grace Stilwell? Horn had no idea.

But find the reason behind these things, he told himself, and he would find the individual.

First, though, find Grace Stilwell.

It was almost time to leave for his nightly vigil at Mad Crow's place but, as he began packing up, the phone rang again.

'This is Maris Felix,' she said, speaking softly as if to avoid being overheard.

He waited.

'I think I know where she is.'

'Tell me.'

'It's a . . . place. It's complicated. I can tell you how to get there, but not right now. I can't stay on the phone very long.'

'Uh-huh.' He was immediately suspicious of her, but he had to play this out. 'You want to meet me somewhere?'

'I suppose. But I can't get away for a while.'

He sighed. 'When?'

'Sometime after ten.'

'All right. Where do you live?'

'Bel-Air.'

Of course, he thought. Where else? 'Meet me in Santa Monica, then. At ten-forty-five.' He thought for a moment. 'There's a bar called the Port-hole on Ocean. Wait for me across the street from it, next to Palisades Park. What kind of car are you driving?'

'A Packard convertible.'

'Don't you have anything a little less noticeable?'

'No.' He heard the edge in her voice. 'Sorry, I don't.'

'All right. Ten-forty-five.'

He finished putting the clothes in the car, then called Mad Crow. 'How's Maggie?' he asked.

'The lady is resting.'

'Is she all right?'

'I think so. She was hurting a lot earlier today, and those pills weren't doing much for her, so I mixed up a couple of my special Bear Slayers for her.'

'That's the one with—'

'A little apple cider, a little rum, a little grain alcohol.'

'Right.'

'She's sleeping comfortably now.'

'Good.'

'You all right?'

'Yeah. But something just happened, and I need to follow up on it. I may not be over until late tonight. Very late.'

'Okay.'

'One more thing: If we decide we need to get Billy to help out, how fast can you get him there?'

'Well, if I can reach him . . . twenty minutes, the way he drives that truck.'

'Good. I'll be in touch.'

He went inside and lay down on the couch, trying to nap, but his mind was adrift and he let it take him along. The thought that he might be getting closer to Grace Stilwell was exciting, but it did little to temper the anger he had felt since the attack on Maggie and Davey. The anger worked at him like an ache in his stomach. Would it take another death to make it go away? He didn't want to think about that.

At ten he went out to the car and opened the trunk. Davey Peake's hunting rifle had been safely stashed in one of Mad Crow's closets, but he had held on to the .38-caliber revolver and its box of shells. He took it out and looked it over. Davey, he knew, had been good with guns, and this one was well cared for, its blue steel finish well oiled and buffed. It had a six-inch barrel, a little long for toting around in a belt or pants pocket, but more accurate than the shorter lengths. Horn guessed that Davey had used it for target practice.

He got in the front seat and loaded all the chambers except for the one under the hammer, put the shell box in the glove compartment, and slid the pistol under the front seat. Then he started the car.

31

He had been waiting about ten minutes when she nosed in to the curb a few spaces ahead of him. The Packard's white top was brilliant, its black finish gleamed with wax, reflecting the streetlights and neon of Ocean Avenue. He pulled up around the car in front of him and parked the Ford just behind her. Then he got out and tapped on her window.

'First thing we should do is go sit in my car,' he said. 'Nobody'll notice it.' Looking vaguely resentful, she locked the Packard and got in the Ford's passenger seat. She was wearing a rich woman's version of casual clothes – pressed wool slacks, a cashmere sweater, and low-heeled cordovans with a man's-style wingtip design – but they did little to soften her brittle image.

'So tell me,' he said.

'Do you mind?' She pulled out her cigarette case and began the familiar ritual. He slid out his ashtray for her to use.

She rolled down her window a little and blew the smoke out. 'I think she's at a place up the coast,' she began.

'Is it called Old McDonald's Farm?'

'Yes.' She looked surprised. 'How—?'

'I heard about it just the other day and guessed. How do you know she's there?'

'I'm familiar with it,' she said wryly. 'I've stayed there a few times myself. It's not the kind of place where you normally make friends, but there's one woman who works there – an older woman, a war refugee – whom I got to know. She's a decent sort. I called up there today, asked to speak to her on some pretext, and talked to her for a while. During the conversation, I managed to get a little information. I didn't want to mention Grace by name—'

'Then how do you know she's there?'

'Will you let me explain? Most of the . . . I suppose you'd call them patients . . . are housed in the main building. But special patients, especially the famous ones, the difficult ones, the ones they need to keep hidden away, are put in a separate location, a small house. I was able to learn from this woman that they moved a new patient, a woman, into the house just last night. Almost no one has been allowed to see her.'

He thought for a moment. He had countless questions, but some of them could wait. What was needed now was a decision.

'Okay,' he said. 'Let's go and see what we can see.'

'I can draw you a map,' she said.

'No,' he said. 'You come with me.'

'I don't know if that's possible. What good can I do?'

'I need you along for the ride. I need you for moral support, for snappy conversation, whatever you want to call it.'

'I'm afraid.' A passing car's lights swept past her face, and what he saw looked indeed like fear. But he didn't care.

'Lady, if it's really Grace who's there, and you want to get her out of there, you're coming with me. I know you'd rather hire this job out and keep your hands clean, but this is one of those times when you can't. Either we both go, or nobody goes. Or you can call the police and let them handle it.'

Another harsh light briefly illuminated her face. The fear was still there, but now something else as well. 'All right,' she said finally. 'Get us on Pacific Coast Highway.'

A minute later he drove down the incline that bottomed out at the ocean and became PCH, and he headed north. On the right loomed the dark, massive bulk of the Palisades, where California broke off and ended. On the left was the uninterrupted row of snug beach houses, and beyond them the Pacific .

After about a mile they passed the huge Marion Davies estate. 'The last of the palaces by the ocean,' his passenger said. 'It's a hotel and beach club now.' She sounded nervous, and Horn guessed she was trying to make conversation.

'You've been there?'

'Of course.' She tapped her cigarette on the edge of the ashtray. Then she added, 'I didn't mean for that to sound . . . snobbish.'

'That's all right. I've seen you in the society pages, Mrs Felix. It's pretty clear to me that you and I hobnob on different levels. I don't hate you for it.'

'I'm so grateful,' she said.

Amid another row of beach houses, he spotted the place where he had met Laura Lee Paisley – just the other night, he recalled, but it seemed long ago.

'Is your husband going to wonder where you are tonight?'

'No,' she answered simply. He decided not to pursue it.

'You want to tell me where we're going?'

'It's several miles,' she said. 'Past Topanga Canyon. I'll recognize the turnoff.'

'I think it's time I knew what to expect there.'

'Yes. It's a kind of clinic. It doesn't have a name, because it doesn't exactly operate in the open. It's run by a man named Pappas who calls himself a doctor. I think he once may have been a doctor, but he isn't any more. He was caught doing one of those things that doctors aren't supposed to do.'

'I can think of a number of them,' Horn said.

'With some help and other people's money, he set up this place where one can get medical treatment done very quietly. Maybe someone's daughter is pregnant and doesn't want to be. Maybe someone drinks too much or has a morphine habit that's proving too costly to a movie studio in lost work or bad publicity. The Doctor, as everyone calls him, will take them in for an exorbitant fee and deal with the problem. Sometimes treatment involves more drugs, or swapping one drug for another. The studios don't care as long as the problem disappears, or at least goes away for a while.'

'Convenient.'

'Only a few people even know about this place,' she said. 'People at a certain level, the ones who write the checks. And, of course, the patients. It's almost never talked about, because it's in everyone's interest to keep it a secret.'

'Why were you there?' He asked out of curiosity, even though he knew she would almost certainly choose not to answer. But she surprised him.

'Without going into unpleasant details, let's just say I was taking a certain medicine a little too enthusiastically. It does not go well with my personality, and the mixture can be . . . volatile. Marvin recognized it before I did, and he persuaded me to go see Dr Pappas.'

'He didn't have you hauled off there in the middle of the night?'

'Oh, God, no. I saw the need for it too. If you're right about Grace, if there was violence involved, that's very frightening. That's why I'm concerned.'

'But not concerned enough to call the police.'

She didn't respond. 'You think your husband's behind this, don't you?' he said. 'Maybe you know it for sure, and you don't want him arrested.'

She lit another cigarette. 'I can see why you might think that,' she said. Out of the corner of his eye, he saw her cigarette tracing nervous little designs of smoke in the air.

'Marvin has certainly sent enough people there, so I suppose if Grace is abducted and suddenly appears at the farm, then . . .' She gestured vaguely. 'But you're not aware of all the possibilities.'

'I'm listening.'

'For example, I haven't told you who helped Dr Pappas set up the place. Who contributed a lot of the money, who made introductions, provided him with contacts.'

He waited.

'It was Laura Lee Paisley,' she said.

Horn whistled softly, Guthrie-style. 'And how did that happen?'

'There are different stories. According to one, he provided either her or a friend of hers with an abortion several years ago, and that was the reason he lost his license. She saw the advantage of having a society doctor in her confidence and helped him establish the farm. She was able to send him rich, secretive clients, and her connection with him made her privy to information.'

'He gives her the goods on them?'

'It's not that simple. No one would go to the farm if they knew their names would wind up on her broadcast. I understand there's an unwritten rule that even though Dr Pappas tells her a lot, she agrees not to use it. At least not publicly.'

'I think I get it,' he said. 'She told me she only uses a small amount of the stuff she collects on people.'

'That's it,' Maris Felix said. 'The rest is just knowledge, filed away somewhere, but knowledge is influence.'

'She knows everybody's secrets, doesn't she?' Horn couldn't keep the bitterness from his voice.

'Yes, I really think she does. If you dislike her as much as everyone else seems to, why were you talking to her?'

'My daddy would say you need to wrestle with the Devil every now and then just to remind yourself how strong he is.'

For the first time, he heard her laugh. 'Laura Lee. The Devil. I like that.'

'Tell me about the layout of the place.'

'All right.' For several minutes she talked as he drove, and he made mental notes. He began to gain a little respect for her. She was certainly high-strung and fidgety, and he had no idea how she would handle a real crisis. But she had a good memory for detail, and she did a creditable job of describing the farm, the physical layout, and the staff.

'Any guards there?'

'No. I mean no one who carries guns, that sort of thing. But some of the orderlies, men and women both, are very imposing physically. Considering the kind of patients they sometimes have to handle, they need to be.'

They rode in silence for a long while. Then she pointed up ahead. 'There's the turnoff.' They were in a remote part of Malibu, where the ocean, lit by a three-quarter moon, glistened to their left and grassy hills rolled away to the right. Except for scattered houses here and there, almost no lights were visible.

235

He took the turnoff and found himself on a steep hill. The road climbed for several hundred yards through high grass and scattered trees, with no sign of life. Then she said, 'Up there,' and pointed to a narrow driveway to the right that led quickly to a tall metal gate flanked by columns of brick. There was no sign.

He drove past the turnoff, continuing uphill, passing a few houses. Some properties had the look of horse ranches, with stables and low fences enclosing grassy fields. Eventually he came to a second road that branched off to the right, and he took it, slowing the car and cutting his lights as he drove. After about fifty yards he pulled over to the narrow shoulder and cut the engine. There could be houses farther down the road, he knew, but none were visible, and he hoped there would be little traffic at this time of night.

This road, lined with young, fast-growing eucalyptus trees, looked down on the clinic. He could make out the rear of the main house, a big two-story structure with a few lights showing, and a sturdy wall enclosing the two or three acres of the property. He could not see the separate house she had described, but he guessed it lay in the near left-hand corner of the estate, obscured by trees. Far below, crawling headlights marked the highway, and the blackness beyond was the ocean.

He asked Maris a few more questions, listening carefully to her answers. Then she listened as he outlined his plan. He checked his watch and saw that it was nearly midnight. 'No need to wait,' he said. He got out, pulled the .38 from under the seat, stuck it in his belt, then sprung the lid of the trunk and pulled out a crowbar he kept there for emergencies.

She got out too, staring at the gun and the crowbar. 'I know it's a little late for me to ask,' she said in a shaky whisper, 'but do you do this sort of thing often?'

He considered telling her the truth, but he knew the answer she needed. 'All the time,' he said.

Beyond the shoulder, the ground dropped off in a slope that was steep but not impossible, marked by grassy dirt and rocks and some shrubbery. Leading the way, he took her hand and descended slowly, feeling out each step before putting his weight down. He had a flashlight in the car but had decided not to use it; the moon gave them just enough light.

Step by step they went down, skidding a little, sometimes setting off little rockslides, but keeping their feet. After thirty careful yards, the slope evened out, and they found themselves on a narrow footpath that ran just outside the rear wall of the estate. The wall was concrete and too high to climb. 'Where's the door?' he asked her in a low voice. She pointed, and they walked along the dirt path until they came to a recess in the wall. She had told him that the wall contained two heavy wooden doors, one on the ocean side of the grounds, the other in the rear. They were apparently there when Pappas bought the place, she told him, and were always kept locked.

Working mostly by feel, he found the door handle and inserted the tip of the crowbar between door and frame just about where he judged the lock to be. Then he put his weight on it to pry out the wood. He kept at it, prying out more each time, trying to keep the noise to a minimum, until he had chipped away most of the wood around the lock. Then, with a quick screech of metal, he dislodged the lock assembly and, putting his shoulder to the door, pushed until it opened.

'Let's go. You first.' He tossed the crowbar aside and she led the way through a small stand of trees, soon finding a new footpath. The main house was clearly visible forty or fifty yards off to their right, its white finish pale in the moonlight, the same lights still burning upstairs. Bathrooms, Horn guessed.

They walked carefully for a few minutes, then she said, 'There.' He saw the house. It was just a cottage, tucked away in the trees, a private place for a private patient. No lights were on.

'Do nurses stay here overnight?' he whispered.

'I don't know.'

'I guess we'll find out.' He delicately tried the front door. Locked. He walked quietly around the house, verifying that it was dark. In the rear, he found the junction where the phone line ran from the main house, and severed the wire with his pocket knife. Then he returned to the front, where he had a quick whispered consultation with Maris.

'Now remember,' he said to her. 'Lots of drama.' Opening the screen door, he rapped on the large glass pane in the door with his knuckle. 'Open up,' he said in a voice loud enough to sound authoritative but not, he hoped, loud enough to be heard at the main house. He knocked three or four times more and was considering retracing his steps for the crowbar when a light went on inside. Then another light went on in the front room, and a woman came to the door, a stout, frizzy-haired woman wearing a nightdress and a sleepy and puzzled expression.

'Open up, ma'am,' Horn said. 'Sheriff's department.'

Her brows knitted. She stifled a yawn and glanced at the doorway behind her for a second. She looked apprehensive.

'Sheriff's deputy, ma'am,' he said, basing his drawl on those of a hundred movie lawmen, with a touch of Detective Pitt thrown in. 'This lady' – indicating Maris Felix – 'is looking for her husband, and we know he's hiding out here.'

'What?' She rubbed her eyes, clutching her nightdress with one hand.

'Howard?' Maris Felix called out, trying to see through the glass into the house. 'I know you're in there.'

'Better open up, ma'am,' Horn said. 'We don't have anything against you. She just wants to get him home.'

'Howard, can you hear me? The little ones are asking about you,' Maris Felix said, sounding on the verge of tears. 'What can I tell them?'

'This is crazy,' the woman said. 'There's no man in here. Just a patient. A woman. Have you talked to Dr Pappas?'

'Better let us in, ma'am,' Horn said. 'If he's not there, we'll be on our way.'

With an expression of disgust, she unlocked the door. They pushed past her. 'That room,' Maris Felix said, heading for the lighted doorway.

He followed her into a bedroom that held a single bed, a few pieces of furniture, and a much smaller portable bed by the window. Its covers were thrown back.

In the other bed was Grace Stilwell.

She lay with eyes closed, tucked in up to her chin, her hair damp and in disarray.

'Grace.' Maris Felix went to her, bent over and touched her face.

'Wait a minute,' the woman said to her. 'I've seen you somewhere before.' She turned to Horn. 'If you're the police, show me some—'

He pulled his jacket aside to reveal the butt of the pistol. 'This is all I've got right now,' he said. 'You stand there and be quiet.'

Maris Felix lowered the bedcovers and began shaking Grace Stilwell gently, then more forcefully. 'She won't wake up,' she said. 'What did you do to her?' Horn heard the beginnings of hysteria in her voice and hoped she could hold herself together until their job was done.

He looked around the room and spotted a tray atop a dresser. On it lay a hypodermic syringe and several vials of liquid. He picked up one of the vials and looked at the label, but it was meaningless to him. 'You,' he said to the woman. 'What's your name?'

'Thelma.' Her tone was sullen.

'We don't want to hurt you, Thelma, or get you in trouble, either. How much of this has she been getting?'

'Three cc's every six hours,' she muttered.

'And what does it do?'

'It keeps her asleep.'

'When did you give her the last dose?'

'Bedtime. About two hours ago.'

His mind churned. There was a lot to consider. An unconscious woman. Another who could raise an alarm. Still another who might come to pieces. 'All right,' he said finally. He turned to Thelma. 'We're going. And you're coming with us. Put some shoes on. Not those slippers.' He pointed to a pair of white, nurse-style shoes with blocky heels and laces. 'Those.'

238

'Now wait a minute—'

'No time, Thelma. I don't like to hit women, but if you don't have those on in about half a minute . . .'

She sat on the edge of her bed and began putting on the shoes.

'Put that on, too,' he said, indicating a sweater hanging on the back of a chair.

He pulled out the .38 and handed it to Maris Felix. 'I know how you like using these,' he said to her with a wink. 'Just don't shoot her unless she does something funny, okay?'

'Okay. Sure,' she said in an approximation of a tough broad's voice. She held the gun in both hands, then pointed it at the other woman. The barrel wavered slightly.

Horn tore the covers the rest of the way off the bed, showing Grace Stilwell in a nightgown. Untucking the edges of the bottom sheet, he folded both sides around her in a loose cocoon. Then he bent and hoisted her up into his arms. 'Let's go,' he said to Maris Felix. 'Thelma first. You give her directions.'

They picked their way along the path through the trees. Grace Stilwell's head lay against his chest, her deep breathing clearly audible. At the door in the wall, he followed the others through, and the three of them stood at the base of the slope. He knew he couldn't carry her up cradled in his arms, so he shifted her weight and slung her over his right shoulder like a sack of grain. 'All right, up we go,' he said to them. 'Thelma first.'

It was rough going. Soon he was breathing hard, and he began to slip on the loose rocks, falling to his knees, cursing softly, almost dropping his burden a couple of times. His legs ached. He fell again, cursed again. Finally he stood at the top. Gasping, he leaned Grace's inert form against the car.

After getting his breath, he had Maris open the passenger door and pull up the seat. He managed to wrestle Grace Stilwell into the back until she was half-lying, half-sitting on the seat. Maris handed him the gun and got in the back next to the unconscious woman.

'Who brought her in, Thelma?' he asked.

'I don't know,' she said, her sullenness gone and replaced by fear. 'It was last night, and I was in the big house.'

'Who gave you your orders tonight?'

'Dr Pappas.'

'Shoot her up every six hours. That's it?'

'That's all.' She eyed the gun. 'Please, Mister,' she said. 'I just do what they tell me.'

'Do what *I* tell you this time,' he said. 'As soon as we leave, you can go on back down. Take your time, because it's dark and very slippery and you could hurt yourself. When you get to the main house, wake up

Dr Pappas. Tell him Grace's friends have come for her. Tell him you tried to fight us off, but we had a gun. Tell him if he doesn't forget about this whole thing, the police are going to find out what he's doing here, and all of you will be out of a job.'

'Yes, sir.'

On the drive back down the coast, he felt exhausted, even as his mind was racing. He checked the road in the rearview mirror frequently, saw nothing to concern him. Once or twice he tilted the mirror to look at the back seat. Maris Felix sat with her arm around the other woman, occasionally brushing hair from her face. 'It's all right,' he heard her say softly, over and over. 'It's all right.'

He desperately needed to know who had delivered Grace Stilwell to the big house with the ocean view. Pappas knew, and maybe there would be a time to apply the screws to him. Maybe the police should be brought in after all. But all he had time for tonight was to find a refuge for Grace Stilwell. A place where no one would look for her. Not her house. Not his place; he couldn't protect her alone. Not, he was sure, the Felix home in Bel-Air. The more he thought about it, only one place seemed appropriate.

Up on the right he saw a fisherman's supply store and, just beyond, neon marking a roadhouse. He slowed the Ford to a halt at a phone booth next to the window with the blinking Schlitz sign. Seconds later he was dropping a nickel into the slot and dialing the operator. Shortly after that, he heard Mad Crow's sleepy growl.

'It's me,' he said.

'It's the middle of the fucking night too.'

'I'm sorry. Listen, I think you'd better get Billy over there.'

'What happened?' Mad Crow sounded instantly awake.

'Things just got a lot more complicated.' He told his story, condensing it all into a few sentences. 'She's in the back seat of my car now, wrapped up in a sheet,' he concluded.

'This isn't kidnapping, is it? You know how serious they are about that.'

'No. She was kidnapped before. I'm taking her back.'

'Hmm. All right, bring her over. The more the merrier. Maybe we can get Woody to come back for a visit. And the Mormon Tabernacle Choir.'

'Thanks, Indian.'

A half-hour later, he pulled up next to the black Packard. Maris Felix got out. 'Where are you taking her?'

'I'm not going to tell you,' he said. 'It's better if you don't know. I'll be in touch with you later.' He leaned over, pulled a pencil and a scrap of paper from the glove compartment. 'Give me a number where I can reach you.'

She wrote it down. 'Thank you for what you did,' she said in a faint voice.

'You were pretty good yourself,' he said. 'Not a word about this. To anybody.'

She nodded. 'Please take good care of her.'

32

It was after two in the morning when he parked in the driveway. He saw Mad Crow and Billy Looks Ahead waiting on the front porch, wrapped in warm coats, mugs of coffee in their hands. Billy, who never wasted words, greeted him with the usual nod. Although both he and his uncle were big men, Billy was taller and more sinewy. Each had the same copper-to-bronze complexion and a face made up of broad planes and edges.

As gently as he could, Horn lifted Grace Stilwell out of the back seat and, with Billy's help, carried her inside. 'Down the hall to my room,' Mad Crow told them. 'Be quiet, because everybody else is asleep.'

They put Grace into the freshly made bed, and they stood looking down at her. She lay motionless, her mouth partly open. 'Damn, she's sure out, isn't she?' Mad Crow said.

'Shot full of some kind of dope,' Horn replied. 'She'll probably be out for hours. We can check on her every now and then. Any chance at getting a few hours' sleep around this place?'

Mad Crow took them back to the living room, where two cots had been set up in the area by the fireplace. 'You get the couch, monsieur,' he said to Horn. 'Go ahead and turn in. Billy and me, we're full of coffee. We'll stay up for a while, look in on Maggie and our new guest.'

Horn needed no more encouragement. Within minutes after bringing his spare clothes in from the car, he was asleep.

He opened his eyes to find Mad Crow shaking him and the room bright with sunlight. 'Phone for you,' the Indian said. 'A woman. She wouldn't say who. I thought you'd want me to wake you.'

Horn groggily picked it up. 'Hello.'

'If you're still interested, tonight would be the time,' Laura Lee Paisley said, without preamble and in a tone that was strictly don't-give-a-damn. 'I just found out that the last of the hotel staff are leaving today, and my people have to start transferring my office first thing tomorrow.'

'I'm interested.'

'Good for you. George will meet you at the back of the hotel at ten.'

He was immediately on guard. 'Why do I need George?'

'To let you in, of course. They've put up fencing all around, and we have a key to the lock on the rear gate. Also to the office door.'

'That's fine, but I don't want him hanging around.'

'Aren't you the demanding one?' Her voice had the taste of lemon peel. 'You just remember our agreement. Don't take anything.'

'I remember.'

'If you're not there at ten, he won't wait.' She hung up.

He lay down again, but the house was full of activity and trying to go back to sleep was impossible. He went to the kitchen, where he found Mad Crow and his nephew eating at the table while Nee Nee busied herself at the stove.

'You hungry?' Mad Crow asked him. 'I'm so turned around I don't know if this is breakfast or what, but it does the job.'

'How's Grace?'

'She's been moving around a little, making some sounds. She's still asleep, but I think she's starting to come out of it.'

The smell of food reminded him how long it had been since he had eaten. He sat down, and soon Nee Nee was scrambling eggs, onions, ham, and peppers in a giant skillet for him. He ate a plateful and asked for seconds.

'Looks like I'll be heading over to the Hollywood Alhambra tonight,' he told Mad Crow.

'Good,' his friend said around a mouthful. 'If you're going to dig through those files, do me a favor and look up Clara Bow. I used to have a great big crush on her, and I'd like to know if there's anything to that story about her and the USC football team. You know, just out of curiosity.'

'I'll see what I can do.'

After breakfast, he showered, shaved, and changed into clean clothes, then went into Mad Crow's bedroom, where Grace Stilwell lay on her side, legs drawn up under the covers, with one hand held in front of her face, as if for protection. Maggie sat beside the bed.

'Thought I'd do nurse duty for a while, give the boys a break,' she said. She wore pajama bottoms and a robe that she had wrapped, shawl-style, around the projecting cast on her left arm.

'Got some news,' he said, and told her about the phone call.

'Well, hallelujah.' She managed a grin.

'How you feeling?'

'Awful,' she said, rolling her eyes a little. 'But better, I guess. I itch like crazy inside these things. I'm getting bored sitting here. And I can't stop thinking . . .'

243

She didn't have to finish the thought. 'I know,' he said. 'We're all proud of Davey.' He glanced at the sleeping form on the bed. 'And now that we've found her, maybe we'll get a little closer to where we're going.'

As if responding to his remark, Grace Stilwell cried out in her sleep. Horn leaned over her. The next sound was a low, prolonged moan. Suddenly her eyes flew open, and her head came up off the pillow. She looked around the room, wild-eyed, breathing hard.

Horn stepped back. 'Don't worry,' he said. 'You're all right.'

She stared at him, then at Maggie, then at the nightgown she was wearing, then at everything else. Drawing out each word, she said slowly, '*Where . . . the hell . . . am* I?'

'In a safe place,' he said. 'Do you remember me?'

Once again, she gave him that familiar up-and-down look. 'Yeah,' she muttered finally. 'But that doesn't answer my—' She stopped, as if suddenly remembering something. 'Oh, God.' She shrank back on the bed.

'I didn't do anything to hurt you,' he said. 'Somebody took you from your house the other night. Do you remember that?'

She raised her hands to her temples. 'Something . . . I remember something,' she said. 'My head hurts, and I feel . . . What's wrong with me?'

'You were doped to the gills when I found you,' he said. 'You've been asleep for a long time. Since night before last.'

She seemed to have trouble absorbing that. She narrowed her eyes at Horn. 'What did you do to me?'

'I told you—' he began.

'He may have saved your life,' Maggie broke in. 'Give the man some credit, why don't you?'

'And who the hell are you?'

'Just another visitor,' Maggie said blithely. 'One who knows who her friends are.'

Grace Stilwell lay back and was silent for a moment. 'Let me start over,' she said, her gaze now on the ceiling. 'Where am I?'

'In the home of a friend of mine,' Horn said.

'And your name is . . . Horn, right? The man with the rude questions.'

'That's me. And this is Maggie O'Dare.'

'Pleased to meet you, Miss Stilwell,' Maggie said with exaggerated formality. 'My father was Owen Bruder.'

'*Oh.*' She sat up again to look hard at Maggie.

'Let me help,' Horn said, coming forward to arrange the pillows behind her back.

'I knew about you,' the woman said slowly to Maggie. 'And I wondered about you. What you were like.'

'How did you know about me?'

'Owen told me.'

'He did?' Maggie looked delighted. 'I didn't know he told anybody about me.'

'Maggie's the reason I'm in this,' Horn told her. 'She's the reason I go around asking all those rude questions.'

'I'm starting to understand,' Grace Stilwell said, looking from one to the other. She seemed to notice Maggie's injuries for the first time. 'You've been hurt.'

Horn took a seat at the foot of the bed. 'The same man who killed Maggie's father tried to kill her the other night. And he shot Maggie's husband to death right in front of her.'

'Oh, no.' She clutched at the bedspread.

'Grace, we think you can help us,' Horn said, feeling awkward at the use of her first name. 'A lot of our questions have brought us to your front door. And just when I was about to have a real talk with you, somebody tried to put you away where nobody could find you. But I did find you. And now we need to have that talk.'

She stared at him as if transfixed by his words, her lower lip caught between her teeth. He could almost see her thinking.

'My throat's very dry,' she said. 'I could use some water.'

'Sure.' He brought her a tall glass of water from the kitchen, which she quickly drained, and asked for more. She drank the refill thirstily, then placed the glass on the bedside table. 'Now I'd like to take a bath,' she said. 'And after that, I need to put something on over this.' She fingered the nightgown. 'And I don't want to sound demanding, but I'm suddenly very hungry.'

'I think you're starting to feel better,' Maggie said wryly. 'The bathroom is down the hall to your left. I'll make sure you have towels.'

Testing her balance, Grace Stilwell carefully made her way out of the room. 'Don't let her go anywhere,' Horn said to Maggie in a low voice. 'Or near the phone.'

'And you,' she said to him, 'don't let her start ordering you around.'

An hour later, Grace Stilwell, her hair wrapped in a towel, was sitting up in bed, looking somewhat out of place in a flannel shirt and a pair of dungarees belonging to Maggie. She had finished eating, and Mad Crow had poked his head in the door briefly to say hello.

'Better?' Horn asked. He had pulled an extra chair into the room and sat near Maggie.

'Hmm,' she nodded. 'I think I've heard of Joseph,' she said. 'Isn't he some kind of gambler?'

'Yep,' he said. 'He'd be flattered you know who he is.'

'And you were in the movies together.'

He nodded.

She laughed suddenly. 'I'm sorry,' she said. 'But this seems so odd to me. I'm rescued by a cowboy, and I find myself in the home of an Indian, wearing somebody else's clothes. It feels like one of those runaway-heiress comedies I occasionally write, where she wakes up in a strange bed, and . . .' She stopped herself. 'Not funny, is it?'

'Not today.'

She sighed. 'You're probably right. 'I'm no Claudette Colbert. And you—' She tilted her head, studying Horn. 'You're no Clark Gable.'

'I already knew that. Can we start?'

'The questions? All right.' She cradled a cup of Nee Nee's hot tea in her hands. Although cleaned up and nourished, she looked exhausted.

'Do you know who grabbed you the other night?'

She shook her head. 'I've been trying to remember ever since you told me what happened,' she said. 'All I remember is working in my study, and hearing a sound downstairs. I went down to see. After that . . . I don't remember anything. Except something cold on my face. And a pain in my arm, a sharp pain.' She shrugged. 'That's it. Until I woke up here.'

A thought occurred to her. 'Have the police been looking for me?'

'No,' Horn said. 'Things moved too fast. Nobody told them you were missing.'

'How do you like that?' she said sarcastically. 'No one missed me.'

'Do you think we should call them now?'

'I don't know.' The sarcasm evaporated. 'I suppose we should talk about that.'

'Your friend Maris Felix felt the same way,' Horn said. 'She had a chance to call the cops but decided not to. I'm not sure why.'

'Maris?' She looked startled.

'Along with me, you can thank her that you're not still up at the farm, bunking with a roommate named Thelma and getting stuck with a needle every six hours.'

'Well.' She looked down at her cup of tea for a long time. 'I guess someone missed me. She probably took some chances, coming after me. If you talk to her, please thank her for me.' She raised the cup and smiled feebly. 'This tastes good, but I'm wondering if a girl could get a real drink in this establishment.'

'Maybe later,' Horn said. 'Let's get back to the questions. I had a long talk with Grover Jones yesterday.' She blinked at the mention of his name, but said nothing. 'He's important to you, isn't he? You sent a note to Owen saying you had figured out that Grover was the one who ratted on him to the Red hunters. Not long after that, you met Owen at Schwab's for a secret talk about Grover and what you planned to do about him. And not long after that, Owen was dead.'

The cup of tea held all her attention. 'You've been very, very busy,' she said quietly.

'I guess so. Having our friends and relatives killed off makes us want to find out who and why. One of the things we found out was that you admitted to Grover that you and Owen had an affair.'

Maggie leaned forward to hear the response.

'Yes,' Grace Stilwell said without looking at either of them. 'We did. A long time ago, when I was still at Paramount. We met at a party. The attraction was immediate and we acted on it. It lasted a while, and then it was over, like a lot of affairs. We both had strong personalities, we set off sparks for a while, and . . .' She gestured vaguely with the cup. 'We acknowledged that we should move on. Owen, you see, was just being his usual impetuous self, but I never doubted that he loved his wife. And it seemed natural that when it came to a choice, he would choose her. I respected him for it.'

'Wally Roland told us he overheard Owen having a talk with you on the phone,' Horn said. 'After he hung up, he cussed you out. You must have gotten him—'

'Oh, yes,' she said. 'I remember that conversation. It was when I admitted something to Owen. Misbehavior, you might call it. He didn't spare the rod with me that day, I have to say. He told me I was being very foolish, making an awful mistake. You know, Owen could be as hard on his friends as he was on his enemies.'

'You don't have to be cute about it,' Horn said. 'I'll bet what you admitted to Owen was that you'd been getting cozy with your boss.'

She looked startled. 'Did Grover tell you that? Well, damn him for a little tattletale.'

It was Maggie's turn. 'We can leave your private life out of it, at least for now. Let's talk about that time you met Owen at Schwab's. It turns out you were right about Grover, he's admitted lying about Owen. But by the time that happened, you and Owen were no longer involved, so why—'

'Why was I trying to find out who was behind his problems? I liked him. He was a terrific guy. Maybe I felt I owed him something for complicating his life. I wanted to help him.'

'How did you find out about Grover?' Maggie asked.

'We're close, he and I,' she said. 'We understand each other. One day we began talking about Owen's problems with the government, and Grover became very emotional about it. I know he never intended to tell me but, as I said, we're very close, and I felt he was carrying around an immense guilt. By the end of the conversation, he had given away much more than he meant to, and I was convinced that he was the one who had informed on Owen. I said so in the note. When I saw Owen at Schwab's, I suggested that we both confront Grover and demand to know why he had done it.'

'We know why,' Horn said. 'Marvin Felix ordered him to.'

Her expression shifted quickly from shock to anger. Then to grim resignation. 'Marvin,' she said simply.

'Your boyfriend. Are you surprised?'

'I don't have anything to say about that,' she said tonelessly. 'I don't know. I need to think.'

'We've run out of time for that,' Horn said. 'If Felix was behind Owen's troubles, I think there's a good chance he had you put away at the farm, where nobody could ask you all these rude questions. And if he's responsible for that, then you know what else he might have done.'

Grace Stilwell shook her head, looking overwhelmed. 'God, I need a drink,' she said. 'Is anyone listening?'

Maggie got up. 'I'll get her something,' she said as she left the room.

'I'm not sure she's earned it,' Horn said, and then, to Grace, 'If the two of you had figured out most of it, I don't see why Owen and Lillian bothered to bring me in.'

'I'm not absolutely sure, but I have an idea,' she said. 'It was all Lillian's doing, hiring you, and that private detective – the one who didn't last very long. If Owen had insisted that he already had some of the answers, that could have led to her finding out about me. And even though we were no longer involved, Owen didn't want to see Lillian hurt, and I didn't want that either. So when she wanted to hire you, he went along.'

She studied him for a moment, almost smiling. 'I have to say I was not at all impressed with you when we met. Your clothes, your manners, the whole rough-cut package. But now that I can see how far you've gone with this . . . well, appearances can be deceptive. Thank you for bringing me back. If I ever write this as a madcap romantic comedy, I'll make sure the Gable part is based on you.'

'Don't bother.' He was as susceptible to feminine charm as anyone, but trouble seemed to collect around her. And until he had all his answers, he planned to keep Grace Stilwell at a distance.

'Lillian already had some suspicions about another woman,' he told her. 'She just didn't know who or why, or exactly what it amounted to.'

'Well . . .' She sipped at her tea. 'From what I know about her, she's an exceptional person. I hope none of this is hurtful to her.'

'You're starting to say nice things about people. Is this the real you?'

'Go to hell,' she said casually.

'Still not ready to talk about Marvin Felix?'

'I told you. I need time to think.'

He took a step toward the bed. 'There's a room down at the Hollywood Alhambra,' he said. 'Laura Lee Paisley calls it her room of secrets. I'm headed there tonight to have a look around. And maybe I'll find out if you're telling the truth.'

She stared at him open-mouthed. 'How in the world . . .'

'Oh, you haven't heard? Me and Laura Lee, we're like this,' he said, holding two fingers close together. 'If she has a file on you, you can bet I'll find it. If there's anything you think I should know, now's the time to tell me.'

Once again she studied her cup of tea. Horn left the room. In the hall he passed Maggie, who was carrying something that tinkled with ice cubes. 'She hasn't earned it yet,' he told her.

The rest of the day passed quietly, with Horn wishing he could speed the hands of the clock around to that time when he could leave. Grace Stilwell, aided by two stiff scotches, sank into a sweaty and uneasy sleep, occasionally calling out in a muffled voice. Horn tried to nap for a while. Then he and Maggie talked, going over the woman's revelations, wondering how much more she had to hide.

Billy Looks Ahead came and went almost soundlessly, a pistol in his belt and a Marine Corps knife in a scabbard. He spent much of his time outside, walking around the property, keeping an eye on the house and other buildings.

Supper was not particularly relaxed. They ate to fortify themselves, barely noticing that it was Nee Nee's good meatloaf. Grace Stilwell slept through it. As the sky darkened, the air felt heavy to Horn, like that moment before the first thunderclap.

Mad Crow produced a deck of cards. 'Anybody for some gin?'

'Sure,' Horn said gloomily. 'Deal 'em.'

'I should warn you that I'm a professional gambler, and I'm likely to own your raggedy cowboy ass before the night's over.'

They played a few hands without much enthusiasm. 'Did Maggie tell you she talked to the police yesterday?' Mad Crow asked.

'No.'

'She called to see if they'd learned anything. Spoke to that guy named Pitt. He's added this one to his case load, figuring there's a connection.'

'Smart. Do they know anything?'

'Just that they think Davey was shot with a Luger. Doesn't narrow it down much, I guess. Probably several thousand GIs brought one of those things back from Europe.'

'I suppose so.' Horn discarded the deuce of hearts. 'I appreciate you sticking your neck out like this. And Billy, too.'

Mad Crow looked at him with surprise, then looked across the room at Maggie, who sat on the sofa by the fire looking through a magazine. 'Somebody killed Davey,' he said in a low voice. 'He was a prickly cuss, and I suppose he wasn't my favorite person. But he could be good company. And he rode a horse like he was born in the saddle. And somebody killed him, and tried to kill my favorite lady over there. If sticking my neck out a couple of inches helps us find who did that, then it's worth it.'

His words sounded strangely familiar. Except for the part about riding a horse, I could almost say the same about Owen Bruder, Horn thought. It wasn't affection for the man that got me into this. It was my favorite lady over there. Maggie O'Dare, whose love life had brought her less than total happiness, nevertheless had the gift of inspiring great loyalty from the various men around her. He wondered if the Indian's feelings for her went beyond simple loyalty.

'Gin.' Mad Crow picked up Horn's discard. 'That's another oil well you owe me. Maybe you should have tried harder to make friends with Roy Earl Briar.'

Finally, just before nine, Horn got up. 'I guess I'll take a trip,' he said to both of them.

Maggie put down the magazine and, after a long pause, said, 'I'm coming with you.'

He shook his head vigorously. 'No.'

'If you find out something, I want to be there.'

'When did you decide this?'

'I don't know. Just now, I guess.' She looked belligerent, daring him to argue.

'We don't know for sure that I'm going to turn up anything,' he said. 'It's just something I have to do. Why not stay here and rest? If I find anything there, you'll know right away.' He considered telling her of his fresh concern about Laura Lee Paisley and her motives since learning of her connection to Pappas and the farm. If George's innocently goofy behavior masked something more sinister, Horn would have to deal with him. If Maggie were there, it would complicate things immensely.

But the look on her face told him it was useless to argue. 'Dammit,' she said. 'Have you ever been hit with a plaster cast? I can promise you it hurts.'

'All right,' he said wearily. 'Let's go.'

33

The Hollywood Alhambra was no more. The place where guests had once gathered, rested, dined, and danced to an orchestra was now a shell of a building. The signs identifying it had been dismantled, except for the gigantic neon marker on the roof that had long been visible for miles. Someone had left the sign burning, either in an oversight or in some last, doomed gesture before the wreckers came. A couple of its letters were blank, and the capital 'A' flickered, as if exhausted after years of duty. The hotel's facade was cordoned off with a high chain-link fence, and trash already littered the broad front steps and the grassy entry yard.

Horn drove down to the corner, turned, and entered the alley that ran the length of the block behind the hotel. When he reached the building, he saw that the rear was also fenced off, its gate padlocked. At the same time he noticed the big Chrysler, its engine idling and George behind the wheel.

'That's him, huh?' Maggie asked.

'Yeah.' He parked by the fence, and George got out to join them. Before leaving the car, Horn slid the .38 into his belt.

'Laura Lee didn't say you were bringing anybody,' George said to Horn. His patch of dead hair stood out in the light from a street lamp. He studied Maggie. 'Have you been in an accident?'

'That's right, she's had an accident,' Horn said to him. 'Can you let us in?'

'Yes.' He unlocked the padlock, and swung the gate open. 'You can go in now. I have the key to the office, too.'

'Just a minute.' Horn stepped up to him and raised his arms to indicate that he wanted to search him. George complied. 'You always do this,' he said, apparently enjoying the joke.

Finding no weapon, Horn said, 'You first.' George led them through a big service entrance, its door already ajar. Horn switched on a flashlight and, their footsteps echoing, they went down a corridor past various storerooms, a pantry, and a sprawling kitchen. Near the end, they crossed a smaller corridor that apparently led to offices on both sides. One more doorway, and they were in the main lobby.

A skylight ran the width of the front of the lobby, and streetlights and other various city lights bathed the high-ceilinged interior in something like strong moonlight. The furniture was gone, but the giant urns remained at the base of the stairs. Across from the reception desk, Horn could make out the mural, and the now silent tiled fountain against the far wall.

George led the way up the stairs to the mezzanine and Laura Lee's office, where he unlocked the doors. They followed him through the solid inner door to the file room and George turned on the overhead light.

They found themselves in a small room, no more than ten feet square, whose walls were lined with filing cabinets bearing labels in alphabetical order. The only other furnishings were a simple wood table with a straight chair in the exact center of the room, and a larger, more comfortable chair in one corner.

'Laura Lee said for me to stay with you,' George said.

'No,' Horn said. 'That's not the deal. Leave the room, George. Hang around outside or go sit in the car. We'll let you know when we're finished.'

'Laura Lee said you're not supposed to take anything.'

'I won't take anything.' Horn felt close to the edge. 'I'm starting to get mad at you, George.'

George hesitated, clearly unsure of his duty. 'She said you weren't nice to her.'

'Well, it's worked both ways.'

Maggie broke in. 'You've been with her a long time, haven't you, George?'

'Yes. Since before I was hurt. She takes care of me, and I try to take care of her.'

'I'm sure you do a good job,' she said.

George nodded. 'She says she loves me. We've lived here for a long time. Now we have to leave. I don't want to, but they're going to tear down the hotel, and . . .' He gestured helplessly. 'I'm going to have a new room at the other place.'

'I'm sorry,' she said. 'Maybe you'll like it there.'

He was staring at her casts. 'What kind of accident was it?'

'Somebody tried to hurt me.'

He shook his head. 'That's not nice.'

'George, if we promise not to take anything, will you leave us here and wait somewhere else?'

They saw him come to a decision. It did not look easy. 'I guess so,' he said finally. He left, and they heard his footsteps fading down the tiled mezzanine floor.

Horn looked around. 'Let's get started.' On the drive over, they had discussed a rough division of duties. Now they went to the filing cabinets, each knowing what to look for.

It took them five minutes. At the end of that time, they closed the last drawers and looked at each other. 'Nothing?' he asked her.

She shook her head. 'None of the files I'm looking for are here.'

He cursed Laura Lee Paisley's name softly, then loudly. 'I am real stupid,' he said. 'After I back her into a corner and threaten her, what makes me think she's going to take it lying down? She's moved them. If I go back and threaten her again, she'll just tell me she never had files on any of those people.'

'Let's not give up yet,' Maggie said. She thought for a moment. 'Maybe they're just not where they belong . . .'

'Out of order?' He shrugged. 'It'll take a while, but it's worth a try.'

One by one, they went through each file drawer to see if anything had been tucked away in the wrong drawer. A half-hour later, they were finished.

Horn went to the outer office, brought in an ashtray and methodically began rolling a smoke, forcing his hands to slow down. Think, he told himself. If they were here, she moved them. If she took them away, I'll never see them. But even if she just hid them someplace around here, I don't have much of a chance of finding them.

Why would she do it? Out of sheer cussedness, to show me I can't push her around? Or maybe because she knows everything, she's behind everything, and she's determined to stop me from learning any of it. If that's true, he thought, she's capable of a lot more than just hiding a few files. He thought of George somewhere out there in the darkened building and grimaced, again regretting that he had let Maggie come along.

'What's wrong?' she asked.

Without answering, he went back to the outer office and checked the door to the corridor. He wanted to lock it, but George had taken the keys.

The keys. He looked around. When he had last visited, a secretary had been busy typing. The receptionist. The guardian of the file room and her boss' office. The typewriter still sat there, surrounded by stationery, so her desk had not yet been emptied. He opened the long middle drawer. There, right in front, was a ring with four keys on it. One for the single desk drawer that bore a lock. One for the outer door. One for the file room. And . . . one for Laura Lee Paisley's inner office.

It took him only a few seconds to unlock the door, the one with her name in frosted glass, and switch on the light. Inside, it looked chaotic. Besides a cluttered desk, telephone, single filing cabinet and a chair for visitors, there were packed cartons everywhere. The lids were not yet sealed shut, and he began looking through them. He found office supplies, books, and other items, but no files. One carton consisted solely of framed photos showing Laura Lee Paisley with Louis B. Mayer, Darryl F. Zanuck, and many of the other nabobs of Hollywood. There was even a photo of her with Hedda Hopper and Louella Parsons at some dress-up event, the arch rivals posing sweetly like sisters.

The filing cabinet had been emptied, and he found its contents in one of the cartons. It was mostly correspondence. He glanced at some of the letters and saw nothing of interest. The desk drawers had also been emptied. Discouraged, he tilted back in the swivel chair and closed his eyes. I could try grilling George, he thought, and maybe he'll give something away without meaning to. He opened his eyes and found himself staring at the light fixture, a large rectangle, fitted with three bulbs and suspended from the ceiling by two chains. He couldn't see the upper surface, but it looked wide and long enough to . . .

He clambered up onto the desk, stood erect, and there they were. A small stack of files resting neatly atop the light fixture. He took them down. There were seven of them, held together by a big rubber band: Owen Bruder. Marvin Felix. Grover Jones. Wally Roland. Grace Stilwell. Cal Stoddard. John Ray Horn.

He carried them to the file room. 'What are you reading?' he asked Maggie.

Without looking up, she gave him a guilty grin. 'Errol Flynn,' she said. 'I could say it's because Davey wanted to know about him, but that wouldn't exactly be the whole truth.' Her eyes darted around the page. 'Oh, my goodness gracious, this is really . . .' She looked up. 'What have you got there?'

'Well, I hate to drag you away from Errol, but I found a few things.'

Her face lit up as she saw what he carried. 'He can wait,' she said, tossing the file on the table. 'Let's get to work.'

He gave Maggie her father's file, and those for Grace Stilwell and Grover Jones. He took Marvin Felix, Cal Stoddard, Wally Roland, and his own. There was no file for Maris Felix, he noted, and was interested – and glad – that there was nothing on Mad Crow.

He rolled another smoke. Cal Stoddard's file was the thinnest, so he started with it. Beyond the kind of bare facts that could have been gleaned from the registry at the Department of Motor Vehicles, there was a single page on the young man's brief connection with communism in 1933. At the bottom of the page, Mitchell Cross' name was listed in a handwritten note as the source of the information. The writing was in green ink and elegantly done. Horn spotted several little notations here and there in the same ink, and guessed that they were made by Laura Lee Paisley herself.

He picked up Wally Roland's file. Again, no surprises. A few pages on his early years and education. A clipping from *Time* magazine identifying Roland as one of a group of 'left-leaning' playwrights active in New York City, with Owen Bruder's name also on the list. A clipping from the *Los Angeles Times* on the arrests in Pyrie in 1939 and the death of Robert Nimm. Next to the sentences dealing with Nimm, Laura Lee had added two exclamation marks and the words *Govt. mum about this.* Finally, a full page of handwritten notes in green ink that read as if taken down from a phone conversation. It was an account of how Roland was identified as a member of the American Communist Party during secret testimony before House investigators, the testimony provided by two former party members. *Subpoena being issued*, the notes concluded. Again, Mitchell Cross was listed as the source.

'How you doing?' he asked Maggie.

'Oh . . . I'm just reading that Owen was a talented playwright and a great screenwriter. That he got involved in things that were supposed to make people's lives better.' She sounded irritated, almost angry. 'That he was often too blunt, and this bothered people. Even the newspapers and magazines that hated his politics usually got around to saying he had integrity. And I'm wondering how any of that could get him killed.'

'Anything on who named him?' he asked.

'You mean Grover? No. It just says Owen's name came up—'

'In secret testimony. I know.'

'I'm thirsty.' She got up and stretched. 'You think there might anything to drink in this big old empty place?'

'I doubt it.'

'I'd settle for a glass of water. Why don't I go have a look?'

'Uh . . . I don't think it's a good idea for you to go wandering around by yourself.'

'Then give me that.' She pointed to the pistol in his belt.

A not-so-subtle change had come over Maggie. She had always had a stubborn streak, but in the past it had been tempered by her fundamental country-girl decency. Since the attack and Davey's death, however, he now saw a woman who would let nothing deter her from her goals – whether finding a murderer or getting something cold to drink.

'All right,' he said, handing her the .38. 'I guess you know how to use this. And take the flashlight.' He locked the door behind her, then picked up his own file. He was relieved that it also held no surprises. Still, he observed, Laura Lee Paisley was interested mostly in the negatives of a life. A man judged strictly by the contents of this file would not come up smelling like honeysuckle.

There was a cursory list of some of his movies. A note from an anonymous source at Medallion stated that Horn had been 'stubbornly insistent' on hiring Joseph Mad Crow, a 'full-blooded Sioux Indian who once lived on a reservation, and a man with limited acting experience,' to play his sidekick, when several white actors at Medallion were deemed at least as qualified for the role. The brawl with Bernard Rome Junior was covered extensively with news clippings, including one that showed Bernie Jr. showing up in court with his face heavily bandaged.

There was an account of Horn's wife, Iris, filing for divorce while he was in prison. Lastly, a short item from *Variety* bearing the headline 'Ex-Cowboy Hero Out of Work' and describing how Horn had come out of prison to find himself blacklisted by every studio in town. Nothing, he was relieved to see, on his medical history during the war. So far, at least, Mitchell Cross had sole custody of that information but that, Horn knew, could change. He was sure that Laura Lee Paisley would rub her hands in glee if presented with it.

He heard a soft knock on the outer door and Maggie's voice. He unlocked it. With the flashlight in her immobilized left hand, Maggie brandished two bottles of Coke in her right. 'Victory,' she said. 'Found 'em in the kitchen. They're warm but drinkable. No opener, though.'

'Any sign of George?'

'Nope. Maybe he's gone out to the car.' She handed him the bottles, then retrieved the pistol from her pants pocket.

He positioned one bottle top on the edge of the table, its cap hooked into the wood. He smacked the cap hard, and it flew off. Then he opened the other one the same way. 'Arkansas bottle opener,' he said.

'I'm impressed. And I thought you Arkansas boys were unsophisticated.' She saw his file atop the stack. 'Anything in that?'

'Just the usual stuff.'

They resumed reading. 'Poor man,' she said after a few minutes.

'Who?'

'Grover Jones. I know I should hate his guts and I suppose I do, but I wouldn't want his life. This whole file is about him sneaking around, trying to keep this one part of his life secret. And all the time, other people have been sneaking around spying on him, seeing him doing something in one place, coming out of somebody's house doing something else. You know. It's all a big game. The secret-keepers against the secret-stealers. And Miss Laura Lee – or Miss Hedda or Miss Louella – sitting here deciding when and if to use it.'

'It looks like somebody finally did use it.' He picked up Marvin Felix's file. 'This gentleman.' He began leafing through the pages. They seemed to be a typical profile of a studio boss, a man who may never have broken a law but nonetheless, in his ruthless pursuit of power, left a trail of enemies behind him – the powerful enemies who still resented him and the weak enemies who wound up broken by him.

On a small sheet of paper he found a note in Laura Lee Paisley's distinctive hand, apparently paraphrased from a report by one of her sources. It mentioned that Marvin Felix had been seen in a restaurant down the coast in La Jolla, having dinner with a woman who was not his wife. It was dated six months earlier. *Woman thought to be Grace Stilwell, writer for Global,* read the last line. *Two seen holding hands.*

'Laura Lee knew about Grace and her boss,' he said.

'I guess we shouldn't be surprised,' Maggie replied. 'But now I'm wondering: What if Marvin saw Owen as a rival?'

'Maybe. But Grace told us it was over between her and Owen before she even came to Global, so where's the rivalry?'

'I don't know, dammit.'

'Let's keep looking. You've got Grace over there. See if you can find anything.'

She opened the file and began reading. He turned the last page in Marvin Felix's file and found two envelopes.

'What's this?' One was labeled *Maris Felix* and the other *Sidney Swain.* He laughed. 'Maris and Sidney, the brother and sister,' he said. 'They're not important enough to have their own files, so she stuck them in with Marvin.'

While he opened the first one, Maggie said, 'There's not much on Grace. And there's nothing on her with Marvin, but I have found something. It's on the page that talks about where she came from and went to school, that sort of thing.'

'What is it?'

'Well, she went to Vassar. Did you know that? She must be very smart. But there's a note here in green ink—'

'That's our friend Laura Lee.'

'It says, *From former classmate. Anonymous. Says G.S. joined radical groups including organization in support of Spanish leftists opposing Franco. In senior year joined CPUSA.* That's—'

'The US Communist Party.' The idea stopped him cold. 'Anything else?'

'Just a note in the margin saying, *Unconfirmed. Needs checking.*'

He drained the Coke bottle and set it down carefully, thinking hard. 'What does this tell us?'

'Well, she lied to you when she said she wasn't political.'

'And?'

'Like a lot of people, she has something to hide.'

'Right. If the committee knew about her, wouldn't they want her?'

'A big-time female screenwriter? You bet they would.'

'So why don't they know about her?' he pondered. 'I mean, all Laura

Lee has is this one item, and it's unconfirmed. But if it's true, I reckon Mitchell Cross and his people would have ways of finding it out.'

'Come to think of it,' she asked, 'why didn't Laura Lee just tell them?'

'Can't say for sure. She's got tons of files here, and maybe this one little item got lost. Also, I get the idea that when it comes to Red-hunting, she doesn't spend much time digging up stuff on her own. Just about everything she's had on the radio came to her straight from the government boys, all tied up neatly with a ribbon.'

That was as far as they could go, and neither spoke for a while. Then Horn got up. 'I think it's time for another talk with Grace Stilwell. Have these phones been disconnected yet?' He went to the outer office, picked up the phone, and got a tone. He dialed Mad Crow's number. Nee Nee answered, and he asked for her nephew. It took a while, but he finally understood her to say that Mad Crow and Billy had gone outside. 'What for?' he asked. Her answer was unintelligible.

'Put Grace on the phone. The woman in Joseph's room. Grace.' Again it took a while, but she seemed to be telling him that Grace was not there.

'What? Listen, Nee Nee, tell Joseph to call me at this number when he comes in. It's very important. Understand?' He read out the number three times before hanging up.

'Something's wrong,' he said to Maggie. 'Joseph's gone out, and it doesn't sound like Grace is there either.'

Uneasily, they went back to their reading. He passed her the Sidney Swain envelope while he began reading about Swain's sister. Maris Felix, it appeared, had been living a colorful life out of the public eye. According to one informant, she had been seen entering a secluded house in Hollywood known to cater to women who sought the company of other women. Another mentioned a payoff made by her husband to a young woman who had threatened to reveal details of her relationship with Felix's wife.

It was explosive, but only if put to use. Horn wondered if Felix knew what Laura Lee Paisley had on his wife, or if the gossip-monger was merely biding her time, waiting for the right moment to use what she had.

He was about to tell Maggie what he'd found when she said, 'I found something.' He looked up.

'It's in the middle of a bunch of other things,' she said. 'Your friend Sidney went to Stanford and got a business degree. After that, there's a lot of drinking and womanizing and some bad debts, and one particular barroom brawl he got into that Marvin managed to keep out of the papers. But you should look at this.' She passed him a single sheet of paper.

A note in green ink, detailing a conversation with a visitor to Laura Lee Paisley's office one day last year. The visitor was an ex-Army sergeant who had served in Europe during the war and was stationed in Austria during the occupation. A military policeman. He had heard that Laura Lee Paisley paid well for useful information.

The next paragraph described what he knew. Below that, she had written in her elegant penmanship, *Confirmed by source at War Department, Washington.*

And finally: *$100 paid in cash.* The informant's fee. Not bad for a few minutes' work, Horn thought.

Maggie watched him as he turned it all over in his mind. To the mix he added a comment Laura Lee Paisley had made at the beach house, something that had made no sense at the time. Now, however, he thought it did.

Mitchell Cross' original target had been a woman. *She'll make a good story for you,* he told Laura Lee Paisley, but he wound up going after Owen Bruder instead. In effect, he moved the cross hairs off her and placed them squarely on him. Why?

With a little imagination, a picture was emerging. If Marvin Felix was secretly infatuated with Grace Stilwell, and if he learned that the woman he loved was about to be denounced as a traitor, possibly threatened with prison, to what lengths would he go to prevent it? What if he were to offer the committee a substitute target, one even better known than she? And what better target than Owen Bruder, one of his employees and a man who had once been involved with her – especially if Felix sensed that Grace still felt some affection for him. Felix was powerful enough, influential enough, to do it. With one sweep of his hand, he could save the woman he loved and condemn the man he saw as a rival.

And no one would know that it was all accomplished with a lie. No one except Grover Jones – until Grace Stilwell and Owen Bruder began to put it together. Then he, of course, had to die, and she had to be put away until she came to her senses and Felix was sure that his secret was safe. He had done it, after all, out of love for her. If she didn't come to her senses . . . well, the farm was a secluded place, where accidents might happen.

It made sense, Horn thought, the way nightmares have their own logic. Was he reaching too far?

But how did Maris Felix figure in this? Did she figure at all? He didn't know. But for the first time since Owen Bruder's death, he began to see a pattern, a reason, a motive. And the outline of a face.

The phone rang loudly in the next room, startling him. It was Mad Crow.

'She's gone,' he said.

'What?'

'She went out the window. Before that . . .' He took a deep breath. 'Let me start over. I'd been out on the porch with Billy for a minute, and when

I came in, I found her hanging up the phone. She gave me some double-talk about starting to call the police and then changing her mind. I told her to get in her room, and I locked the door. Figured it was smart to lock her up till you got back, worry about apologizing later. But it looks like she pulled on a pair of Maggie's shoes and one of her sweaters and went out the goddam window.'

Horn sighed loudly, making static over the line.

'I thought she was still woozy, never would have guessed she'd . . . Anyway, she waited till Billy was making his rounds in the back, and she took off in the Caddy.'

'Because you always leave the keys over the visor,' Horn said.

'Yeah. I always figured, who would steal a big, show-off car like that one? They'd never be able to hide it. Damn, I'm sorry.'

'It's okay,' Horn said. 'I don't know what harm she can do us. I would've liked to ask her a few more questions, that's all. You think there's any chance she could have overheard us earlier, when we were out in the living room?'

'Then, I would have said no. Now I'm not so sure.'

'Right. Well, at least I've got an idea where she might have gone.'

'Where?'

'Tell you later. We're headed back pretty soon. See you then.' He hung up.

As the phone hit the cradle, he heard a sound, startlingly loud, from just outside the office door.

A gunshot. Then rapid footsteps. Then silence.

34

He grabbed the .38 off the table and hit the switch that killed the overhead light. The outer office was lit, and he suddenly recalled that he had forgotten to lock the door to the mezzanine when Maggie had returned. Peering out of the file room, he saw that it was still closed, and only blackness showed through the frosted glass. He quickly turned off the light in the outer office.

'Come on out,' he called to Maggie, and heard her make her way out of the file room to where he knelt behind the receptionist's desk. 'Get down here.'

They crouched there for several seconds, hearing nothing outside the door. 'What the hell?' he said almost to himself. George? Although Horn had frisked him, he could have stashed a gun in his car and gone to get it. But if so, what was he shooting at?

'George,' Horn called out loudly. 'Are you out there?'

No answer, and not the faintest sound from outside.

'Do you think anybody could have heard that?' she asked. 'And maybe called the police?'

'I doubt it. Even if they did, people expect to hear noises at a demolition site. I think I need to take a quick look.' Crossing to the outer door, he opened it a crack, then wider, extending first his gun hand through the opening, then his head. After the dark of the office, the exterior seemed bathed in dim light. He saw the waist-high balustrade that edged the mezzanine, supported by fat stone columns spaced about four feet apart. He saw the shop windows glinting on the far side, just above the tall windows over the lobby doors. And, down below, the deeper shadows of the main lobby.

One other thing. To the right, just short of the point where the balustrade made its right-angle turn, he saw a shape on the tile floor. A body. He squinted, then saw the patch of white hair on the left side of the head. And the small, dark pool underneath it.

He pulled back inside and closed the door. 'I think George has been shot,' he said quietly.

He heard her reach out for the phone and locate it. 'You think we should call for help?' she asked.

'And have the cops find me here with a body? No. Even if they decide the bullet didn't come from this gun, I don't want to give them a crack at me. They'll find some way to tie me to it.'

Her silence sounded like agreement. He shook his head to clear it and tried to think. 'I don't want to stay in here all night either, because people will be showing up. Let's look at it this way: we don't know if he's still there or gone. If he's there, he's not the only one with a gun, and visibility's as bad for him as it is for us. There's no point waiting.'

'What do you want to do?'

'I'll go out and look around. You lock the door behind me—'

'No.'

'And when it's all clear—'

'No.' All her stubbornness surfaced again. 'You're not going out there alone, leaving me here alone. If you go out, we go together. Don't even think of arguing.'

He knew what she meant. *I've lost two people. I'm not losing another.*

He formed a mental picture of the layout. The mezzanine ran around the second floor in a big square about sixty feet across, with shops and offices on all four sides. The grand staircase was close to them, about twenty feet from the office door, and would take them down to the lobby and the way they came in. There was a back stairway somewhere, but he couldn't remember if it lay to the left or the right, and he didn't want to waste time trying to find it. To the left and around one corner of the mezzanine was the elevator. But he didn't know if it was still running, and even if it was, he didn't like the idea of not knowing what awaited them when the doors opened below.

It looked like the main staircase was the best choice, exposed as it was. In a few seconds they could be downstairs and on their way out.

'Listen,' he said. 'We can't help George, at least not right now. Don't look right or left. Just stay at my side. Careful but not too slow. Down the stairs, right turn, and back to the exit. All right?'

She answered by squeezing his hand with surprising strength. 'All right, cowboy.' She sounded tense, but then he supposed he did too.

It took about ten steps to reach the top of the stairs. One fast look around. All his senses were tuned, reaching out for sights, sounds, smells, anything. She was to his left, leaving his right hand free for the .38. Still awkward carrying the extra weight of the casts, she used her good arm to hang on to him.

Without pausing, they began to descend. One step, then another.

The shot sounded like a cannon. He saw the flash off to the right, behind one of the columns. At the same instant, he heard the slap of the

262

bullet's impact right next to him. Maggie yelled hoarsely and stumbled against him, almost dragging him down. He raised the gun, barely took time to sight, and fired, hearing glass shatter at the far wall as the .38 bucked in his hand.

Oh, God. She's hit. He turned, scooped his gun hand under the cast on her arm, and dragged her back up the stairs, tripping over the top step, scrambling to reach the corner of the stairway. She was on the floor, he was on his knees dragging her behind him. He had her by the collar now, yanking, but the collar ripped and he came up with a fistful of cloth.

Another shot cracked against stone a foot away. 'Come on!' – an urgent, shouted whisper, as much to himself as to her. Reaching out for anything, he grabbed a handful of her hair and dragged her the final few feet to cover.

His lungs pumped air, he could feel his heart pounding in his head. Maggie's breaths were interspersed with groans. Frantically, he ran his free hand over her, feeling for blood. Nothing. Wait. His hand came away from her upper arm with crumbled bits of plaster. The bullet had struck the cast. She groaned more loudly. Her arm, he knew, might be broken again.

'Maggie,' he whispered. 'Can you hear me?'

'Uh-huh.'

'Lie still.'

'Son of a bitch shot me.'

'I know. Try not to move.'

He raised his head a few inches to peer over the stone railing. A shot sprayed grit from the column directly in front of him. He saw the muzzle flash clearly, took a second to sight on it and squeezed off another shot, then ducked down. The guy is good, he thought.

'Sidney Swain,' he called out. 'Is that you?'

'Why, yes, as a matter of fact,' the man answered. The voice came clearly over the thirty feet or so that separated them. The tile surfaces lent the sound a slight echo that made it hard to judge his precise location. But there had been the muzzle flash. Now, Horn thought, if only he doesn't move. He tried to fix the spot in his mind. Four columns from the corner, he thought.

He knelt there with Maggie directly behind him. George's body lay no more than twenty feet away, just this side of the corner of the balustrade. Since he had left the extra shells in the glove compartment, he knew he had three shots left. Swain was not exactly hoarding ammunition, and Horn wondered how much he had to go.

His stomach churned with the old familiar fear, the knowledge that someone wanted him dead and had the means to kill him. Given free rein, fear could take him over, drain him, leave him without the strength to raise an arm to defend himself. He knew how cowards felt. He wondered how Mitchell Cross, the war hero, would handle himself here. Or George, who scaled the cliff at Normandy with German fire pouring down on him. Horn knew that one of the hallmarks of heroism was simply not to doubt. The man who doubted was doomed by his own hand.

He heard Maggie panting, and knew she was in pain. 'Easy,' he said. 'Try to take deep breaths. We'll get out of this.'

'You wouldn't kid me, would you?' she said through clenched teeth.

'Who, me? Listen, I'll have you back at Mad Crow's in time for a good breakfast.'

Another shot, which struck the wall behind him. He aimed a little high that time, Horn thought.

'What are you two talking about?' Swain called out.

'Nothing.'

'Well, I'm feeling left out.'

'Why did you shoot George?'

'No good reason. I thought it would be a good way of getting you to come out. Worked, didn't it?'

'Sure did. Looks to me like you're a pretty good shot.'

'Thank you.'

'Military police, right?'

'Good memory, John Ray. Is it all right if I call you John Ray? Last names seem a little unnecessary when you're about to kill someone.'

'I've been reading about you, Sidney.'

'Uh-huh. Marvin and I were afraid you'd find something here. And I suppose you did.'

'Lots of things. About him. About Grace Stilwell. The most interesting one was you, though.'

'You're just saying that.' Horn heard a slight scuffing sound. He raised his head carefully and thought he saw Swain shift position to his left, bringing him a few feet closer to the corner. If he tries it again, he thought, I'll take a shot.

'You told me you were an MP,' Horn went on. 'You didn't tell me you beat a prisoner to death.'

'No, I didn't. It was just one of those things that happen under stress. You go along living your quiet little life, and then they throw you into a war and, in a second, you find out what you're capable of.'

'I found out some of that myself.' *If I can keep him talking*, Horn thought, *maybe I can get him to make a mistake.*

'It's something I think about a lot,' Swain said, sounding as if he were settling in for a good talk with amicable company. 'But I've told only one other person about it.'

'Marvin?'

'Exactly. Marvin's very curious about what I do. About those things he sends me to do, I mean. It's the one time . . .' He paused. 'It's the one time I can feel superior to him. Telling him about experiences he can never have. I've actually taken a life – taken *lives* – and you should see the expression on his face when I describe the sensations. He looks almost . . . *sad*, knowing he'll never be able to do what I do, have what I have. It's about the only time I feel close to him.'

Another scuffing sound. 'Pardon me.' Swain's voice came over the space between them. 'Just shifting position, so I don't get too cramped. I was telling you about the first time. This was in a POW camp in Austria, after the armistice. I had been called to the cell of a troublesome inmate, a lieutenant in the Waffen SS. One of the hard core of arrogant bastards who refused to accept that they had lost the war. We exchanged words, and, amazingly, he came at me. I was ready for him, though – I have very quick reflexes.

'I wore a sidearm but didn't need it. I just unlimbered my billy club and laid him down with a well-placed blow to the head. He lay there, half-conscious, and I realized I was alone in the cell. A little voice told me I might never get this chance again – to end a life with the strength of my right arm – and I raised the club and brought it down again, and again, and again. I actually felt the skull crack and come apart, and I think I could even feel the cushioning effect of the brain underneath . . .' Horn thought he could hear the man sigh.

'And then it was over. It looked very suspicious, of course. But my commanding officer, after some debate, decided that my life had been threatened and my response was within the limits. Not long afterward, I was quickly mustered out with an honorable discharge and I went back to my old life as my brother-in-law's fixer, his right-hand man.'

'Until he found out you had other talents.'

'Oh, he already knew. Marvin has tentacles everywhere. He knew of my other talent. The only question was when and if he would ever need to use it.'

'And then Owen Bruder and Grace Stilwell started asking the wrong questions.'

'Yes, well, Marvin had been a fool. He's always led with his pecker, but he usually picks brainless starlets who are grateful for his attention. Grace was different, a very complicated woman.'

'I've heard her called that before.'

'Yes. Very smart, very independent. And, to make things more complicated, she's been known to stray on both sides of the path, if you know what I mean.'

Horn recalled the sounds from the back seat as he drove Grace Stilwell

265

and Maris Felix down the coast. The sounds, almost, of a mother caring for a child.

'And did she find your sister on one side of the path?'

'Don't say anything against Maris,' Swain said. 'She's been good to me. But I'll tell you a secret, one I hope you'll take to your grave. Grace has not been involved with Marvin for very long. She and Maris have been together for years, and although Marvin knew everything, Maris never suspected.'

'That's hard to believe.'

'I know. I told you Grace was smart. She also has a talent for being whatever you want her to be. She's a chameleon. I'm sure she loves Maris, and the various men in her life have been just . . . trips over to the other side of the path. But I think she takes too many chances with other people's emotions. And she can be careless. From some of her comments, Marvin could tell that she was becoming suspicious of Grover Jones. He knew that she would eventually make the leap from Grover to him. And so . . . next stop, the farm, with me as her chauffeur.'

'It must have been hard to do.'

'Not really. Marvin didn't want her hurt. In the beginning, I think he saw her as a kind of challenge, someone to be possessed. After a while, though, I think he loved her.'

'So when I saw the four of you at the theater that night—'

'A lot of play-acting and pretending. There was Maris secretly enjoying the knowledge that Grace was hers, and Marvin congratulating himself that once again he was proving that he could conquer anything in skirts. And, especially, the lovely Grace, knowing that she was the sun around which all the planets revolved.'

'And what about you, Sidney?'

'I was doing my job, being indispensable, helping keep up the various fictions. You see, I like the status quo. If Marvin gets a thrill secretly poaching on his wife, and if Maris stays happy in her ignorance, I'm content to leave things alone. I have loyalties to both, and I don't want to see either one miserable.'

'You're a considerate man, Sidney,' Horn said. 'Thanks for telling me. But I can't promise you that I'll take it to my grave.'

'That's all right. I'll make sure that you do.'

Another groan escaped Maggie.

'Your lady friend is hurting,' Swain said solicitously.

'Don't worry about her. She's tougher than both of us.'

'Maybe you're right,' Swain responded. 'I thought she'd be easy the other night, and I could get the job done before her husband came back. I was very surprised when things became difficult. I had to use my war souvenir here on the hubbie – not my first choice of weapon – and to make things worse, she almost blew my head off with that big shotgun. The plan was her first, then you. Things had to be postponed. But here we are, and I'm finally getting around to it.' He raised his voice. 'Can you hear me, missy? I'm finishing you tonight, then your boyfriend.'

Horn knew what kind of war souvenir he meant. A Luger. The gun that killed Davey Peake. Horn tried to recall what he knew about them. They fired a smaller slug, which was good news. But he was pretty sure their magazine carried more shells, which was not. How many had he fired? He couldn't remember.

'How did you know we were here, Sidney?'

'I'm a mind-reader,' he said with a laugh. 'No, it's simpler than that. It seems Grace, wherever you had her stashed away, overheard some talk about you coming here tonight, and she called Maris to warn her.'

'About what?'

'That their particular cat might soon be out of the bag. But more important, it was starting to look like Maris' husband was behind the murder of Owen Bruder. Meanwhile, neither one of the girls knew that Marvin often enjoyed listening in on his wife's phone conversations. This was one of them.

' "Sidney," he said to me, "will you please clean up this mess?" "Sure, Marvin," I said. "And have you been thinking about how much of a liability Grace has become?" I asked him. "Yes, I have," he said. "And when you're finished with Horn and the O'Dare woman, you can take care of her as well." He sounded sad when he said it, though.'

Keep him talking, Horn told himself. 'Any idea how Grace Stilwell would react to the idea that people were dying because of her?'

'Hmm.' Swain seemed to give that serious thought. 'She'd be horrified. Flattered, maybe. How would I know? I'm not much good rooting around in the minds of women. I've had better luck with polo ponies.'

Horn looked carefully through the gap between columns. He thought he could see Swain's form between numbers four and five, wearing something pale. He's moved to his left, he thought. Trying to get closer. That's a good thing for me too.

He took careful aim at what he could see and squeezed the trigger. He heard the slug ricochet off the stone.

'Ow! That hurt.' Swain sounded peeved. 'I think you got me with a pebble. Good shot, though. Almost.'

Horn cursed. Two bullets left. They would have to count. That meant he needed to close the distance between himself and Swain. Since he couldn't leave Maggie, he had to bring the other man closer.

Without turning around, he reached back to touch Maggie. His hand met her neck, then her face. He laid the hand on her cheek. 'How you doing?'

'All right,' she said, sounding a little more relaxed. 'Like I told the doctor, I've broken bones before. I just don't want to make a habit of it.'

He called out to Swain. 'So tell me about your first choice of weapon, Sidney.'

'Well, it's the standard military cop's nightstick,' the other man said. 'I've got one right here. It's only about a foot long, fits neatly under a jacket or a longer coat, fastens onto your belt with the lanyard. Smoothed and varnished. Nice example of woodworking. But since it's not really made to be lethal, I've sunk a few extra ounces of lead into the tip. It adds just the right amount of weight. You can actually kill a man with one blow. Think about it.'

'Just like you did with Owen.'

'Exactly.'

'You know, for a long time, we all thought it was his politics that got Owen murdered.'

'That's what Marvin and I wanted you to think. Pretty smart, huh?'

'Owen must have been an easy target, standing there by the pool, but Maggie was too much for you, wasn't she? I guess that's because she didn't have her back turned.'

The remark was followed by a volley of three shots that sprayed shrapnel all around them. Horn fell backward against Maggie, making her yell in pain. He heard a clink of metal against tile, then a more solid click of metal against metal. 'Just needed a few seconds to reload,' he heard Swain say. 'I like these semi-automatics, don't you?'

Horn felt despair and the return of fear. The man was carrying extra magazines. With two bullets left in the .38, he couldn't stand against him. And with the shape Maggie was in, they couldn't run for it.

All they could do was wait.

'I think we've talked enough, don't you?' Swain called out. 'I'm getting cramped over here, and a little bored. Let's wrap this up.'

Two more shots, more singing ricochets. The floor in front of Horn was a mess of grit and chipped stone. Slowly he eased himself up to get a look. His eyes were fully adjusted to the low light now, and he clearly saw Swain between columns two and three. Still moving my way, he thought. I need a good shot. He reached out and picked up a golf ball-size chunk of stone, hefted it, and drew back his arm. There was a time when I could pick a squirrel off a log at twenty paces, he remembered. Let's see . . .

He threw as hard as he could, and the rock struck Swain solidly in the side, causing him to cry out and spring up. Horn leveled his gun at the middle of the form and squeezed the trigger. Swain yelled again, flinging his arms wide. Sighting as carefully as he had time for, Horn fired once more. The man sank out of sight.

Silence. Then a chuckle. 'John Ray, I think you just put a big hole in my trench coat,' Swain said. 'I paid good money for this at Brooks Brothers in San Francisco.'

Now he could see the face of the fear. It was his own face, but ugly and twisted. He didn't want to look at it. He and Maggie were about to die, and there was nothing he could do about it.

Three more shots from the other side. The air was dense with clouds of dust from the chipped stone, and his ears rang with the echoes.

He heard Swain slowly getting up. 'I've got an idea,' the man said. 'I've counted five shots from that revolver of yours. I'm pretty sure the cylinder holds six, but I know that a careful man sometimes loads only five, to guard against accidents. I'm guessing you're a careful man. If you had a sixth shot, or a reload, you'd have answered those three of mine just now. Am I right? Or am I wrong? I think I'll come over and find out.'

'You don't want to make a mistake,' Horn told him.

'No, I don't. But here I come anyway.' He stood up and began walking along the mezzanine. Horn saw him turn the corner and carefully step over George's body. A few steps more, and he stood over the two of them. He looked bigger than Horn remembered, a solidly built man. A polo player, with a good right arm. Even in the low light, Horn could see his square, handsome face clearly. Something lit up the eyes. It looked like anticipation.

Just as Horn noticed that Swain had shifted the Luger to his left hand and was holding a long object in his right, the man abruptly swung the stick at him, catching Horn on the side of his head and sending him reeling backward to land on his side. His ears clanged with demonic music.

'Just a tap.' He heard Swain's voice from a long way off. 'You stay out of the way. But I'd like you to watch this.' He swung the club once through the air, easily, like a cop walking the beat, taking pleasure in the feel of the weight in his hand.

Then he raised it over Maggie. 'Goodbye, missy.' His voice was almost gentle.

Horn tried to scramble to his feet, but he knew the blow would fall before he could get there. An animal cry gathered in his throat . . .

'You hurt me.'

The sound came from behind Swain. The club halted. He awkwardly swung his left hand around, the hand with the gun, and gaped as he saw George raise himself to one elbow.

'What . . .' The gun leveled at George. Horn drove with both legs, covering the distance in less than a second, piling into Swain at the knees, bringing him down. He heard the gun fire, heard more glass shatter, heard Maggie yell.

He had no grip on Swain but reached out and found his gun hand. The club was free to strike, he knew, but he moved in as close as he could. They went from their knees to their feet in one movement, then stood wrestling, grunting in each other's ears. Swain was strong, but Horn was powered by the image of Maggie about to die. He got his left arm around the other man's waist, and they grappled for a second in a parody of a dance. Then Horn's legs surged and he drove the man backward against the stone railing, heard him gasp at the impact. Swain tried to butt with his forehead, but Horn swung his head away. He tried to bend the man farther, but Swain went rigid. They froze there.

Then Horn heard Maggie groan with effort and pain as she appeared on the edge of his vision. She grasped the pant cuff of Swain's right leg with her good hand, lifted it off the floor. Swain kicked out at her, but she got her shoulder under his leg. Then Horn gave a heave, and Swain went over. He let out a small gasp, just *Oh*, and he was gone. They heard the wooden club strike the tile floor with a crack and, a split second later, the slam of his body.

35

They leaned over the parapet for a long time, their labored breathing
the only sounds in the big, vacant space. Horn felt nauseous for a
moment, but it passed. Then they heard fresh sounds from George
on the floor, and Horn knelt down next to him.

'I heard a loud noise,' George said slowly. 'Then I don't remember
anything.'

Horn fingered the side of his head, where the scalp was viciously torn.
Some of the bleeding appeared to have stopped. Just under the scalp, he
felt an indentation where the bullet had struck the metal plate. 'George,'
he said, 'You're a hard-headed cuss. I hope you realize how lucky you are.
He shot you in the one spot where you could take a bullet.'

George reached up to feel the spot. 'I've got a big headache,' he said. 'I
want to go home. I mean the other place, where I'm going to be living.
The new place. Can Laura Lee come and get me?'

'I'm sure she can,' he said. 'We'll call her.'

He turned around, but Maggie was gone. From the lobby below, he
heard a sound. An impact. Something being struck hard. Then another
sound, and another, each accompanied by what may have been a sob. He
stood up and saw Maggie slowly mounting the broad stairs with something in her hand. When she reached him, he saw what it was and took it
from her. Pulling out his shirttail, he wiped the handle clean, then tossed it
over the railing and heard it clatter to the tiles below.

'Are you all right?' he asked.

'Fine,' she said in a normal voice.

'Did the fall kill him?'

'No.'

At ten-thirty that morning he entered the lobby of the Roosevelt Hotel
and was directed to Laura Lee Paisley's new office suite on the third floor.
In the large main room overlooking Hollywood Boulevard, her two assistants were unpacking cartons, shifting furniture around, and answering
telephones. Laura Lee sat behind a desk next to one of several windows,

her back to the busy street. She was picking at a crab salad served on the hotel's china. She looked up as he came in and watched him expressionlessly as he approached.

'You're coming up in the world,' he said, looking around the suite.

'Police were here for half an hour,' she said. 'One of them knows you. They find Marvin Felix's brother-in-law dead just outside my office, the Alhambra shot up like the OK Corral. They find a weapon they think could be the one that killed Owen Bruder. They're trying to put the whole thing together, and they're going around in circles. Naturally they want to know what I know.'

'And what do you know?'

Instead of answering, she speared a piece of crab.

'We had a deal,' he said.

'The deal was you could go in and look around.' She sounded defensive. 'I didn't promise you any results.'

'You didn't tell me you were going to hold out on me, either. What I'm wondering is whether you hid those files because you just wanted to stick your thumb in my eye, or because you—'

'I didn't like getting pushed around,' she said abruptly. 'I'm supposed to make it easy for you? No, sirree. I wanted to say thanks for getting snotty with me. You didn't even tell me which ones you were interested in. I had to guess. Look, I've got a few million facts stashed away in those files of mine. Some of them jump up and say, "Look at me." Others sit there for years. Sure I'd been through those particular files, but I look for gossip, I don't look for murder. I still don't know if you found anything important.'

'You don't need to know.'

She looked almost amused. 'You owe me something.'

He pulled the familiar envelope out of his jacket. 'You mean this?' He tossed it on her desk. 'You didn't hold up your end, but I don't care. You won't hear any more about this from me.'

He paused, thinking. Then: 'What did you tell the cops?'

She opened the envelope, peeked inside, then put it in one of the drawers. 'That I have no idea what Sidney Swain was doing at the Alhambra. Maybe he wanted to look through my legendary files, to see if I had anything incriminating on him. As for who killed him, well . . .' She made a what-the-hell gesture with her salad fork, almost losing a piece of crabmeat, then plucked it off daintily with her teeth.

'Don't get any wrong ideas,' she said, chewing busily. 'It's not because of that old stuff on me. I told you before I'm not afraid of you. That was more of an inconvenience than anything else.'

'Then why?'

She put her fork down. 'George told me you saved his life.'

'Maybe we saved each other's,' he said.

'Maybe. But that's what he said.' She studied his appearance more closely. 'You look like holy hell, by the way.'

'How is he?'

'George? He'll be all right. He's got his story straight, that he was home with me last night. And he's at a place up the coast for a few days, where they'll take good care of him.'

'I'm sure they will.'

'And now, I'd appreciate it if you'd get out of here. If I didn't see you again, it would suit me just fine.'

As he turned to leave, one of her assistants called out, 'Harry Cohn on line two, and he's not happy.'

'Harry!' The old Laura Lee was back. 'Don't use that tone with me, you bald-headed weasel . . .'

Ten minutes later he was on the Cahuenga Parkway, headed over the hill to the Valley and Mad Crow's house. The promise of breakfast he'd made to Maggie had been too optimistic. Instead, he had dropped her off at the same hospital. By now, he thought, she was outfitted with a fresh plaster cast, Mad Crow had picked her up, and all of them could meet for lunch.

Something on the radio interrupted his thoughts. An urgent voice, and familiar names. He turned up the volume.

'. . . to repeat, police this morning were called to the Bel-Air home of Marvin Felix, president of Global Studios. According to unconfirmed reports, investigators found Felix's body there, apparently shot to death, and took his wife, Maris, into custody. No other details were available. This has been a news bulletin from KFAC. We now return you . . .'

I'll be damned, he thought. Maris. Even gutsier than I gave her credit for. Or finally just plain crazy. It had to be Grace who touched this off. Grace, who pulled up in Mad Crow's Caddy with a message for Maris: Your husband's a killer.

Was it a three-way showdown from the beginning, he wondered, or did it start out as just a private talk between girls? And exactly how did the secret about Marvin and Grace come out? Did Grace decide to confess? Or did Maris see a guilty look pass between the two of them? However it happened, it was enough.

And were you really surprised by any of it, Maris? he asked her silently. Or did it just confirm what you already knew? Was Grace there when it happened, or did you send her home, to keep her out of it?

And most important, when you picked up the popgun, did you remember what I told you? Make sure you're not wearing gloves. And step in close.

★

273

'Thank you.' Lillian handed him a tall, cold glass. 'For everything.'

He looked around the apartment, noting that it was now free of all those cartons, those symbols of exile or impermanence. Maybe she has a home for a while, he thought. She deserves one.

'I wish Maggie could have come,' she said.

'Me, too. But believe me, she needs a rest.'

He had spent the better part of an hour telling her, in effect, that it was over. She asked a few questions, and he answered them as best he could, holding back only a few details that might be hurtful to her. As for Grace Stilwell, he said simply that she had felt guilty to learn that Marvin Felix was trying to protect her by implicating Owen and had decided to help Owen find out the truth. And as for what happened in Pyrie back in 1939, it was a simple decision to let that remain buried.

'Marvin Felix,' she said sadly. 'It's so easy to hate him. I think I will, for a while. And then I'll just toss away the hate so it doesn't eat me up.'

'Good. Well, plenty of people hate him already. And by the time his wife gets through talking about him, they'll have some brand new reasons.'

She gestured towards the writing desk. 'My checkbook is ready,' she said.

'Lillian, that check you wrote me at the beginning will do just fine. I should return some of it to you.'

'I won't hear of it.'

'All right. You know, this isn't what I do, really. It's time I went back to collecting debts for my friend Joseph. Debtors are a better class of people than murderers.'

'I'm sure. And I suppose I'll go back to my painting. Which reminds me . . .' She got up and went over to one of three easels in the room, one with the drop cloth covering it. She removed it. 'Come take a look.'

He went over. It was the landscape she had been working on earlier, now finished. The scene was somewhere in an idealized West, a place of rugged hills and deep, red-rock canyons. To the right of the middle foreground was the silhouette of a lone horseman, the man looking out over a chasm that dropped away into shadows. Most noticeable, though, was the sky over the far hills, a sky washed in reds that ran from the palest pink to the deepest golds and oranges. Poised atop the highest peak was a setting sun the color of blood.

'What do you think?'

'It's really something, Lillian.'

'It's yours. The artist's way of saying thanks.'

'I appreciate it. Does it have a name?'

'Well, I don't name all my paintings, especially not the ones I give to

274

friends. I usually let them call it whatever they like. But I was thinking of calling this *Requiem*.'

'Requiem. Isn't that a kind of funeral?'

'It's something for the dead. It can be music, but it doesn't have to be. It's just that all the time I was working on it, I heard music in my head. Sad and lonely.'

Like a lament, Woody Guthrie might say. 'So who's dead?' He regretted the question as soon as he asked it.

'Oh . . . take your choice. The West, at least the one you see here. The West of your old movies. And, I suppose, the cowboys. If I wanted to be gloomy, I'd go beyond that and say a whole way of life. Just a year ago I thought the universe was stable and solid. Now I don't know.' She laughed quietly. 'Forgive me for being morose. You can call it anything you like.'

'That's quite a sky there.'

'I know. The setting sun is usually peaceful, but I wasn't feeling particularly peaceful at the time. And the fires were burning, and the sky looked ominous every night . . .'

'They're still burning,' he said. 'It's just that they're farther out now. Word is, we won't be able to control them. They'll burn from now until the first rainfall of the winter.'

One afternoon two days later, Horn was on his way home. Nearing the end of the canyon, he saw a car back out of his entryway and onto the road. He pulled abreast of the car and recognized Frog Face behind the wheel. The other man looked at him coolly, appraisingly.

'I just left something in your mailbox,' he said.

'Is it ticking?'

'No. See you around.' He put the car in gear and drove away.

In the box Horn found a large, fat brown envelope. He took it inside and opened it. It was his file, the one Mitchell Cross had referred to in the hotel room. Attached to it was a handwritten note.

Interesting stories in the newspapers lately. I guess it's over. I won't be needing this.

It was signed with the initial 'C'.

Lou's Quick Stop was a roadhouse attached to a gas station on the way to San Bernardino. The food was just edible, the floors were seldom swept, and the place stank of stale beer. But Lou's had a band every weekend, and Cal Stoddard and his boys had managed to book an appearance.

Horn and Maggie sat on a rough bench near the back of the audience, next to Mad Crow and Rusty Baird. All had made the long drive in Mad Crow's Caddy. He had retrieved the car the previous morning, when he found a haggard Grace Stilwell sitting behind the wheel in his driveway. Mad Crow, ever the gentleman, had driven her home.

Things were not going well at Lou's. Cal was resplendent as always, in a royal blue rodeo shirt with white fringe, and white trousers tucked into mahogany-toned hand-tooled boots. His band members were almost as well-dressed. But they looked jarringly out of place on the knotty-pine stage, and the crowd of truck drivers, fruit pickers, and assorted rough-necks seemed to regard them as visitors from a far-off country. Except for one forlorn couple, the little dance floor in front of the stage was empty. The audience, arrayed on eight rows of benches, was noisy and likkered up, with little appreciation for the Rhythm Wranglers' selection of sweet-tempered cowboy songs and ballads. A screen of chicken wire protected the band from any audience mischief.

The band wrapped up 'Faded Love' to unenthusiastic applause. Whooping laughter erupted on one of the benches as one prankster emptied a beer bottle down the back of someone's collar, and their friends moved the ensuing fight outside.

The musicians launched into 'San Antonio Rose', which had gone over well at Maggie's picnic just a few weeks earlier. This crowd, however, was indifferent.

Mad Crow went to the bar and brought back four beers. Horn turned to Maggie. She was still wearing the casts, but he was pleased to see that the color was back in her cheeks. Although the smiles were still infrequent, she seemed peaceful and relaxed.

'He's too good for this crowd,' she said to him, speaking up to be heard.

He nodded. 'It's the only job his manager has found for him in weeks. You've got to hand it to him, though. He won't quit.'

Horn felt like changing the subject. 'You know, Woody turned out to be right about Owen's murder,' he said. 'He thought it had to be something more personal than politics.'

'I suppose so,' she said. 'But look at it another way. It was the Red Scare that gave Marvin Felix the excuse for killing him – to protect Grace – and also the smokescreen to help him hide. So . . . no Red Scare, maybe no murder.'

'Maybe.' Horn though about that. This whole thing had been a tangle from the beginning. Why expect it to make perfect sense at the end? Then he heard Maggie say, 'Why don't we tell him what we think?'

He turned around and saw Woody Guthrie coming their way, guitar under his arm. 'What are you doing here?' Horn said. 'Aren't you supposed to be in New York?'

'Oh, I s'pose. I keep changing my schedule. Hell, I don't *have* a schedule. I called Joseph here yesterday, just to say goodbye, and he told me about Cal's first public appearance in a coon's age, and I thought, well, them New York advertising boys can just wait a few more days. So here I am. See you later.' He headed for the stage. Cal spotted him and, grinning, summoned him up.

The crowd hooted when the scrawny, wild-haired little man stepped up to the microphone. 'Howdy-do,' he said. 'My name's Woody Guthrie, and I play the git-tar.' Horn noticed that stepping in front of an audience seemed to intensify Guthrie's nasal accent and his cornpone pronunciation. 'You don't know me, and I don't know you peckerwoods neither.' That brought a laugh or two, and scattered muttering that seemed to suggest that some in the audience had actually heard of him. An empty beer bottle arced toward the stage, bounced off the chicken wire, and shattered on the dance floor. More whooping.

'Next time, make it a full one, okay, boys?' Guthrie said, drawing a few laughs.

'I'm standing here because I heard my friend Cal Stoddard was playing here. And I happen to think he's one of the gutsiest old boys around. A lot gutsier than me, and more than most of you too, I bet.'

He strummed on his strings a bit, then glanced down below, where a drunk had passed out sitting with his back against the stage. 'And this here's my friend Corncob Quinlan from Kokomo. He's going to get up and do a buck and wing for us in just a minute.' The audience liked that one, and a few of them clapped.

'But I came here to play with Cal, and that's what I'm going to do—'

'You play some first, Woody,' Stoddard insisted.

'Well, all right. This here's for my friend John Ray Horn. Any of you out there remember hard times? This song promised us things were going to get better. 'Course they never did, but . . . What are you going to do?'

It was 'Big Rock Candy Mountain' and it seemed most of the crowd knew it. When he got to the line '. . . *And the bulldogs all have rubber teeth,*' everyone laughed. And the line *'There's a lake of stew and of whiskey too'* drew cheers.

By the time he strummed to a close, the crowd was on his side.

'Just one more,' he said. 'Then I'm going to sit down and listen to Cal and his boys, and I hope you do too.' He began playing, and the chords sounded familiar to Horn.

'I stole this tune from the Carter Family, but if the po-lice show up, I'll deny it,' he said. 'Here's a song for anybody who ever had to work for a living. For anybody who's ever been cold or hungry, who's had to sleep under the stars, who's had to go hat in hand to the man, begging for a job.' The audience grew quiet.

'Who's ever looked around at this country and thought it was full of promises that never got fulfilled. I wrote this for you. Some of you've heard a new version of it, and that's nice enough, I guess. But this is the one I wrote first. You may know some of the words, but not all of them. I called it "God Blessed America" – I almost stole that from Mr Irving Berlin – but you probably know it by another name.'

And he began singing 'This Land is Your Land', but it was not like the song Horn had heard before. It was angrier, and Guthrie's voice sounded like a preacher invoking God's blessings even as he itemized the sins of his congregation. Cal and his band came in, falteringly at first, then stronger, as Guthrie sang, in an unvarnished baritone:

> *Was a big high wall there that tried to stop me,*
> *A sign was painted said: Private Property.*
> *But on the back side, it didn't say nothing—*
> *God Blessed America for me.*

These were new words, strange words, and although no one in the crowd knew them, some tried humming along. Cal's backup playing picked up, and he began embroidering on the melody. Guthrie was almost shouting the words now:

> *One bright sunny morning in the shadow of the steeple*
> *By the relief office I saw my people—*
> *As they stood there hungry,*
> *I stood there wondering if*
> *God Blessed America for me.*

Cal looked up, caught the eyes of his four friends near the back, and winked. Horn reached over, took Maggie's good hand, and squeezed it. There was no answering squeeze, but he hadn't really expected one.

It's all right, he thought. *I can wait.*